CAUSE OF DEATH

MIRRORS IN THE DARK BOOK 3

KT BELT

RUBBER TREE BOOKS

CONTENTS

1

ANOTHER DAY IN THE OFFICE

Here, surrounded by nothing, the cold penetrated all. Time stood still until there was just this singular moment. Only a glance at the clock in front of her told otherwise. The dark, lonely nothingness warped and clouded everywhere else she looked. This was her life for longer than she could remember. Her only company, the only thing that let her know she still existed, were the small pinpoints of light all around her—and, of course, Red.

"I'm telling you, Winter, they're not going to show."

Winter smiled as she flexed her fingers and rubbed them together. Their starfighter was a nice, dim hunk of metal floating freely in space. Almost every system, major or minor, had been shut down to lower their signature on any passive sensor scan. Unfortunately, that also included the life support systems. The air was getting mighty stale, but what was more of a bother was the temperature. An ice cube would have felt warm in her hand.

"Perhaps," she remarked casually. "Doubt it, though."

"They aren't *that* stupid. We can't get them again, same tactics, same place."

She smiled for a second time. "As I said, perhaps. We'll know in…one minute," she added, glancing at the clock. "Frankly, they better. I don't want to be out here flying picket and freezing my ass off for nothing."

"Bet?"

Winter thought about it for a moment and then shook her head. "Unless you got a heater stuffed in your flight suit, there is nothing you can give me that I want." The fighter pilot let out an annoyed huff. "I'm pretty sure my eyelashes have icicles now."

Red laughed, which made Winter purse her lips, but she said nothing else. He was seated behind her, and she could only imagine his face.

"Traveler One-One, Cerberus, thirty seconds, comms check," spoke a soft voice on their fighter's communicator.

So it's Leena this time, Winter thought. The *Griffin's* operations officer, Ensign Leena Swanson, always had a calm, soft voice no matter the situation. Her words just had way of knifing through maelstroms to soothe racing pulses. Most in the squadron had come to appreciate it.

"Cerberus, Traveler One-One, four by five," Red responded. "Anyway, they're not going to show," he teased, turning his attention back to Winter.

"Well, when you work by algorithms and efficiency, it does make you predicable. You call it stupid, but it's smart in a way."

"Uh huh." She well knew her backseater was rolling his eyes. She grinned as she thought of the expression she saw far too often. "We're too far away anyway. It will be hard to pick them up at half a light year," he continued.

"Ten seconds," Leena remarked.

Winter glanced at the clock before she spoke. "I think you'll appreciate the separation if they do show. Baby and TR escaped with about half their Screamer," she remarked, referring to their Banshee starfighter by the name most pilots called it.

Half a Screamer was a bit of an exaggeration. She'd heard the phrase, 'A wing and a prayer,' but even merciful angels would have ejected from that ship. It was barely worth saving as scrap.

Red must have been considering what she said, as he didn't respond immediately. "No doubt about that," he eventually muttered.

Winter barely heard him. She was fully focused on the clock now. All things considered, and despite the monumental waste of time it would be, she'd rather freeze here for nothing than suffer some other less pleasant alternatives. *Five, four, three,* she counted down in her head as she stared at the clock. The expected time till intercept came and then went, but there was nothing. Her gaze went to where the Eternal fleet would be dispelling their Ghost Drives. She had no hope of ever seeing anything with the naked eye at the expected range, but the reflex couldn't be helped.

"Good thing I didn't bet."

"No shit," Red responded. "Cerberus, Traveler One-One, negative contact. I say again, negative contact."

"Traveler One-One, copy negative contact, cleared RTB," Leena said back.

Winter sighed softly as she flexed her fingers once more. At least she'd be able to get warm soon. "All right, let's get out of here. Plot a course. I'll start powering systems."

There was no response from Red; not at first. "Winter!"

"What?" she asked, annoyed that he was practically screaming at her.

"Winter! Winter!" he said, his voice so rushed that it was cracking.

"What? What is it?"

"Multiple contacts all around us. Closest contact is just eight light seconds away!"

She turned on her helmet-mounted display and looked rapidly in every direction. The enemy didn't drop out of light speed half a light year away as expected but right on top of them.

"Do they detect us?"

"Not that I can tell," Red answered.

"Phone it in."

He nodded, though she'd never be able to see it. "Cerberus, Traveler One-One, enemy contact, datalink established, confirm," he said hurriedly.

"Easy, Red." She spoke softly, though admittedly her breath came short. "We've still got a job to do. Focus on that." But she couldn't fault him for his nerves.

She was the Hustlers' CO, a veteran from the beginning of the first Terran-Sorten War from the very first battle. There were few pilots who weren't either retired or dead who could say they'd seen more combat than Winter had, but now even her hands were tingling, and it had nothing to do with the cold.

The two of them waited for several more seconds, but Leena gave no response. Winter swallowed hard. "Are we being jammed?" she asked. If so, that wrinkle would ruin the entire plan.

Red opened his mouth to speak and then cursed softly. Winter raised a confused eyebrow as she turned her head toward him. He continued muttering to himself.

"No," he finally said. "It's just... Damn it, I'll leave that on."

"Red?"

"Cerberus, Traveler One-One, enemy contact, datalink

established, confirm," he repeated, ignoring her. At least his words were crisp and professional this time.

She considered what just happened and felt a wry smirk come to her freezing lips when the only possible explanation dawned on her. He had forgotten to hit the transmit button.

"Traveler One-One, Cerberus, confirm," came Leena's steady, calm reply. "Wow, great tracks. Hold position. All Hammers inbound, enjoy the fireworks. Twenty-two seconds."

Well, there's a reason for the great tracks, Winter thought, but neither she nor Red said anything. She could hear his breath quicken. It made her realize that hers also worked to keep up with her thudding chest. Her mouth was dry, and she swallowed hard.

Just then, there were small pinpoints of lights all around them. They were brighter than the stars and had an odd bluish-white ethereal glow. They grew ever brighter as the missiles streaked to their targets. In time, long thin beams of light streaked out to meet them from where she knew the Eternal fleet was. Everywhere she looked, all around them, the light show grew and grew in intensity until it came to its inevitable climatic end. The first explosion turned their fighter's cockpit canopy almost completely opaque. She still had to squint her eyes. On and on the explosions came until she felt like she was in the center of the sun.

"Winter, they've begun active scanning. Several smaller contacts inbound…fighters."

"They've made us. All systems on, let's get out of here," she said quickly but without stress. She could almost feel the abrasive certainty of the noose tightening around their necks, but hysterics never helped.

There was, however, a voice that could be calmer than hers no matter the situation. "Traveler One-One, please hold position for battle damage assessment," Leena said, seemingly unaware of the enormity of the request.

"BDA?" Red shouted in disbelief. "Are they fucking crazy?"

"Traveler One-One, Cerberus, I didn't copy your last. Say again," Leena said.

Red muttered curses under his breath again while Winter smirked once more. When he forgot to transmit, he must have turned on his VOX to avoid making the same mistake. Politeness aside, Leena had heard him five by five.

"They really want to get us killed this time," Red continued, but only after double-checking that it was a private conversation.

"No more than any other day," Winter said with a shrug. "Time till intercept?"

"Fifteen seconds."

"Time till full power?"

"Full power…now. But we won't have weapons for about a minute."

Winter groaned loudly. At least the cockpit was getting warmer. In any case, not only were they flying alone, but also, other than their six laser cannons, they were unarmed. Nine times out of ten, it was better to be lighter for a quick escape. The tenth time? Well, those usually made great stories at the bar, if you survived to tell the tale.

"Cerberus is outbound at this time. Rendezvous at alpha three. Good luck."

Red muttered more curses under his breath; Winter ignored him. Now was a perfect time for the *Griffin* to get away. The carnage of the attack, which was rapidly dissipating, disrupted long range sensors, allowing a brief window for the starship to power her Ghost Drive without being tracked by whatever was left of the Eternal fleet.

The more immediate, however, came to the fore. Their pursing fighters opened fire. The energy rushed toward them like an impossibly fast missile, but at this range, maneuver was still an effective defense. Her IF/A-1000F Banshee was operated with a fly-by-thought flight control system. In an instant, they were burning on an evasive course that sped them to safety—at least for the next second or so.

"Still want to take that bet?" she teased.

"Fuck you, Winter," Red snapped. "They're firing again."

She took a deep breath and, a fraction of a second later, they reversed their vector. The violence of the turn would have crushed her into putty and turn her sleek starfighter into a pile of disheveled junk, but the inertial inhibitor trimmed the force out to no more than an annoying weight on her chest.

Winter took the briefest of instants to glance at her sensor display and was quick to see the Eternals closing on them in an ever-tightening net. The machines weren't capable of vengeance, as far as she knew. Perhaps a lone starfighter wasn't even worth the trouble. But algorithms and efficiency were quite predicable. When you encounter the enemy, you kill them.

"Get us a hole, a weak spot, anything. We don't have much time!" she shouted.

Then she threw the fighter in an erratic weave while Red cursed continuously behind her. Several shots now burned uncomfortably close. She worked the problem herself, glancing everywhere with her helmet display, but there was no immediately apparent solution.

"I think I got it. Two fighters slightly apart from the main group," he said.

"Where?"

"Designated Master One and Two."

Winter glanced at the relevant pair and accelerated her fighter toward them at full power. The Banshee's twin matter-antimatter annihilation engines spooled to their second stage, and it was like an explosion. Her vision grayed as the inertial inhibitor struggled to keep up with all the acceleration forces. White-hot plasma belched behind the fighter for hundreds of miles. Their opposition fired at them, and her counter with a small change in vector almost blacked the two of them out.

"Winter, shoot list is up," he said. But nothing happened. It was only maybe a half-second or so, but it seemed like an hour. One of the enemy's shots even burned their shields down to a critical level. "What's the matter? Shoot 'em!"

"We don't have lasers yet."

"Shoot 'em!" Red yelled again, before he heard her response.

"We don't have lasers yet!" she repeated, yelling over him. "Give me a missile lock."

"Winter, we don't have missiles either," he pointed out.

"They don't know that."

Her words made his hands fly over his console. Back-seaters made due without a fly-by-thought system. The response was immediate when it was done. "They're turning cold."

"Charging Ghost Drive," she announced as she put the fighter through another series of violent vector changes.

All throughout, an ethereal light built all around them. Their acceleration slowed from engine power feeding the system. At the last moment, Winter pointed the fighter on its proper course. Then, all at once, there was nothing. No fighters and not even any stars—nothing other than black all around them. Winter breathed easy.

"You did record all that for their precious BDA, right?" she asked after a sigh. Red said nothing. "Right?"

"Aw... Shit, I'm sorry. With everything going on, I forgot." Winter leaned forward and then turned, trying her best to see him. He smiled at her. "I got it all, don't worry."

"Fuck you, Red," Winter said as she turned to face forward again.

"Hope it makes them happy, Fleet officers."

"Either way, the result's the same," she replied.

"What's that?"

"We do it again tomorrow."

2

DEPARTURES

Carmen stepped onto the deck of the spaceport, Phaethon and Inertia right behind her. *The Lady* was a small ship, making the expanse of spaceport whatever's hangar a welcome respite. She stretched her arms and shoulders but felt too pressed for time to do much of anything else. She looked to Inertia, as she unknowingly found herself doing more and more often. He tipped his head in a direction and started walking. She followed, and Phaethon was right behind her.

This was a military spaceport. Rows of starfighters were parked at various stages of alert status. Another group was getting readied by crews with multiple kinds of ordinance. There were other corvettes as well of the same class as *The Lady*, but of course they weren't customized for the sort of extralegal work the Rogue Wolves were known for. She watched the scene casually as they walked and considered the past day or so.

The Rogue Wolves, she thought, slowly grasping what those words meant. She had somehow become one of them over the course of all this, though that wasn't her intention at the outset. Indeed, Phaethon was the odd member of their trio. She wore body armor of the same style and color of Inertia's. Phaethon, by contrast, wore some of Inertia's civilian clothes, which were too large for him.

They exited the hangar soon enough and entered a large room with several corridors leading off from it. Inertia went to consult a map posted nearby.

"Do you think we'll be able to find a transport here?" Carmen asked.

Phaethon looked at her as she spoke, but he didn't say anything. They'd had more than one argument about him staying with her instead of going back to the facility on New Earth. The subject was put to rest when, after a particular heated session, Inertia gave his opinion by staring down at her charge with narrowing eyes. She was pretty sure Phaethon hadn't spoken once since then.

"Hopefully," Inertia answered. "This port serves the sector. We should be able to find him something. Then we can continue on our mission. Have to do some checking first."

Carmen nodded. "What do you need me to do?"

"I might need some time," he answered after a few seconds of thinking. "Why don't you get something to eat?" he suggested. "Maybe even find him some of his own clothes," he added, glancing at her charge. Phaethon cowered under his gaze, but it contained no malice.

"Makes sense," she said softly as she thought it over. "You find me?"

Inertia nodded, and the two groups went their separate ways. Carmen walked in the lead with Phaethon following just a step behind. She found it a little weird that everyone ignored them. She was well used to the extra attention being a Clairvoyant brought, but more than that, both she and Phaethon were civilians walking around, free and unescorted, in a military base. Except maybe it was an odd circumstance only for her. She guessed she looked the part of a mercenary now—because she was—and Phaethon was obviously with her. It might be nowhere out of the ordinary for a Clairvoyant merc to be going about her business in a port like this. For what it was worth, they weren't walking in any place that seemed sensitive or critical.

"I don't think we'll be able to find you any clothes other than Space Force uniforms," she said as she looked around.

Before Phaethon could respond to her, the two Clairvoyants felt prompted to move to the side of the corridor. Scores of medical personnel with a fleet of gurneys and other equipment came running past them seconds later. Carmen didn't hear everything they said, but it was something about an incoming starship called *Hunter's Moon* suffering mass casualties. The Clairvoyants continued on when the medical teams were gone. Her charge still didn't say anything.

"Phaethon?" she asked, turning toward him.

"I just can't deal with him. I don't know how you handle it," he said.

"Deal with who?" she asked, confused.

"That guy with you."

"Inertia?" she questioned, wondering how the conversation could possibly be about her partner. They'd probably still be stuck in Solitary without him. "What's the matter with Inertia?"

The boy slowly shook his head. "That guy scares me…"

Carmen laughed lightly. "Scares you? You? Phaethon? I never thought I'd live to hear you say you were scared of anyone."

"I'm being serious," he said through gritted teeth. "He might not bother you, but I think he hates me."

"In that case, I should tell him about your weakness with chess," she joked.

"Edge!"

"Phaethon," she began. She spoke calmly, but she did stop walking to look at him fully. "Think of it this way. Even if Inertia is one of the evilest men to have ever lived, I wouldn't have gotten you back without him. I'll admit there are times he…unsettles me, but I'll always be thankful for that."

Her charge paused for a moment. "I guess, when you put it like that, I understand."

"Right," Carmen said with a sharp nod. "If he bothers you, just stay out of his way. You should be on a transport out of here soon anyway."

Phaethon nodded a couple times himself. "You should come with me."

"No," she responded immediately, shaking her head. It seemed more likely that she'd be convinced she had a third arm growing out of her forehead than to leave. "I came to find you. But I can't do that to him, not now." She started moving forward again. Silent clocks were ticking down to the deadline of their mission, and she felt hastened with almost everything she did now.

"But I thought you don't like fighting?" Phaethon asked as he followed.

"I don't. Hate it, even. But, though he never says anything, Inertia needs my help. This is bigger than him now. It's bigger than me and bigger than just saving you. I have to see it through."

Just then, more medical personnel ran by with yet more equipment. Carmen and Phaethon made way and then continued on.

"If he never says anything, how do you know?" he asked.

Carmen's gaze fell as she struggled to come up with an answer. She'd never tell Phaethon, but Inertia had encouraged her to leave more than once. Her lips contorted as her mind considered several possibilities. Nothing was said, though. Nothing she could say made any sense.

"So, do you want that Space Force uniform or not?" she asked, changing the subject.

"No. I think I might be done with fighting."

Carmen looked at her charge in a state of stunned shock. No expression came to mind until, at last, a small smile graced her lips. "Let's at least get something to eat," she suggested as she noticed a few signs for food.

Phaethon nodded, and the two made their way to an eatery that was mostly empty. The décor led her to believe it was a civilian-owned establishment. The staff also didn't wear any sort of uniform. It was actually relatively pretty inside. The lights were dimmed, and though they were deep in the heart of the spaceport, transparacells were set up on the walls like windows. Even Carmen had to take a moment to watch the inbound and outbound traffic of the spaceport. It wasn't every day that she was able to see near mile-long starships. Eventually she and Phaethon took a seat at the bar—anything to save a little time. An older man approached them in short order.

"What can I get for you?" he asked.

"Phaethon," Carmen said, motioning politely to the man with her head. He ordered, and she turned to look at the bartender. "I don't want anything. We're in a bit of a hurry."

"Sure. Everyone is nowadays," he said. "I'll take care of you, special." Then he left at a brisk walk.

Carmen took a deep breath and relaxed in her chair. Phaethon said nothing to her. Clairvoyants weren't really known for idle chatter. He seemed to take the moment to relax as well. She glanced at her charge from time to time, and he glanced back. Sitting here, now, Solitary seemed another lifetime ago. They had only talked about it once, and it was a subject she had no interested in bringing up again.

Her eyes drifted away from him. The front of the restaurant was an open view of the corridor they'd come from. As she silently people watched, she wished she could somehow contact Kali, if only to give her the good news about Phaethon. Her previous handler had to be worried about her to some degree. Now that she thought about it, though, Kali hadn't been too concerned when Carmen told her she was leaving. Just then, she heard someone screaming down the corridor.

"Clear corridor, clear corridor! Make a hole!" someone yelled.

Seconds later, the medical team they saw earlier came rushing past. Every gurney was filled; blood dripped and spilled from several. Some of the crew of *Hunter's Moon* were so mangled that she wondered what was keeping them alive. They reminded her of the Constructs the sorten doctors worked on back at Solitary. After that first group there was a second. These crew members weren't on any gurneys, as there were none left. But if they couldn't move solely under their own power, there was a helping hand or two to support them on their way. Both Clairvoyants turned just before the bartender returned to the room.

"Here you go," he said, handing the food to Phaethon.

Carmen casually glanced at his plate, grabbed a couple of French fries, and ate them. Phaethon, for his part, gave his handler an annoyed look but made no other protest. She didn't notice.

"Like that more and more often," the bartender said as he watched the crew of *Hunter's Moon* go by. Carmen nodded though offered no comment. She had no idea about much of anything with the war. The bartender was quiet for a time afterward. "See stuff like that every day now—men and women your age, sometimes even as young as your friend here," he continued, motioning to Phaethon, "tore up, wrecked, you name it. It's a damn shame. I fought in the first Terran-Sorten War. Lost some friends there, but nothing like this." He paused once more as his mouth grew tight. Eventually, he shook his head. "If you don't mind me saying, it looks like you've seen your fair share of fighting yourself."

Carmen thought about it before touching the burnt side of her face with her burnt hand. Phaethon visibly cringed as she did so. She glanced at him, and he looked away. "You can say that," she said softly, turning her attention back to the bartender. "But shouldn't it be getting better? I thought the sortens surrendered?" she asked, turning her body to be in line with her attention.

The bartender nodded a few times. "You'd be right to think that, but not from what I hear." Carmen made no comment other than to gesture him to go on. "I see all sorts— troopers, Fleet, pilots, even Clairvoyants like you. You get to hear things."

"Like what?" she asked, swiping a few more French fries off her charge's plate. He groaned.

"If you go by the news, everything is under control. Nothing to worry about," the man said. "But I've heard tell that, even with the sortens' surrender, the Eternals still outnumber us more than two-to-one. Heard that the fleet sent to destroy the sorten home worlds barely made it back. Heard that Space Force is stretched to the limit to meet the Eternal counterattack at Leevi. You know anyone from there?" he asked. Carmen shook her head. "Well, seems like the planet is under siege. If it falls, Eternals can use it as a beachhead for deeper strikes. Might be no stopping them then."

Carmen nodded glumly. *Bigger than me and Inertia indeed*, she thought. "Did you hear anything about New Earth? Is it still safe there?"

"Far as I can tell. Haven't heard any mutterings about there?"

Carmen nodded again. She thought twice about what she was going to ask next but eventually decided the question couldn't hurt. "Did you hear anything about a Clairvoyant who goes by the name Charon? He attacks Clairvoyant training facilities. Hear anything about something like that happening?"

"Other than that time on New Earth, no. But everybody knows about that."

Carmen sighed and then gave an annoyed puff to the bangs that had slipped in front of her face. "Bill, please."

"Yes, ma'am," the bartender said, leaving once more.

She leaned back in her chair and groaned. 'You're done, right?"

"Yeah."

"Good." She looked outside the restaurant. "Come on, Inertia," she muttered to herself in an annoyed tone. Her foot even began tapping the ground.

"Why are you in such a rush?" Phaethon asked.

She didn't answer right away. Instead, she took a moment to look around. Unlike most of the bartender's customers, it seemed, she wanted to make sure sensitive information remained a secret.

"The sortens have another facility like Solitary, except this one is a freighter. We know where it is now, but it will move on in less than a week. We probably won't be able to find it again after that."

The bartender was returning, so Phaethon only nodded. Carmen was out of her chair the instant she paid. Her charge was right behind her.

"You two take care of yourself," the bartender said.

Carmen nodded as they made their way out. She stopped when they entered the corridor.

"So, what now?" Phaethon asked.

She let go a pained smile. *So, that's how Inertia feels*, she thought. In any case, she scanned slowly back and forth as she considered what to do until she could only shrug. "I guess we should go back to the hangar area and wait."

Phaethon offered only a shrug as well in response, and with that settled, they headed back in the direction from they came. They walked quietly, but there was one question Carmen was keen to ask her charge. It had been on her mind for some time, except it was a subject she had yet to muster the courage to breach. She didn't want to talk about Solitary again, for his sake as much as hers, but she needed to know. She glanced at him a few times. If not now, never.

"Phaethon, is there anything you can tell me about Charon?" she asked as softly as she could. Despite that, she felt his entire being shudder. "I didn't want to ask, but if there's anything you can give me, it might help."

She watched him over her shoulder as he started slowly shaking his head. "I'm sorry, Edge. I don't know anything."

"Nothing at all?"

Phaethon shook his head again. "I fought him and he beat me. I don't know what he put me under with, but I was unconscious the entire time." Carmen nodded. It was difficult to drug a Clairvoyant into unconsciousness, let alone for extended periods. "I woke up in a cell in Solitary," he concluded. "Sorry."

"It's fine," she said, raising a hand.

When they arrived back at the hangar, there was no sign of Inertia. Carmen went to lean against a wall. Phaethon followed her lead.

"You're going after Charon too?" he asked.

"If we can," Carmen answered after brief hesitation. She figured it was best not to mention Gungnir or Widget.

"Be careful. He's stronger than he first appears. It was almost like he was toying with me when we fought."

Carmen nodded, steeling herself for the battle she didn't look forward to but hoped was inevitable. She may have been understating the issue. She didn't *just* hate fighting; she was utterly sickened by the thought of it. But, as she'd learned, it was sometimes necessary and even prudent to suffer certain ills. She looked down the corridor a few seconds later. Inertia was coming.

"Good. I hoped I'd find the two of you here," he said. "Follow me."

She nodded and quickly joined her partner at his side. Phaethon followed slightly behind them. After a while of watching the two of them walking, he shook his head. Edge was still Edge—she hadn't changed. But he wasn't used to seeing her like this. She and Inertia fit together as surely as gears in a watch. Inertia was the most dangerous man he'd ever met. And then there was Edge. The meek, gentle handler he'd known back on New Earth was still in front of him. Except maybe that was never really her, at least not fully. She still seemed like she'd go out of her way to avoid stepping on a flower. There was something else, though, quiet and menacing, yet obvious. Yes, she wouldn't step on a flower unless absolutely necessary, but if she did, it was because the flower *deserved* it. Behind her pearly blue eyes and soft voice was judgement. Final, complete, and absolute. Seeing it for the first time, even when not aimed at him, made Phaethon scared of more than just Inertia. It was a wonder that he had never noticed before. He wondered if even she was aware of that aspect of herself.

"I was able to find an SDF troop transport to a local colony," Inertia said. "From there, I booked him passage back to New Earth."

Carmen turned to smile at her charge and then looked back at her partner. "Thank you."

Inertia nodded casually. "We have to hurry. They're holding the shuttle just for him. It's in an auxiliary hangar."

She nodded and increased her pace to keep up. In a minute or so, they entered another hangar vastly smaller than where *The Lady* was parked. Before them was open space, held at bay by a magcon field. The shuttle was a boxy, ugly craft meant to contain the maximum number of troopers as was volumetrically possible. Carmen could see the pilots in the cockpit turn to look at them when they entered. The deck crew, standing by to launch the shuttle when ready, did the same.

"Make it quick," Inertia whispered to her before he moved away.

Carmen turned to face her charge and smiled. "End of the road for you," she said. "I'm not going to have to worry about you, am I?" she teased tenderly.

"Do I have to worry about you?" Phaethon asked back.

She shook her head. "Inertia is with me," she remarked, looking his way. Her partner stood impassively. "We take care of each other."

"Still, be careful," Phaethon said.

Carmen nodded a few times. "I'll try. Come here," she said, holding out her arms.

Handler and charge hugged awkwardly. It was not a skill taught at the facility, nor one they had much practice in.

When it was done, she motioned toward the shuttle with her head, and Phaethon began walking toward it. Carmen watched him go. Each step he took produced a wave of emotions best described as bittersweet.

In time, she noticed that Inertia had come to stand next to her. With no prompting or conscious thought, she rested her head on his strong arm. She didn't know he glanced down on her when she did so. Then he turned and left so abruptly that Carmen lost her balance for a moment. As she stood there alone, watching him make his way out of the hangar, she felt another emotion. It would never, in any sense, be described as sweet. She rushed to join him, but this time they didn't walk side by side.

"So, what about us? Our mission?" she asked. "Can we do it?"

"I don't know. But it's definitely not something we can do on our own."

"Who can help us?"

"There is only one person I could think of." He took a deep breath before he continued, which made Carmen swallow hard. "I had to call in a marker—one I've been saving for an occasion like this. I just hoped I would never have to use it."

3
____

HOPELESS

ISS *Griffin* ICD-775
Captain Renee Brown commanding
Mission: Interdiction

Every ship was different. Even sister ships built to the exact same specs on the exact same yard weren't truly the same. There was minutia that no engineer could find on a schematic or design brief but which the crew lived by. Over time, they became myths and legends to the crew who manned the ship and even sometimes to the wider fleet. It could be little things, like the inertial inhibitor trimmed .2% slower unless it was kicked in the exact right spot at the exact right time in the exact right way, or that showers on deck six were never as hot as those on deck eight. All existed to some degree for the crew of the ISS *Griffin*. However, if there was one constant of the universe—one enduring truth that let everyone know, truly and forever, the inevitable and predictable nature of reality—it was that Lt. Tawny Crowe would never EVER win a poker game.

Tawny stared at her cards and then at the dwindling pile

of money in front her. Her eyebrows scrunched together. It was the same every time. She'd start with a pile and, slowly but surely, it was would get smaller and smaller until nothing was left. That she always lost in and of itself wasn't too bothersome for her. She never bet anything she couldn't stand to lose. No, what was utterly infuriating was that she couldn't even add one stinking credit to the pile before she lost everything.

"This is good, right?" she whispered to her coach.

Commander Frederick Reeves leaned close to her and looked at her cards. She couldn't help a small shudder. She couldn't stand him. More times than not, Tawny pondered how to eject him out an airlock without getting court martialed. But he was the only person willing to teach her how to play…which was a bit suspect. She heard a rumor once that he had paid off a couple crew members who were interested in teaching her to not do it. But it was a rumor only and nothing she could prove. Anyway, the fat slob was close enough now that she could smell the alcohol on his breath. He loomed over the small woman, and if her short hair could stand on end, it would have been as erect as steel pillars.

"Oh, these cards are terrible. You should bluff," he said, louder than she would have preferred.

Her opponents looked at her, waiting for her to make her move, but they gave no reaction to Frederick's outburst. Perhaps they didn't hear? Either way, Tawny let go a dejected sigh.

"Why do I do this to myself?" she muttered.

Frederick laughed, and she was sure she heard a demonic howl behind the mirth. "Hey, you want to win, right?"

"Well, yeah, but why should I bluff? My cards are all the same suit. I thought that was good?"

He looked at her as if she was a rare species of moron and

batted her words away. Tawny bit her lip in quivering frustration. The closest airlock was just down the corridor.

"Good?" he began. "It ain't bad, but there are definitely better. You got it all wrong, anyway. You don't play your hand, you play your opponent. Look there," he continued, pointing across the table and speaking louder. "You see that bastard, Ensign…Bastard," Frederick said, fumbling to find a name. Everyone at the table gave a soft chuckle, except Ensign Bastard, who stared at his cards while giving a hard sigh. His actual name was Zhou, and he was a new addition to the game, a replacement assault shuttle pilot. Hardly anyone knew him, including Tawny. "I've been watching him. Every time he has a good hand, he scratches his nose twice. He's had to have scratched his nose fifty times this hand already."

Everyone in the room except Tawny looked at Zhou suspiciously. Her attention was on Frederick. Her face leaked puzzled annoyance while she bit her lip again. She was an officer—most everyone else in the room was too—but there was a level of decorum that had to be kept, even in the face of…well, Frederick.

"You said he scratches his nose twice. So, he scratched it twice fifty times, or he scratched it twenty-five times, twice each time?" she asked.

Frederick rolled his eyes before downing his drink in one gulp. The commander gave a thunderous burp before he spoke again. "You're thinking about this too hard."

"I just want you to help me and stop messing with me," Tawny said as she fanned the smell of his bile away. *Maybe codes of conduct apply to just junior officers*, she thought.

"I am helping you!" he exclaimed loudly.

"Commander," Zhou said, looking at him over his cards. "I haven't scratched my nose once since I've been here."

Frederick's face turned a deep shade of flummoxed as the silence built in the room. But a few seconds later, as if on cue, Zhou smirked and then made a show of scratching his nose twice. Frederick pointed at him and laughed, as did everyone else. Replacement drinks were passed around. After taking a sip of hers, Tawny turned back to her cards, her smile rapidly diminishing.

"So, what should I do?" she asked again.

"Bluff."

"But why—" she began to say, until Frederick leaned back in his chair to the point of absurdity, brought his refilled cup to his lips, and drank slowly, all the while waving her on. "Why? Why do I do this to myself?" she whispered as she rolled her eyes.

She looked at the other players for this round. If she was supposed to play them and not her hand, she had no idea where to start. They were as readable to her as a two-year-old's scribble. Her eyes subconsciously went to her captain then. As usual, Renee sat casually alone, with but not part of the group. She merely looked back at Tawny with no expression, which made the lieutenant sigh. She didn't know why she bothered; Renee never helped.

Tawny looked back at her cards, thought about what Frederick said, and thought about her first instinct. *This isn't a bad hand, but they had to have heard him. Why is he always so loud when he gives advice?* She rolled her eyes once more. Frederick was loud no matter the occasion. In that moment, her meager pile of money caught her attention.

She took a deep breath and placed her cards on the table. "I fold." Frederick scoffed, but she would have none of it. They had to have heard him.

Renee watched the scene and couldn't help but shake her head. No one noticed her reaction though, and that was just as well. The card games in the officer's mess had become quite the shipwide event. The game was usually poker. Out of tradition, Fleet had to buy in, as the Hustlers had started the game themselves, but it was a small price to pay. Almost every officer on the ship had played at least once at this point, if not regularly. Winter was in there somewhere. Noncoms were allowed as well, except Phalanx Troopers. The joke was that they couldn't count well enough to play cards. She guessed they entertained themselves in other ways, perhaps by punching or stabbing each other or something. Whatever the case, the captain also wasn't allowed to play. Not since Thycol. It was still fun to watch though.

The game continued, but Renee turned to see her executive officer, Commander Terry Fletcher, enter the officer's mess just before he opened the hatch. She'd been expecting him. He walked toward her slowly, a PDD in his hand, but his attention was on the game.

"Lt. Crowe win a hand yet?" he asked when he was finally within earshot.

Renee could only smile as she shook her head. "Pigs can't fly in space," she remarked.

Terry nodded and then took a seat next to the Wiz Kid. She was a good ten years his junior. No other starship captain in the fleet was as young...at least now. She had her strengths, but she wasn't the best commanding officer he'd served under. Damn capable, if unorthodox at times, but not the best. Frankly, Renee would be the first to admit that. She sat leaned back in her chair with her feet resting on a table. Though she was wearing her uniform, she looked more ready in this pose to go to the mall than to skipper a starship. As a few cheers and curses went up from the game table, Terry decided, on second thought, that perhaps she was the most professional looking officer here.

She was about his height, which made her a bit tall for a woman but not noticeably so. Her black hair complimented her mid-brownish skin tone well. It was trimmed to just above her shoulders and cradled her cheeks. The captain was pretty—worth a casual backward glance, at least. He'd heard and tried to forget some of the comments the embarked Phalanx Troopers made about her.

The two of them watched the game in silence for a long moment, but it was by no means silent in the room. Bellows and curses from Frederick filled the air, joined by various threats from an exasperated Tawny on the bodily harm she'd commit on him. Some of the descriptions were quite vivid.

Terry slowly shook his head. "Commander Reeves has all the command presence of a pile of pudding," he said with a hint of disgust.

"Well, then it's a good thing he's not actually in command of anything," Renee said with a smirk.

"Political officers are supposed to be the face of the UTE, representing us in diplomacy and contact with other species."

Just then, Frederick burped again, but this time with enough force to cause an actual tremor in the officer's mess.

Renee smirked while she rolled her eyes. "Terry, we're in a state of total war. Who are we talking to that we're not also shooting at?" She sighed. "Don't worry about him. I'll take care of it."

"Like last time?"

She glanced at her XO and tipped her head, acknowledging his point. "Fine. I'll have Tawny deal with him."

"Captain, you do that and there'll be nothing but bloody rags left," he said after a chuckle.

Renee smiled and looked back at the game. "What have you got for me?"

"BDA from the last strike," he answered as he handed her his PDD.

"That was Winter's flight, right?" Terry nodded as she looked over the figures. "They got out of that one by the skin of their teeth. I don't think we're going to get away with it again. Schedule some sim time to game out new tactics. Let's change up."

"Yes, ma'am."

Renee was quiet while she continued to read. After a few more seconds, she took a deep breath. "All right, what's the bad news?"

"Our replenishment inventory came in. 0500 tomorrow."

She flipped to the relevant page of the PDD and groaned. Her eyes became narrower and narrower as she read. "At least they're giving us a full refuel. No replacement personnel, a third of the requested Hammers, and basic food stock."

"I must say, Captain, when you piss people off, you make them good and mad at you," he remarked.

Renee was not amused. "I get that, but how do they expect us to fight with a skeleton crew, hardly any weapons, and starving?"

"We've got the fuel to run away," Terry pointed out after a pause.

She looked at him hard, and as always when she did that, it was like her eyes pierced straight through him. She wasn't actually angry—not at him anyway. He knew her well enough to know that. He swallowed nervously anyway.

"Anything you can pull?" she asked.

Terry slowly shook his head. "Not this time. We're fast becoming a ship of pariahs. Even so, the fleet is in pretty tough shape. I can't even get a loaf of bread from my usual sources."

Renee cursed softly under her breath and handed the PDD

back to him. Then she stared off into the distance. He knew that big brain of hers was calculating, thinking as was its wont on how to circumvent the problem before it. Whatever her conclusion, she either decided it was best to keep it to herself or, ultimately, there was no solution.

"All right," she muttered, her head falling slightly as she spoke. A second later, she relaxed and regained her usual calm determination. "Look at that. Tawny made it to the last round of a hand."

The lieutenant's hands were shaking, such was her excitement. All eyes were on her. Frederick screamed advice in her ear, all of which contradicted itself. But, such was the skill of his bullshittery, it seemed like even he believed the nonsense coming out of his mouth. That or he was too drunk to care.

"Come on!" he bellowed. "You can't let Ensign Bastard win again!"

"Right, not this time!" Tawny yelled. Then she pointed at him, subconsciously imitating her coach from earlier. "He's pulled his ear and, like, blinked three times," she said. So caught up in the moment was Tawny that it was hard to tell if she even believed what she said, or if she was too drunk to care. "This time, this time, I know he's bluffing." Zhou took a moment to scratch his nose twice and then smirk. "I call," she concluded, slamming her cards down on the table.

Zhou also placed his cards down, with infinitely more calm, and then it was over.

THE RIGHT TOOL

The universe was logic and order. Everything happened for a reason and could, with enough patience, be traced back to a causal source. That was the nature of reality for now and forever. Catch was knowledge. No one knew everything or could know everything. As Widget stared at her computer screens, that was frustratingly apparent.

"Nothing? How is there nothing?" she asked.

"That is what I'm telling you," replied a disembodied masculine voice named Quinn.

She did not know if she was actually talking to a man or a woman. She didn't even know if it was one person or multiple. That was the nature of her sources, the world she played in. Her identity was similarly disguised, though everyone knew she worked for the Rogue Wolves—too hard to hide that. But to anyone who would ask, she was a nine-year-old boy named Billy. Even the words she spoke were not only coded to sound like that of a boy but also translated into current Earth slang from Australia with a Spacer accent from habitat Reagg 45A.

"That's what I'm telling you. There is no record of a

Clairvoyant named Charon prior to the attack on New Earth. Considering the mythological origin of the name, it suggests that he is from the original sorten-trained generation of Clairvoyants."

"I think so too, and if that's true, there should be some record of the name somewhere. Someone named him," Widget said. "I need to get at least that."

"And I'm telling you that no such person can be found. The only possibilities I can think of are that the Clairvoyant who named Charon died in sorten captivity, so no such record exists; that there was a record but it was erased; or that Charon named himself."

Widget sat back in her chair and thought through the possibilities. She turned to one of her screens a few seconds later and began typing everything that came to mind. It was a long-learned habit but a helpful one. It was better to risk typing something meaningless than to forget an idea that could potentially have merit. At any rate, she didn't much care about Charon's name or even who named him. Not exactly. What she actually wanted was a physical description. No one knew what Charon looked like. The Sentinel stated in his interrogation that he'd never met Charon personally and that he always wore his mask if they spoke via holo. Even the sortens had no facial record in the data taken by Inertia from Solitary. If anything, Charon should have been named "Ghost." It was a more apt description.

"Clairvoyants don't usually name themselves unless as an alias, but even then that's rare. Even for Clairvoyants in the business," she pointed out. "Our Clairvoyants don't," she added, thinking of Gungnir and Inertia among others. "The only time I've ever encountered it is when a Clairvoyant wants to hide their identity for a specific mission. Kind of pointless, though—a Clairvoyant's bioelectric field has a unique traceable signature. Clairvoyants can even sense it. They say it's like seeing a face."

"Was there a scan of Charon's signature from his attack on New Earth?"

Widget shook her head even though her camera was off. "Dozens of Clairvoyants were fighting, and many more live there. My sources in the investigation are telling me they found nothing so far. I don't think there's anything on that lead."

Charon really is a ghost, she thought. What she said was essentially correct, but it wasn't the whole story. Every bioelectric field from the attack had been catalogued. It was helpful that the Clairvoyant Constructs' bioelectric fields were slight variations on each other and not wholly unique. Nevertheless, there was no Charon—no unknown bioelectric fields whatsoever.

Just then, Widget heard something behind her. She went stiff for a moment. "Stand by," she said quietly.

So practiced was she by now that, in her mind, it was like shifting a gear. Focus gave way to whatever fleeting thought entered her head. Logic was a curse word. All she wanted was random swirly bits of plum fairies on granite rocks made of Tiffanies.

"Widget, how's your investigation going? Any leads yet?" Gungnir asked.

"Yes, frogs. Lumpy crumpy frogs. Bullseye!" she said.

"Widget…you're being stranger than normal," the Clairvoyant replied, which was as much a warning as a statement.

She leaned over backward in her chair to look at him. Gungnir eyed her curiously. "Lamron?" she asked.

"I'm turning in for the night. Inertia sent some updates on their situation. We'll discuss it in the morning," he said after a sigh.

Widget closed her eyes but grimaced fiercely. Gungnir sighed again and then left the room. She returned to sitting properly and sighed herself when he was safely gone.

"I hate to tell you this, but mature Clairvoyants really only read someone's mind when they have to," Quinn said.

"Who told you that? A Clairvoyant?" Widget remarked dismissively.

"Yes, but I have data I can share with you."

"Topic for a different day."

"Indeed. But speaking of Clairvoyants and reading, I have to inform you that every data query I made about Charon was somehow traced back to me."

"What? Your network probes are encrypted, right?"

"Yes, they are. I was equally as surprised as you," the disembodied voice said. "It's never happened before to this degree."

"Any retaliation?" Widget asked quickly.

"None so far, but security measures are in place just in case. Needless to say, though, we have thus far been unsuccessful in tracking Charon. He most certainly knows we are looking for him, and he might be tracking *us*."

Widget nodded several times and wrote that fact in her notes in big bold letters. Then she sat back in her chair and thought deeply. *So, the ghost appears from nowhere and no one knows what he looks like. He then attacks a Clairvoyant training facility—probably one of the most dangerous places in the galaxy—seemingly as a lark...and then just disappears again,* Widget thought as she considered everything. *He also works for the sortens, which no Clairvoyant ever willingly does. But they trust him enough to use him to hire talent for wet work.*

"Billy, you still there?"

"Yes, just thinking," Widget responded.

"About?"

She took a moment for a deep breath, her many ideas coalescing into something coherent. "How did Charon and his army of Clairvoyant Constructs get on New Earth?"

"With a ship, of course."

Widget stared at her screen, completely dumbfounded. Gungnir could have fried an egg on her head. "Is that it? Why am I even talking to you? With answers like that, I may as well start reading tea leaves."

There was a laugh on the other end of the line, and for one brief moment she thought she heard more than one voice laughing. She wasn't completely sure though. The conversation was being recorded, so she wrote a note to check later.

"I'll rephrase what I said to something more intelligent. It stands to reason that Charon and his army didn't originate on New Earth, and you told me one of your teams sighted him somewhere else after the attack, meaning he is not still on New Earth."

Widget nodded as Quinn spoke. She didn't mention any real details of Solitary. This source was as much an information broker as it was an investigator. There was no reason to let slip every tidbit she had just for it to be sold to someone else in a transaction she couldn't control.

"More intelligent, yes, but no better than tea leaves," she mocked.

There was another laugh from her counterpart, but he continued undaunted after that. "If what I said is the case, he obviously used a ship both to get to and leave New Earth. Cloaking or other stealth systems could do the job."

"Normally I'd agree with you, but not now," she said, shaking her head. "New Earth is a core system of the UTE in a time of war. There are regular patrols by both Space Force and New Earth SDF. *No* ship," she continued, emphasizing the point, "can approach without being detected."

"If that's true, why aren't the Rogue Wolves constantly intercepted by these same patrols?"

"Figured you'd ask that," she began. "Our ship is very small. Enough to escape detection—"

"But you said no ship could do that," Quinn pointed out.

Widget rolled her eyes. "Fine. *Very few* ships can escape detection by both Space Force and SDF. Certainly not one large enough to house the Constructs Charon brought with him. Anyway, we also pay some bribes so certain people look the other way."

"Charon could also have given some bribes. With sorten backing, I doubt he is short of funds. Probably makes your operation look like a bake sale."

"Probably," Widget agreed. "But I doubt any Space Force or SDF officer would be too keen on taking a bribe from a Clairvoyant who never shows his face. We have history with certain *relevant* people. And we don't go attacking Clairvoyant training facilities. If Charon bribed his way in, he'd never be able to bribe his way out."

"True. Anyway, I know you, Billy. You wouldn't bring this up if you didn't already have an idea."

"I might," Widget said hesitantly. "It's really the only thing that makes sense to me. I just need a little help from you to see if it proves true."

"As always. Besides, it's either me or those tea leaves you talked about."

Widget smiled. "Don't get too confident. I can also fall back on fortune cookies."

5

___

THE NEW GUESTS

Like bees at a hive, they came to and fro in mass swarms. This was one of the few safe areas left; the sentries and patrols on the outer parameter saw to it. Yet, even without them, this was not a place for the unwary.

Giant metal behemoths were staged in long lines that stretched nearly across the solar system. Battleships, dedicated starfighter carriers, freighters, and troop transports, all tens of miles in length, lumbered along in parade. The laser and direct energy cannons alone that belonged to some of them dwarfed their maritime counterparts from long ago. The ships came for fuel, food, ammunition, repairs, and replacements for crew lost in battle. Another group of vessels also traveled to and from the spaceport to feed the war machine. Their labors were unceasing. Packed to the brim and surpassing even the size of the battleships, these super starfreighters formed a second line. There, and with the utmost urgency, the crews of Spaceport 168 unloaded these ships before they jetted off at maximum speed to return in time with another load.

And this was just one sector—one of dozens across the

whole of terran space. Numbers, unfathomably large and growing, told the story of the scale of the effort. It was the responsibility of someone behind a desk in some far-off place, but the trials of battle were reflected more coldly and more immediately here.

At times, only half a ship returned. Others bore unsightly scars of the carnage. Twisted metal and burnt hulls were suffered by most. There were holes blown in some that looked more akin to the puncture wounds of teeth, as if the ship had been preyed upon by some great and foul beast. A few couldn't even move under their own power, reduced to being towed by tractor tugs. And then, of course, there were those who didn't return at all, of which only memory remained.

In the midst of all of this, unscathed but weary, was the ISS *Griffin*. Though comparatively diminutive at just under five thousand feet in length, she stood proudly on the line nevertheless. The starcruiser was new and young, like her captain, and was one of the most advanced ships in the fleet, the seventh in the new Peacekeeper class. And, like her sisters, she was one of the fastest machines ever built. In her hangar was a squadron of Banshee starfighters and enough assault shuttles to get her battalion of embarked Phalanx Troopers to the enemy, wherever it may be. Her direct energy domes (DEDs) and direct energy cannon (DEC), as well as her complement of Mjolnir missiles, made her a formidable opponent in and of herself. Yet, for all that, in this place of relative peace, the crew of the *Griffin* never knew they were being stalked.

Renee stretched in her captain's chair and enjoyed the pleasure of a long, slow, deep breath. There was content-ment to be found in no one trying to kill them, at least until after they were replenished. *And I volunteered for this*, she thought with a reflectively satisfied but pained smile. Terry was beside her, as usual. No words were really said between them. She didn't dislike her XO, but they just didn't have the same casual acquaintance she had with Winter or Frederick. It was probably more appropriate that way, anyway.

She glanced at him in that moment. The man seemed more manufactured than born—an observation and not an insult. He was professional, usually proper, and disciplined when required but aggressive when necessary. If Fleet Command could roll Terry Fletchers off an assembly line, they'd break the handle turning the machine to high. The thought made her smile. His career, however, was as doomed as that of every other senior officer of this ship, assuming they survived the war.

With that in mind, Renee turned her attention back to her chair display. She was currently studying the latest intelligence report. It was anything but light reading, but it passed the time.

"Captain, our requisition list has been confirmed. We are currently number thirteen in line," Leena said from her operations station.

"Very well," Renee replied casually.

Leena nodded and returned to communicating with the spaceport. The captain listened, if distantly, but the transfer was quite routine. Frankly, at least on the bridge, Leena was the only person actually working. Even Tawny at the helm could have fallen asleep for all the difference it would have made. Automatic systems and sophisticated computer cores were a wonder when kept to their purpose. The engineering section would say that, for all the gizmos to function correctly, the technology had to be, in some cases, literally hammered into place after long hours of work. But here, the end result was almost magically simple and precise, and she was thankful for that.

"I was able to pull some strings," Terry said. "Food stocks mostly. I was even able to get some ice cream."

"What flavor?" Renee asked.

"Cherry or strawberry. Can't really remember."

"So, it's red."

Terry thought about it and then laughed lightly, more at himself than anything. "Yes, it's red. I'm sure of at least that."

"Ice cream. It's not much, but the crew will appreciate it," she said with a shrug.

"Sorry, Captain… There won't be enough for the entire crew."

"How much were you able to get?" she asked.

Terry groaned softly. "Perhaps enough for a senior staff meeting." He paused for a moment as he thought about it further. "If Frederick isn't there."

Renee sat back in her chair. She then smirked evilly as she considered how she'd pull that off. She didn't care all that much for ice cream, let alone "red" ice cream, but it gave her something to think about that didn't deal with the war. A few options came immediately to mind, which she filed away for later.

"I'll see what I can do," she said, still smirking.

Terry smiled. He knew her well enough to know she meant what she said. She always meant what she said. "I also got—"

"Captain, we have a situation," Leena interrupted.

Renee snapped her head to her like a shot, her conversation with Terry instantly forgotten as the familiar focus of command was summoned. "Go on," she said.

Leena nodded. "The spaceport is receiving a distress call. High priority code."

The captain looked at her sidelong and raised an eyebrow. "Half the ships here are in distress."

"I understand, ma'am, but this is different. It's coming from an Archer-class corvette from out of the system."

"What's the nature of their problem?" Terry asked. "And what does that have to do with us? The outer patrols can take care of it."

"They can't, sir. I don't even think there's a problem with the ship," she said, her voice increasingly rushed. Then she was quiet for a moment, obviously listening to some new transmission. "They are asking for you, ma'am…by name. They say they want to come aboard."

Renee looked at her operations officer, at a loss for what to make of her. Leena was quiet as a mouse unless she was on a commlink. She was so demure that she didn't even attend the card games in the officer's mess. Renee had never seen her actually rattled before, even during combat. But now her soothing, calm voice was almost shrill.

"Who? Who wants to come on board?" Renee asked.

Leena gripped her console and swallowed hard before she answered. "The Rogue Wolves," she said softly.

There was utter silence on the bridge after that. Renee nervously clenched her jaw as more than a few officers looked to her for direction. Others stared off into the distance, too dumbfounded to even think of that. In time, what felt like an eon at least, the hums and whirs of the bridge displays and instruments reentered perception. For some, awareness of their quickening breath or shaking hands soon followed. And yet, for one, there was a thought—a clear grasp of the incredible situation. However unlikely, it was also felt in clean, crystal clarity and just as easily expressed.

"We're fucked," Frederick uttered loudly.

His comment snapped Renee from herself. "What's the spaceport's response?"

"They haven't made any, ma'am," Leena answered.

They're waiting to see what we do, she thought. Her first impulse was to close her eyes and take a deep breath. This seemed more like a nightmare than reality. But she didn't— everyone was watching her. Instead, the captain activated the *Griffin's* communication systems.

"Colonel Lanser, meet me in the hangar with a security contingent." *Might as well fight fire with fire*, she thought.

There was a pause of no more than a second before a chirp came back. "Aye, ma'am," replied the commander of the embarked Phalanx Troopers.

"Captain?" Terry questioned quietly as he leaned close to her.

Renee ignored him. "Sound battle stations counterboarding."

"Aye, ma'am. Sounding!" Leena said.

A second later, a loud klaxon was heard throughout the ship. Leena rallied from her hesitation earlier, her voice returning to its even, steady rhythm as she gave direction through the intercom system. Renee could feel hundreds of men and women responding smartly and calmly to the command. They had no idea what was going on.

"Ms. Crowe, intercept course. Execute when ready," Renee continued.

Tawny repeated the order and entered the appropriate data into the navigation computer as she spoke.

"Contact the spaceport and inform them of our intentions." She considered the situation for a few more seconds. "Also ask them to keep our place in line." *If we survive this*, she didn't add.

The main engines flared to life as she turned her attention

to Terry. It would be a short burn. The Rogue Wolves weren't far away. She felt the acceleration distantly, in an odd way. It wasn't physical sensation but a broader subconscious awareness. She shouldn't even have felt it with the inertial inhibitor operating. Yet, as with many things now, she didn't know how she knew. She just did.

"Mr. Fletcher?" she asked softly.

"Captain, is this wise? Even with the troopers?" Terry asked.

Renee slowly shook her head. "The colonel is a Clairvoyant. Has to be worth something," she suggested.

"Any other time, I'd agree with you, but against this?"

She turned away to think. "We don't know if they even want to attack us," she pointed out as she turned to look at him again. "Perhaps they really do need help?"

"Why would they ask for you by name then?" Terry asked. "You're the only person who can help them?"

Renee knew his point better than he did. Try as she might, there really was no other way to see it. "If we can't hold them in the hangar, deploy SCS."

"Charging Ghost Drive," Tawny announced, though the immediate operation of the ship was on neither Renee's nor Terry's mind.

He nodded sternly. "Aye, ma'am."

"Might as well not keep them waiting," Renee said as she stood.

Despite what she said, though, she did have one other task to deal with first. She walked toward Frederick, who was seated behind her, and looked down on him expectantly.

He slowly shook his head as his eyes grew wide. "Oh no," he began. "You don't expect me to commit suicide with you."

"Ghosting…now," Tawny announced, and Renee swore she heard a giggle in her voice.

For the captain's part, she couldn't help a small smirk. But it was a commanding, resolute smirk that, by itself, could send brave men rushing headlong into certain doom. She had never used it before. It didn't work on Frederick, who began to protest.

"Captain—"

"You're the political officer. You're supposed to be the face of the UTE, negotiating for us and the like."

"And if those damned Rogue Wolves want an export treaty, I'm sure you're up for the challenge."

"Frederick," she said softly but sternly.

He grumbled and cursed under his breath, but he said nothing that was intelligibly important. Smirks were one thing, but he never argued against her when she used that tone. Renee exited the bridge and heard him continuing to grumble behind her as he followed. Soon she saw her second destination, an arms locker just outside the bridge.

"What do you know about the Rogue Wolves?" she asked as she strapped a pistol to her side.

A rifle would be more appropriate, but she'd have a squad of troopers for backup and Colonel Lanser. Frankly, if it came down to her, everyone in the hangar was dead anyway. Even so, she had no intention of going there unarmed.

"Same as everyone else," Frederick answered. "That they are a group of powerful Clairvoyants who hire out to the highest bidder."

Renee heard him but made no response. They were alone in the corridor, and she used the moment to finally take her deep breath and close her eyes. Frederick was an unquestionable fuck-up of the highest order and a fool. But he was *her* fuck-up and *her* fool, and he always held her closest confidence. Her moment over, she opened her eyes, slammed the locker closed, and started for the elevator. Two armed and armored troopers had just appeared from it and were running to guard the bridge.

"That's it? Nothing else?" she asked as the troopers ran by them.

"What else is there, Captain?"

Renee glanced at him. "Who they work for, how many there are, who they are, etcetera..." she said, as if it were obvious.

"As I said, Captain, the highest bidder."

"You know what I mean," she added after a quick sigh.

Frederick nodded as they entered the elevator. She pressed the button for the proper deck, and he continued. "No one really knows who hires them. Just guesses based on their supposed activity. It really is another world out there, Captain. People like you and me never see it. Had a friend once—" Renee silently raised her hand, ending the story. There was no time for it. He nodded and decided to change tack. "As for the rest of your questions, there's no way to say. There could be a hundred Rogue Wolves or just one."

Renee nodded a few times before she began pacing around the elevator. She always walked slowly in circles when she was thinking deeply. Frederick couldn't stand the habit.

"How strong are they?" she asked.

"There are only stories. I don't think anyone has survived one of their attacks, to tell the truth."

"Well, what kind of stories?"

"Heard it said once that if an average Clairvoyant can be considered a gun, a Rogue Wolf would be a...a—"

"Would be a what?" Renee asked as the elevator doors opened.

"A force of nature."

She looked at him for a moment, and he stared right back.

It was obvious that the captain was considering his words, but she said nothing and exited the elevator. He was right behind her. On this deck and almost every other, troopers and crewmen prepared for the possible confrontation that all hoped wouldn't come. Weapons were passed out; armor was donned; tactics and procedures were reiterated. Renee and Frederick moved through the machine like salmon making their way upstream. She walked confidently and deftly, fully switched into command mode. Frederick followed behind her slender frame as she made a hole in the crowd. Every now and then, a young trooper or crewmate would glance at the captain as she walked by, and each time she returned a nod, if however slight, in acknowledgement. It wasn't much, but he saw a spark of vigor and resolve ignite in the crewmember every time it happened.

They reached a hatch for the hangar, and she paused at it. It was hard to discern if it was fear or nervousness that made her wait. If he knew her, however, and he was quite sure he did —rather well—then she was engaged in her one and favorite pastimes: thinking.

"Well, Captain, I'll wait out here for you," he said. "Yell if they need to negotiate one of those export treaties."

"Would I be in my rights to shoot you for cowardice before the enemy?" she teased.

"What's the difference?" the political officer said with a shrug. "I'm just as dead in that hangar."

Renee gave an amused smirk, grabbed him by the shirt collar, and dragged him inside. Colonel Melvick Lanser looked at them when they entered. Frederick grumbled and cursed as he staggered off balance. She let him go and assumed a more dignified poise, which almost made Frederick fall over. He made no more protests though. The Clairvoyant before him, for the moment, was a more halting sight than the Clairvoyants who were on their way. The colonel wasn't a very tall man. Indeed, he was shorter than Renee and several of the troopers he commanded. He was bald by choice, natural balding having been eradicated centuries ago through genetic massaging. There was a quiet tenseness about him, much like the tautness of his muscles. Frederick drew no closer, but Renee approached calmly with hands on her hips and an air of a smile.

"Mel," she said respectfully but softly enough for only him and Frederick to hear.

Frederick shook his head. He'd seen fat kids more intimidated by a jumbo ice cream sundae than he'd ever seen her with their resident Clairvoyant. Not every ship had Clairvoyant crewmembers. In fact, most had none. He didn't know of any…incidents ever happening, but it was just so uncomfortable being around them sometimes. Though, when he thought about it further, that wasn't always the case with every individual.

"Captain," Mel said back with a nod.

Renee looked from him to the troopers, who were conversing quietly amongst each other as they got ready. "If they attack, can we hold them here?" she asked.

"No chance," Mel replied casually, matter-of-factly, as only a Clairvoyant could.

Upon hearing that, Renee clenched her jaw and then took a deep breath, but she said nothing.

There was a chirp from the hangar's intercom system. "Contact established with target corvette," Leena said. "Inbound, ready to dock in approximately one minute and seventeen seconds."

"You know, Captain," Frederick said, leaning close to her, "you can always give the order to blow them out of the sky right now. Might be doing the galaxy a favor."

"They could actually need help," she responded.

"And what if they don't?" he offered in return.

The option had never crossed her mind and she wasn't tempted to act on it now, but the idea did have merit. Pursing her lips, Renee accessed the ship's intercom. She hated indecision. "Bridge, this is the captain. Have you scanned them? Do they have any damage?"

"That's a negative, Captain," Terry answered. "Their function appears normal."

Renee nodded, though there was no way for him to see her.

"Captain," Frederick began.

"No," Renee said firmly.

"Thirty seconds," Leena announced.

Frederick didn't try again, but Mel began giving orders to his troopers. They formed two firing lines, one knelt before the other. Renee, Mel, and Frederick were behind, but she could tell the Clairvoyant was ready to leap into action the moment it became necessary. She even thought she saw one of the lights flicker a moment ago.

"Opening hangar bay doors," a crewmember announced from the control room that overlooked the hangar.

The doors opened relatively quickly to reveal the starfield of the empty void of space. Only the magcon field kept everyone and everything from being sucked out. Nothing could be seen—not at first. But gradually the arrowhead-shaped craft came into view. There was utter silence by all as the surreal became reality.

"Ten seconds," Leena said.

The ship glided closer and closer, like a predatory bird about to swoop on its prey. The point of the arrowhead was aimed like a dagger at the defense team. Sweat beaded on foreheads, breaths were caught in throats, and Renee noticed that one of her hands shook. Slowly, finally, the ship came to rest before them on its landing struts.

"Closing hangar bay doors."

There was no command to do it, but every trooper brought their rifle to the ready. Renee swallowed hard. "All right, let's go," she said softly to herself. She didn't pull her pistol, but her hand tingled in anticipation of doing so.

Nothing else happened for who knew how long. The ship simply sat. Then, finally, there was a hiss like a coiling snake as its boarding ramp descended. The troopers' grip on their rifles tightened. A few seconds later, a young woman walked down the ramp. She was blond and, in fact, very pretty. Renee even heard Frederick whistle to himself, but he soon choked the sound back into a gag. The woman was striking in more ways than one. One side of her face was covered in rather unsightly burn scars.

Carmen descended the boarding ramp of *The Lady*, eager to continue her and Inertia's mission. She'd never been on a military starship before. Other than *The Lady*, she'd only been on a passenger ship when she went to Evonea to hunt for the Sentinel. She wasn't exactly sure what to expect. Her mind had run with the many possibilities from when Inertia told her what they'd be trying to attempt, yet for all that, she never would have guessed the start of their journey would begin like this.

She paused, almost frozen in surprise. In front of her were two dozen Phalanx Troopers, all with their weapons pointed at her, and two Clairvoyants. She could read one of the Clairvoyants pretty easily, but the other was near impossible. Next to her, strangely, was an overweight, middle-aged man who seemed so terrified that Carmen wondered if urine was running down his leg. She looked at the female Clairvoyant curiously. The woman wore a Fleet uniform and not body armor like her male counterpart. She was also armed with a pistol. Carmen had never heard of Clairvoyants using firearms before. What would be the point? In any case, she stood in front of the ramp, unsure of what to do. Her first thought was to raise her hands to show she wasn't a threat, but before she could, her partner stood at her side.

"Inertia?" she questioned softly, glancing at him.

He said nothing. By his countenance, the rifles the troopers carried shot water instead of bullets. Carmen wasn't particularly worried herself, but there was a vast chasm between helping someone and shooting someone. Their mission was dead as a doornail if this endeavor turned to the latter. For his part, he stared at the female Clairvoyant, who stared right back. After a time, there was a change in her from tense readiness to tense curiosity. Carmen looked back and forth between the two many times, and the longer she did so, the more curious she became as well.

The woman began walking toward them slowly. The fat man protested, but she ignored him. She didn't pull her pistol. There was no threat about any aspect of her approach. She stared at Inertia and seemed captivated, as if she were witness to the impossible. Eventually, the woman stopped in front of him and just stood there. She was almost as tall as him, which made her taller than Carmen by a good measure. Nothing was said by anyone, though she leaned close and her mouth teased several words. It seemed like she didn't want to break the spell. In time, she said one word—one solitary word, with apprehensive hesitation.

"Will?"

Inertia's lips twisted into a wry smirk. The woman gawked at him and, like a shot, punched him very hard in the arm. The reaction made Carmen jump. The fat man at the other end of the room almost fainted.

"You asshole! You scared the shit out of me!" Renee said loudly. Inertia laughed before the woman grabbed him in a tight hug. Carmen even thought she saw a tear in her eye.

"Inertia? What's going on?" Carmen asked, even more confused now than a moment ago.

Renee let him go, and he turned to his partner. "Edge, this is my older sister, Captain Renee Brown."

Carmen's face turned a deep shade of perplexed. "You have a sister...your real name is Will?"

Inertia rolled his eyes, but Renee spoke before he could. "Long lost sister," she said, wiping away a tear. "I haven't seen you since they took you. I didn't think I'd ever see you again."

"I know," he said gently. "We need your help."

"Anything."

THE WARMONGER

Inertia didn't always tell her everything. Indeed, she always knew what she needed to know, but he had a rather annoying habit of being coy with information she didn't know she needed to know. There was no malice behind it—from what Carmen could tell, anyway. But as annoying as it sometimes was, she simply concluded that he was more comfortable than most in allowing events to play out at their own pace. At least she wasn't the only irritated person.

Captain Brown and her partner walked in front of her as they made their way through the *Griffin* to the main briefing room. No words were said by anybody, and it seemed like Renee was near the end of her discipline to keep the silence. The captain glanced at Inertia constantly. Carmen looked between them as well, but with less urgent curiosity. All of Renee's being was bent toward her brother. Her shoulders were angled toward him, and one hand's fingers danced restlessly, as if it were a spider attempting to hypnotize its prey into coming closer. Yet her mouth stayed still...sort of. Her lips teased words that went unsaid. Her mouth sometimes opened randomly to voice something, anything, but after a flash of prudence, it would shut with a frustrated quiver.

Only Carmen noticed. Beside her was the fat man, who she learned was named Commander Frederick Reeves. He was more interested in her than the drama between his captain and her partner. He stole glances when he thought Carmen wasn't looking. She found the idea of it conceptually odd, because of course she always knew he was looking, whether she saw his little peeks or not. His eye surveyed her as completely and thoroughly as a master cartographer would an unknown landmass. She most certainly tried *not* to read him then, but she did glance back from time to time, though nowhere near as covertly.

There were very few fat people after the advent of genetic massaging. She had to work to think of any she knew. His bulbous belly, however, seemed welded to his otherwise fit frame. His hair looked like it had been dropped on his head like a bad toupee. It could have been styled into something handsome, but he didn't seem to care. There were streaks of grey here and there in the otherwise brown. He was easily old enough to be her father. All in all, he was quite the odd duckling compared to the trim and proper Space Force officers and crew who passed them by.

The other atypical standout was Colonel Lanser at their back. The Clairvoyant reminded her of Mugal in a way. His tense, ready bearing was obviously bent to the protection of the ship, same as the sortens' had been to Solitary. But he had none of the security director's apprehension. In fact, he was the only person who didn't pay herself and Inertia any attention whatsoever. She looked at him once, and he merely gave a polite nod in return. She guessed it was some sort of Clairvoyant comradery. She didn't have much experience socializing with Clairvoyants out of the facility, now that she thought about it. He wasn't in her and Inertia's generation, though; he looked maybe half a generation older than Gungnir and Kali.

The group entered an elevator, exited a few decks up, and continued on. They arrived at the briefing room a short while later. Renee opened the door for them and waved her guests inside. The room was larger than Carmen expected, and a large round table dominated the space. Projection equipment was built into the ceiling. The decorations were modest, mostly pictures of starships, which she knew nothing about.

Renee sat at a chair that was noticeably larger than the rest, and unless Carmen missed her guess, it was slightly elevated as well. She and Inertia sat opposite the captain. Colonel Lanser took a random seat, but Frederick sat on Renee's immediate right. At that, Renee paused a moment then took a deep breath. Afterward, she lazily turned her head toward the political officer and groaned as she glared at him.

"All right, all right, all right," he said hastily as he stood. He then sat down on her left.

Renee groaned again while shaking her head, but she smiled as she did so. "If you'll give us a moment, I'd like to wait for the rest of my senior officers."

Carmen nodded. Inertia relaxed in his chair. The Clairvoyants didn't need to wait long, though. A rather tall woman entered after only a few minutes. She was alone and unarmed, unlike Renee, and she wasn't wearing body armor like Colonel Lanser. Her uniform was not like Renee's either. It was black with dark blue stripes that ran along the arms and outer seam of the pant legs, in contrast to the captain's black and silver. Her head was topped with a mess of short, blonde curls that otherwise hugged her scalp. She paused at the doorway when she saw Carmen and Inertia, but she regained herself quickly.

Renee looked at her with a smile and a nod. Frederick looked also, but there was a mischievous gleam in his eye. "Wint—"

"Fuck off, Frederick," the woman said sharply before he could even say her name. She had a strong New Earther's accent.

The fighter pilot then took a seat at the table, nowhere near the rest of the group. Frederick chuckled. Carmen noted that, though the woman's response was aggressive, she wasn't actually angry. A quick read told as much.

The next to enter were two men who were casually talking to each other. One was Asian, well-groomed, and alert, like a proper Space Force officer. The other's only remarkable feature was the complete lack of any remarkable feature. He wasn't ugly in any way, just plain. He sat next to Renee after the two exchanged a respectful nod, and the other man sat next to him.

"Okay, we're all here," Renee began. She then gestured to her right. "This is my XO, Commander Terry Fletcher. Beside him is my fire control and tactics officer, Lieutenant Commander Hiroshi Fujita." Both men looked at the Clairvoyants and nodded in turn. "Colonel Melvick Lanser is the CO of our embarked Phalanx Troopers," she continued as she gestured toward him. "And that is Commander Nadia 'Winter' Silver, CO of the Hustlers. And lastly…lastly," Renee muttered as she took a deep breath and rolled her eyes. Frederick tapped a tune on the table for his impending announcement. "This is my political officer, Commander Frederick Reeves. You can safely ignore him."

"Hi," Frederick said, waving at the Clairvoyants, though mostly at Carmen. She looked at Inertia after pursing her lips, but her partner actually let go a small smile of amusement.

"This," Renee said, gesturing at their guests, "is Edge and

Inertia of the Rogue Wolves. They have something very important to tell us."

Carmen looked at Inertia again, who leaned forward in his chair. Across the table, Terry took out a PDD to write notes. Renee came to sharp attention in an almost cat-like manner. Hiroshi also came to attention but couldn't muster the laser-precise focus of his captain. Mel was…well, a Clairvoyant. Winter was ready to listen but seemed more interested in taking a walk in a park than hearing anything they had to say. Frederick burped.

After pausing to take a breath, Inertia laid it all out. Carmen listened attentively, even though she knew every-thing he was going to say. He went over the timeline in detail, from the Sentinel, Charon's attack on New Earth, and their time at Solitary. Last, he spoke of the sortens' research base concealed aboard a freighter. Carmen found the entire tale incredible to believe, despite having lived it. She thought about all she had done then, all she would do, and all she may have to bring herself to do in the future. She meant it; she was in this all the way. But here now, sitting across from trained professional Space Force officers aboard a heavily armed starcruiser on the verge of beginning the next leg of the jour-ney, she began questioning the wisdom of her resolve. Inertia eventually finished his brief and leaned back in his chair while she still considered everything.

"Intercepting and destroying a freighter shouldn't be too hard," Hiroshi said.

The comment snapped Carmen from her reverie. "No, you can't destroy it," she said quickly, as she was reminded why she was here.

"Why not?"

"To you, it's just a ship. But back at Solitary, the sortens were abducting Clairvoyants for their research, even going as far as kidnapping children. There's no telling how many they could have on that freighter. You have to understand that it's a rescue mission as much as it's about stopping a threat. It can't be risked." She spoke firmly, passionately, and the words came out with such speed and force that they were halfway across the galaxy before she even realized she was capable of uttering them. Winter raised an eyebrow, and Frederick stared at Carmen, his face blank but his eyes serious.

"I agree," Renee began, her voice providing a welcome soothing calm. "The freighter shouldn't be destroyed. But there is one thing you haven't told us yet. Where is it?" Carmen looked at Inertia, who said nothing. "Where is it?" Renee asked again after a few seconds of waiting. The silence continued, and she began to look at her brother with a hint of worry. "Where?"

Inertia raised a hand just off the table and looked at Terry. The XO got the hint and slid his PDD across the table to the Clairvoyant. Inertia inputted the coordinates and slid it back. Carmen didn't know what the big deal was. It was in sorten space, of course. She would have answered herself, but she didn't know its exact location. When Renee looked at the PDD, however, her body instantly went rigid. Her face twitched in pained grief as her eyes fell. She knew she had the room's attention, but the captain was unable to stop the reaction. She rotated her chair until her back was turned to everyone, unable to think of anything else to do.

"So that's why you came to me," she said, her voice quivering despite her best efforts. "I'd hoped it was something else."

"Where is it?" Hiroshi asked.

"Sorten space," Terry answered seriously after glancing at the PDD.

Carmen looked at them, at the back of Renee's turned

chair, and at Inertia several times, unable to make any sense of what just transpired. Her partner had no real expression. He looked expectant, if anything.

"What? What is it? I don't get it?" she asked.

"This is a military starship," Terry began. "We can't exactly go waltzing into another empire's territory without provocation."

Carmen's eyebrows scrunched together. "But there is provocation, I told you, they're abducting Clairvoyants and they staged an attack on a training facility."

"Yes, we heard. But Charon is a terran, as was the Sentinel—"

"Working for the sortens," she interjected, cutting him off, as frustration made her shake her fists. To believe they'd come this far to be stopped by this, of all things.

"Can you prove that?" Hiroshi asked.

The comment made her pause. She knew Charon was working for the sortens; Inertia even saw him at Solitary. When it came to hard, tangible evidence, however, her hands were empty. She didn't know what secrets the files of Solitary revealed. She glanced at Inertia with that in mind. He glanced back but said nothing.

"Yes," she answered hesitantly.

Just then, Renee turned her chair back around. "That doesn't really matter," she said. "The situation is more than that." She looked directly at Carmen. "Do you know how this war was started?" Her tone suggested that the Clairvoyant didn't.

Carmen didn't see the point of the question. "Everyone knows that. One of our ships had a malfunction and drifted into arkin space, who we've never encountered before. They attacked, despite us saying the incident was inadvertent. After the battle, they declared war on us. The sortens and Eternals followed suit."

Renee nodded slowly. "That isn't the whole story." Carmen couldn't read her. The Clairvoyant, however, raised an eyebrow when she saw the starship captain take a deep breath and then let it go after a shudder. "We've been aware of the arkins for approximately two years. I won't go into detail on how. But what matters is we dispatched several starships deliberately into their territory for reconnaissance. One of them, the *Growler*, was detected and unable to escape. Fleet Command intended to sacrifice the *Growler* to keep the peace. An arkin recon ship was previously intercepted and destroyed in our territory, so it would have been one for one. They got a black eye, we would get a black eye, and that was where it would have stayed."

"It obviously didn't," Carmen said.

Renee nodded again. "Against orders, the officers and crew of the *Griffin* entered arkin space and rescued the *Growler*. Oh, there was a battle. But it wasn't the fleet flying to gloriously save one lost little ship that mistakenly wandered behind enemy lines. No, it was the mutinous crew of a cruiser that wouldn't trade the lives of comrades to keep the peace. In short…*we* started the war."

Renee didn't say anything else, but she looked like she wanted to. How she spoke, detached and analytical, couldn't save her from the conclusion. Carmen looked at the women across the table and felt an odd tinge of pity. There was no torture more complete and unending than self-torture. Carmen had played that game more times than she could count and always came on the losing end. There was a second part to the sentence that went unsaid but all heard anyway. It wasn't: "In short, we started the war." It was: "In short, we started the war, and billions suffered for it."

Carmen considered the new pieces to the puzzle and subconsciously licked her lips. It wasn't just hitching a ride on a military starship, and it wasn't just that the captain of the ship was a blood relative of her partner. It was all that, plus that they were with the persons who had started the conflict in the first place.

Renee continued. "And somehow you knew all that. It's why you're here." Her words sounded more for herself than to edify the room. She spoke softly yet with a tone that could cut. The captain stared at Inertia as she spoke. "To think I only wondered how you were able to find me. The location of a starship is classified enough outside the fleet, let alone the true beginning of the war."

Carmen looked at her partner as well. She never had any hope of reading him, but she liked to think she knew him now, at least somewhat. What thoughts churned behind his piercing eyes, however, probably no one would ever know. He looked at his sister calmly but blankly, as if he didn't want to betray anything. Carmen did not know how difficult that was.

"If that's what happened, why aren't you all in jail or something?" she asked Renee.

The woman gave a cheerless laugh. "Jail?" she muttered, laughing again. "I pissed off Admiral Wright so much that I'm surprised he didn't execute me. We honestly thought he hired you two as a last dying wish to take care of the job. Anyway, we can't go to jail. By the official story, we're heroes of the battle to rescue the *Growler*. Know this, though: I myself and every officer of the ISS *Griffin* are living on borrowed time. Higher command can't just get rid of us, nor can they reassign anyone, since they don't want us influencing anyone else. So, we are assigned the difficult missions. We live fine. We die just as good.

This is a ship of pariahs, as far as the rest of the fleet is concerned."

The captain's subordinates nodded seriously when she made her conclusion, except one. Winter stared at Renee and looked like she was biting her tongue. She held her peace though, just like Carmen noted but held her comment about the reaction.

"I understand," the Clairvoyant said gently, looking at each officer in turn. "But we still need your help. Will you help us?"

"Yes. It can't be done any other way," Inertia added, finally entering the conversation again. However, he only looked at his sister. "It can't."

Renee took a deep breath as she leaned back in her chair. She then looked at Terry. The two exchanged a few seconds of silent consideration until, at last, he nodded and Renee turned her attention back to the Clairvoyants.

"It's not up to me," she remarked. Carmen deflated in her seat, sighing as she did so. Renee glanced at her. "A ship of pariahs or not, it is nevertheless a ship of war. It is not mine to command as I please. We have responsibilities, others depending on us."

Inertia leaned forward before he spoke. He carried a confident twinkle in his eye that Carmen had seen before, and she stopped worrying if they were going to get the starship's help.

"With all due respect, Captain, your interdiction efforts, while important, aren't vital," he said.

Renee's eyes narrowed. "So, not only do you know our location but also our mission. I can't just leave the sector; I have to speak to my superiors first. Though, I suppose you already know what they are going to say?"

"I do, and you're wasting time. We have less than a week."

"Perhaps, and perhaps you do know, but I will speak to them first." She took a deep breath. "Anything else?" The two Clairvoyants glanced at each other. Then they looked at Renee. Carmen shook her head, and Inertia simply leaned back in his chair. Renee said something to her executive officer that no one else heard and then stood. "It will take a little time to establish a secure connection with Fleet Command. Until then, let us show you to your quarters."

Carmen leaned close to Inertia. "Should we pretend we're married again, so they don't separate us?" she asked out the side of her mouth.

He glanced at her and smirked. "No, we got divorced. Forgot to tell you."

Carmen smiled. "You'd forgotten to tell me we were married in the first place."

"Yeah, that's why we got divorced. Don't you remember?" He allowed a brief smile before he grew more serious. "I don't think we have anything to worry about here."

Carmen nodded and then stood with everyone else.

"I'll escort Inertia myself," Renee said. "Mr. Reeves."

"Aye, Captain?" Frederick responded.

"Can you please escort Edge to her quarters?"

Frederick pointed at his chest with a shaky finger. "Me? Alone?"

"Of course alone," Renee said, rolling her eyes. "Maybe she's interested in an export treaty," she added with a shrug.

Carmen had no idea what they were referring to, nor did she hear Frederick's grumbling response. But eventually he stopped muttering to himself, stood up straight, and pointed a thumb at the exit. "You ready?" he asked.

She glanced at Inertia, who nodded. His attention was barely aimed at her, though. He stared at his sister across the room with the same tense readiness he faced the sortens with. Renee's posture, outward expression—everything about her—was much the same. It was quite obvious that they both were and were not looking forward to their time alone. That, however, had nothing to do with her. Carmen left her partner to it and began walking toward Frederick, who opened the door for her.

She didn't read him; she didn't *want* to read him. But she got enough of an emanation from Frederick to start walking in the correct direction before he said anything or took the lead. He followed a touch behind as he scratched his head. He glanced at her as they went, but not like before. He wasn't nervous, exactly; it seemed more like he knew how he wanted to proceed but was unsure if he should take the first step. It made her think of when she first met Michael and of his bumbling attempts to just say hello. While she doubted he and Frederick were anything alike, just like then, she knew she'd have to take the lead now in whatever Frederick wished to say. She glanced at the *Griffin's* political officer with soft, inviting eyes as she tried to coax him out of his shell.

He coughed gruffly. "You spoke pretty passionately back there. This seems to mean a lot to you," he said.

"Yes, yes, it does," she said casually.

"May I ask why?" he asked, his voice tentative—even meek.

"It's not complicated," she responded after a quick smile. "As I said, the sortens are abducting people for these experiments, even children. They have to be stopped."

"Ah, yes, that's right. Just—"

Carmen glanced at him as they entered a new corridor and then looked straight ahead. "I must say your captain is shrewd," she remarked matter-of-factly as she cut him off.

"Oh yeah, she's definitely that," he agreed without even thinking. Then he paused and looked at her with a start. "No, wait, what do you mean?" he asked quickly.

The complete abrupt change in his demeanor made her shake her head with a small smile. "She doesn't fully trust us. She's probably questioning my partner right now, and she hopes you'll be able to get some details from me." He looked at her with ever-widening eyes, which made her smirk. "You don't even realize that's why she asked you to escort me. I can see why she trusts you. She probably figured I'd take your inquires as awkward flirting," Carmen mused aloud.

"How do you know she trusts me?"

She paused a moment. "For the life of me, I can never figure out why people ask Clairvoyants questions like that."

He barked out a laugh that echoed down the corridor. *Bird is fully out now*, Carmen thought. "Yeah, you got me there. I wasn't thinking. Anyway, there's something odd between the captain and that partner of yours. Never seen her act like that with anyone before. Do they know each other?"

Carmen didn't answer right away. She realized now that no one else knew Renee and Inertia were related. Everyone had been at the other end of the hangar when they told her. She didn't know why, but the two of them seemed to think no one else should know, for whatever reason. She decided to follow their lead out of respect, though she didn't really see the point of it—they looked exactly alike.

"No, I don't think so," she replied.

Frederick nodded a few times, then looked at her and smiled. "So, is it working?"

She couldn't help but raise an eyebrow. "Is what working?"

"The awkward flirting."

The eyebrow was soon joined by a wry smirk as she rolled her eyes. "I'm at least half your age," she pointed out.

"Aye," Frederick agreed, nodding. "But I think I can endure that burden if you're up for it," he remarked, his voice serious and contemplative.

She looked at him, nonplused for a few seconds, until the brazen stupidity of his statement made her laugh. It felt good to do so. A few passing crewmen looked at her curiously, but Frederick only smiled.

"I must say, for a blood-thirsty Rogue Wolf, you're a bit more normal than I was expecting."

"Thanks I guess," she said, still laughing lightly. His statement got her thinking, though. "I know Renee is one of those Wiz Kids—I remember seeing her on the holo—but I didn't know she was a Clairvoyant. I didn't know there were any Clairvoyant captains."

Frederick stopped smiling. "She'd say she's not." Carmen looked at him as his demeanor changed yet again. "There was a lot she didn't say back there. The captain of the *Growler* was a friend of hers, another Wiz Kid. Think his name was Garvin Brook. I believe they were quite close, but I don't know all the details," he said with a shrug. Carmen thought she remembered hearing the name somewhere. She nodded and Frederick continued. "Not too long ago, the two of us were assigned the evacuation of the planet Thycol. It was bad. The Eternal fleet arrived early and the *Growler* was lost with all hands. The captain and Captain Brook were stuck on the planet with a small team when we had to fall back. They held on as the Eternals laid siege. I don't know exactly what happened—I wasn't there and the captain doesn't talk about it much—but Captain Brook was killed. Something happened to her after that. She somehow became one of you."

They had stopped walking. She assumed they were at her

quarters. "It's possible for someone to become a Clairvoyant as an adult. I've heard of it but never seen it happen. Extremes of emotion can cause it."

"Well, she hasn't been the same since," Frederick said. "She's still her, and most of the crew probably wouldn't notice, but there's another part hidden that she keeps to herself. It's like she's separated from everybody. It's weird too, because she almost always knows what everyone's thinking."

But no one knows what she's thinking, Carmen added. She was tempted to explain it to him but was unsure if he'd understand. Her mind was on other things anyway. "So, she inadvertently started a war to save her friend, who died in that war."

Frederick nodded, his features grim. "Kick in the guts, ain't it? Never can tell how things will turn out."

He looked her dead on and tried his best to hide a wince. She reflected that, during their walk, he could only see the undamaged side of her face. Now that she was facing him, there was no hiding it. Carmen touched her burnt, leathery skin and sighed softly.

"Is it really that bad?" she asked.

"Like a pile of shit on a master portrait," he answered without missing a beat.

Carmen sighed again as her eyes fell. The comment made her think of Inertia, oddly enough. He never said anything about her burns. He never even made any reaction to them. She'd found it comforting. Yet now, the more she thought of it, the more anxious she became. She was his partner and he hers. She'd do anything for him, and she was quite certain he'd do the same. But there were distinct times it felt like she could only see him through a telescope.

"Hey, tell you what," Frederick began as her eyes fell

lower and lower. "I can have a talk with the medical staff. I've seen them patch together troopers who looked worse."

Carmen forced a smile. "All right."

He nodded sharply. "Just have to wait till we get some time. If that friend of yours is right about what the higher-ups will say, we should be setting off pretty soon. The captain will send for you as soon as we establish a secure connection with Fleet Command."

"Thank you."

DETOURS

Carmen lay in bed and stared at the ceiling the way she did almost every day. Yet this time was different. This time, she was aboard a Space Force cruiser and wearing the body armor of the Rogue Wolves. That had been on the forefront of her mind for quite some time, but not now. She had rested in her new quarters for what she guessed was a few hours since Frederick dropped her off. The exact time didn't really matter; it had felt like only a few minutes actually. No, it wasn't her present circumstance that occupied her thoughts and annoyingly refused to let go. As she stared, with her untied blonde hair splayed out on the pillow like a flower, she touched her burnt face yet again. Then she touched her burnt hand with the other and sighed.

She'd never cared about her injuries before. Frankly, her physical appearance was never really much of a concern to her, other than the rare instances where it mattered, like her countless job interviews, which felt like another lifetime ago. But here, now, on a starship about to go into battle against a powerful and cunning foe, her grotesque appearance, for some reason, seemed to matter more than anything else. She had no idea why, and that more than anything was silently driving her crazy. It was with some relief that she sensed a crewmember approaching to retrieve her.

Carmen sat up and tied her hair into a ponytail before he reached the door.

"Ms....Edge, may you follow me, please?" he said after opening the door, clearly unsure of what to call her.

She said nothing and walked out. The crewman took the lead, but even a glancing read let her know they were going to the main briefing room again. In any case, this really wasn't like Solitary. There were no guards to escort her and no one watching her every move and scanning everything she did. The crewman even seemed younger than she was, hard as that was to believe.

They reached the room soon enough, and he opened the door and gestured for her to enter. "Ma'am," he said politely.

Carmen gave a polite nod in return. Renee was already inside, as was Terry. The two sat at the table, much as before. Frederick was there also, as was Inertia, but the men stood off to the side. Carmen walked toward her partner. When she got closer, Frederick offered a smile, which she returned, but her attention was fixed on Inertia. Without even thinking about it, she walked past him to give him the good side of her face. Other than a glance when she first entered the room, though, he didn't seem to even notice her.

"Edge, can you take a couple steps back, please?" Renee prodded gently.

Carmen adjusted herself despite not knowing why it mattered. She didn't really care anyway. She gave Inertia a quick look. "How'd it go between the two of you?"

He closed his eyes and took a deep breath. "Don't ask," he said simply.

"That bad?" she asked softly.

"As I said, don't ask."

His words had rolled off the tongue as harshly as one would coo a baby to sleep, yet they hit her like a quick jab to the ribs. "Sorry," she muttered.

"Don't be."

"Captain, receiving secure transmission from Fleet Command," came a voice on the intercom.

"Understood," Renee responded casually. "We're ready."

The holoprojection equipment turned on a few seconds later, and Carmen now knew why Renee asked her to step back. A soft light enveloped the captain and Terry where they sat as an image became more and more coherent at the opposite end of the table. It was obvious that Renee didn't want whoever they were about to converse with to know there were other people in the room. That person began as a ghostly image of a man which eventually became indistinguishable from a *real* person.

Carmen thought she may have seen him in a news program once or twice, but she wasn't sure. He looked about Frederick's age, but stress had turned his hair solid white. His bearing, stiff and resolute, also had an element of weakness about it. He couldn't sit straight for long, despite the obvious determination to. His face, almost everything about him, looked like overworn leather. The cracks could no longer be lacquered away and ignored. In his eyes was fierce aggression but also pain. It reminded her of Eli.

"Captain Brown, Commander Fletcher," he said, nodding to each in turn.

"Admiral West," Renee said, respectfully bowing her head.

"I received your report and it reads like a treasure map, not a battle plan. Do you truly have no information on what exactly you're seeking? Expected enemy strength, reinforcements, anything? Just a location to find some freighter, and we don't even know what she's carrying, her complement, or even what exactly she is?"

"I'm sorry, Admiral, we do not. We also only have a few days to execute this, or what we do know becomes null and void," Renee said.

West groaned hard but then swallowed away his ire. "Well, I don't know who these Rogue Wolves are or who they have connections to, but the mission was approved not five minutes after I sent it. No questions asked."

Carmen glanced at Inertia. It was a question she wondered herself, but her fellow Rogue Wolf made no reaction.

"Our orders, sir," Terry asked.

"You have free and total leave to investigate this freighter. Capture if possible, destroy if necessary. The Rogue Wolves are to be your advisors. I don't care what anyone says; this is still a Space Force starship, even if we have to play ferry for someone else." Renee and Terry both nodded. West continued. "But there is one thing you must be aware of, Captain. This operation is not officially sanctioned by Space Force or the UTE. Only I and a few others will even be aware of it. Get detected, captured, or destroyed, and we will disavow all knowledge. The official cover story will be that the captain and crew of the *Griffin* went rogue on some sort of vengeful crusade through sorten space."

"Wouldn't be the first time," Frederick muttered under his breath.

Renee coughed to cover the comment and then gave him a quick pointed glance. Carmen's eyes narrowed as she thought everything through. Inertia was right. This genuinely couldn't be done any other way. No other captain would accept their mission from the outset, and if they were ordered to, the fact that Renee was his sister ensured a level of commitment and loyalty. Furthermore, there was no risk of sparking a wider conflict if they failed. It also meant something else—something Carmen had never really considered until now. The ship and her crew were expendable. Carmen now understood why Inertia seemed so hesitant to come here and why Renee was so upset earlier. She looked at her partner again and, as before, he didn't notice her. *Telescope indeed,* she thought.

"Good hunting, Captain," West said. The admiral then paused a moment. "And good luck." After that, his image faded away.

Renee stared at where it had been. "Shit," she said softly after a deep breath. Then she rolled her eyes. "Well, I did say *anything,*" she muttered more to herself than to anyone in the room. She pressed a button hidden in her shirt collar, activating the *Griffin's* communication systems, and announced calmly, "Battle stations."

A loud klaxon sounded an instant later, and there was a flashing red light. Carmen took it all in with a start.

"What, right now?" she asked hurriedly as Renee and Terry came to their feet.

"Clock's ticking," the captain said over her shoulder.

Everyone was out of the room in seconds with Carmen the last to leave. Renee moved at a fast walk. Frederick was at her side, and the two talked in increasingly animated fashion. Carmen ignored them as she turned to Inertia.

"I just didn't think everything would move so fast," she said telepathically.

"It didn't. They prepared while we were waiting. Gaming different scenarios; thinking of different contingencies; plotting the optimum course. This is Space Force. They're professionals, military. They don't play by chance like we do—"

"Or stick their hands down rat holes, wondering what they'll find," Carmen posed.

Inertia smiled wryly. *"I don't think anyone can avoid that."*

She smiled as well and, indeed, what Inertia said seemed to be the case. Crew rushed past in both directions down the corridor with well-ordered haste. Some were still putting on their uniforms, obviously having been roused from their sleeping racks; others wore protective firefighting equipment and discussed among themselves how likely they were to need it. There was no fear or worry in their voices. In fact, the average office worker deciding which report to file would appear more stressed. They didn't even seem to notice the Clairvoyants; only their captain drew any attention.

With that in mind, Carmen changed her focus to Renee and Frederick. The two were interesting to watch. Renee was visibly more relaxed around the political officer, her tone and movements livelier and more animated, much more so than anyone else Carmen had seen her with. Also, unlike everyone else she had seen around Frederick, the captain looked interested in what he had to say. Indeed, when the group reached an elevator, Renee turned fully to him.

"Frederick, if you call me the Dread Pirate Renee one more time, I swear I'll throw you in the brig!" she said pointedly.

Terry watched the exchange and sighed loudly while rolling his eyes. Carmen couldn't help a small smile. She barely knew him, but if Frederick had any one talent, it was certainly provoking reactions from people. Even the ship's captain wasn't immune.

"Aye, Captain, aye. I'm sorry," he muttered sheepishly, though with a mischievous gleam in his eyes. Renee looked at him with a raised eyebrow and pursed lips as the elevator arrived. "The Dread Pirate Renee takes no prisoners," he added under his breath though easily loud enough for everyone to hear.

Carmen smiled again as Frederick's antics made her think of Widget. There was a certain charm to outwardly useless people that were actually useful, despite how annoying they sometimes were. She did not know what use Frederick had, but Renee obviously kept him around for some reason. For her part, the captain groaned loudly, mouthing, "Why me?" but she neither threw him in the brig nor shot him as she looked like she wished to. Instead, Renee walked into the elevator and everyone followed. The doors opened again and, after a short corridor, the group entered the bridge.

The only starship bridge Carmen had ever been on was on *The Lady*, but she doubted that counted for much of anything. The activity here reminded her of birds chirping in a tree. Everyone was seated, but they talked quickly amongst each other in acronyms and shorthand phrases that she couldn't hope to begin to understand.

"Captain on the bridge," someone announced.

"As you were," Renee said back.

She then glanced at Frederick, who nodded respectively before he took a seat in the back of the room. And just like that, as if flipping a switch, the tenor changed. Any hint of a smile no longer graced Captain Renee Brown's lips. The already tall woman somehow became three inches taller. She turned to her XO, her gaze now filled with an intense determination that looked as ready to waver as the oceans were to turn to dust. Terry nodded, but it was different than with Frederick. Both men dripped with so much respect that it seemed the gesture, if however small, infected everyone else in the room. They came from different foundations, though. Frederick took to her as a friend, warm, open, and steadfastly loyal. Terry was a colleague, a fellow soldier bound by duty and shared hardship. It was a respect of what she could do versus who she was.

Renee took a seat at the captain's chair in the center of the room. Terry sat next to her on her right. Both chairs had a large display affixed to the left armrest. The movement to her chair had only been a few steps, but she commanded the room as surely as any Clairvoyant. The attention, however, while similar, was not of the same kin. There were no nervous eyes looking away or hushed whispers when Renee moved. No, the bridge crew sat with the same tense readiness of a trained dog awaiting its master's command. But it was not something Renee seemed to outwardly acknowledge. It was a quiet confidence, secure in its ability and ready for a challenge just to prove that which everyone already knew: that it was never a challenge in the first place. In a way, it reminded Carmen of Inertia. They didn't just look alike.

Renee gestured to two chairs beside her. "Please take a seat," she said.

The Rogue Wolves looked at each other and nodded. Carmen wondered for the first time how they would they be evaluated if someone watched them. Were they colleagues? Friends? Mere partners? She bit her lip to stop herself from thinking about it any further. Inertia took the seat closer to his sister and Carmen took the other.

"Edge, you should use the belts," Renee suggested softly.

Carmen had sat on them without even thinking about it. The seats on *The Lady* had belts, but neither she nor Inertia had used them. She took a quick survey of the room and noted that everyone else was strapped in. Even Inertia was presently attending to them, so she did as well.

"Tighter," he said.

She'd thought she made them pretty tight, but she pulled

again after his suggestion. He didn't say anything but gave them another tug as well. Satisfied, he gave her a quick nod, which made her smile. He didn't return it, and her smile left just as quickly as it came, joined by a somber sigh.

"Battle stations manned and ready, Captain. The Hustlers have a two-ship on alert status. An additional four-ship will be ready in…ten minutes. All armed for anti-ship," a woman to Carmen's left said.

She was a rather unassuming person, though her voice was anything but. Soft, even, clear, her words cut through noise like a rock standing in the middle of a waterfall. There was a comforting quality to it. Nothing was rushed; each sentence was given just enough time to be understood and not an instant longer.

To Carmen's right, on the opposite wall and facing the wall, sat Hiroshi. Several large screens dominated his station. "All weapons charged, Captain," he said.

Renee nodded. "What's our plot?"

"Three legs, ma'am," a short woman said at the front of the room. She faced away with an aircraft-style control yoke in front of her and several smaller screens. Her skin tone was darker than both Renee's and Inertia's, and her hair was shaved to the point that she was near bald. "Going fast. First leg one-point-five days; second leg point-six days; and final leg just over two days, ma'am," she continued.

"Likely opposition along projected course?" Renee asked.

"Light to none," Terry answered. "Especially at our destination. Hasn't been any activity there for months." After that, both he and the captain looked at Inertia and Carmen.

"The intel is good," Inertia remarked. "The ship will be there."

Carmen glanced at him before turning her attention to the Space Force officers. "I'd say that's actually encouraging at the destination. The sortens would want to lay low," she interjected.

Renee nodded and looked toward the helm. "Ms. Crowe, execute when ready."

"Aye, aye, ma'am. Charging Ghost Drive," Tawny said.

More orders were repeated in the background that Carmen paid no attention to. Neither she nor Inertia had any part of the operation of the ship. She sighed softly as she turned to him. "Four days. Considering the time we already spent, isn't that cutting it a little close?"

Inertia agreed with a small nod. "We should consider ourselves fortunate. Peacekeeper-class cruisers are easily the fastest starships in the galaxy."

No other way, she reflected again. Tawny announced that the Ghost Field was established, and it got Carmen thinking. "This might be a stupid question, but how does all this *Ghost* stuff actually work? I've always wondered but never thought to ask."

Inertia eyed her with an ever-raising eyebrow. "Do you really want to know? It's a lot of math."

"Yeeeah…how does it work conceptually?" she asked, amending her question after a pained grimace. She hated algebra and shuddered to think of the math beyond that basic foundation.

"Well…speaking conceptually," he said after playfully rolling his eyes, which made Carmen smile, "it's as simple as the question, how fast can something travel that doesn't exist?"

"I don't know. You tell me."

"Think, Edge. I can't feed you everything."

Carmen grimaced again but did take a few seconds to think the matter through. "It wouldn't go any speed at all. It doesn't exist," she said, unable to think of anything but the obvious.

"Exactly," Inertia responded.

"So…"

"So," he continued, cutting her off from her usual question but not before giving her an accusing glare. Carmen couldn't help a guilty smirk. "That is exactly what happens inside a Ghost Field. When it's active, all contained within cease to exist."

"I'm pretty sure I still exist now," she pointed out.

"What is existence?" Inertia asked in turn. Carmen opened her mouth to answer, and he held her off with a raised hand. "To an outside observer, right now we exist only as a void of nothingness speeding through the galaxy at tens of thousands of times the speed of light. Yet, for you and me, there is no change."

"Are we dead?"

He thought about her question for a moment. "Before you were born, before you were even conceived, were you dead?"

"No. I didn't exist yet."

"Right. Something has to exist for it to die or be killed. And now, by all the rules of the universe, you don't exist."

"Does that mean that, when I'm in a Ghost Field, I *never* existed?"

Inertia shook his head. "Time is another dimension from place and being. Look here. For the moment, my arm is on the armrest." Carmen nodded. "If I raise my arm off the armrest," he continued, doing just that, "my arm now exists in this new location, but it also existed a few seconds ago on the armrest. If my arm then no longer existed, it still existed a few seconds ago on the armrest."

Carmen nodded again. "I think I understand. But then why does it seem like I exist now?"

"You don't."

"But it feels like I do."

"Yes."

Carmen sat silently for a few seconds as she waited for the explanation. When none came, she let go an annoyed sigh. "You'd have me circle that philosophical drain all day, wouldn't you?"

He gave that knowing, confident smirk of his. "Yes."

She pursed her lips. Without a doubt, there were times she wanted to strangle him or smack him or something. He was well practiced at being a bastard. Yet she didn't. How he was able to prod her so easily she'd never know, and that more than anything made her want to smile as much as she wanted to frown. Unable to decide on either, Carmen bit the inside of her mouth while her lips trembled in amused rage. Her partner saw her predicament and laughed for the both of them. He stopped suddenly just as she was about to smile fully in response. The emotion was arrested so quickly that it was almost like Inertia was chastising himself for having felt it. The smile left Carmen's lips as his face turned more serious.

"To answer your question, there are more fields active than just the Ghost Field. There are others that allow the perception of reality for those inside, at the expense of efficiency of the Ghost Field," he said, his tone little different than if he were talking to the bulkhead.

The transition made her pause. She didn't think she had done anything wrong or had upset him. He was as relaxed, calm, and confident as he normally was. But all of a sudden the mere inches between them felt like an insurmountable chasm. She tried not to think about it as she turned her attention back to their conversation.

"So, is what's happening right now actually happening?"

"Yes," he answered, "in a matter of speaking. If I fill a coffee cup in a Ghost Field, it will be filled once the field is dispelled. But as I said, this comes at great cost to efficiency. As it is, it takes almost all the power of the ship to establish a Ghost Field. The field emitter, when it is powering up, is easily as bright as a small star, visible for light years."

"So, what's all this going fast stuff that everyone always talks about?"

"That is when a starship turns off those fields. The speed increase is easily an order of magnitude, and for anyone on the ship, the trip will feel instantaneous."

Carmen considered what he said. "What's the catch?"

"The catch is that a completely stable Ghost Field can never be dispelled. For the moment, we are a void with a definite vector. We can even be intercepted. A perfect field, though, would in theory exist everywhere in the universe simultaneously."

"Or said another way, it would exist no place in the universe? Not even as a void?"

Inertia gave an approving nod. "Right. The end result means, especially when going fast, that once the field is established, it is done with a stability error timed to dispel the field at the destination. That calculation is neither easy nor reliable. The greater the distance, the harder the calculation."

"That sounds like fueling your car with just enough to coast to a stop at your destination," she remarked after considering everything.

"Exac—"

"Going fast," Tawny announced. "Ghost Field dispelled," she added an instant later.

"Tly," Inertia finished.

"Shields up, active sensor scan," Renee ordered.

Her orders were repeated and carried out, and as before,

Carmen paid them no attention. "Why shields? We haven't arrived yet."

"As I said, it takes an enormous amount of power to establish a field. That energy doesn't just go away when it's dispelled. Every ship in the sector will know we're powering our field, and every ship in the sector we arrive in will know we just dropped it," Inertia answered seriously.

Carmen took it all in and then groaned softly. "And because we can't be completely precise with where we arrive, we don't know what we'll find when we get there or who will find us." *I'm beginning to see why Renee was so nervous about this*, she thought. Inertia nodded.

"Multiple contacts…no threats, ma'am," Hiroshi announced.

"Displacement from projected course eleven-point-five percent, Captain," Tawny said.

Renee cursed under her breath. Carmen heard it, as did Inertia and Terry, but no one made a comment. "Can we do better than a double-digit course error?" she asked, her voice a forced calm.

"I apologize, ma'am. I'll compensate better for the next leg," Tawny replied.

The captain's lips became thin lines before she muttered a curse out the side of her mouth. "Begin the second leg when ready," she ordered, her usual poise returned.

"Captain, I doubt Ms. Crowe made any error. Engineering reported trouble with our Ghost Drive weeks ago. We just haven't been able to get the normal service," Terry said just loudly enough for her and the Clairvoyants to hear.

"Mr. Fletcher, if we all die from this, remind me to track down Admiral Wright when we get to hell," Renee said after a sigh. "I'll have a few words."

Terry chuckled lightly but seemed as amused as if he'd

stepped on a thumbtack. "The S-O-B probably has a queue for just that."

Carmen looked at Inertia nervously, and her partner could only shrug. *No other way*, she thought again.

"Charging Ghost Drive," Tawny announced.

As the *Griffin* powered her Ghost Drive, the fairing that housed her field emitter grew ever brighter. Her three engines belched white-hot plasma for hundreds of miles in her wake, turning the ship into a spectacular comet that would be seen on worlds years later. On and on the light built until it suddenly ceased, gone, as if it had never been there in the first place.

"Ghost Field dispelled," Tawny announced after going fast. "Displacement from projected course three-point-seven percent."

"No contacts, ma'am. Scope is clear," Hiroshi said.

Renee nodded, but there was a faraway look in her eye. She closed them both after a deep breath, and when they opened, it was obvious she had returned to the here and now. She glanced at her XO, who nodded, and then she looked to the Clairvoyants. Inertia nodded as well, though not in the same way as Terry. The commander indicated his readiness; the Clairvoyant, however, silently told her to proceed. Carmen made no gesture other than to grip her chair with tense, strained fingers. After a second or so, she realized her breath was coming in shallow pants.

"This is it," she said so quietly that even Inertia didn't hear her. Then she swallowed hard to regain her composure.

Renee did the same. "Final leg, Lieutenant."

"Aye, aye, ma'am. Powering Ghost Drive."

There was no countdown, but Carmen felt like there was. No one on the bridge said anything. Her partner sat still, his face contemplatively neutral as he rested his chin on a fist.

She wished he'd tease her or prod her or piss her off or something—anything to take her mind off the next few seconds. The entire mission would be decided in a minute or so, and the outcome was completely out of anyone's hands.

"Ghost Field established…now," Tawny said. Carmen gave a small start and then kicked herself when she remembered the ship needed to accelerate after establishing the field before it could go fast. It only took a few minutes. Tawny gripped the control yoke tightly before she made her announcement. "Going fast. Ghost Field dispelled."

"Shields up, active scan. Give me a full sweep," Renee said. Hiroshi nodded as he repeated the order.

"Displacement from projected course…seventeen percent, ma'am," Tawny said. "I apologize."

"Can't be helped," the captain replied. She turned her attention back to Hiroshi. "Got anything?"

"*Seventeen percent sounds really far,*" Carmen spoke to Inertia.

"*It is. Especially considering the distance we just traveled.*" He glanced at her. "*Don't worry,*" he continued, seeing the concern on her face. "*It'll just be a short hop from here to where we need to be, and that jump should be much more accurate.*" Carmen nodded.

"New contact, Captain," Hiroshi said.

"Just one. We're too far off course for it to be our freighter," Terry remarked.

"I don't think it is, sir. She's small; I'm surprised we even picked her up at this range."

"Suspend active scan," Renee ordered.

"Aye."

"What is she?"

"Appears to be a sorten patrol frigate, ma'am."

Terry stared hard at his screen. "Captain, they haven't

reacted to our arrival yet. We can blow her out of the sky before they relay our position to anyone."

The suggestion froze Renee so completely that she didn't even blink, let alone breathe. Carmen watched her, and the weight of the decision appeared to hang as heavy as a crown made of lead.

"Crew complement of that class of frigate?" she asked.

"Two hundred and eighty-six, Captain," Hiroshi answered.

Renee slowly shook her head. Carmen unknowingly gripped her seat again. "Why?" Renee asked softly to herself. "Why did it have to be manned? Why couldn't it have just been a probe?"

"Captain, contact maneuvering. They are powering shields," Hiroshi said.

"They spotted us?" Carmen said at a rush.

"Captain, we can still fire," Terry suggested.

She shook her head once more. "No, no, I can't. We're not starting another war," she said softly but firmly and as much to herself as to him. Terry stared at her, his mouth saying nothing but his eyes protesting with the same vigor as a man arguing against his execution. Renee would have none of it. She looked at her display screen. "New course 113 minus 57, ahead flank. Launch decoys and power the Ghost Drive."

Tawny responded smartly. Carmen felt a heavy weight on her chest from the acceleration before the force was trimmed to nothing by the inertial inhibitor. She did not know it, but the ship had already accelerated past twenty percent the speed of light.

Renee rested her chin on the point of steepled fingers. "We'll get away and reset, then we'll be able to continue our mission."

Terry relaxed in his chair. "Yes, ma'am," he said simply, but he sounded like he wished he could say more.

Renee then looked at her brother, who looked back dispassionately. She didn't know him well enough to get any read from his stern silence, but he casually looked away as a period on whatever he was thinking. He turned to his partner then, who looked at him with hope and worry, but he only gave her a small reassuring nod.

"Captain, the frigate is attempting to send a transmission. I am jamming them, but I can't guarantee I was able to stop everything," Leena said.

Renee let go an annoyed puff. "Very well. Ms. Crowe?"

"Ghost Field established…now," the helmsman announced.

Carmen breathed a little easier after that, secure in the relative safety of the Ghost Field. She turned her attention to Inertia. He didn't seem to share her ease. If anything, he appeared to be thinking deeply. His eyes scanned back and forth as new ideas came to the fore.

"So, what now?" she asked.

Inertia licked his lips then swallowed. "I don't—"

"Ghost Field disrupted!" Tawny yelled.

Hiroshi gasped. "Captain, we have incoming. Three seconds!"

"Evade at will, cleared emergency G!" Renee said at a rush.

A loud klaxon sounded and this one was even more urgent than the battle stations' alarm had been. Inertia sat upright immediately, as did everyone else in the bridge other than Carmen. She even heard some of them grunting. She didn't know what to expect; she didn't even really know what the captain meant. It began as a weight bearing down on her entire body. She had felt that before whenever she flew exceptionally violently, but it overwhelmed her almost instantly. Her vision went gray in less than a second before being overcome by black. Then there was nothing. She didn't know how much time passed, but the next thing she knew, she was trashing about in her seat while the room spun. Sound came back first, and she heard Inertia speaking to her.

"Calm down, calm down. I'm right here," he soothed.

His voice led her back to her senses. In time, she was aware of a different kind of weight on her shoulder. It was Inertia holding her in place, gently but firmly. She frowned. No Clairvoyant could control their bioelectric field when they were unconscious—indeed several lights still flashed on the bridge. It must have been acutely painful for him to touch her.

She grabbed his hand and squeezed tenderly. "Sorry," she said, unable to help embarrassment from bleeding into her voice. He pulled his hand away and she felt worse.

"No damage reported, ma'am. Injury reports on your display now," Leena said.

"Later," Renee replied after raising a hand.

Carmen stopped thinking about herself long enough to hear a groan behind her then. She turned and saw Frederick nursing a large bruise on his forehead. He must have hit his face on the console. He gave her a thumbs-up after he noticed her worried face. She nodded and faced forward again.

"Open the range; we're at a disadvantage at this distance," Renee continued. "What's our opposition?"

"Two sorten fast attack destroyers, ma'am," Hiroshi said. "I have a firing solution on both."

"They're no match for us," Terry remarked under his breath but loudly enough for Renee to hear.

If she heard him, she didn't even glance in his direction. "FCT, ready three Hammers per target. Fire when ready."

Hiroshi glanced at her over his shoulder, an eyebrow

raised in confusion as he did so. "Ma'am, three missiles are not enough against their point defense systems."

Renee looked directly at him. "Fire!"

"Aye, aye, ma'am. Firing."

She sighed softly. "It will get them defensive at least," she said to no one in particular, though Carmen knew, as she always *just knew*, that the comment was intended for Terry. "Launch decoys, power the Ghost Drive. Get us out of here."

Seconds passed; Renee's foot tapped nervously. The captain of the *Griffin* sat still otherwise, lost in thought as contingencies and plans played out in her mind.

"All missiles shot dow—"

"Ghost Field established…now," Tawny announced again, cutting Hiroshi off.

Renee let go her breath and seemed to relax. Carmen, however, did no such thing. She gripped her chair to the point that she couldn't feel her hands. Her pulse raced through her so quickly that she was starting to get lightheaded. She hated fighting, but this was altogether worse. Any other time she fought, whether she lived or died was up to her. Now every-thing—their entire mission—was completely out of her hands. Even Inertia had no power here. He sat tensely, unmoving but ready.

"Ghost Field disrupted," Tawny announced.

Carmen's breath caught in her throat as she was sure she was going to black out again. But this evasive maneuver was nowhere near as violent as before.

"How do they keep doing that?" she asked Inertia.

"They go fast and jump ahead of us. The only way to break free is to have them lose our track before we Ghost."

"Same destroyers as before, Captain. New contacts inbound, a cruiser and another destroyer. There are a half dozen others I don't have a classification on yet," Hiroshi said.

"Captain, we stirred up the hornet's nest. We have to fight back—effectively," Terry growled.

Renee looked at her XO and her eyes narrowed. "Then do so. Buy me some time," she said as she turned to her display.

"Yes, ma'am," he answered, determined despite the odds.

He then made orders Carmen didn't listen to. The ship maneuvered hard as it fought, and she was happy Inertia had ensured her belts were tight. Her attention, however, was on Renee. Her hands flew over her display, not in desperation but with a focused calm that once again made the captain appear Clairvoyant, even though she insisted she was not. She leaned back in her chair when she was done.

"Ms. Crowe, destination on your display now. Execute when ready…best possible speed," she said.

Tawny looked at her display and went rigid as her eyes grew wide. "Ma'am?"

"Execute when ready, Tawny," Renee ordered softly.

"Aye…ma'am. Charging Ghost Drive."

"Shall I launch decoys, Captain?" Hiroshi asked.

Renee shook her head. "No need."

"Captain, what are we doing?" Terry asked.

"The only play we have left," she answered.

The ship Ghosted seconds later. She emerged from her Ghost Field at a site forever immortalized in history: the graveyard of multiple planets torn asunder, a collapsing star, more than twenty billion sortens, and the blackhole of the doomsday weapon Medusa. Utter silence persisted on the bridge as the starship slipped through the ever-changing gravity waves and planetary rubble.

Renee broke the gloomy stillness with a sharp exhale.

"Start powering down the ship; make her good and dim," she ordered, her voice calm and even.

The lights were the first to go. They were dimmed until the bridge was just barely visible. Displays began shutting off next.

"Multiple contacts," Hiroshi said.

"I know," Renee responded, her voice still calm. "Even with an active scan, they'll have trouble detecting us in all this. At the first opportunity, we'll slip away and continue our mission," she added as more displays were shut off. "Until then, contact Fleet Command and inform them of our situation."

Inertia sighed softly and glanced at his partner. "We might be here a while."

Carmen made no reply. Instead, she looked at the clock and counted down how much time they had left.

8

HOW THE MERC CROSSED
THE ROAD

"Two plus two is four. Two plus two is four. Two plus two is four…" Widget sang over and over again. Her Clairvoyant company sitting on the opposite side of the room gripped the table in front of him hard enough to leave permanent imprints. "Two plus tw—"

"Widget!" Gungnir yelled.

She paused for a moment in genuine surprise. She didn't even know he could yell. It was only a moment, though. "Two plus two is four," she continued, this time adding a small dance in tune with the rhythm. "Two plus two is—"

"Widget," Gungnir said. This time he didn't yell. No, this time he was calm and spoke evenly. It was probably the most intimidating sound she had ever heard, and it stopped her song immediately. "If you don't stop singing that song, I will pluck every hair from your body individually as if you were a pheasant."

She looked at him over her shoulder and he was staring right back. She swallowed hard. He meant every word. She turned back to her computer, blinking nervously a few times.

Then she sighed softly. "One times one is one. One times one is one. One times one is one. One times one—"

The air filled with an abrupt screech as Gungnir slid his chair back and bolted out of it. He came toward her. Forget plucking her hair out—fire burned coldly in his eyes, and she doubted she'd see the next morning. She held out her hands. "Yes, yes, no yes, no."

"Widget."

"Don't hug me, don't hug me, I figured it out!"

"Figured what out?" Gungnir asked.

"That…two plus two is four! Two plus two is four."

Gungnir groaned loudly and then returned to his chair at the opposite end of the room. He sat down with a loud huff before he telekinetically damped the noise. It would be minorly fatiguing, but it would be less of a bother than cleaning Widget's blood off his hands.

"What's going on?" Kali asked on the other end of the phone.

He wished he could speak to his old colleague holographically. He was in the Lair, though, and while she had a vague idea of what he did, and was probably intelligent enough to guess he was a Rogue Wolf if not their leader, for both their sakes, it was better to not confirm the suspicion. Mere voice communication would have to do.

"Nothing too important, just contemplating the murder of a brilliant nincompoop."

"I see… Not a big enough bounty then?" Kali remarked. The urge for him to defend himself passed in a fleeting second. That wasn't worth the effort either. "Heard you haven't been to the facility for days. Is everything all right?"

Gungnir sighed, though not from Widget. "Just business, as always. Sometimes it's more difficult and slippery than expected." *Or can't be found at all*, he didn't add.

"Hmm," Kali hummed softly. "I know you won't tell me more, but I'm sure you'll figure it out."

He sighed again. "Or kill the one trying to figure it out," he remarked. Widget was now out of her chair and doing a full dance number to go with the song. Toddlers were more coordinated.

There was silence on the other end of the line for a few seconds. Undoubtedly, Kali had no idea who he was talking about. He never talked much about his business with her, let alone described his personnel. Widget was beyond description anyway.

"Do you have any word on my charge? Is she okay?" Kali asked.

"I can't say for certain. My world is one of rumor and innuendo. Even a credible report has to be considered with suspicion, and I receive few credible reports. Last I heard, they were seeking outside help," he said, referring to Space Force. "But you know I can't be too loose with information."

"Yes, and it is quite annoying. I just want to know if she's okay."

Gungnir shook his head. "You shouldn't worry; she's with my best man. I'm sure she's all right."

"Not worry?" Kali said after a pause. "Gungnir, you've never been a handler. Not everything is about bounties, business, and rumor. Not everything is as cold and clinical as you make it out to be. If you descended from your ivory tower every once in a while, you'd see that. There is only one world, not yours, not mine, one: the *real* world. It is full of death, hatred, horror, and war. When has it not been?" she asked rhetorically. "I'll always worry about my charge."
There was no anger in her voice and she didn't speak at a rush. If there was any mar to her soft, melodic tone, it was a hint of annoyance.

"I always considered the world is how you perceive it. That perception creating the world all around you," he said back.

He couldn't see her scoff, but he did hear her irritated sigh. "No lectures, Gungnir. I'm not one of your desperate prospects sitting in your office and clinging to hope." He was quick to note that Edge, who she cared so much about, had been sent to him exactly in that state by Kali. There was nothing to be gained, however, by making that point to a fellow Clairvoyant. Normals ignored the obvious to spare their egos, but not Clairvoyants. "I respect what you do," she continued, "but not all of us can sit and analyze happenstance from afar. We live it day by day. It pains us day by day. If you tried living it for even a moment, you'd understand. Even Edge does…now anyway."

Gungnir's jaw tightened. But once again, the urge to defend himself passed momentarily, if only just. He'd known Kali for years; a few barbed comments here and there were just rocks thrown in a lake. It wasn't the first.

"When I know anything about Edge, you will be the first to know," he said, assuming worry was the source of the frustration soaking her every word. "Edge's charge is on his way back to the facility. I'm sure she'd appreciate you looking after him," he added, changing the subject.

"I'll…see what I can do."

His eyes narrowed. He didn't see what the issue could be, but it was not a subject worth pursuing. He sensed someone behind him and rolled his eyes. "Excuse me," he said to Kali as he turned around. Widget stood bent over right in front of him. She held her mouth with bulging cheeks while her entire body shook. He rolled his eyes again. "Yes?" he asked, though he already knew what was about to happen.

She dropped her hands, took a massive breath, and then said quietly, "Twelve times twelve is one hundred forty-four."

Gungnir wiped his face with an aggravated hand and turned back around. "Kali, I think we'll have to continue this conversation later."

"All right, take care."

At that, he stood and walked out of the room. Widget watched him go with her hands on her eyes like a pair of binoculars. She let go a contented sigh and went to her computer when he was safely gone.

"Billy, I don't think all that is really necessary. If you want to talk to me alone, just tell him you want to talk to me alone," her contact said. "Clairvoyants are very direct people. They don't even understand why everyone else isn't."

"Why do whatever Clairvoyants want?" Widget remarked derisively.

"Better for your health, for one," Quinn pointed out.

She rubbed her neck and reflected on how Gungnir looked at her earlier. She doubted he would ever harm her, but perhaps she was pushing her luck? She typed on her notepad, "Could be killed by boss, consider being less annoying," and then turned back to her main screen.

"Anyway, what do you got for me, Billy?"

"I cracked it," she said triumphantly.

"Let me guess…it has something to do with two plus two is four?"

"In a manner of speaking," she answered after laughing lightly.

"You got me curious; how does kids' arithmetic give you a Clairvoyant merc?"

"It didn't give me the merc, not exactly, but it did give me the army of clones."

"Go on."

"How did Charon and his Clairvoyant clones get to New Earth?"

"We already established that. It is very unlikely they originated on New Earth, meaning they arrived by starship. Did you find the ship?"

Widget cracked a satisfied smile. "I didn't find *the* ship; I found the *ships*," she said.

"More than one… Are you sure? Why use more than one for an op like this? It increases the likelihood of being discovered—adds difficulty of coordination and extraction. I honestly never considered the possibility. How many ships are we talking about?"

"Twenty-three," she said confidently.

"Shit, that many? Billy, you might actually be a nincompoop." Widget pursed her lips while she smirked. "Well, if it's true, I want to hear all about it. Might even take notes on how to get something like that done. Popcorn is ready."

Widget laughed lightly. "I have to hand it to Charon or whoever planned this. It is stupidly genius," she said. Just then there was a sound of crunching. Either her contact actually was eating popcorn or they just added the sound effect. She gave a wry smirk and continued. "It was civilian flights, dozens and dozens of civilian flights from as many locations. Individual clones' travel arrangements were booked with forged IDs. All flights were timed to arrive at roughly the same time."

"Meaning they were able to stage at the local starport and continue planetside from there."

"Exactly. Conveniently solves that logistics problem, doesn't it?"

"As I said, I would have never considered checking civilian flight logs. Too much of a security risk flying civilian, smuggling the weapons onboard for the team."

"But Clairvoyants don't need to smuggle weapons; they are the weapon. We've sent Clairvoyants civilian before, but only as a single. That's usually enough to do the job anyway. It would never cross our minds to send a team that way either," she said.

"I understand. But how was extraction supposed to work? They could have taken civilian in but not out. All outbound flights were checked by New Earth SDF after the incident."

Widget shook her head. "They never planned to leave, at least not the clones. I never found any return tickets booked, and all the ones in the assault were killed. It's a bit of an advantage to logistics when you consider your entire team expendable."

"Truly. But Charon left," Quinn pointed out.

"He did, and I can't find the method. The only thing I can think of is that he has his own ship. It must be small and have one hell of a stealth system."

"Hmm. How were you able to confirm this, anyway?"

"Facial recognition scan of the dead clones compared to all travel records of the past month. Not two plus two but one plus one."

There was a long silence on the other end. "That's a lot of work, Billy."

"It is," she agreed with a quick nod. "But it's worth it when it pays off."

"Yes, but the more important piece is does it give you Charon? A name, a face, anything?"

"It doesn't."

"Were you at least able to get a point of origin? It may have been separate flights, but they all probably started from the same location."

"I thought of that, but every flight had a connection before New Earth. Honestly, it's too much data," she said.

"Doubt it even matters. The sortens move their operations constantly, and this is probably the most thorough op I've ever seen."

There was a long silence again. "All right, Billy, we're on the same page now. You wouldn't contact me unless you needed something."

"I do," she said. "I can crunch data after the fact, but I don't have enough capacity for anything that's useful real time. I'll transmit the template I used and you can start from there."

"Start from there to do what? What am I looking for?"

"A large number of flights arriving at a planet at roughly the same time, with individual or pairs of Clairvoyant passengers."

"To what end?"

"If Charon attacks again, we want to catch him in the act," she answered. "We just need his target soon enough so we can be in place to intercept."

"I assume to capture him?"

"That's the plan."

"Well, Billy, seems like my tea leaves are useful after all."

Widget smirked and teased, "Though not as useful as fortune cookies."

9

SETTING THE TABLE

Carmen placed a hand lightly on the corridor wall to steady herself. She didn't really need to. Her partner, walking in front, didn't even wobble. Frederick almost fell over.

"Sorry," he muttered sheepishly.

She waved the apology away. It had to have been the third or fourth time he stumbled. The *Griffin* hadn't moved, relatively speaking anyway, since she'd parked herself in the harshest, most treacherous region of the maelstrom that was Medusa. The inertial inhibitor, however, was operating at minimum power. Carmen knew nothing about natural black-holes, but she was told gravity fluctuated wildly and randomly around Medusa. Each time they were hit by a wave, the ship would lurch, and sometimes she could even hear the structure groan all around them.

The lights were dimmed as well. Most of the crewmen walked with flashlights. The Clairvoyants needed no such illumination, nor did they notice the cold. Carmen's breath was visible in front of her, and Frederick wore a light coat, but it all meant nothing to her. It had taken several minutes to convince him to not give it to her. She appreciated the gesture, but there were times that unnecessary politeness got annoying. The subject was put to rest when Inertia casually asked if he had a coat for *him*. The political officer soon got the hint.

"Damn it," Frederick said softly as he almost went face first into the deck again.

Carmen placed another hand on the wall as she let her body rock to the side. It took a bit of concentration to make the effort look natural. Clairvoyants, at all times when they were conscious, partially supported themselves telekinetically. Sure, she could lose balance, trip, and stumble the same as everyone else, just like cats didn't always land on their feet, but she'd be hard pressed to remember when she'd done it. The action was so subconscious that she hadn't even been aware of it until Kali mentioned the reflex offhand back when she was a tenant of the facility. That was all too much to explain to Frederick, though. He'd eyed her curiously from the start of their trip when he noticed she was completely unaffected by the wallowing ship. The look birthed the ruse.

"We're almost there."

"I know," Carmen said.

"Yeah, I forget you Clairvoyants always know," he remarked. There was a hint of affection in the comment, which made her give a polite smile. "Wonder what that's like," he mused out loud.

"We really don't know everything. We can't tell the future," she replied. "I can't speak for Inertia, but I try really hard *not* to know everything." She looked at her partner as she spoke, but he didn't even turn his head when he was mentioned. He was speaking to her less and less, and Clairvoyant or no, she had absolutely no idea why that was. It was almost like she had offended him somehow. "As for what it's like," she continued, still watching him walk silently and sternly in front of her. "It's confusing."

"Aye, I can—"

Just then the ship twisted and bucked as if an invisible hand had thrown it across the room. The inevitable happened as the distracted Space Force officer crashed to the deck. Carmen winced when he hit and then knelt to help him to his feet. Inertia kept walking.

"I'm all right," Frederick said as he brushed himself off.

She remained unconvinced. "You sure?"

"Yeah, I've abused and poisoned my body enough to know what it can take," he said with a chuckle, though there was a slight limp in his step now. "Head down to the officer's mess with me after this; I'll show you."

Carmen knew what he was referring to. "It's very hard for Clairvoyants to get drunk," she pointed out.

"No shit. They also don't need to touch a wall to steady themselves," he said.

"How—" she began, raising an eyebrow.

Frederick chuckled loudly now. "Read about it," he said quickly. "You really don't need to bother. You and your partner here are thoroughbreds in your prime. No one gives any mind to a rotund, old bastard like myself gyrating through the ship like a pig in the mud. It's only the first time I've done it sober."

His comment made her grin, which caused him to smile. "I've been meaning to ask… What does a political officer do, anyway?"

He lifted his chin and stretched to his maximum height. "Officially, or what do *I* do?"

"I think I have pretty good idea of what you do," she said, eyeing him suspiciously for effect. He gazed back with a small, mischievous twinkle. "Officially then."

"Officially, this is a combat ship for Space Force Fleet Command, designed to operate by herself at long range for extended periods. The captain and the crew are trained to meet the enemy, any enemy, with resourcefulness and without reinforcement. Where I come in is whenever anyone wishes to talk. We do get diplomatic missions from time to time. The captain commands the ship, but officially she can't speak for the UTE. I basically have nothing to do with the ship, but I *can* speak for the UTE."

"Then why are you on the bridge?" Carmen asked. "And included with the senior officers?"

"I'm supposed to remind her and them of any treaty stipulations, obligations, or violations. Things of that sort."

She nodded a few times. "So, Captain Brown is right. Most of the time, you are useless."

Frederick looked at her nonplussed before he barked a laugh that echoed down the corridor. He even needed to take the time to wipe a tear from his eye before he spoke again. "As you said, she is shrewd." Carmen smiled. "I still can't figure you out, though. I know you can kill me ten times before I hit the ground, but you seem so normal. Can't square why you're here."

"I have to do what I can to help," she replied. "I wouldn't think there was anything complicated about that."

"I get that piece," he remarked, "but not the rest of you. I've heard about the Rogue Wolves before. Your friend fits," he continued, nodding to Inertia up the corridor. "You don't. I'd sooner expect to see you on a beach drinking a piña colada than wearing body armor."

Carmen thought about what he said for a few seconds. "I've never been to a beach before," she reflected, nor had she ever had a piña colada. She didn't even know what that was. The idea, unfortunately, got her thinking. If that was what *normal* people did, then she lived in a completely different universe. She shook her head briskly to stop the idea from growing roots. "I don't really have anything other than this."

"Nothing?" Frederick scoffed. "I don't believe you." She looked at him and nodded several times with raised eyebrows. "All right, let's see. What's your family like?"

"I don't know," she said with a shrug. "I barely remember what my parents look like. I don't even know if they remember me. They could have had ten children after me, for all I know."

"You can always reconnect with them," he pointed out. Carmen thought about it and shuddered before waving the idea away. "Okay, what about a boyfriend? You have to have that."

"Had. He was sick for a long time and…died. I couldn't even say goodbye."

Frederick leaned away from her and paused. "A friend?"

"I had one, I guess," she said, thinking of Artemis. "I helped her get away after I was sent to kill her when she took hostages in a mall. I don't know where she is now, or what she's done since." *Hopefully nothing extreme*, she didn't say.

They arrived at the main briefing room, and Inertia walked inside without even a backward glance. Her eyes fell as she sighed. *It seems I no longer have a partner either*, she thought dismally. Frederick saw her increasingly dejected expression and gave a few words of encouragement, but he was totally unaware that her reaction had nothing to do with their conversation.

"A place to live?"

Carmen shook her head. "I lived in a roach infested apartment. Not a nice place," she added, shaking her head again.

"It was blown up. Everyone who lived there was killed. I was sitting on the windowsill."

"A pet at least? Wait, don't tell me. It was in the apartment when it blew up."

"No. I had a dog… I cut off her head."

Frederick took a deep breath and let it out sharply. "Shit. Now I'm depressed," he remarked as his eyes fell.

Carmen looked at him, forced a smile, and shook her head. "Don't be. I'm not."

"How's that possible?"

"Not without a lot of effort, that's for sure," she said more to herself than to him. "I try not to dwell on it. Others have had worse. Even then, it doesn't matter. I accept that what happened happened. Some of it was done to me, and some of it I did to myself. I think it's best to focus on the future, not the past."

"What do you see in the future? With a past like that, it's hard to imagine the future being any different."

Carmen stopped to think about it for a moment. "Perhaps it won't be. I don't know," she finally said. "I've never known. That…terrifies me sometimes. But I try to accept that knowing isn't the point."

"What's the point then? I've burned out so many brain cells; make it simple, please. It's hard enough to follow you as it is," he said with a grin.

She smiled. Frederick seemed to almost instinctually know when someone's mood needed a boost. "It's…" she began, but she trailed off before she said anything else. She was still coming to grips with everything herself and had never thought to put what she felt—what she hoped—into words for anyone else's consumption. "For me, it really comes down to one thing." Frederick waited eagerly for her response, and in a way, it reminded her of the rare times

Phaethon wanted to know her perspective. "People, circumstances, life, can't turn you into anything you don't already believe you are."

He nodded a few times. "Now I really don't get you," he said casually.

Carmen shrugged. "I'm used to it; I'm a Clairvoyant. Tell me, though, with all that's going on, will we still be able to find the freighter in time? Honestly."

"Better than even chance," Frederick answered without having to do any searching. "Trust the captain. We've been in tougher scraps than this."

"That's good to know," she said softly.

He nodded thoughtfully. "Aye."

After that, the two of them walked into the briefing room. They were the last to arrive. Renee and Terry were seated as before, and as before no other officers were present. Carmen took station next to Inertia, who might have blinked when she walked by but nothing more. She wanted to say something to him, anything would do. She didn't mind Frederick and could even see why Renee tolerated him so easily, but the dynamic was ultimately just a distraction.

She'd drowned in distractions. Distractions had nearly driven her crazy. Her entire relationship with Michael had been a distraction. They were a diabolic comfort that she was painfully used to. She looked at her fellow Rogue Wolf and wondered why they could risk life and death together but that, lately, she had to gather her nerve to mutter just a simple hello. But the hologram of Admiral West came into being before she could attempt to say anything. She let go a regretful sigh.

The admiral groaned loudly before he spoke, and Carmen swore he looked even more worn than before. "Well, this situation has turned into a disaster," he began.

Renee clenched her jaw. "They haven't started another war, have they?" she asked, her voice wavering and dripping with worry despite her best efforts to hide it.

"No, nothing like that," West said quickly. "Just know the sortens have an entire fleet hunting for you with orders to destroy on sight. I pushed for purely your arrest and extradition, but they would not have it. If you are captured, expect your immediate execution."

She and Terry spared each other a glance. "I understand, sir, but we still need to complete our mission," she said.

Carmen couldn't help a small smile when she heard that, but West took a deep breath and exhaled through barred teeth. "I can see how you pissed off Admiral Wright so much," he remarked. "Can it still be done?"

Renee took a deep breath herself as she thought the matter through. She closed her eyes for few seconds and, when she opened them, she tipped her head. "Seems like either we will or we'll die trying."

"How succinct, Captain," West replied. "There is something else you should know. It won't be just the sortens hunting you. In the interest of keeping the peace and showing this was not a sanctioned action, two Peacekeeper-class cruisers have been dispatched to join the search. They are already on their way."

"Are they aware of our mission?" Terry asked.

"No," West said. "They have very specific orders to destroy the ISS *Griffin*. They also have a sorten observer aboard to guarantee those orders are carried out. I suggest you ensure that isn't allowed to happen. I am transmitting details of your opposition now."

Renee nodded as Terry pulled out his PDD and began reading. "Thank you, sir. We are going silent after this. It's a bit of risk even talking to you now."

"I understand, and that's prudent. I don't know what's on that damn freighter and why it's so important, but to say the obvious, there is a very narrow path to victory here." Renee pursed her lips and nodded glumly. "I'd wish you luck, but I fear it's already forsaken you. I'd tell you good hunting, but you're going to be fighting our own. I'll just say find a way, Captain. West out."

The hologram faded away and there was silence in the room. It broke when Renee let go a sigh that was almost a groan as she rolled her eyes. "What are we facing?" she asked Terry.

"The admiral wasn't exaggerating when he said a fleet," he began. "Two battlecruisers, eight fleet cruisers, twenty destroyers, a carrier, and support ships…including sensor pickets."

Carmen glanced at Frederick when the ship's XO finished. Inertia would have probably ignored her. The political officer, however, didn't notice her interest either in the dim room. He stood still with his arms folded, his hands gripping them tensely, and she noticed his breathing was very shallow. He eventually realized the Clairvoyant was looking at him and he stopped and gave her a confident nod. Carmen swallowed hard but decided she'd trust Frederick's faith in his captain even if it didn't seem absolute.

Renee cursed softly under her breath. "What about on our side? What are we facing?"

"ISS *Mercury*, Captain Biggles commanding. You know him?" Terry asked.

"No," she answered after thinking about it for a few seconds. She turned to look at Frederick, who shook his head.

"Well, West sent personnel files on the entire crew," Terry continued.

She nodded. "And the second ship?"

Terry looked at the PDD in his hand and groaned. "Shit, they really do want us dead." Renee eyed him curiously. "ISS *Jaeger*, Captain Holder commanding. *Him* I know. Never served with him, but he previously commanded a Renegade-class cruiser. He probably came in the top three if not first in every fleet combat readiness evaluation since he became a skipper. The man's a warrior."

"I've heard of him," Renee said.

He kept reading. "His XO is a Wiz Kid," he pointed out, glancing at her over the device. "Lieutenant Commander Mortis… You know him?"

Renee grinded her teeth upon hearing that name, as if a hard piece of leather was stuck between them. "Yes, sadly, I do. An annoying pissant of a man. No one could stand him when we were training. Hell, Garvin gave him one to the gut once to shut him up. There was no reprimand—the trainers couldn't stand him either. He has a mind of nothing but gears… Unfortunately, his imagination is limited to what's in the book."

"Why unfortunately?" Carmen asked. "That sounds like it would be good for us."

The captain glanced at her and then took a deep breath. "Because he knows *everything* in the book. The only reason Garvin and I were rated higher was because he's about as commanding as a boy scout who hasn't realized he's crapped his pants. Vicious as a horde of ants when he has the advantage, though."

"Oh," Carmen muttered.

"Worse, I've fought him before, many times in simulations. He knows how I fight," she continued.

"Doesn't that also mean you know how he fights?" Frederick asked.

"Yes," she responded. "I gave as good as I got, but no one

—*no one*—executes as well as he does. At least, from what I've seen. It's hard to be consistently more brilliant than perfect fundamentals."

"The admiral also mentioned there would be a sorten observer. Do you have any information on him?" Inertia asked.

"Yes, Fleet Commander Kril."

"What do we know about him?" Carmen asked.

* * *

"The Fleet Commander's shuttle is approaching, sir. They are requesting docking clearance."

Captain Holder awaited the sorten delegation in *Jaeger's* hangar. His XO was with him. "Stand up straight, boy," he said gruffly. The commander had an annoying habit of slouching.

"Yes, sir. Sorry, sir," Mortis said as if he'd just been stuck by a cattle prod.

Holder shook his head. "They are clear to dock. We are ready," he said after accessing the ship's intercom.

His XO then took to straightening and pruning his uniform. The garments were custom cut for the individual, and it was hard not to look striking in the black and silver of Space Force Fleet Command, but somehow his executive officer managed it. His soft, almost babyish features would make him look prepubescent probably well into his sixties. His hair was a slick midnight black; no strand was ever out of place. Even now he tended to it as he licked his lips in anticipation of their guest. Holder also turned his attention toward the approaching shuttle.

It was visible now. In the far distance, about the size of his finger, was the battlecruiser from which the shuttle had come. The size was a misnomer; the ship was easily three times the size of *Jaeger*. Details couldn't be made out, but that was not the case for the shuttle. Sleek, elegant, and functional like most sorten construction, the craft drifted into the hangar like a shark gliding over a seabed. The two Space Force officers stiffened when it set down, the first time a sorten craft that wasn't captured or a prize of war had ever boarded a terran starship.

Mortis glanced at his captain, but he didn't notice the attention. Tall, broad shouldered, and proud, the captain stood in his hangar like a great big oak. The XO came to about his chest. As the boarding ramp for the shuttle lowered, Holder placed his hands on his hips with a look like he was preparing to battle the entire sorten fleet with nothing but his bare hands. In time, their guest appeared, flanked by two guards. Holder's eyes narrowed upon them. He was unarmed and alone, other than the hangar crew and his XO. Kril eventually stepped onto the ship proper, and Mortis strode forward to greet him.

"Fleet Commander Kril, it is with great pleasure that I—"

The sorten and his guard walked right by Mortis to stop in front of the master and commander of the *Jaeger*. Neither side said anything. The sorten's fur was light grey with a black stripe on either side. He came to his hind legs and towered just over the terran, who stared right back. His guard remained on all fours with their weapons still stowed on their backs. Mortis looked at them and licked his lips again. The sortens, always thin to the point that they appeared sickly, were an odd contrast to the powerfully built captain, but Kril came across as no less intimidating. He had an air of command of more than just muscle and sinew. In time, he gave the sorten equivalent of a nod.

"I can deal with you, terran," he said. "We are not

conducting pleasant business; I can tell that you understand that."

"No, we're not," Holder agreed. His deep voice always made even the simplest words resonate far beyond their importance. "I never thought I'd cooperate with a sorten on anything, least of all this."

"Indeed," Kril said, dropping to all fours. "Let's begin."

10

———

PLAY YOUR OPPONENT

They were alone, and if all went according to plan, they'd be the first sacrificial course for the meat grinder. It had been hours, with relief still hours away. Their backs by this point were a dull, stiff tingle that protested every now and then with a quick shot of pain that radiated throughout their bodies. The patrol was of a graveyard. But at least it wasn't cold. Winter always hated the cold.

Red busied himself with his sensor readout, trying to pick out contacts while removing false returns, echoes, and duplicates. It was no easy task in their present circumstances. He hummed an old academy fight song while he worked. Winter had never gone to the academy; it hadn't existed at the start of the first Terran-Sorten War, but she'd heard the tune enough to know it word by word. Red always sang or hummed it when he was sick of talking to her during especially long missions. She could talk about her family, which she hardly ever saw, all day, but sadly not everyone found the domestic monotony as interesting.

"Winter, new navpoint," he said.

She nodded and guided the fighter toward the coordinate

with a thought. Such was the ease of the system that her mind drifted elsewhere rather easily. It was like reading and walking at the same time.

What she was reading in this case had nothing to do with the operation of her starfighter or even their mission. Her gaze darted everywhere she could see as she took everything in. She knew intellectually what had happened here—a doomsday weapon had claimed the lives of billions of sortens and ended the war, on that front anyway. Yet, she had never thought she'd see the devastation in person. It was altogether different than Winter had expected.

She'd seen ships go down with all hands. She'd easily lost more friends to the business than she had fingers and toes to count. Some of them bought the farm, screaming to the end, and some met their death with an eerily silent calm that still made her pause when she thought of it. She'd seen cities burned to the ground and had regrettably carried out orders to attack anything that moved, even when it was against her better judgement. The toll of all those actions paled in comparison to Medusa, the weapon that didn't kill with heat, light, or a concussion wave. The entire system was dead, but by the naked eye, there was no horror to be seen.

The star at the heart of the system orbited the artificial blackhole; a long stream of fiery orange shot from it like a punctured water balloon to circle around and around that invisible, all-consuming mass like water circling a drain. The sheer force of Medusa had ripped the planets apart. The crusts were torn open in a way that oddly reminded her of the oranges she hastily peeled for her daughters. The planetary cores were visible in some cases, pulsing molten and angry as they were destroyed. Debris was everywhere. It wasn't just stellar matter but also that of ships that were unable to escape Medusa during the running battle of its deployment. The entire system was an utter mess, but when close enough to see it, the destruction was almost pretty to look at. Furthermore, the time distortion from the gravity froze the scene in place from an outsider's perspective and would for eons. No quick explosion and done; no decompression or being left to float in the icy cold of space. Everyone here had died instantly, yet they remained almost exactly as they were, as if spectral statues.

The fighter arrived at the navpoint. She'd flown with Red long enough to know better than to ask the question. In all this disaster, the ISS *Griffin* and the sorten fleet trying to find her were hidden. It was Winter and Red's job to find the fleet before that happened. Their squadron mates were searching in other subsectors.

"Just an echo," he announced after a few seconds. "I don't know how they expect us to find anything in this. They should have used probes."

"They are," Winter responded.

"Yeah, I got that, but you know what I mean. A starfighter is too small a flashlight for too big a room."

"Better than nothing," she remarked. "Besides, if it's hard for us to find anything, that means it's also hard for them."

"It's all a waste of time. The ship should just Ghost and make a run for it."

Winter shook her head. "Wouldn't work. Sortens aren't stupid. They'll have ships stationed out of the system monitoring for exactly that. Not too hard to set up an intercept with other ships in adjacent sectors, even if we went fast."

"I think we're boned, Winter."

"Probably," she agreed. She took a deep breath and let it out slowly. "Hope you took care of your will and everything."

He gave no reply. It wasn't the first time she'd said as

much to him and he to her, but it was the first time she actually meant it. She wished she hadn't said it.

"New contact. Navpoint set for bogey," he said, completely ignoring her comment.

"I see it," she said after turning her head.

The point in space looked, on her helmet-mounted display, like an outline of a diamond encasing a solid diamond. She glanced at her fuel gauge and sighed. It was at just the perfect distance to be too close to efficiently Ghost to but far enough to make the trip at sublight quite the haul.

"You got something else? I've been in this seat too long. My toes are going numb."

"You know, Winter," he began. She rolled her eyes, knowing she was in for it now. "Whenever I read about the exploits of the famous Grim Reapers, they never say how whiny you are."

"Fuck off. That was more than fourteen years ago. I was younger than you then."

"No excuse."

"Huh, please… You'll find out," she said. *If you live that long*, she didn't add. "But Red, you're making me wish I'd stayed in single seaters." Her backseater laughed. Winter smirked. "Find another contact to investigate."

"Yes, Skipper," he replied in a tone he might use with an overbearing mother. Winter smirked again. She did occasionally call her squadron mates her kids; it had to come back on her sometimes. "On your HMD now."

"Got it," she remarked after turning her head again.

A thought sent them burning toward the new coordinates at just under a quarter of the speed of light. Red went back to humming, and she sighed and tried to get comfortable in the seat, for as much as that was possible at this point. In her long career, it always amazed Winter that even in situations like this, when they were literally surrounded by enemies, the job was unending boredom punctuated by moments of stark terror rather than the other way around. The bewildering nature of space travel didn't help matters. The reference points were so far away that it didn't seem like they were moving, despite the relative velocity scale stating otherwise. The only thing she could think to do was stare at the ETA clock as it counted down. The stupefying dreariness of it dulled the aches somewhat. Well, it didn't, but it was better than nothing. The clock eventually reached zero.

"Anything?" she asked. She usually never asked, but the tedium was making her hand irrationally snake toward the ejection handle. "Red?" she asked again when he gave no reply.

"We might have something. Should we phone it in?"

"No, not unless we need to. The communication could give the ship away," she answered. Their datalink was turned off for the same reason. "What is it?"

"Can't tell at this distance. I could give it an active scan?"

Winter considered the benefits versus the tradeoffs for a few seconds. "No, I'd rather not. That would give *us* away. Work us in closer, low G approach."

"Yes, ma'am…plotted."

Winter got the fighter going on the new vector with the barest minimum of a burn. The aches and pains of the past few hours faded away to be replaced by a familiar focus. She didn't need to remind herself that she'd done this hundreds of times before; the habits of battle merely came to her on their own accord. The genius of the fly-by-thought system made itself known in these moments. With conventional controls, her well-practiced hand almost kissed the control stick and throttle to command the fighter in a gentle but deliberate fashion. She'd gotten no small measure of pride from the knowledge that she could coax every bit of performance out of the craft while staying in complete control. Now she didn't even think about it. The action was as natural as transitioning from a walk to a run.

"Contact maneuvering, definitely no echo or sensor ghost."

"Mark as hostile; we don't have any friendlies out here," she ordered. "What is it?" she asked again.

"Looks like a sorten sensor picket."

"And they haven't detected us yet?" she said with surprise.

"Doesn't look like it. She appears to be running good and dim. Probably in transit to a position to begin her search," he said. He then asked the most important question. "What do we do?"

"How good is our track?"

"Enough for a firing solution…barely. You want to attack?"

I'm not Renee, Winter thought. "We're armed, aren't we?" she asked rhetorically while she eyed the six anti-ship missiles under their wings.

"Well yeah, but shouldn't we think about this? Who knows what will happen if we destroy that ship? It might even start the war again."

Winter swallowed hard as the idea crossed her mind as well. "We're already past that. All I know is, while this isn't a battleship, the sortens need these pickets to find the *Griffin*. Taking it out gives us a better chance." She then took a deep breath, rolled her neck a few times, and made sure her straps were tight. "Weapons hot, give me two javelins."

"Ready," Red announced.

Her HMD symbology indicated as much, she could fire now, but it was much too soon. She instead started another low G burn. Any relative speed they had would be imparted on their missiles, and every little bit helped. The humming and idle banter was forgotten as they bore down on the target. Her adversary was shown plain as day on her display as a pulsing red square with a cross inside it, but it was far too distant to be seen by the naked eye. That was the case with most of her targets, such was the nature of space combat. Just then, there was a light on her console associated with a mild beeping noise.

"They've painted us," he remarked.

Winter already knew the obvious and made no comment. The attack was now solely under her control. Sorten sensor pickets weren't very well armed, but a good hit from a feebly armed target could kill them just as well as a glancing hit from a well-armed one. She brought the fighter to full power, and they streaked ahead.

"Go active."

"Roger. Multiple contacts," Red said.

We've stumbled on the sorten fleet, she thought as the number of red squares multiplied.

"Two sorten Swifts inbound."

Winter cursed under her breath. An individual sorten starfighter was more than a match for her Banshee, let alone a pair of them. She glanced at her sensor display and noted they weren't in a threatening position yet and that she had a positive vector away from them, though that was shrinking. She turned her attention back to the picket and opened up with her fighter's six laser cannons. Three blue-white ribbons of energy lanced from each of the Banshee's two wings to splay out on the picket's shield. The sorten ship returned fire but was unable to get a bead on its nimble adversary. Again and again, the fighter darted and danced in the exchange, scoring hits while never being in danger itself. She could have downed the ship with lasers alone, but they didn't have that kind of time.

"Missiles away," Winter announced. As soon as the missiles were clear, she put the fighter on an escape course—though not completely. "Red, shoot list."

"Up,"

She didn't want to tangle with two Swifts if she didn't have to, but her sorten counterparts could accelerate faster than she could, especially loaded down with weapons as she was. It was better to give them something to think about now than to be run down later. She readied a Viper anti-fighter missile for each. A moment later, the Banshee shut off its main engines and then flipped in place to point at the incoming sortens.

"Missiles away, two," she announced.

She then got her Banshee burning on their original escape vector. At this range, the sortens would probably defeat the missiles kinematically easily enough, which was beside the point. Winter didn't really intend to kill them, just disrupt their intercept. They were already maneuvering to defend themselves. The picket was destroyed.

"Send to the *Griffin*. They're coming," she said.

* * *

Mortis entered *Jaeger's* CIC and felt a sudden surge of confidence. In the dim room, surrounded by computer screens and with a large holographic display in the center, he was home. Here, he was a god. A few of his shipmates spoke casually amongst themselves, but it all stopped when they noticed him. There was utter silence now. He walked deeper into the starcruiser's nervous system and the dead calm continued. Everyone, even Captain Holder, had to admit that, while he might make mistakes from time to time, and while there were whispers and jeers behind his back, *none* were better than Mortis when he was in his element. Those mistakes were hardly ever his fault anyway.

The short man walked around the room with his hands behind his back while he eyed the crew manning the consoles throughout the room. They always returned the look, but all he had to do was stare that extra bit longer. Just those few extra seconds of deadpan authority, and they eventually looked away. He returned to the center of the room once he was finished leaving his mark.

"Ladies and gentlemen," he began. A couple of the women present rolled their eyes. They always did around him, despite his rank. He just couldn't figure out how to get them to stop. He ignored it for now. "As always, I need precision and efficiency. Carry out my orders to the letter and without hesitation. Anyone have a problem with that?"

He smiled when there was no challenge. Holder was right, at least with this, that speaking strongly and with the proper posture was all it really took. People wanted to be led. But, strangely, no one was looking at him. They all stared at something behind him. Mortis licked his lips before he turned around. When he did, Fleet Commander Kril and his two escorts were standing in front of him. The sorten looked around the room slowly. Mortis wanted to shoo him out as if he were a disobedient dog. Most members of the crew weren't even allowed into the CIC, but Holder had said to allow full access.

"What are you doing, terran?" Kril asked.

Mortis licked his lips again. "Commanding the fleet, of course."

Kril didn't even look at him when he gave the response, and he felt a small boil of rage as the action made him feel two inches tall. The sorten looked at the crew, *his* crew, and when Kril's gaze fell upon them, they looked away promptly. The sorten didn't even appear angry, just passively curious.

"By whose authority?"

"My own. The captain agrees that I'm the best for the job," he answered, stretching to his full height as he spoke.

"Oh please, boy," Kril remarked dismissively. Mortis's hands balled into fists behind his back. The captain sometimes called him that, but he called everyone that. He had probably popped out of his mother and called his own father "boy." But that was the captain—he had to take it from him, not from some sorten on his own ship. Why even give them any deference at all? They'd been defeated in war...twice. "This isn't a terran expedition. Remember, *you* are aiding *us*."

Mortis eyed the sorten directly, and Kril stared right back. Seconds passed, several seconds, as Mortis's fists became tighter and tighter while Kril became more and more amused. Mortis broke the standoff by pretending to look up to think.

"I know Captain Brown," he said. "I know how she thinks, how she fights. I know exactly what her ship is capable of. I've beaten her before."

"Have you now? Accomplishment must come in all sizes," Kril said, looking the Space Force officer up and down. As Mortis's cheeks flushed red, there was soft laughter in the room; he chose to ignore that, as well, while noting which voices they were. "In real battle or merely in simulation," the fleet commander continued.

"Makes no difference. You haven't fought her ever."

"True, terran," Kril said, though he still looked amused. He even took a moment to glance at one of his guards who shared the same look. "As you wish. The fleet is yours to command." Mortis nodded, which caused the sorten to outright laugh. He didn't know what the problem was. It was only after a few seconds that he realized he was trembling slightly. "I see there is already a target," Kril said, turning his attention to the large holographic display.

"Yes, a single starfighter. It's no threat."

"Indeed. I see, though, that it downed one of our pickets," Kril pointed out with rising aggression in each word.

"It did, but a single fighter is immaterial. The objective is Captain Brown."

Kril stared at him with narrowing eyes. Mortis licked his lips and took a subconscious step back. "She is. But know this, Lieutenant Commander Mortis. Waste a single sorten life unnecessarily, and I shall visit you after this incident is concluded…and it will be no simulation."

There was utter silence in the CIC after that. Mortis looked at the sorten and swallowed hard. He then looked at the holo display while he wiped the sweat from his brow. He'd intended to make a longer speech to the CIC crew, but he didn't have the heart for it anymore.

The display showed a large three-dimensional representation of the system and all the ships in it. He didn't know where the *Griffin* was for now, but he had a few good guesses. Knowing Renee, she had to be wedged in the most treacherous, foolhardy place a starship could go.

"Tighten the net," he ordered.

* * *

Carmen paced her quarters, groaning every time she completed a lap. She knew nothing about starships; nothing about starship combat; nothing at all that was a help for anyone. She may have been one of the most powerful beings to have ever lived, but her mounting uselessness was driving her to literally pull out her hair. She'd long since turned off the clock in her quarters; nevertheless, she could still hear its incessant ticking throb through her soul. It made her so antsy that she couldn't lay in bed and stare at the ceiling like she usually did.

"Inertia," she said through gritted teeth.

This was his plan. She could agree it was the best shot they'd had at the start of this. Now…now, what difference did it make if she agreed? She'd never really had any choice or influence in any of this. Perhaps she never truly had. He hardly even acknowledged her existence now!

She stopped at a wall to try to force herself to calm down, but she instead pounded it with her fist. The lights, dimmed to almost darkness, even flickered. She grabbed her hair, pulled, and then sank to the deck, still pulling. There was no respite. She thought about finding the freighter. She thought about fighting Charon. She thought about Inertia. Then she was annoyed that she thought about Inertia. And then she thought about being annoyed that she thought about Inertia. Then she was annoyed about that! She didn't think it was a mistake to continue after Solitary, but she was certainly reconsidering the reason why she did.

Carmen closed her eyes and started banging the back of her head against the wall softly. "I really *don't* have anything else," she said.

The realization didn't fill her with quiet dread, make her anxious, or even cause a sigh. It was merely a statement of the obvious. She'd known it for quite some time. Everyone who knew her, even in passing, knew it. Inertia knew it. She rolled her eyes as her mind strayed to her partner/not partner again. It was like a switch had been turned off between them. He'd flipped it just when she was starting to realize it was there, and she had no idea why. If he just came out and said he hated her and never wanted to see her again, well, she wouldn't exactly appreciate it, but she could live with it. But the cold ambiguity now was absolutely vexing.

Just then, there was a loud alarm. "Battle stations, battle stations, all hands. Man your battle stations!"

Carmen remained seated. She wasn't a member of the crew. The ship could be blown to atoms in the next few seconds and there was nothing she could do about it. That realization made her sigh. She was tempted to just wait in her quarters and accept the inevitable, but an idea came to her. She stood and started her trek to the bridge.

The relaxed readiness she'd previously seen in the crew was nowhere to be seen. They weren't panicking, but there was an extra intensity born of the unease of a possibly unwinnable battle. She knifed through them and ignored whatever feelings she sensed. She didn't know the situation, but she was absolutely certain it wasn't hopeless. She'd long since learned that nothing was beyond hope. Sometimes that was all that was left to go on.

She found the elevator for the bridge easily enough on her own. It helped that starships were arranged logically, especially compared to Solitary. She got off on the proper deck, and after pausing a moment to sense who was inside, leaned against the corridor wall and waited. After a small groan, she closed her eyes and resumed banging her head against the wall. She was alone for less than a minute.

"Trying to get as dumb as me?" Frederick asked.

She smiled but didn't say anything. She didn't even open her eyes. She did stop banging her head, though; it was a bit ridiculous, and now she had a headache to go along with all the other annoyances of the past few hours.

Some other bridge crew walked by and some others left, but none said anything to Carmen. When the time came, there was no soft pinprick on her subconscious; it was more like an icepick to the back of the neck. Her eyes shot open, and she stared at the elevator. She couldn't say she was nervous. She'd battled worse foes than Inertia. She couldn't say she looked forward to the next few minutes either, but they had to happen. The elevator doors opened and her fellow Rogue Wolf began walking toward her. He couldn't help giving her a quick glance, but after that she may as well have not even been there. She couldn't tell if that was good or bad, but she didn't care for the moment.

"Inertia, we need to talk," she said, getting off the wall.

He stopped and looked at her. "Yes?" he said simply, nonchalantly, as if whatever she was about to say could be handled with all the effort of tying shoelaces. The tone made Carmen pause. It was utterly disarming. She hadn't exactly been full of vim and vigor, but she had certainly intended to finish what she started. Now it felt like her tongue had been stung by a scorpion.

They stood there in silence, looking at each other. Carmen's mouth opened in a vain attempt to speak, and Inertia watched her like a germ in a petri dish. Renee exited the elevator then. She was still buttoning her uniform and moving at a fast walk. She looked at the two Clairvoyants, first Carmen then Inertia and back. Whatever went through the mind of the captain of the *Griffin*, she kept it to herself, but she did raise an eyebrow at them before she entered the bridge. The expression snapped Carmen back to her senses.

"Inertia, what are we doing?"

"Getting ready for an attack. The ship may have been discovered," he said.

She bit her lip. He was incapable of being that dense. "You know what I mean."

"I do?" he remarked, letting the question hang.

Carmen looked at him and hesitated. She couldn't read

him, telepathically or otherwise, but he made a reaction, if infinitesimally small, at seeing her state. From what she could tell of it, it made her hesitate more. "I don't think we can find the freighter," she said softly. "Not like this."

"What do you suggest?"

"I don't know," she said, shaking her head. "You're the one who always has a plan, not me. You're the one always two steps ahead of everybody."

"Not this time," he said after a pause.

Carmen looked at him sidelong. "Nothing? That's it? Nothing?"

"Edge, you wouldn't come at me like this if you didn't already have an idea."

"Well, why don't we take *The Lady*? It's small. The sortens might not even notice it."

"They may not, but if they did, we would be defenseless. Doesn't matter anyway. *The Lady* is meant to stealthily travel from place to place, maybe even light combat when pressed. It can't take a freighter."

Carmen shook her head again. "At least it's an idea. It's better to take our chances trying than to wait here, doing nothing. We're running out of time."

"We are," he agreed. She waited for him to say something more, but nothing came. She pursed her lips in disappointment. He gave a barely perceptible sneer. "I think Solitary gave you the wrong impression. Operations fail—that's part of the business. Nothing is certain. Here is another thing you need to accept. Even if we do succeed and shut down everything the sortens are planning, it makes no difference. There will always be more. There will always be predators hunting the weak. I can't stop them all and neither can you." He didn't raise his voice—he never did—but he was yelling at her, loud enough to make the entire ship shake. "You know that."

"I do."

"Then why does this mean so much to you? You already rescued your charge."

Carmen looked at her partner and slowly shook her head while her eyes glistened in disbelief. "How can you not know?" she asked softly. "How can we have gone through all of this and you not know?"

The Rogue Wolf gave no reply other than to stare at her angrily with narrowing eyes. Then he walked past her and entered the bridge without even a backward glance. Carmen stood alone in the corridor and, for the first time, was unable to think. Eventually she placed her weary forehead in an open palm and took a deep breath. Then she entered the bridge herself.

The bridge crew talked quickly amongst themselves, except for Leena, who was talking to someone else through the ship's comm gear. Inertia was already seated, resting his chin on a closed fist. Carmen took the seat next to him. She ignored her partner while she attended to the belts. When she was done, she noticed he was watching her out the corner of his eye. He studied the belts without appearing to do so and, when satisfied, nodded to himself. Carmen didn't know what to make of it after their argument in the corridor.

"Datalink established now, Captain," Leena announced.

"Good. On holographic," Renee said.

A large image appeared in front of them and behind Tawny. Renee studied it quietly. Most captains preferred to fight the ship from the CIC. It really was the best place—the space was designed for it. She always preferred the bridge, though. It seemed more proper in a stupidly romantic way.

"Looks like there's a screen of destroyers coming our

way. Moving fast, pulsing active," Renee said, thinking out loud more than talking to anyone specific. She also noted that Winter was well clear now and moving away smartly. It helped that she didn't need to worry about them.

"Nothing behind us?" Terry asked.

"Not yet, sir," Leena answered. "None of our other fighters or probes reported any sightings."

Terry nodded and turned his attention to the captain. "Seem suspicious to you?"

"Very," she said. "My guess is they're the hounds driving us to the hunters." She leaned forward and looked at the image intently. "What are you planning, Mortis?" she asked herself, though she wasn't entirely sure if that was who she was fighting.

Carmen looked at her with a start. "How could they get here so quickly? It took us four days."

"We were a lot farther away. *Jaeger* and *Mercury* were pulled from patrol of the sorten border," Terry answered.

Carmen considered that and nodded after a soft groan. *How can things get any worse?* she wondered dismally.

"Mr. Fletcher, would you rather fight the hounds or the hunters?" Renee asked.

"In this case," he said, "I think I'd rather fight the hounds. At least they are a known quantity."

She sighed. "I agree, and that's what concerns me." She leaned back to sit straight in her chair. "Shields up. Ready all weapons. Set an intercept course."

* * *

"New contact, identified as Peacekeeper-class starcruiser! On holographic now."

Mortis smiled when he heard the report. She was almost

exactly where he expected. *Yes, that's it, fight*, he thought as he watched the dot that represented the *Griffin* begin to move. The sorten destroyers opposing it reacted precisely in accordance to their preassigned role. They may have been defeated in war, but even he would admit they made formidable adversaries.

"The *Griffin* has gone active," someone else announced.

"Of course she did," he said to himself. "Are the sorten battlecruisers in place?"

"Yes, sir. They haven't appeared to be detected."

I expected more, Tenacious, he thought. Garvin had coined the name. Renee couldn't stand it, but it was well earned. She did have a way of pushing through everything with nothing more than dogged determination. She didn't solve problems; she ground them into paste. But not today and not now. Her undoing would be everything that made her what she was. He'd defeated her before.

* * *

"Multiple contacts. Holy shit, they're everywhere!" Hiroshi reported.

Carmen stared at the holographic display after the ship began active scanning and her eyes went wide. She had known what they were up against, but seeing the red dots arrayed in a sphere around their current position put that realization into stark reality. She gripped her armrest tightly—not from fear, though she did worry that she might blackout again, but from the frustration of knowing that, no matter what happened, there was nothing she could do to affect much of anything.

"We all knew what was coming," Renee said calmly.

"Other than the destroyers, the fleet isn't really closing on us," Terry remarked. "They're more holding position than advancing."

"I noticed. Time to optimum weapon range on the destroyers?" she asked.

"Ah…twenty-three seconds with energy weapons. Hammers available now," Hiroshi answered.

"Save the Hammers." She thought for a few seconds. "Give the leading destroyer a spread from bow torpedo… Let's get him defensive. New course, right 15 degrees minus 3 from ship's head. Burn for point-one-five c."

"Aye, ma'am," Tawny said after she repeated the order.

"Captain, that course puts us in the heart of their strength," Terry told her under his breath.

"I know," she replied. "FCT, fire at will—energy weapons only."

"Fire at will, energy only. Aye, ma'am. May I shoot to kill?" Hiroshi asked.

Renee hesitated for a long second. "Yes."

The terran starship accelerated smartly on its new course, preceded by a brace of torpedoes fired from its two bow torpedo tubes. The projectiles fired electromagnetically, shot forth at a significant fraction of the speed of light. The intended target turned away, completely spoiling the intercept. Streams of impossibly bright energy poured from the *Griffin*, lancing toward the sortens' probable vector. The sorten starship changed course again and burned on a vector that ensured its safety but which now placed the ship completely out of position, spoiling the formation. Its counterparts responded in kind. Their lasers spewed like a geyser, destined to blanket the ship no matter how she turned. Yet they didn't.

Tawny glanced at the captain over her shoulder. "May I maneuver, ma'am?" she asked anxiously.

"Hold present course," Renee said calmly while her hands flew over her display.

Carmen looked at the Wiz Kid, unable to help a questioning raised eyebrow. The first thing she'd learned way back when was that the best defense was to not be there. Renee didn't look suicidal. If anything, she seemed almost serene. The Clairvoyant looked at the XO and Frederick next. Neither man seemed concerned.

Renee stopped whatever she was working on suddenly and took a quick breath. "Ships, head toward the center of the sorten formation. Maximum forward shields," she ordered.

Tawny and Leena responded immediately. The starship turned into the sorten attack for no change in vector. The brunt of the fire went all around the ship. The little that hit splayed harmlessly against the cruiser's shield. Carmen's eyes narrowed when she realized what was going on. *She is shrewd*, she thought. The sortens were aiming with the expectation that their target would maneuver. It reminded her of not falling for a feint in hand-to-hand fighting.

"Current heading plus 90, ahead two thirds," Renee said. She counted silently to herself for three seconds. "Left 90, ahead full. Even shields."

The sorten destroyers had corrected for their mistake before their first volley even arrived. The mass of the second and third were focused on where the terran would be if it didn't change course or speed. The now-maneuvering cruiser, however, evaded the majority of energy as both volleys passed behind it. As the *Griffin* moved, she returned fire, spoiling the enemy's aim and scattering the sorten destroyers in turn.

* * *

"What fools do they give me?" Mortis yelled to no one in particular.

The sorten fleet commander growled behind him, and the lieutenant commander froze for a moment. He'd forgotten that they had company. He turned to look at Kril, whose eyes drilled straight into his chest, but he said nothing.

It was no matter anyway. This was merely the anvil for the hammer.

* * *

The sortens buzzed toward and away with slashing attacks that entered their opponent's optimum weapon range for only the briefest of instants. The two sides traded like that for several volleys with the destroyers partially surrounding the cruiser, which was more than twice their size, in a hemisphere.

"They're trying to wear us down," Terry said.

Renee agreed with a nod. There was no damage, but energy reserves were steadily being depleted. That got her thinking. *Why don't you just overpower us with more ships?* The destroyers could hurt them, and they were certainly trying, but they couldn't kill them—not without more effort than was necessary. Mortis had to know that as well; he wasn't an idiot.

There was a small planet relatively close by, a matter of light minutes. Medusa had ripped the planet to shreds. The back half was cratered in on itself, and the side facing the blackhole was torn away, leaving a long stream of debris that trailed the orbit. Renee looked at it on the holographic display, and the opportunity to move the battle to more favorable ground seemed obvious. They couldn't hide there for long, but that didn't even enter her mind. What did, to the point that it was annoyingly hard to ignore, was the advantage to giving the sortens something else to contend with when the rest of the fleet decided to engage.

"We got one, a destroyer slightly apart from the main group," Terry announced.

Renee hadn't been paying attention to the battle. "Intercept course…take him down."

The starship abruptly changed vector and leapt on the sorten destroyer like a bird of prey. Maneuver was rendered useless at the close range, but the cruiser could take the hits from its lighter opponent. The destroyer's shields buckled. A hit to the bow spouted fire as if it were a bloody nose. Another to the ship's engineering spaces broke its back. The large explosion bent the once-sleek war machine into twisted metal slag. A secondary explosion snapped it in two. The pieces spun off in separate directions.

"The destroyer is down, ma'am," Hiroshi reported.

Renee made absolutely no reaction. "New course," she began, as she then said a set of coordinates.

Terry glanced at her. "The planet?"

The captain nodded, though her expression was about as readable as a sundial at night. She looked neither stressed nor calm; she came across as contemplative, for whatever reason. "It seems the obvious choice, doesn't it?"

* * *

"That's it, Tenacious, run," Mortis said under his breath. "Get to that briar patch. It's too good to pass up."

The ship had broken through the destroyer screen and was now accelerating toward the closest planet. Once there, it would be harder to track amongst the rocks and other debris. Worse, the stellar matter would also work as a funnel, restricting any approach vector to but a few, effectively reducing the sortens' numbers the same as a bottleneck.

Kril took a few steps forward to stand beside him. "This captain appears no fool. She will know it's a trap."

"I want her to know," Mortis said triumphantly. "There's no point in winning if she doesn't know who was finally superior."

Kril looked at him with barely hidden disgust. "What is your stratagem, terran?"

"To kill her."

* * *

"They are still pursuing," Hiroshi announced.

"I see," Renee replied, a frustrated edge infecting her voice. The tone was not caused by the report of the destroyers, though. "What am I missing? The bastard has something planned…" she muttered as she stared at the holoprojection. Her jaw clenched ever tighter to the point that it was a wonder her teeth weren't dust.

"Captain?" Terry asked.

She groaned loudly. "Something's up. We're completely outgunned and outnumbered, but their fleet just sits there."

Carmen looked at them, then at the holoprojection and back. The situation reminded her, for some reason, of the fight rooms at the facility and Solitary. "It's like they're spectating," she remarked.

The comment made Renee look up with a start. "That's it!"

"That's it? Why is that relevant?" Terry asked.

"*He's* spectating," she answered.

"I assume you mean Lieutenant Commander Mortis? What difference does that make?" Terry asked. "Of course he'd direct the fleet from a distance, if he's actually commanding it."

Inertia looked at his sister. The Clairvoyant, who had been silent through all this, tipped his head as he came to the conclusion of the chain of logic. Renee saw it and nodded in turn. Carmen watched them and began making a few educated guesses herself. She didn't know anything about starship combat, but she'd been in enough fights to know how people worked.

"It makes a difference if you know the man," Renee said. "This isn't a spectator sport; we'll have to remind him of that."

"Aye, Captain," Terry said, though he didn't sound like he understood where he was being led.

"We're approaching the debris trail, ma'am. Shall I alter course?" Tawny asked.

Renee snapped back to more immediate concerns. She considered her options for a few seconds. "No, wait for it."

"Um…aye, ma'am."

Renee rolled her eyes and kicked herself. It wasn't the clearest order she'd ever given. Anyway, she figured they only had a few more seconds. "Let's do something about those trailing destroyers. Hammers, two missiles each. It should be enough to make them disengage. Fire when ready."

"Missiles away!" Hiroshi announced after a sharp nod.

The captain sighed deeply. "If we were able to get a full reload, I'd actually try to kill them," she said to Terry.

"Keep that in mind when you tell off Admiral Wright," he remarked. "It might be all too soon."

"Not if I can help it."

Just then, Hiroshi gasped. "New contacts, two sorten battlecruisers, dead ahead! They are turning broadside and firing!"

"Ms. Crowe, now's the time. Alter course at will," Renee said with surprising levity.

Tawny didn't waste an instant to repeat the order. Carmen watched her aggressively pull and turn the yoke, which caused the Clairvoyant to grip the armrest as her face turned white. The ship yawed harshly enough that, despite the belts, she was thrown into her partner. After that, it was almost like they were somersaulting through space. There were no windows to tell, but Carmen's stomach was certainly doing barrel rolls. She'd telekinetically flown in flips and loops without even thinking about it. It would even be a fun pastime if the activity wasn't so tiring. But the experience was altogether different when she was a passenger. Her vision greyed and black gathered on the outer edges, but then, just like that, it was over. She sat, breathing hard, for a few seconds until she swallowed to regain her prior composure.

"Shields heavily drained, Captain. Probably won't withstand another direct hit," Leena reported.

"They must have been hiding in the debris," Terry said.

"Yeah, I figured there had to be something," Renee agreed. She then spoke with a calm rush. "Escape course. All ahead flank. Lead battlecruiser: engage energy only. Second battlecruiser: engage with Hammers, single volley. Fire when ready."

Carmen was pressed into her seat as the starship turned to the new course and accelerated. The inertial inhibitor trimmed out the force after a few seconds until it was no longer felt. Affirmations of Renee's orders rang throughout the bridge. And Carmen could only sit and consider everything that was happening. She had killed before. She'd washed blood off her knuckles and clothes and had been haunted by the experience to this day. But that was a single person or groups of people killed in equal combat, at least as equal as it could be when faced with a Clairvoyant. She quickly realized that, until now, she didn't know what war was.

Yes, she was presently employed as a mercenary, but both she and Inertia were really just highly skilled duelists. There were rules to their battles. It was never completely about killing the enemy as quickly and efficiently as possible. It was a small distinction that made a very clear difference. She'd freely admit she was a killer—a murderer, a mercenary, and even in quiet moments, a monster. But she was no solider. Yet, as Carmen watched the battle unfold on the holo-projection, she couldn't help a small taste of disgust. She hated fighting. The stinking smell of it, feeling the pain, seeing the pain of her opponent. This, however, was amazingly antiseptic. It was just dots. She had to remind herself that each contained hundreds if not thousands of souls. However, when she watched the tracks that were the missiles they had just fired hit the sorten battlecruiser and heard Hiroshi report the damage, the dot was removed as if it were a light that had simply burned out. A person could give more care to stomping ants.

* * *

Mortis heard the report of the destruction of the sorten battlecruiser and may have blinked.

"Terran!" Kril roared. "I do not know what you hope to prove, but I warned you about wasting our lives to prove it!"

Mortis didn't even turn to look at him. "Tell me, Kril, are you always this squeamish over a little bloody nose?" he replied.

The sorten reared and brought the Space Force officer to the ground where he clutched him firmly. Mortis cried frantically for help from the crew of the CIC, but no one made a move other than to stop what they were doing to watch. He cursed them furiously when he realized no one would be coming to his aid.

"And you speak of being squeamish," Kril bellowed.

"Don't you dare hurt me!"

"I should. The little terran playing war with brave soldier's lives…"

"Not a game—no, not a game," Mortis said quickly, shaking his head. "What did you think? That you'd be able to just roll over a Peacekeeper-class cruiser with no loses? You don't know her like I do; she won't just give up. I have to wear her down first." The sorten glared at the little man and squeezed harder. He cried out like a frog that had gotten its leg run over. "The ambush wasn't supposed to attack in force," he managed to wheeze out. "They were overeager. She would be expecting the attack. Let me finish the job. The snare is almost set."

Kril wrenched one of Mortis's arms, and he moaned in pain. "You'd better," Kril said coldly before he let him go.

Mortis coughed and wheezed on the ground for a few seconds before he realized his subordinates were still watching him. "Mind your stations!" he screamed. Then he stood, straightening and fixing his messed hair as he did so. *Dumb brute,* he thought. *The captain will hear about this and about how all of them did nothing,* he added as he looked at the crew of the CIC with fire burning behind his eyes.

"Tell cruiser squadron five to engage," he ordered.

* * *

"Multiple cruisers inbound. One minute and thirty seconds until they have optimum firing range," Hiroshi said.

Renee cursed under her breath. *Had to happen sometime,* she thought. "Shield status?" she asked. Leena looked at her and answered by slowly shaking her head.

The captain cursed again. There was nothing she could think to do that would be an immediate benefit. As always, a few Hail Mary plays remained, but now was not the time. The debris was doing its job, even though they were slowly losing the contest. There were able to fight the battlecruiser at a shorter range than would be prudent in open space, landing several hits. Their lumbering opponent just wasn't small enough to take advantage of the fleeting cover. If it worked against one, it would work against many.

"Move us into this section of the debris field," she ordered, having already sent the relevant coordinates to Tawny via her chair display. The greater density there would help.

"Aye, ma'am," Tawny responded.

The *Griffin* reversed course abruptly, its adversaries ever pursuing. Closer and closer to the planet it went. The debris which had previously been the size of mountains now approached and, in some cases, surpassed the size of continents. The ship darted between them, using the cover to shield itself from the advancing battlecruiser that spat energy like a venomous dragon. In the far distance blazed exhausts of the rapidly-approaching cruiser squadron.

"We can at least make some sort of stand here," Terry remarked.

Renee nodded. "Yes—"

"Captain!" Hiroshi yelled, cutting her off. "Incoming sorten heavy fighters to port at point-blank range! They are firing!"

"Maximum power to shields!" Renee screamed, but the shots were already striking home.

The lasers battered the protective screen mercilessly until it finally failed. The armor shroud protecting the ship's vitals was next to suffer the onslaught. It ablated off in superheated embers like the kindling of a burning log.

"Ventral DEDs to anti-fighter mode," Renee said.

"Additional cruisers, same bearing. They will have optimum firing range in…five seconds," Hiroshi added.

"Ms. Crowe, escape course. We stumbled into the thick of them."

"Aye, ma'am."

Everyone on the bridge grunted as the ship made a hard turn and accelerated.

"We could try our own fighters?" Terry suggested.

Renee thought about it for a quick second before shaking her head. "No, they're spread across the system, and it will just get them all killed. They're no match against all this."

"Fuck me! Mines dead ahead!" Hiroshi called.

The captain's eyes went wide. "All back emergency. Lock on closest mines and fire."

The two retro-engines mounted amidships spewed white-hot plasma for hundreds of miles throwing everyone into their belts. Highly accurate weapon fire vaporized a half dozen of the small deadly devices, but it wasn't enough. One mine detonated slightly earlier than its planned fusing, perhaps due to its exploding neighbors. Carmen sensed the explosion before it could be physically felt. It was strange. The bow of the ship was at least a quarter mile away from her, and the shockwave travelled up the ship like a tuning fork. She could feel everything around her twist and bend when it reached the bridge. As the lights flickered and displays shorted out, she gripped her chair, sure that the belts were leaving bruises if they hadn't already. And then it was over.

"Are we dead?" Frederick asked.

Both Renee and Terry ignored him. "He's reading us like a book. They pre-staged the ambush to drive us into the mines," he remarked.

Has to be Mortis, Renee thought with clenched teeth. "Let's bring the pipsqueak into the battle. Mr. Fletcher, fight the ship. I only need a few seconds." *And then I'll fold you like the house of cards you are!*

"Aye, Captain," he said. Then he immediately began giving orders.

Renee focused on her chair display. Carmen watched. The Wiz Kid had done this before—the desperate plan that had gotten them here in the first place—and by Terry's reaction, it seemed to be a regular occurrence. This time, she busied herself with math equations and ship status reports. Carmen hated math, but Renee breezed through the equations in mere moments.

"My command," she told her XO. "Set collision course with the *Jaeger*. All ahead flank. Call out the speed."

"Collision course, aye. Present speed point-one-five c and accelerating," Tawny said. "Point-two c. Point-three c."

Carmen looked at everyone with her mouth agape. Her skin was tingling with rising anxiety. No one questioned what Renee had just said, even though the order was suicidal. She looked at her partner, who glanced at her and gave a confident nod. The Clairvoyant's concern abated, if only just.

"Point-five c."

* * *

"The *Griffin* just set a collision course," one of the CIC crew reported.

Mortis looked at the crew member and rolled his eyes. "With what?"

"With *us*, sir. Speed now sixty-five percent the speed of light and climbing."

The lieutenant commander felt his legs turn to jelly for a moment. *You won't take me with you, Tenacious,* he thought. "Evade! Evade! Why must I give such simple orders?"

"The *Griffin* is opening fire. I don't understand…nothing is aimed along our projected course."

"So she's crazy and inept," Mortis remarked bitingly.

"You damn fool!" Fleet Commander Kril roared. "She's trying to hold us in place, keep us from maneuvering."

Mortis stared at the rapidly approaching dot that represented the *Griffin*. It seemed to be almost leaping across the projection. "Is that so? We'll see. All weapons, all ships, destroy it now!"

"No, belay that." Kril's counterorder drowned out all other noise in the CIC.

Mortis shivered. "How dare you! I am in command of this fleet!"

"And your stupidity would kill us all!" the sorten shot back. "Don't you see? You can't attack! Even if you destroyed it, whatever's left of its hulk would spear through this ship with enough momentum to hull a small moon!" Mortis said nothing back, but he rapidly licked his lips while his fists shook. "I think I understand what she is doing," Kril continued. "She intends to Ghost right through us."

"Confirmed. The *Griffin* is powering her Ghost Drive," someone else reported.

"I don't know if it's courage or desperation. A simple miscalculation and she won't be able to establish the field in time," the sorten observed.

Closer and closer the starship came, traveling faster and faster. There was utter silence in the CIC. Everyone's computer station was forgotten as they watched the holoprojection with bated breath. A few jumped when the collision klaxon sounded. It was the most urgent alarm of them all; its high-pitched scream could be heard throughout *Jaeger* where not a soul moved. Then, right before the next leap the dot would have made, where it would have landed on the other side of them, it was gone.

"The *Griffin* has Ghosted, sir."

"Course track?" Kril asked.

"Can't be resolved, sir. She was too close to us for an accurate track, two-tenths of a light second."

"Track from the screen outside the system?"

"That's also a negative, sir. If she left the system, they didn't pick it up."

"It couldn't have just disappeared!" Mortis shouted. "Find that ship!"

"Sir, Captain Holder is ordering you to report to the bridge…immediately," a different crew member said.

Kril looked at the lieutenant commander and gestured to the exit of the CIC. Mortis swallowed hard. He made a show of straightening his uniform and then started walking. After they were gone, one of the CIC crew looked at the holoprojection. It contained dozens of sorten starships and fighters, the *Jaeger* and the *Mercury*, but no ISS *Griffin*.

"Incredible," she said softly under her breath.

* * *

"Ghost Field dispelled," Tawny announced.

"All engines stop. Make the ship good and dim," Renee ordered. As when they first arrived, the light level went down and displays shut off. "Any sign of pursuit?"

They'd Ghosted to the other side of Medusa but remained in the system. The blackhole would hide their signature from any ship that didn't have a line of sight, but it wouldn't take long for anyone to realize what they'd done, and then the game would start again.

"Negative, ma'am. Scope is clear," Hiroshi reported.

She and everyone else on the bridge took a deep inhale and then breathed easy.

"Captain, I swear, if I didn't know you..." Terry said while grinning.

Renee smirked. "I don't think we'll be able to get away with that again," she remarked. Terry nodded.

"So, what now?" Carmen asked softly.

The captain closed her eyes for a long moment, sighed contently, and then groaned. She glanced at Frederick before turning her attention to the Clairvoyant. "I think it's time I should be the Dread Pirate Renee."

11

THE ODD COUPLE

It was always hard to say what you'd find in a "backwater" colony. The local flavor could usually best be described as "in progress." The people that lived here almost never had a shared history. They had no nationality, no customs, and no rituals. That all came in time, often after several generations. The food was a hodgepodge of a variety of different cultures, though strongly characterized by the local fauna. The clothes were in a similar state. The only thing that united the young, old, wealthy, and desperate was the pioneering spirit of setting off on your own with limited resources and little to no help but endless prospects.

It was thus quite the event when the two New Earthers arrived at Davison City's small airport on Planet Eris. New Earthers weren't known to be the most well-traveled people of the Great Colonies, let alone to a place as small and insignificant as Eris. They tended to never leave their planet, content at quietly declaring their superiority over everyone else, especially Earth. Yet here the New Earthers were, a man and a woman, walking down the street as if they owned it after mere minutes planetside. In the rare instances they spoke, however, their voices didn't carry the distinctive accent of New Earth, nor were their heads topped with the golden blonde that New Earthers were famous for.

The man's hair was blonde, though it was almost white in color and tied in a short ponytail. He was tall, though not markedly so. He strode forth confidently, as if his legs were pistons. His eyes were fixed straight ahead. His entire manner was trim and exact. The slightest extra effort in a glance, his stride, or even his breath appeared almost sinful. Men, women, and children parted his path with a start, though he didn't even glance at them. He didn't slow his pace to give them time to move out of the way either. He merely expected them to move, and they did. His clothes were equally as exacting. He wore a black business suit tailored perfectly to his thin, athletic frame. The Clairvoyant was striking in a way only Clairvoyants could be. He commanded attention, though he didn't actually want it. He expected respect, though it was respect tinged with fear. And all of these were not traits that could describe his companion.

The woman wore no suit and was certainly not striking in any measure. She was dressed in a bright orange T-shirt with short, dark green pants. Her dark brown hair was barely tended, and on her face was a pair of glasses. Glasses were an anachronism in an age of genetically-massaged perfect vision. Those who wore them did so for style only, and they were but a few. Indeed, on Eris, the woman with glasses was rarer than her Clairvoyant friend. Unlike him, she looked around the street as they walked. Their course was taking them directly to the newly-built Clairvoyant training facility that served the needs of this planet and several others in adjacent sectors. It looked like she wished to survey everything along the way, but the action was too deliberate for mere curiosity. The intention was anyone's guess, but a pistol was strapped to her hip. She wore bright blue bracelets on each wrist, which were a rather "off" style, and strangest of all was the large silver storage container floating after her.

The container drew more attention than either the Clairvoyant or the woman. It was cube shaped and took roughly the square footage of a transport pallet. It could be argued that most had moved out of the way to avoid the container, which spanned the width of the sidewalk, more than the Clairvoyant. Small access panels were built into it in asymmetrical locations all around it to the point that the container itself appeared functionally useless—that or the person who created it was a wacko. What was the point of making something that large just to make retrieving whatever was inside it pointlessly difficult? A large door at the front would have been more sensible.

The duo reached a rather sizeable building, for Davison City anyway. It was a mere five stories tall. The man looked at the woman, who nodded several times while she frantically waved her hands as if whatever he was suggesting was horrifyingly terrible. The incongruity made little sense to all those watching. But the man appeared used to it, strange as that seemed. He shook his head and then took to the air. The container floated after him on its antigrav tray. The woman entered the building shortly thereafter.

Gungnir landed on the roof of the building and couldn't help frowning at the Phalanx Trooper platoon that awaited him. It was half the size he was expecting. The platoon was currently unwrapping their gear and looked like they had arrived only a matter of minutes before. The only thing they had ready for immediate use was their rifles. It was understandable, given the short notice of this op, but he'd hoped for more. Presently, they were configuring a surveillance drone for launch. A better equipped colony in a better equipped sector would be able to get an orbital bird, which was more reliable.

"Sir, we have company," one of the troopers said to his CO when he noticed Gungnir.

All of the troopers turned to the Clairvoyant, but one in particular stood tall and took a couple steps forward. "Yes, we do," the man said. "I'm Lieutenant Dewitt," he announced as he extended his hand.

The Clairvoyant ignored the gesture so completely that he didn't even glance at the Space Force officer's hand. "Lieutenant?" Gungnir said dismissively. This was probably the first time he'd ever spoken to a Space Force officer of such junior rank. "I explained quite clearly what we will be facing. I expected at least a brigade, not an understrength platoon."

Dewitt pulled his hand back after it was obvious that it wouldn't be accepted. "Yes, we are aware. An army of Clairvoyant clones—"

"And a very formidable natural Clairvoyant who leads them," Gungnir pointed out.

"Yeah, we got that. But we're also fighting a war. Troopers on short notice are hard to come by," Dewitt replied. "Anyway, when can we expect this attack?"

"Difficult to say. The only thing I can say is that, based on certain activity we observed, an attack is probable."

"Probable?" Dewitt scoffed. "You can see how it will be difficult for me to get reinforcements against a *probable* attack." Gungnir's eyes narrowed as the lieutenant spoke, but he made no challenge to the statement. "Especially to protect a facility of no strategic importance in a sector that has no strategic importance."

The Clairvoyant's countenance of annoyed irritation

broke with a nod. "I understand, Lieutenant. We will make do with what we have."

"Trooper's motto," Dewitt said with pride.

Just then, Widget arrived on the roof. She made a show of huffing and puffing from the effort. Gungnir turned to her. He was certain that, despite her dramatics, there was an elevator. "Widget, look after the troopers. I'm going to the facility to make sure they are prepared."

She motioned to give him an exaggerated salute but in actuality gave her boss a middle finger. Either the Clairvoyant didn't see it or didn't care as, a second later, he shot off toward the facility a couple miles away. The troopers stared at Widget for a long while after he was gone.

"Look after us? I know he's a Clairvoyant and all, but is he cracked, sir?" one of them complained.

"Yeah, what the fuck?" said another.

Widget looked at them and brought the middle finger at her brow to her chest, aimed toward all of them. The troopers continued to stare, though this time they were silently dumbfounded. She walked toward the container, which now rested on the roof, opened one of the access panels, and started rummaging inside. After a few seconds of searching, she found her computer. It was more capable than a mere PDD. She took the small device to the ledge nearest the facility, which could be seen in the distance, set it down, and opened it. Immediately, several holographic images appeared in a semicircle. They were flat images, like floating pieces of paper. Widget ignored them all and went back to the container.

This time she stuck her arm far into a small access panel. It was almost comically stupid how half her body was wedged inside to give her just a few more inches of reach. The stress on her face was plain for all to see as her hand blindly searched. On and on she went, cursing softly every now and then when there was the sound of something falling or crashing together. Then she smiled when she grasped her prize. The troopers watched, transfixed, while she slowly pulled it out.

When he saw it, one of them muttered, "What the actual fuck?"

It was a helmet, though nothing like the tactical gear the troopers wore. It looked preposterously ridiculous, and protection didn't appear to be its first function. Its dome-like top was dark green, in the same color of her shorts. There was a gold band on the bottom that gleamed bright in Eris's sun. Part of the helmet extended downward to cover her right ear and only her right ear completely. A mike jutted out from the protrusion. As Widget fixed and tightened the chin strap, the troopers all wondered who, or more exactly *what*, they'd been stuck with.

"Calibration check?" she asked as she walked back toward the ledge.

"No, go," Gungnir replied.

Widget cursed to herself and took the helmet off. She then produced a small toolkit from a back pocket. She fiddled with the helmet for about a minute before placing it back on her head. This time, she let the chinstrap dangle free.

"What about now?" she asked.

"You're good. I can't sense you at all now."

Widget smiled when she heard that and began tightening the chinstrap again. She always wondered why Clairvoyants constantly lied about not casually reading people's minds, but the more powerful of them could sense a specific individual from miles away. She knew what she ate for breakfast, how many times she burped a day, and most important, what color she'd make her fingernails next week. No Clairvoyant need know.

"The facility is as I feared. They haven't prepared much of anything either. I will be busy organizing the handlers and suppression teams. Only contact me if necessary," he continued.

Widget answered by double keying the mike. Then she took a deep breath. Eris was a hot and humid place. It was like jungle air, though not a tree was visible. She was already starting to sweat. That was the origin of the term "wet work," as far as she was concerned, and she hated it. It was worse to think that she and Gungnir could have sat right next to Charon on the shuttle down here and not known it. She'd never known a target so difficult to identify, let alone catch. Gungnir had said, for what it was worth, that he couldn't sense any Clairvoyants in the vicinity. But no matter.

She spoke a soft command which made her blue bracelets glow red for a second. A large sniper rifle flew from the container an instant later and into her waiting hands. One of the troopers swore loudly, surprised, when it happened.

"Wait, wait—that gun has no trigger! That crazy woman brought a gun with no trigger!" the trooper exclaimed loudly.

His comment got the others going again, but she ignored them. It was true, though. Her custom rifle had no trigger, nor did any of her weapons. Where the trigger would be was only a small pad to rest the trigger finger. Widget placed the weapon on the ledge and took the next few seconds adjusting the fore and rear mounts to get it dialed in to a comfortable position while sitting. She looked through the scope when she was satisfied, briefly surveying the grounds of the facility. She doubted anything would be happening for a while, but it was always good to be ready just in case. At this range, Widget would have preferred to use a laser, but lasers were useless against Clairvoyants—the energy just bent right around them. Bullets would have to do, but that was no major slight. It did help, though, that she had excellent sightlines in all directions. Their presurvey picked their perch perfectly, which wasn't always the case.

Davison City was similar to most colonies in the early stages of immigration. The buildings were ramshackle and temporary. All around them was the continual process of tearing down the previous temporary structures to be replaced with new temporary structures as the needs dictated. In time, who knew how long, more permanent establishments would be created as the colony found its footing and itself. After a few hundred years, it could be a New Earth, Evonea, or Leevi. It was unlikely but possible.

For now, Widget focused on her boss as he talked to the handlers of the facility. Annoyingly, her laser range finder and radar were just as useless against Clairvoyants as lasers were in killing them for the exact same reason. It would have to be old style optics. It was a curious question if Gungnir knew she always range checked with him as the target. He probably did; he was a Clairvoyant. He was also probably ready to telekinetically stop the bullet in case she actually did try to shoot him. It was always tempting, if only to keep him on his toes. After her rifle was set, she crosschecked what its scope was telling her against her glasses and nodded when they agreed. Then she leaned away from the rifle and looked around the city, marking good landmarks with the glasses as she did so.

The preliminary work was complete, and there were other tasks to take care of. Widget preferred these, as they took place behind a computer screen. But she was also hungry. She walked toward the container again and reached inside.

"What the fuck is she doing now?" one of the troopers

asked rhetorically. They were back to setting up the drone, but their attention was clearly on her.

She glanced at them as her hand closed around exactly what she was looking for. She pulled it out and then heard a gasp.

"Fortune cookies?" one of the troopers bellowed. "Triggerless rifles, clown helmets, and fortune cookies. Lieutenant, what is this detail?"

"Yeah, this can't be serious," another agreed. "It's one thing to cook our asses off out here, but do we have to do it with her?"

More and more troopers began complaining, and Dewitt had quite clearly had enough. "Shut up, all of you!" he shouted.

"But, sir," one of them began before he could continue. "She'll get us all killed. We can't be fighting Clairvoyants while dealing with her perpetual nonsense machine getting in the way. What's she going to do? Throw her rifle at them?"

"Perpetual nonsense machine?" a different trooper questioned. "You know, Cole, that almost sounds intelligent. What are you, Fleet?"

"Hey, shut the fuck up, motherfucker!" Cole spat back.

Widget watched as Dewitt unsuccessfully screamed at all of them to regain order. She put her hand back in the container. She'd planned for this.

"Over here," she called. All the troopers turned to look at her, and she tossed cans of beer to several. They caught the cans, and once they realized what they were, snapped them open and took a quick swig in the hot Eris sun.

"Never mind, Lieutenant. She can stay."

"Damn, they're cold too. What else she got in there? A barbeque?"

Widget smiled, took her fortune cookies, and went to sit

at her computer. She pulled the fortune out of the one of the cookies before she ate it and read: *Escape chaos through those closest to you.*

"Well, that's worthless. I should have brought the tea leaves," she muttered.

12

MUTINEERS

"Are they dead?"

Winter let go an exasperated sigh. It had to have been the fifth or sixth time Red had asked that. "I don't know," she answered.

"They have to be dead. They went up against that entire fleet. No way they survived."

"Well, we did see them Ghost," she pointed out.

"True. Probably everyone on *Jaeger* is changing their underwear right now," Red said, grinning as he spoke. Winter smiled. The comment had to be not too far from reality. In any case, if the *Griffin* was destroyed, it had certainly put up a respectable fight before it went down. "There's no place to run. They have to be dead," he continued.

"It's certainly a possibility," she remarked after another sigh. "I'll just point out that they *might* be dead, but if they are, we're *definitely* dead."

Red swallowed hard when he heard that. "So…you think they're dead?"

Winter made no reply and just shook her head. "I didn't say that."

"True. You think they made it then?"

"I didn't say that either." She took a long breath. "It doesn't matter what I think. They're dead or they're not. Either way, we have to figure out what we're going to do. We can't stay out here forever if they are dead, and they can't hide forever if they're not," she said, her words heavy with thought and experience.

"Yeah…but are they dead?"

She rolled her eyes. "For shit's sake, Redeye," she said in one of the rare instances she spoke his full callsign. "I don't know."

"You've got to think something, though. Are they dead?"

Winter groaned loudly. "Yeah, Red, they're dead. Very, very, *very* dead," she spat. "All hands gone. The sortens blew away any escape pods they found, and when they find us, we'll be skinned alive and strung up in their town square as a message to the others."

He was quiet for a long moment. "Hmm. I don't think they're dead. They have to be alive."

Winter's eyes bulged to the point that it was a wonder they didn't pop out of her skull. "Red, pull your handle and get fucked. I want to go back to single seaters. Damn!"

"Aye, aye, Skipper," he said with a grin.

She didn't know whether to smile or pull her own ejection handle just to get away from him. That's when something very unlikely for dead people happened.

"Rabbit One-One, this is Briar Patch," Leena said through the communicator.

While Winter hadn't thought they were actually dead, and who knew what the hamsters in Red's skull were doing, both pilots sat for a moment, stunned that they were being addressed directly. The ship should have had bigger worries than them.

"Briar Patch, this is Rabbit One-One. Go ahead," Red responded.

"Rabbit, umm…" Leena began, but her voice trailed off. Winter couldn't remember the last time that had ever happened. "Rabbit One-One, we have a rather unusual request of you."

Renee is up to something, the pilot thought.

"We're ready to copy," Red replied. Winter's eyes narrowed as she tried to figure what would come next.

"Rabbit, I don't really know how to say this, but we want you to get captured," the *Griffin's* operations officer said.

They both sat frozen in place. It had nothing to do with the temperature, though, despite the bone-piercing chill in the cockpit. They had found a quiet place to hide during the battle among a cloud of assorted rubble—rocks mostly. All systems had been powered down as soon as they arrived. Winter had been gaming out how to get back to the ship between Red's stupid questions. Before now, she might not have known the *Griffin's* fate, but she'd been near certain of theirs. Either they would get intercepted before they could rendezvous with the ship and would be blown out of the sky, or they'd run out of fuel while running…and then be blown out the sky. The only request she considered even possible to make was a reconnaissance run along their egress.

"Do you copy?" Leena asked when the silence persisted.

"Yeah, we copy," Winter said evenly. Red began protesting behind her, and she ended it with a raised hand. "Okay, I'm guessing—hoping—you guys didn't go insane during that last battle, so what's the plan?" she asked, noting it was a lot easier to be professional when she could feel her hands, toes, and face, and when Fleet officers weren't trying to get her killed on suicide missions.

"Winter, it's the only way," came the response, but it wasn't from Leena. Captain Brown spoke directly.

Winter was certain that was completely true, as Renee only spoke to her over the comm when the situation was dire. Even still, she asked, "How do you figure?"

"We can't escape this system without being tracked. If we try, we'll only be intercepted out in open space, where we'll have no cover and where we'll be completely overmatched," Renee said.

"And how does us getting captured solve that problem?" Winter asked.

"It doesn't," the captain admitted after a pause, though her voice was quite confident. "But we're not going to try to escape the system. You're going to convince the fleet that we already did."

Winter's eyes were bulging again. Perhaps they had gone insane? "Renee, tell me you have some plan for how I'm supposed to do that. Please tell me you have something."

"You tell them we left."

And she's supposed to be a genius. "We tell them? Why would they believe us?"

"Reputation," she said simply. "You're a hero of the first Terran-Sorten War. Every officer on this ship is a step above dog shit, as far as the rest of the fleet is concerned, but you are still respected. You tell them you took the first chance you could at mutiny and that you're seeking their help. Tell them the ship was able to Ghost out of the system without being detected and that you have the coordinates on where you are supposed to rendezvous with us. Give the sortens that, and it might be enough to get them off our back."

Winter nodded a few times. It made a stupid kind of sense. In a certain way, it was even true that she was separate from every other officer. She hadn't agreed with saving the

Growler, which had started the war in the first place. Some people even knew that, including her old CO, Admiral Lance Calbry, who was now effectively in command of the entire fleet—at least until a proper replacement for Admiral Wright could be found.

"I can see your logic," Winter muttered softly.

She could almost feel the captain nod when she said that. It was just her way. She somehow had a knack for taking insurmountable problems and stepping over them as if it was all part of a Sunday stroll.

"Winter, bit of a problem with that," Red began. "If we're supposed to be mutineers, why would we destroy that sorten picket?"

She'd forgotten about that. "Briar Patch, one hitch with this plan. We destroyed a sorten picket and alerted you to the sortens' approach. They have to be aware of both actions. Kind of shoots down our credibility."

There was no immediate response. It seemed Renee hadn't remembered that either. "Sorry, I don't really have anything for you there," she admitted sheepishly. "Stand by."

Stand by? Yes, Renee had a knack for defeating the insurmountable on the regular, but there were many times it was by the skin of her teeth, with the help of a little luck. Winter grinded her teeth for a few seconds before she spoke. Luck had a way of running out.

"Well, for one thing, if I didn't want to mutiny before, you're strongly convincing me to do so now," she transmitted in frustration.

"Use it," a third voice said. It was Frederick.

"What?" Winter questioned.

"Use it," he repeated. "Don't lie, use it. You were on board with everything until after the battle. After the battle, the Dread Pirate Renee became completely unhinged. The

Dread Pirate Renee made a grand speech about how she will make all who wronged her pay. That she'd unleash a thousand Medusas on the sortens. That there will be blood for blood for all that they've done. Until then, you were under the impression that this was a sanctioned mission, and you were just following orders."

"So pretend the captain is as crazy as I think she is right now… I can manage that."

She heard Frederick laugh, but if Renee was in any way amused, she hid it well. "Good," the captain said. "We'll have fighters and probes monitoring the sorten fleet to confirm that they took the bait. Rabbit One-One, good luck…for you and us. Briar Patch out."

The line cut off shortly thereafter, and the only sound left was the steady, deep breathing of the two pilots. They received a transmission a few seconds later with the coordinates they were to give the sortens. Winter glanced at them and then rested her head against the headrest. She knew Renee. She knew her quite well, in fact. She was not one to burn lives or even risk burning lives unless she had to. Perhaps she shouldn't have been so snippy with the captain. While Renee sounded completely calm and confident in ordering her friend to her possible death, Winter well knew that she was not. The captain spoke to Frederick about some things, spoke to her about others, and probably kept the darkest revelations for herself. It really should have been, "Yes, ma'am. Absolutely, ma'am." It was bad enough to think of how many sleepless, tear-filled nights her family would suffer if she were ever vaped. There was no reason to add another person to the list with guilt.

"Well, Winter, looks like they're trying to kill us again."

"No more than any other day," she replied.

13

THE DESPERATE BRAVE

Winter's hands seemingly took on a mind of their own as they flipped switches, pressed buttons, and readied the starfighter for what she didn't know. Such was her training and experience that she could have found everything blindfolded. Procedures and rationale were similarly engrained to the point that she didn't even need to think. Red was the same behind her. No amount of training, however, could stop her left leg from going painfully numb. It wasn't from the cold, though the cockpit was thankfully getting warmer, but from how long she'd been sitting in her seat.

Hunger was gnawing at them both as well. She took a sip from her drink tube and made a quick assessment. She'd made several over the past few minutes. This one, however, was not of their fighter or their situation but of herself. Fatigue was an insidious adversary. She didn't really feel tired, but she knew she was. She had to be, as was Red. They'd been operating at a high level for hours with periods of intense stress. Her body screamed protests that she knew wouldn't go away for at least a week—if they survived. There was no way she could sit, no position she could place herself in, to alleviate the dull aches that came from everywhere.

She just wasn't as young as she used to be. Back when she was Lance's XO, she'd go through missions like this without a thought, get drunk that night, then fly the next day nursing the hangover but still no worse for wear. It was hard to think back on those days—where every battle was fought against long odds, where they'd lose half the squadron and consider it a victory—and feel anything approaching nostalgia, but she did. It was a miracle she'd managed to survive the entire war, as most hadn't, but she'd never really thought about it. Yet, here and now, in another battle with long odds to live, let alone for any hope of success, she thought about it. Sure as she loved her husband and daughters, she thought about it. Perhaps she was getting old in more than one way?

"Up. Good ship," Red announced.

"I'm good here too," Winter announced when the last of her systems came back online.

"Okay, Skipper, how the hell do we do this?"

She took a deep breath while she closed her eyes. "I don't know. You have any ideas?"

"Nothing."

"One step at a time then. First we need to find them, or let them find us," she said. Then she glanced at the most important gauge in any starfighter. "Don't have much fuel to search though." Her comment prompted him to look at his own back-up fuel gauge, wherein he cursed softly. She stared at the ordnance under their wings while he did so. "Let's jettison our remaining weapons," she continued. "Maybe we can convince the sortens we weren't the ones to down their picket?"

"They aren't that dumb," he remarked.

"Worth a shot. Anyway, start a continuous omnidirectional active scan, full power. That should get someone's attention."

"You got it, Winter."

She heard him work behind her, and it was done in a few seconds. She looked at her display, and when it reported nothing encouraging, she had to ask. It was probably a pointless question, but he had more readouts to work with than she did.

"Anything?"

"Sorry, Winter. Clean, clear, and naked."

"Shit," she said softly. "All right, let's get out of here. It will be harder for them to find us in this."

"Where do we go?"

"Anywhere but here."

"Want a navpoint?"

She thought about it for a second then shook her head. "No." She picked a direction and, after a brief burn, the Banshee glided from the debris.

She looked all around them. The distances were too far for her eyes to be of any use, and certainly her fighter's systems would detect any approaching ship long before she'd see it, but it was a habit born from her time when she flew civilian. The high-altitude skimmer she'd cut her piloting teeth on was laughably underpowered and primitive compared to the Banshee she was sitting in now. But it had only taken a couple close calls back then to make her visual scan instinct, as vestigial as it was in this realm.

"Think this plan will work?" Red asked.

It's a Renee plan, she thought, which meant many, many things, not all of them good. "I think it will."

"What makes you say that?"

"Because if it doesn't, we're screwed." She sighed. "Got anything yet?"

"Nothing. Well, some sensor ghosts, but nothing promising. And we don't have the fuel to go chasing after those."

Winter pursed her lips. "I agree."

"Well, we could…no wait, picking up something now." She looked at her display as he spoke to see what he was talking about. It was *something*, but that wasn't saying much. "Definitely following some sort of course. Approaching rapidly."

"Hail them."

Red nodded. "To approaching ship, this is Space Force starfighter. We unconditionally surrender and are seeking asylum."

There was no response, and as Red repeated the message, one of Winter's eyebrows subconsciously raised. Other than fast, this sensor ghost…now track, was very small and on a collision course. *It's a missile!* she realized. There was a warning alarm an instant later when the missile went active.

She cursed herself as she began maneuvering against it. They were so busy broadcasting their position that she didn't think about being shot at by someone outside their sensor range. There was a bright light in the distance as the missile's engine flared to life to counter her evasive action. Winter shut off her own engines to save fuel and watched. The threat warning indicator's shrill alarm was going bonkers, but she was calm. She'd done this more times than she cared to count, and panic never led to a high probability of success. The light disappeared after a time and she maneuvered again. The light reappeared instantly, and again she waited. Twice more the sequence went until finally the missile was out of fuel and it passed harmlessly behind them.

"Multiple contacts. Sorten Swifts…four of them. I'll start transmitting. This is Space Force starfighter. Don't attack, don't attack! We surrender!" Winter didn't wait for any response and got them burning on an escape vector at full power. Four lights, brighter than the missile that had been shot at them, blazed in pursuit. "Hey, what are you doing? You're running away!"

"You want to surrender to the people who just tried to kill us, Red?" she asked at a rush.

"No, but we don't have any choice." Winter's jaw clenched tight. He had her there. But it wasn't in her nature to raise her hands and give up when someone put a gun to her forehead. Just then, there were more lights ahead of them, off to the right. "New contacts! They're firing!"

It was a brace of three missiles this time, once again fired at long range. Winter turned the fighter away and began the sequence again. Sorten missiles weren't very good against a maneuvering fighter; they were meant to take down heavier craft. They just didn't have the fuel capacity to sustain drastic changes in course. Their rather large warheads were a different matter, though. If the weapon hit, perhaps her atoms could be buried. In time, the missiles passed behind them harmlessly and this new flight joined the pursuit.

"Winter, we can shoot back!" Red yelled. "We've got Vipers!"

She gritted her teeth. That was true—their wingtip anti-fighter missiles couldn't be jettisoned—but still. "And then what?" she yelled back rhetorically. "We kill them and then surrender to the next group of sortens?"

"I know…but what else can we do?"

Winter didn't answer, as she really didn't have any ideas herself. Worse, they didn't have the fuel to fight and they certainly didn't have the fuel to run. She glanced at the gauge as she weighed all their options.

"Red, give me a shoot list."

"You got it Winter. Up," he replied.

She took a deep breath. *Maybe we can scare these guys into listening,* she thought. She shut off the engines and then pointed the nose of her fighter at the closest formation of sortens. She heard a solid lock-on tone and then heard Red's loud complaints about why she hadn't fired yet, but she did nothing other than maintain the threat. The sortens responded by slowing their advance in anticipation of dodging a missile shot or laser blast.

"Hail them again," she ordered.

"But Winter—"

"Hail them!"

"To sorten squadron, this is Space Force starfighter. We surrender. I say again, we surrender. Stop your attack."

The sorten response was instant. Both flights fired at them with lasers. Starfighters, and starships for that matter, were equipped with time dilation systems. The device worked automatically and intelligently to slow the perception of time to aid crew reaction and decision making. It was that system, in combination with the fly-by-thought flight controls, and the fact that they were operating with their shield up, that saved them from a fiery ignoble end.

The beams of energy rushed toward them in long streaks that perceptually came across as an impossibly fast missile. A thought set the Banshee on an evasive course. Winter made it on reflex, but the fighter's computers were able to translate the myriad fears and worry into an intelligible set of actions. Slowly, all so slowly, the fighter responded. The perception of time could be changed, but the fighter existed in and was limited by the laws of reality. Its most aggressive max performance action appeared as a turtle gingerly making its way across a street.

Winter groaned and grunted as the field of stars began to gyrate. The distant lights, always disorienting as a point of reference, moved around them as if they were stuck in a kaleidoscope twisted by a drunk, lazy child. Her vision turned grey from the g force. Then there was black creeping in from the periphery. It closed upon her tighter and tighter until it seemed like she'd fallen to the bottom of a deep well. Then she held the fighter to no more than that level of acceleration.

Red grunted behind her, but she focused on her own g-strain, working to keep the blood in her brain. Sharp breath, grunt, squeeze. Sharp breath, grunt, squeeze. Unfortunately, the time dilation system also had the side effect of elongating the torture. Sharp breath, grunt, squeeze. The black was set to completely take her as her body weakened from the stress… and then it was over. A stray shot burned their shields to almost nothing, but they were still alive. Winter made their flight straight and level as she panted and trembled in recovery. She then turned offensive; there was no point in holding back against people who wanted her dead.

The shoot list Red set up before was still valid. She placed the first target in a large circle that represented the field of fire for her fighter's six laser cannons and went on the attack. The needles of light stabbed toward her sorten counterpart. As she had, he maneuvered violently to avoid the beams. She scored no hits, but he was out of the fight for a moment. She did the same thing with the next target for the same effect. The effort wouldn't be repeated for a third time as the sortens returned fire. Another crushing turn sped them to safety, but now they were totally defensive. The first flight of sortens was able to catch up, and the two groups took turns firing. She did her best to keep away from them in a spiraling defensive weave, but the options were rapidly diminishing.

"Winter, minimum fuel," Red announced.

She cursed under her breath. She didn't really want to down them. Some small part of her held out hope that this plan, as insane and foolhardy as it was, could potentially work. The lives of everyone on the *Griffin* depended on it. But sometimes fate turned against the wishes of the best intentioned. She selected the Vipers with a thought. Might as well get some new Swift silhouettes to paint on her soon-to-be slagged fighter.

"New contacts inbound," her backseater said.

"We're surrounded by contacts!" she screamed. Forget the sortens—perhaps she'd finally act on her dream of turning around and strangling Red to death.

"These are different. It's a pair of Screamers!"

"Ours? I mean, from the *Griffin*?" she asked quickly.

"Negative, they're C models."

Winter nodded. The Hustlers flew two seat F models. "Where?"

"Ten o'clock."

She turned her head and immediately saw what he was talking about. She timed their breakout precisely, jetting toward the inbound Banshees at the opportune moment to avoid a missile or laser up their tailpipes. The sortens floundered for a moment and then renewed the pursuit. Winter rubbed her fists. She didn't know what her Space Force colleagues would do or what their orders were, but she'd rather take her chances with her own people than keep fighting the sortens.

"Hail them," she said.

"Aye, aye, Skipper. To incoming Banshees, this is Space Force starfighter. We surrender and are seeking asylum."

There was no response, and the moment of silent dead calm seemed to stretch for an hour. Winter checked that the time dilation system wasn't operating and then groaned when she realized it was just her nerves.

"To Space Force starfighter, this is Angel Three-One.

Power down your weapons and lower your shields. You are to be escorted for docking with ISS *Jaeger*. If you take any hostile action, you will be destroyed," came a stern, crisp voice.

"Angel Three-One acknowledged. Powering down. Boy, are we happy to see you!" Red said.

Winter didn't really care for the enthusiasm even though she felt the same way. There was still no real confirmation that they were on the same side; they just weren't shooting at them yet. For all she knew, they would be executed as soon as they set down on *Jaeger*.

Whether that would happen or not, their sorten pursuit disengaged, and a few minutes later there was a Banshee off their left wing in close formation. It was close enough that she could plainly see the craft. The fighter was sleek. Most races didn't bother with aerodynamic shaping for their starfighters, but terrans had kept the practice of their ancient forebearers, as Space Force did expect its starfighters to be capable of and excel in atmospheric combat. The wings were forward swept and blended into the fuselage, and large, leading-edge extensions started just before the cockpit. The cockpit itself was raised and placed forward with a "bubble" canopy. Vision was largely irrelevant for a starfighter, but the Banshee gave spectacular sightlines in almost every direction. Irrelevant or not, her bacon had been saved more than once by simply looking behind herself, and she'd always been grateful for it. The fighter itself was difficult to see, though. It was dark grey in color and had darker splotches to visually break up its planform across several spectrums.

The pilot of Angel Three-One hand signaled them to follow, and Winter signaled her assent. Angel Three-Two, however, maneuvered behind them and locked on. She didn't doubt their words; she knew they would shoot them down if they had to. Now they were in the perfect position to do so at the slightest provocation.

She tried not to think about it as the trio angled toward *Jaeger* and accelerated. Winter glanced at her fuel gauge, but the starship was closer than she'd first assumed. It wasn't alone either. *Mercury* was relatively close by, as were several smaller and larger sorten vessels. It looked like they were in the process of regrouping. Her best guess was that the cat and mouse and stratagems were about to be over. They would sweep the system in force and simply overwhelm the *Griffin* with numbers and mass firepower. It seemed this ruse was timely.

In due time, *Jaeger* could be seen by the naked eye. Military starships were always hard to see. If one was in orbit and you pointed a telescope at it, you still wouldn't see it. The visibility—dimness, as it was often called—extended to more than just the visible light spectrum, just like her fighter.

Winter examined the cruiser as it loomed ever larger. It looked exactly like her home, the *Griffin*, but she felt none of the relief she usually did during the approach after a long mission. The ship was sleek as well, almost menacingly so, though that had nothing to do with any sort of atmospheric streamlining. It would be disastrous for multiple reasons if the ship ever entered an atmosphere. In any case, the ship was long and narrow, like its oceangoing counterparts from eons ago.

Most starships were configured similarly. It was a product of optimum Ghost Field efficiency. The large, armored bridge tower extended roughly a quarter of the ship from the bow. In front of it was the direct energy cannon (DEC). Behind the bridge was the boxy housing for the ship's complement of Mjolnir missiles, of which at full load there were about five hundred. On the ventral, mounted equal distance from each other, were three direct energy domes (DEDs). Another was mounted on the dorsal side at the stern. The most distinctive feature of the *Peacekeeper* class, though, was the armored shroud that pointed out from the flanks of the hull like a sideways V. It began at the bridge tower and had a large cutout to allow the retro-engine's exhaust to clear. The back end, however, was flat. The shroud protected the Ghost Field emitter and the guts of the ship.

Angel Three-One rocked his wings and then flew off. Angel Three-Two joined him. *Jaeger's* tractor beam grabbed Winter's fighter a few seconds later. She could see the troopers waiting for them in the hangar. It was about then that she realized the predicament she and Red were in. She'd been mostly worried about how they were going to engineer their own capture without getting blown out of the sky. Now that they were in custody and hadn't been blown to bits, yet, she dismally wondered how she was going to convince anyone that they were defecting while also convincing them that somehow the *Griffin* had escaped without anyone noticing or tracking it. Renee was literally a Wiz Kid and arguably a genius, but she wasn't a wizard. She wouldn't buy it if the situation was reversed.

Jaeger's hangar appeared to almost swallow them whole as they silently glided in. They eventually came to a rest on their landing gear and then just sat. Red was busy shutting down his systems, but Winter could only think, with an annoyingly blank mind, about what she'd say as she stared at the troopers pointing rifles at them.

"My systems are down," Red said.

"Oh yeah, right," she muttered to herself as she shut down everything on her end.

She popped the canopy when it was done, took off her helmet, and took a deep breath of *Jaeger's* synthesized air. It was no better or worse than the synthesized air from her flight suit, but it was better to breathe while not encumbered by the confines of a helmet. The culmination of everything since the start of the battle passed through her then, and she shuddered as she ran her fingers through her short blonde hair. It wasn't the getting shot at that bothered Winter. She'd been shot at before and laughed about it. No, the sheer physical exertion had taken its toll. She was drenched with sweat, and she took another deep breath to relax her body.

"With your right hand, remove your sidearm and throw it out of the fighter, now!" a trooper commanded.

"We're not armed," Red said quickly as he raised his hands. It was true; they hadn't bothered to carry pistols for this flight. There would be no point—escape and evasion was impossible after an ejection in space. "You think they'll actually skin us alive?" he whispered.

"Perhaps," she said after a soft sigh. Then she swallowed hard as her eyes narrowed. "Time to get in character," she said more to herself than to him.

The ship's crew extended the boarding ladder from the Banshee's leading-edge extension. Red stood hesitantly, his arms still raised, and then started down it. Winter watched him go, but when it was her turn, she couldn't move.

"Shit," she said softly. Her legs felt like pudding. She tried to force herself up and her right leg cramped painfully, causing her to give a sharp cry.

The troopers' grip on their rifles tightened when they heard it. "Get out of the fighter...now!" the leader commanded.

Winter glanced at him, unable to keep the pained expression from her face. She gave no reply, but she did massage her calf for a few good seconds. There were times before in her career when she had to be physically pried and carried from the cockpit after a particularly grueling flight. Here and now, however, help didn't appear on offer, and she wasn't of the mind to ask for it. With all things, dignity had to be maintained. Yes, she was technically surrendering. Yes, their situation was near hopeless. But she'd never ever considered herself helpless with anything, and she wasn't about to start now. When her leg felt better, Winter placed her hands on the canopy rails and forced herself up. She tested the leg by putting some weight on it. Pain shot through it and up her spine. This time, she was able to keep it to a small whimper that no one heard, but it would have to do. She hopped down the ladder on one leg and then limped to Red, who still had his hands raised.

"Put your hands down. You look ridiculous," she whispered to him.

"Would look more ridiculous with a bullet in my guts," he said back.

She had no time for a reply as a trooper approached them with handcuffs at the ready. The pilot glared at him. She would not be handcuffed. *All right, let's see how this goes,* she thought.

"I demand to speak to the captain," she said to no one in particular. "Urgently, in fact."

"You can speak to me," said a voice from behind the troopers. "You will during your interrogation, but we can start now."

Winter cocked her head to the side as she watched the short Space Force officer emerge. His uniform and grooming were impeccable, but she was decidedly unimpressed by the man before her. Even Frederick could probably beat him in a fight with an arm tied behind his back. Red made no real reaction, but she had to choke back a small bit of bile just from looking at the man. He made her skin crawl.

"And who are you?" she asked.

"Lieutenant Commander Eugene Mortis," he answered.

Ah, so you're Mortis, Winter thought. Renee had told her about him, but her description of the man was *polite,* as she usually was with most everything. Winter had handled men like him before.

"Ma'am," she said sharply.

"Excuse me?" he muttered.

"It's Lieutenant Commander Eugene Mortis, *ma'am.* Or do you have no respect for rank?"

Mortis licked his lips, and there was a quiver of anger in his brow, but he said nothing. *Bullseye,* she thought with such force that she almost mouthed the words. That was exactly the reaction she was looking for. The trooper with the cuffs gestured for her hands, and she turned her gaze to him and then quickly back to Mortis.

"Call off your dogs," she commanded. Red glanced at her nervously, which she didn't notice, but he slowly dropped his hands as his CO placed hers on her hips. "Where's the captain?" she asked, an angry tone enveloping her voice. "While I'm wasting time with you, they're getting away."

She also didn't notice that, while she was talking, the door to the corridor had opened. No one had noticed. A strong, deep voice echoed throughout the hangar. "I'm the captain."

Winter saw who the voice belonged to instantly. "Yes, sir. Thank you for rescuing us, sir," she said quickly while she brought her hand to her brow in the crispest salute she'd ever given in her life. "Salute, salute," she said to Red out the corner of her mouth.

"Oh, yeah," he muttered before he aped her movement.

"I'm Commander Nadia Silver."

Holder stepped forward confidently, and Mortis seemed

to shrink in his shadow. A sorten was with the captain. Winter's best guess was that he was Fleet Commander Kril. She swallowed hard. The stage was set; now she only had to put on the performance of her life.

Holder nodded a few times as he looked the tall woman up and down. "I've heard of you. Fought in the Terran-Sorten War, all the way from the beginning. Some academy classes are taught from your missions with the Grim Reapers."

"Yes, sir."

"Now what is this you're talking about? Who is getting away?" he asked.

"Captain Brown. She was able to Ghost out of the system after the battle, sir."

"Impossible!" Mortis shouted. He even stomped his foot. "No ship was tracked leaving the system. Even if the *Griffin* could cloak, it would have been spotted."

Winter made a show of rolling her eyes, and Mortis was visibly taken aback. "There was a hole in your net. Captain Brown was able to move your ships out of position strategically during the battle. It was all planned. I don't know how she bypassed your outer screen, but she did. I was sent the rendezvous coordinates only a matter of minutes ago."

Kril's head shot to Mortis. "Is that possible?" the sorten asked.

The short man's cheeks flushed pink. His hands balled into fists and even began to shake. "No, absolutely not!" he yelled, his voice becoming a screech. Holder and the leader of the troopers groaned when they heard it. "There was no hole and certainly not one she engineered. I know Captain Brown—I know what she's capable of. She's certainly not capable of that! If there is anything going on, I bet this, right now, is part of some plot. Captain, let me conduct a full interrogation of this pilot. I'll find out everything she knows within the hour!"

Holder sneered. "This *pilot* is a war hero, boy! You will give her the respect she deserves or it will be you in the brig." Mortis's mouth snapped shut, but he did glare at Winter afterward. The captain took a deep breath. "Still, it begs the question. Why are you here?"

"To help, sir," she said as sincerely as she could. "Captain Brown has gone too far. We took the first opportunity we could to break away."

Kril looked at her, nodded, looked at her fighter, and then back at her. "One of our pickets was downed by a Banshee. It was shot by two missiles, and a Banshee can carry six. Your fighter has no anti-ship missiles. That is most curious. Was it you who destroyed our ship?"

"Yes," Winter admitted. Red coughed roughly next to her, but she agreed with Frederick that it was best to lie with the truth. She tried to stop her eyes from moving back and forth as she thought quickly. "Captain Brown lied to everyone. She told us this was some sort of secretly sanctioned mission. She never shared her orders, even with me. It was only during the battle, where we saw *Jaeger* engage, that we began to question what was going on. After the battle, she raved, babbling about finally getting revenge for something or whatever. She's become quite crazy." Winter took a deep breath. "So yes, I destroyed your picket. I'm sorry I had to, though I don't apologize. I'm a soldier and that was my enemy at the time. I'm sure you understand."

"Yes…yes, I do," Kril responded.

"We jettisoned our remaining missiles when we decided to join you. We didn't want you to think we were making another attack run," she added.

"Will she suspect that you turned against her?" Holder asked.

Winter dropped her head and brought a hand to her chin. This time, she worked to make it appear that she was thinking deeply. *They just gave me an out*, she realized as she was getting her story straight. She'd worried that the game would be over as soon as they arrived at the designated coordinates and saw that nothing was there. Until now, she wasn't sure how she'd circumvent that problem.

"Probably," she concluded. "I questioned her more than anyone, sir. We need to act quickly and in force. If she suspected anything, and she may, she'll immediately transit to a new position, and who knows if she'll ever be reacquired again and how many people she'll attack before then."

"I agree," Holder said with a sharp nod. "Mr. Mortis, retrieve the coordinates from that fighter and prepare the fleet to redeploy immediately."

"Sir, I must again protest. I severely doubt—"

"Now, Mortis!" Holder barked.

The lieutenant commander immediately fell silent and stood as if frozen. "Yes, sir," he said sheepishly.

He started walking toward where the hangar crew watched the drama, but not before he shot Winter a glare. She gave a small smirk back, for Renee's sake, and tried to capture the image of his enraged response to tell her later…if she ever saw her again. He knew. In that moment, it was absolutely obvious that Mortis knew. Just as it was obvious that she knew he knew. Worse for him, she knew he knew and that he'd never be able to convince anyone otherwise. The man looked like he was going to explode.

"Commander Silver, I do of course demand a full debrief. Her possible targets, motive, anything you can tell us that can help."

"As would I," Kril agreed.

Winter's smirk was gone instantly, though it still warmed her tired, aching body. "Absolutely, sir. But if you don't mind, I would like to get out of this flight suit first. It's been hours."

"I completely understand, Commander. I'll arrange guest quarters for you myself. We can talk on the way. Come with me," Holder said.

Winter gestured to Red with her head to follow. Her back-seater gave her a small thumbs-up, and then the Space Force officers and the sorten exited the hangar. Mortis glared at them and cursed under his breath the entire time.

*	*	*

The comm system was currently tied into the speakers on the bridge, as it had been for the past few hours. The heavy silence was broken first with a crackle of static and then a voice. "Briar Patch, this is Rabbit Two-One," it said.

"Rabbit Two-One, Briar Patch, go ahead," Leena replied.

Most everyone, including the Clairvoyants, looked the operations officer's way, though they didn't have to with the speaker relaying everything. Carmen gave Inertia a quick glance. He at least looked back, which was better than it had been lately, but he didn't say anything. Neither did she.

"Briar Patch, the fleet is on the move. It appears they are entering some sort of formation," the Banshee pilot reported.

"Probe telemetry confirms," Hiroshi said.

Only their displays were operative in the darkened room. Renee had to stop herself from checking hers, which was off. It wasn't the only thing she had to stop herself from doing. She had felt like she was going to throw up from the start of this. They'd been monitoring Winter and Red's progress as best they could. She'd almost had to leave the room when the sortens started shooting at them. Watching and not being able to do anything at all was one of the most trying tests she'd ever faced. Only Frederick noticed her unease. Now—for the past few seconds at least—there had to be permanent fingernail gouges in her palms.

"Fleet is charging Ghost Drive! I say again, fleet is charging Ghost Drive!"

"Confirm!" Hiroshi yelled.

Renee nodded. "What's their track?" They could just as well be Ghosting toward them.

"Stand by," Hiroshi said. He studied his display for a few seconds before he turned to look at her. "Track is for out of the system, exactly for the dupe coordinates."

"Briar Patch, the fleet has Ghosted."

"We got 'em," Terry said triumphantly.

He wasn't the only one; everyone on the bridge cheered in their own way. Frederick whooped loudly. Renee sighed with the same relief as someone who'd just dropped a heavy weight and then leaned back in her chair. Leena said, "Yes!" quietly to herself with a clenched fist. Tawny howled. Even Inertia smiled and tipped his head to nod at his sister. Everyone let the elation wash over them, save one.

Carmen looked twice to make sure, and then the pit of her stomach froze as if she had eaten ice. The burning cold chilled her veins. Her eyes grew wide while she stared at the clock. It was already too late. The sorten freighter was already gone.

14

KEEPING SIGHT

Renee smiled contently as she sighed. "All right, let's get all these rabbits home," she said.

"Aye, ma'am," Leena replied before she began giving instructions to the fighters.

The lights were coming on, as was everyone's chair displays. Terry looked to his captain and suppressed a shiver. Running the ship as dimly as possible was hardly a comfortable event for multiple reasons, but Renee never seemed to notice the cold—not anymore. The two Clairvoyants didn't react to it either. The mechanism of how that was possible was beyond his understanding. They could exhale more frost than an ice maker and not even chatter their teeth. That, however, was of little concern for the moment.

"I must admit that, when you posed it, I didn't think this plan would work," he said.

"Honestly, Mr. Fletcher, when I posed it, I didn't think it would work either," Renee confessed, though only loud enough for him to hear. Terry smiled. "What am I going to do to thank Winter?" she mused out loud. "Assuming we ever see her again."

"I don't know, Captain. We may yet. Better than even chance now, I'd say."

"It's too late," a third person remarked.

Renee and Terry looked at Carmen, who was slowly shaking her head. "What?" they asked.

"It's too late," she said again. "The sorten freighter has already left. We missed it."

Both officers looked at the clock, as did Inertia.

"Shit," the captain said softly.

The rest of the bridge crew looked at Renee in that instant. Smiles and elation melted away as they tried to figure out what was going on. Carmen looked at her as well, but the Space Force officer wasn't on the forefront of her mind. The familiar hopelessness that was her most faithful companion was knocking on her door, asking for dinner. It all came flooding back so easily. *Why wouldn't Inertia listen to me?* she thought. Perhaps he was right that they would have been blown away at any attempt to escape the system with the fleet still here. Perhaps they couldn't take the freighter on their own. Perhaps. But, as she reminded herself, *perhaps* was not certainty.

"Is there anything you can do?" she asked Renee. "Maybe the freighter didn't leave yet? Maybe they'll delay?"

"Edge, that's unlikely," Inertia replied. "Sortens are too precise a people and their operation too regimented to delay without reason."

Carmen glared at him. He looked back and appeared totally at ease with being the subject of the one-percenter's ire. She never could faze him. Possibly no one and nothing could. He really was a professional in this trade she wanted nothing to do with. But being angry with him—and she was angry with him—didn't solve anything. She didn't know whether he utterly detested her or was hopelessly in love with her, but either way he never let it get in the way of anything that actually mattered. It forced her to start thinking of solutions, even though none immediately came to mind.

"Well, there must be something we can try," she said while she considered it herself.

Renee sat with a pronounced frown on her face. The Wiz Kid muttered angry tirades at herself that no one else heard. She took a deep breath after a second or so. "I agree with Inertia. It is very, *very* unlikely that the sortens didn't leave when they were scheduled to," she finally said.

"Is it possible the sortens left early?" Terry asked. "They would have had to be aware of our incursion into their space. It would be prudent for them to relocate immediately. This entire mission may have been null and void from the moment we were detected."

"That I doubt," Inertia said confidently. Carmen looked at him, but the tone she'd come to trust didn't fill her with its usual comfort. Not with the situation as it was. "The sortens were operating in an almost completely compartmentalized manner. The sorten military might not even be aware of this research program. If they were, and if they even so much as suspected that we were tasked with destroying it, they probably wouldn't have allowed Space Force's assistance in the first place."

"Could they have another base somewhere else? Possibly fixed, so it would be easier for us to attack?" Terry asked.

"If they do, we don't know anything about it," Inertia answered.

"Could they have another base?" Carmen asked quickly. "Is that possible?" If they could have two, why couldn't they have three or more? She hadn't considered the possibility until now. Inertia shrugged, and she gave an annoyed puff to her bangs. She took a deep breath before she spoke again.

"So, what do we do now? What can we do?" she asked no one in particular.

Renee had been listening to the exchange with her hand on her chin and was the first to answer. "Let's stick with what we know. There is no point speculating about other bases and other operations, agreed?" She looked at Carmen and Inertia, who both nodded, and then at her XO, who did the same. "We don't know their procedures or what they do in the event of a comms failure. They might still be there. We haven't failed yet," she continued. Carmen nodded again, and in the first time since the fleet's departure, she smiled. Perhaps she'd just overreacted. "Time to our original destination, best possible speed, and not going fast?"

"Thirteen hours and twenty-four minutes, Captain," Tawny answered.

"Not going fast?" Carmen questioned. "Isn't it better to save as much time as possible, just in case?"

Renee shook her head and sighed softly. "It is, but starships don't really work that way. Put simply, it's too close to go fast. We could go fast on a reciprocal vector to open the distance and then go fast to our destination—that would be quicker—but I don't want to increase the risk of being detected again."

"I understand," Carmen said after a solemn nod.

"Besides, we all need to sleep, and it will give us time to effect repairs." She turned to Terry. "Get it started. Then make sure you hit your rack."

"Yes, Captain," he replied, immediately turning to his display to get to work.

"We'll get underway as soon as all fighters are aboard." She took a deep breath and let it out sharply. She then looked at the Clairvoyants. "You two should get some sleep as well. Tomorrow might be a big day."

Carmen nodded and stood, as did Inertia. She noticed her partner hesitate for whatever reason, but he said nothing. She was tempted to ask what the problem was, but a latent worry stopped her from speaking. It wasn't the possible answer that bothered her but the possibility that there wouldn't be an answer at all. The two of them left the bridge with him in the lead. She was his shadow, as she usually was, watching his every move and waiting with bated breath to hear what their next course of action would be or what bit of advice he'd offer for tackling the coming trial. Nothing came, though. She didn't know why she expected something, anything, even a respectful nod. Just before the hatch to the bridge closed, she turned and saw Renee watching them closely with an eyebrow raised. She'd done that before. Carmen didn't think much of it, though, and the expression was soon forgotten as she and her partner waited for the elevator.

They did so in complete silence. She glanced at him from time to time; he did no such thing back. He said nothing and did nothing. Carmen could swear it felt like he was annoyed just to be near her. His foot began tapping after a while, though the wait for the elevator was no more than a minute before they walked inside. He pressed the button for the deck to his quarters and she pressed hers, a deck below his. She would have pressed both for them, but he was faster on the draw. This was the first time they'd been alone since their argument at the entrance to the bridge. It was the first time they'd been alone since they had boarded the ship, really. They could have talked to each other telepathically and no one would be the wiser, but having a conversation that no one could hear while surrounded by people was quite different than talking while genuinely and completely alone. Solitary had been an expert teacher in that.

She gave her partner a long look. She couldn't read him—

never could and probably never would—but she could feel his energy. He was not a reserved person by nature. He said few words, but that wasn't born of restraint. Only prudence seemed like it could actually stop him from anything. She knew that from experience and could sense it. Her partner spoke how only a Clairvoyant could speak: directly, accurately, and with no trepidation. Here and now, though, Inertia was restraining himself, just as sure as he was breathing. A Clairvoyant couldn't hide themselves with themselves—she knew that better than anybody. Her and his bioelectric fields interacted and danced with each other subconsciously. Everyone, Clairvoyant or not, experienced those around them in the same way, though most were unaware of it. His energy, though, retreated from even her slightest glance, despite him physically holding firm. She could feel it as surely as a hammer dropped on her foot, though the sensation was hard to describe.

She was angry with him. No, that was an understatement. If given a choice between fighting Inertia or Charon, she'd be hard pressed to choose her actual adversary. But she was angry at his restraint; his restraint was not because of her anger. She doubted Inertia would care how angry she was anyway, even if she were cursing at him with her sword at his throat. She didn't understand it. Any of it. And though that made her blood boil, it was not the strongest emotion she felt.

"Inertia," she said gently right before the elevator doors opened. He shot out of the elevator as soon as there was an opening wide enough for him. "Inertia, why won't you talk to me anymore?" she asked. He didn't even give her a backward glance. "If I did something wrong, I'm sorry." The elevator closed again and she was alone. "I'm sorry," she said again.

The words echoed in the small space, and it was fitting, as she seemed to be the only person to hear them. Carmen touched the burnt side of her face with her burnt hand and sighed. The elevator opened again on her deck and she stepped out. There was more crew here. Word must have passed quickly; they spoke excitedly to each other, and there was a general atmosphere of light-hearted cheer. It was the first of it she'd seen on the ship. They made a hole for her, but other than that she was totally ignored. They were well used to her by now. It made her think.

She'd used to find being ignored refreshing. It certainly beat having people run away from her in fear or the quivering, whimpering nothings people would turn into whenever she looked at them. She wasn't so sure what she felt now. People at least acknowledged her existence when they were afraid of her. She may as well not even exist when she was ignored. Here she was, walking down the corridor, surrounded by people, and it didn't matter to anyone that she was there. She could sense them—read them—all, but she was a bubble to them, as unknowable and transient as the Ghost Field they were presently encased within. And she was the only person among them to notice the dichotomy or even care that it existed.

She arrived at her quarters and stepped inside. Then Carmen sat on her bed, undid the tie for her ponytail, brought her knees to her chest, and wrapped her arms around them. She wanted to scream. She wanted to throw her table into the wall. But instead the Clairvoyant dropped her head to her knees and let her hair splay across her shoulders. Here she was, one of the most powerful beings in the galaxy, and she felt just like the weak and helpless little girl she was all those years ago back at the facility. Maybe that had been the point of her training? She didn't know, and thinking about it was driving her crazy—along with everything else that was driving her crazy. She wished she could talk to Kali, but that wasn't possible, as it could give away the ship's position.

"Shit," she said. Then she cursed again because she cursed. Apparently she couldn't keep promises now either. She apologized to Eli as she squeezed her legs hard.

Her mind was painfully blank, save for one thought. She knew the pains of the past would always be with her, but she never would have believed they could find her so quickly and easily at the smallest provocation. They seemed to know to strike when she was exactly at her most vulnerable. Carmen closed her eyes and imagined the demons playing and laughing as they flew around her head and then them sighing with glee as they drank her nightmares like fine wine. The Clairvoyant groaned while she threw her body back to lie flat on her back.

She didn't know…she didn't know anything. But Renee was right that she needed to rest. So she shut off the lights and attempted to do just that.

* * *

It was the worst kind of sleep, at first happening not at all and then all too much. Carmen's eyes shot open, but the world came to her slowly as she awoke from her stupor. There was fear then, that she had overslept and missed the rendezvous with the sorten freighter. But as she became more aware and more logical, she realized there was no way she'd slept thirteen hours. She looked at the clock, confirming as much. There were still a few hours to go.

The Clairvoyant sat up and thought about what to do to pass the time. There was always her usual diversion of staring at the ceiling in bed, but that would not do. She may not have been over absolutely everything that had ever happened in her life, but she was quite done with that method of trying to solve it.

She stood and telekinetically retrieved a change of clothes. It had been some time since she last wore her body armor. She actually hoped she'd need it for a change, but that still wouldn't be for a while. She was out of her quarters a moment later.

Her destination, the closest mess hall she knew of, was an enlisted man's mess. There were a large number of people here divided into several groups. The ship's crew sat at their own set of tables; the Phalanx Troopers sat at another; and the smallest group was the personnel who armed, tended, and maintained the embarked starfighters and assault shuttles. It was somewhat fascinating how it was possible to guess who belonged where just by looking at them.

The troopers were brawny and loud, bellowing curses almost poetically in crude humor. A couple of them on the *good* side of her face pointed thumbs her way as they talked amongst each other. The troopers on the burnt side of her face paid her no mind, other than muttering under their breath.

The ship's crew were sometimes brawny but usually of a slighter build. By percentage and absolute number, there were more women among them than the others. The crew spoke in just as animated a fashion as the troopers but used fewer curses and more words she could only guess the meaning of. Acronyms flew, technical details were argued as if life and death, and in a way, Carmen found the spectacle more ridiculous.

The maintainers, by contrast, didn't talk much. Their uniforms were dirty, often stained and ripped in places. Their knuckles were usually bruised, and there were sometimes bandages on their arms and even faces. Their conversation was the most unusual of all, as they spoke as if the fighters and shuttles were alive. More than that, it seemed like the machines were always plotting, figuring when was the best, most inconvenient time to break. She didn't understand any of it.

The Clairvoyant, a cohort of one, made her way across the room. She grabbed a tray telekinetically, and food flew to it by the same unseen force. Frederick had told her the food in the officer's mess was better, which was true, as she'd tried it once, but all the food on the ship was consistently quite good. It was certainly better than the nuclear waste she'd made in her meager, now blown-up apartment. The crew watched her telekinetically fill her tray with only slight interest. She was fast becoming a regular. She then went to a quiet corner of the room and sat down.

The din was vivacious. She listened to none and all and couldn't help being transfixed. She'd often wondered how the officers and crew dealt with it—how they dealt with being away from their family and friends for months and maybe even years at a time. Yet, as she watched the goings-on in the mess hall from her corner where she was completely alone, the camaraderie, the cheer, and the open rumination over shared hardships began to give her a clue.

There was a soft pinprick on her consciousness then. She looked to see what it was and was quick to note that she was no longer the only Clairvoyant in the room. Colonel Melvick Lanser was walking toward her with his own tray. He stopped in front of her and gestured with an open hand to an empty chair. Carmen nodded, and he sat down.

"Edge," he greeted respectfully before he began eating.

"Colonel Lanser," she said back.

"Call me Mel."

She nodded. "Then call me Carmen."

She paused as soon as her name left her mouth, overcome

by a sudden realization. No one on this entire ship knew her name—her real name, anyway. Not even Inertia knew it. She could be dead in a few hours, and she'd be buried by her Clairvoyant sobriquet, "Edge." It was a name she had no great care for, given to her in a place that had given her nightmares by a man she was terrified of.

She knew Inertia's real name: Will. William Brown. She never called him that, and he'd never indicated that she should. She never wished to call him anything else. She knew him as "Inertia," and it fit him. It was comforting to not think of him as anything else. He terrified most everyone around him, even other Clairvoyants, by just existing—and for good reason. Moreover, he appeared to know almost everything and was always calmly ready no matter the situation. He was Inertia the Rogue Wolf, second in command of one of the most feared and dangerous mercenary bands in the galaxy. And he was also *her* partner. She was certain, no matter what happened between them—no matter how angry she ever got at him and he at her—that, when push came to shove, he'd be the first to help her in her hour of need.

That was Inertia. That was her partner. But that was here on this ship, deep behind enemy lines on what was practically a suicide mission. If circumstances were different, though, and if they weren't stuck together by their situation, would that still be the case? Carmen didn't know what *Will* would do. She had no idea whatsoever. She'd never considered it. She had always thought she viewed her partner distantly, but now she realized she didn't know him at all. And though he didn't know her real name, he certainly knew her. There was no professional veneer covering anything she did. She was just being herself. Perhaps that was why he no longer talked to her? Perhaps he saw something distasteful enough in her that it was uncomfortable for him to even be near her. She didn't know. And it was hard not to think about it now that the idea was in her head.

"Carmen," Mel repeated after a nod, trying the name.

The remark was enough to thankfully break her thoughts. "Mel," Carmen repeated as well.

The two Clairvoyants took a couple bites of food. Carmen watched the commander of the Phalanx Troopers and he casually watched her. It wasn't an uncomfortable silence. It was just silence—calm, cool, and somehow relaxing in a way. She opened her mouth to speak after a time, though. She'd rather talk to Mel than think about Inertia yet again, or the freighter, or anything else going on. There was a question on her mind, anyway, if a small one.

"Why don't you eat in the officer's mess?" she asked.

"I prefer to eat here with my troopers," he responded. "Many of them are younger than you. They are asked to do dangerous and terrible things, some of which extract a heavy toll. Some of them will give their lives. The least I can do is dine with them."

Carmen nodded a few times; she could respect that. "But you're not with them," she pointed out.

"Indeed," he began seriously. "Clairvoyants are well known for their incredible powers of observation," he said. Carmen felt the rap on her knuckles despite how softly it was given and couldn't help a guilty smile. Mel didn't appear annoyed in any way, though. He even gave a thoughtful nod before he continued. "I shouldn't be with them, not totally. Fleet takes the idea further than the Phalanx Trooper corps, but the practice of separation between leader and subordinate is sound." Carmen nodded again and wondered if that same practice extended between Clairvoyant mercenary partners. She bit her tongue to stop her mind from going on that annoyingly familiar journey. "Besides, even with them I'm not with them, nor can I ever be. I sensed you here, and I'd much prefer to be with a fellow Clairvoyant."

"I understand," she said.

She was more comfortable around Inertia than any *normal* she'd ever known, except maybe for Michael. But being around her boyfriend had often felt like admiring finely decorated porcelain. He was always wary of her, if sometimes only subconsciously, and she was worried she'd shatter him in some way. He was sweet and sensitive, but he'd never really understood her and never would have been able to. There were times that it had been rather frustrating.

"But the captain is a Clairvoyant," she remarked.

"She can be called a Clairvoyant, but she is not like you and me," Mel responded. "Her abilities are grossly underdeveloped and, more importantly, she's never gone through the experiences we have."

Carmen thought about that as she ate. She wondered if it was better or worse to be halfway between Clairvoyant and *normal*. Captain Brown acted normal enough, yet she was also very isolated. Carmen always assumed it was because she was the captain, but maybe there was more to it. Then she thought of something else.

"But you aren't completely like me. You've never been interned at a facility. Your generation was trained by the sortens."

"Yes, that's true. However, most of the training of the facility is modeled after the sortens' methods."

"I can see what you mean."

"One major difference, though, is that Melvick Lanser isn't even my name. Unlike you, I don't know what my actual name is." He paused before he spoke again. "Names show care. You have to care about someone or something to take the time to name it. I was always just a number."

Carmen wondered what that meant. She'd never considered it before. It was a small thing and, when considered further, a chasm of difference between them. She thought of her given name—well, second given name—Edge. She had been too petrified of Janus at the time to notice how much effort he'd put into choosing it. She also thought of Caelus, the sorten scientist who had just called her *beast*. She didn't know if that was better than a number, but she couldn't imagine the sorten's mind of gears producing a name that didn't make her throw up in her mouth.

"What's your Clairvoyant name?" she asked.

Mel shook his head. "I never had one. I was a control."

"What do you mean?"

"The sortens had several training centers. Many of them were run independently, but some were tasked with specific research. To this day, no one understands where a Clairvoyant's abilities come from, but there is an emotional and psychological element involved. Most assets were allowed to socialize with each other. My center was the control group. We didn't socialize...at all. I never knew anyone to name me," he said. He spoke calmly, evenly, but Carmen gawked at him.

"You were completely alone?" she asked. "For years?"

"Yes. The sortens taught us with a disembodied AI. Its personality and voice changed daily to prevent us from becoming attached to it," he said. There was no stress at all in his voice or manner, and Carmen was amazed by that. "The only individuals I ever saw, I fought...and killed. Unfortunately, I killed several of the troopers who liberated the center. I didn't know any better. It's why I became a trooper myself."

"To pay it back?" she asked.

Mel nodded. "It took a long time to recover." He didn't

speak for a few seconds. He looked directly at her when he did, though. "Carmen, it is a noble thing you and your partner are doing. I hope we succeed. All Clairvoyant research should have stopped after the war—at least of the kind we endured."

She was quiet for a moment. "You're not the only one to say that," she said softly as she thought of Eli. She looked at Mel and hesitated to say what was on her mind. But he was so open and calm that it was worth asking. "The Clairvoyants of your generation never talk about what the sortens did to them. I have some idea," she said, thinking of Solitary. "But what was it like?"

Her Clairvoyant counterpart was quiet for a long time. He didn't seem bothered by the question; it just looked like it was difficult to describe the experience with words. He reminded her of Gungnir in a way. Both men came across as *mature*. She knew she was young. There were a few things she'd been able to figure out about life, what she was, and her place in it all, but those two appeared to be near the end of the journey she was just beginning.

"Perhaps it's best that it is not said," Mel mused out loud. Carmen gave a disappointed groan, and he glanced at her. "If you must know, imagine the worst thing anyone could do to you. Imagine them taking everything you knew about yourself and everything you'll learn about yourself and destroying it—"

"Can't really say my situation was much different," she muttered, cutting him off.

"In a way yes, and in a way no," he said, his tone unstressed but firm. "Yes, your training was modeled after the sortens' training of my generation, but you weren't studied in the same manner as pulling wings off a fly. Imagine that— being the fly. Whatever you can dream in your worst nightmare pales next to the reality of living it."

Carmen blinked a few times. It wasn't what he said but how he said it. When he spoke, there was no anger or pain cloaking his voice. She, on the other hand, couldn't maintain the same serenity despite how hard she tried. It made her feel small all of sudden. She could fully acknowledge what happened to her. She still had nightmares from time to time, but it wasn't a period of her life that colored her day-to-day very often. Yet, a level of resentment remained. She wasn't sure she'd ever be able to reach Mel's level.

"After considering that, why ask? Why now?" he concluded.

"Curiosity, I guess…but not really," she began, taking a moment to think. "I would like to understand—understand all of you, why you are how you are. My previous handler often spoke offhand about the treatment she suffered under the sortens. She's still bitter about it. I always wondered why."

"Many are," Mel said. "It's a pity. If I'm resentful of anything, it is killing some eighteen-year-old kid who liberated me, who only wanted to stop fighting and go home to his parents. That is worse than anything the sortens did. Even then, it's best to move past it. They tortured us for a time; no need for us to carry on the work ourselves for the rest of our lives."

Carmen nodded several times. "I well know that," she muttered. "I don't like what happened to me, but I'm not…" She was quiet for a moment as she thought of the lie she was just about to say out loud. She shook her head. "I'm trying, I really am. I'm not special. I just don't know why I can attempt to get over it but others can't. It's hard. I won't deny that. But I…I don't want to stay like this."

"It is hard," he agreed. "Why you and not others, I can't say. In that there's not really any advice I can give you, Carmen. I'll just say that some never get there. Some don't want to. But if you don't at least try, you're on a ferry to hell."

"That's most of the reason I'm here. To stop others from getting on that ferry," she said.

Mel looked at her and slowly shook his head. "You can't stop it, Carmen. No one can. There will always be those like the sortens who are seeking to exploit others for their own gain."

"Have to try, though," she shot back.

Carmen nodded then, more to reassure herself than anything, and went back to eating as she contemplated what Mel had said. She agreed with most of it, and though their conversation wasn't light and carefree, she appreciated it. She also appreciated the silence after, and she could read him well enough to know he did too. Clairvoyant company really was different. There was no need to ignore or butter over reality. She and her cohort lived it, through its pains and pleasures. It was all around them. They couldn't escape it, nor did they want to.

She glanced at the clock when she swallowed the last morsel. It wasn't time yet, but it was getting closer. She stood, happy that she could just leave instead of searching for some social justification for doing so. Mel looked at her.

"Carmen, there is one thing you should keep in mind," he began. She met his gaze and waited attentively. "I don't know how old Charon is. If he is willing to work with the sortens, he's most likely among your age group. However, if he is not, be careful. You are very powerful and can kill, but you're no killer, and you're certainly no soldier. Sortens trained us to fight and nothing else. It was more intense and disciplined than your battles against Constructs at your facility. Remember that. He is more than likely weaker than you, but he might be a better fighter. Don't underestimate that advantage."

She considered his words and nodded. "Thank you, Colonel Lanser," she said respectfully.

Mel nodded in turn. "Be well, Edge. I hope you find your path. Just remember, no matter what it is, there are no finish lines."

She paused. No one had ever told her that before. The idea of it made Carmen shudder. "Thank you," she said anyway.

She made her way out of the mess hall after that, the troopers, crew, and maintainers making way as necessary. She was in the corridor in seconds, her destination the bridge. She thought about her enemy. Could he beat her? He beat Phaethon, who was respectfully powerful. Her charge, however, was also young and reckless. She consoled herself with the knowledge that Charon might be able to defeat her, but he couldn't defeat both her *and* Inertia. She'd be hard pressed to think of any single opponent who could do that. Perhaps it would be her, Inertia, and Mel? She didn't know what the colonel could do, but he was a Clairvoyant, and that had to count for something. And it would be a freighter against a cruiser. For once, the opposition was outgunned. They just needed to be found first.

She stepped into the elevator for the bridge, hoping the prospects for that weren't impossible. When Carmen entered the bridge a short time later, she paused. She was the first here…well, that she knew. The bridge was always manned, but she didn't know who any of these officers were. They looked at her with some surprise but didn't say anything. She went to her observer chair and sat down.

"Ma'am," the watch officer said respectfully from the captain's chair.

Carmen nodded back but didn't say anything. She looked at the clock. *Just a little while longer*, she thought.

* * *

The first to arrive was the helm officer. Carmen could never remember her name. In any case, the short woman glanced at her when she entered, but neither said anything. She went to the helm and spoke briefly with the officer stationed there before she took his place.

Next to enter was Leena. She looked at the Clairvoyant and opened her mouth, though no words came forth. Carmen returned her gaze and the two were locked like that for what felt like several minutes. She could read that the ensign just didn't know what to do. Should she say hello? Should she just think hello and assume the Clairvoyant would read her mind? Should she ignore her or run from her? Carmen settled the matter by casually looking away and sighing. Clairvoyant company *was* less annoying most of the time.

Commander Fletcher and Hiroshi arrived after that. They spoke quietly to each other, and once in the bridge proper, the two men nodded and went to their respective stations. The watch officer left.

"Edge," Terry said, nodding in her direction. He possessed none of Leena's tentativeness.

She nodded back. "Commander."

She heard Renee and Frederick, well mostly Frederick, before they entered.

"I told you I'm not taking odds," Renee said in an exasperated yet not exasperated tone she used only with him.

His trademark gleam came to his eye, and Renee sighed loudly when she saw it. Carmen couldn't help thinking what an odd pair they were—the most important and least important officers on the ship joined together in almost all things. She had some pretty good guesses as to what they were talking about, but that all fell away. She licked her lips. Her partner was coming.

She heard the hatch open and forced herself to not turn to look at him. That lasted about two seconds. There was a hopeful look in her eye as she watched Inertia approach. She didn't register it consciously, but she turned her head to give him the good side of her face. She forced her body to relax, suppressing a tense tickle here and there. Ultimately, she was betrayed by her shoulders and arms, which almost trembled in anticipation. She didn't want much. A glance or nod would do—anything that let her know she existed.

Nothing came. He sat next to her, and she might as well have been invisible. Yet she looked at him and still waited. There was nothing else to do, and he couldn't ignore her forever. She'd almost be happy if he just turned and slapped her. It was then that she noticed Renee was looking at them. Her wayward eyebrow raised again, making Carmen turn her attention to the captain and pretend it had always been trained on her.

"How much longer?" Carmen asked, though she already knew the answer.

Renee glanced at Tawny, who may not have been a Clairvoyant but who always knew when her captain was looking at her.

"Four minutes and ten seconds, ma'am," Tawny answered.

Carmen nodded glumly as Renee turned to her XO. "Mr. Fletcher," she said simply.

"Aye, Captain," he said. "Sound battle stations," he ordered a second later.

The loud klaxon that Carmen couldn't stand but

welcomed in this case sounded. Terry gave additional orders, all of which she had heard before in the unfortunate battles that delayed their arrival here. She ignored them. She even ignored Inertia as she faced forward and placed her hands on her knees. Every second counted down in her head. She tried to ignore that as well, but it was futile.

She didn't know what was on the freighter—no one did. It wasn't even listed in the records of Solitary. But she expected at least Charon; there was no place else for him to go. She really did hate fighting, despite being here now and resolute of purpose. And soon she'd be faced with it, with him. The Clairvoyant who worked with sortens. The Clairvoyant who aided their experiments. The Clairvoyant who'd abducted her charge. She knew she had to kill him if she could. This wasn't like with Artemis way back when. Some crimes were truly unforgiveable and some people unredeemable. She knew that. She was certain of it. It was only when Tawny began audibly counting down that Carmen realized she was squeezing her knees so hard that her hands were numb.

"Ghost Field dispelled," Tawny announced.

"Shields up, report all contacts," the captain said.

Her order was repeated, and all eyes turned toward Hiroshi. "Scope is clear, ma'am," he said after a few seconds.

Carmen's breath caught in her throat. Renee and Terry glanced at each other. "Go active," he ordered. "Full power."

"Switching to active search, full power. Aye, sir," Hiroshi replied. After a few seconds of dead silence on the bridge, he shook his head. "No con—no, wait," he began. Then he shook his head again. "No contacts, ma'am. I thought I had something for a moment, but scope is still clear," he said, turning to look at her.

He wasn't the only one. Everyone looked at Renee, and no one said anything. The Wiz Kid leaned forward to set her chin upon steepled fingers. Her eyes darted wildly back and forth as she thought about their predicament. Everything fell away as the problem turned over and over again in her mind. Carmen couldn't read her, but she knew if there was anything that anyone could do, Renee would find it. She'd learned at least that much about the captain. Eventually, the woman leaned back in her chair and sighed softly.

"Secure active sensors," she said. Then she looked at Leena and spoke in a rush. "Send to Fleet Command: We failed. Could not locate sorten freighter. Returning to terran space at best possible speed." Her attention turned to Tawny. "Plot a course to—"

"We can't give up," Carmen interrupted.

Renee ignored her. "Plot a course to the closest starport at best possible speed."

"No, stop!" Carmen yelled. "We can't give up! There has to be something else we can try?"

"What else can we do?" Terry asked. "The freighter isn't here, and there's no way for us to know where it went."

Carmen heard him and couldn't think of anything herself. Nevertheless, she began slowly shaking her head.

"Edge, I'm sorry, but we gave it our best shot," Renee said. "Frankly, we'll be lucky to escape sorten space without getting intercepted again."

You can't save them all, Carmen thought over and over again as she shook her head. She stopped abruptly. "No. No, I can't believe that. I won't! It can't end like this. I can't believe that, after everything we went through, it's ending like this."

A soft voice that was firm in its gentleness graced the air. "Edge, we both knew this was never certain," Inertia said. He placed a hand on her shoulder. "There is nothing else we can do."

She slapped his hand away. "I don't accept that. We have to find something. We have to find a way," she said, her voice growing more and more desperate as she spoke.

"I don't want to accept it either, but Inertia is right. Unless you happen to have the coordinates they Ghosted to or can go back in time to when they were here, there really is nothing we can do," Terry said.

Carmen looked at the officer and then at everyone in the room, all staring at her. She didn't have coordinates and she couldn't go back in time. And now she was thinking about how crazy her determination sounded. Here she was, the Clairvoyant, the one-percenter, whining like a spoiled schoolgirl to seasoned Space Force officers about *their* profession. She sat quietly, head downcast, as more than just her hands turned numb. It was hard to breathe at this point. Her chest was so tight that it felt like she was trapped in the coils of a snake. And then she could feel—could sense her partner looking at her. He didn't say anything, and though she could never read him, Will's concern pierced through the wall of ice between them. She appreciated it. She always had, and she especially yearned for it now, but just then there was something else on her mind. *Time machine*, she thought.

"Course plotted, ma'am. Ready to Ghost on your order," Tawny said.

"Exec—"

"No, wait," Carmen said quickly.

The master and commander of the *Griffin* gave the Clairvoyant an annoyed glance, but she was able to hold herself to just that. "Yes, Edge?"

"What's all this talk I always hear about light minutes and light seconds?"

"It's a unit of measure of how far light travels in the stated time in a vacuum. What of it?" Terry asked.

Carmen nodded a few times. Then she looked at Inertia. "You said that when a ship charges its Ghost Drive, it is very bright. Even as bright as a star."

Her partner looked her in the eye, and she saw the exact moment he grasped her line of logic. She smiled as he nodded.

"So, so what?" Terry asked.

"I…I think she might have something here," Renee said quickly when she also realized it. She again rested her chin on her fingers as she thought the matter through.

"What? What do we have?"

"A way to track them," Frederick said. "All we have to do is get far enough away to record the light from their Ghost Drive when it reaches us."

Terry shook his head. "Wouldn't work. Been tried. The only way to get an accurate track is to know precisely when they Ghosted. Light can be produced by anything. A random light gives a bearing but no course track or range."

"But we do know precisely when they Ghosted," Carmen began. "Instead of thinking the sortens Ghosted late, let's say they Ghosted exactly on time. They're a very precise people, right?" she said, looking at Inertia. The Rogue Wolf nodded, which made her smile again.

"Ms. Crowe, give me a plot," Renee said.

"Plotted, ma'am."

"Best possible speed, execute when ready," she ordered as she relaxed in her chair.

"Best possible speed. Aye, ma'am. Charging Ghost Drive."

"If this works, it puts us back in the game," Renee said to no one in particular.

Her brother nodded. "It helps that some partners are better than others."

Carmen heard him, though he wasn't speaking to her or even looking at her, and grinned. Forget being numb; it felt like there was fire shooting through her veins.

It was a quick trip. Almost as soon as the Ghost Drive was established, it was dispelled. All eyes turned to Hiroshi. The FCT officer sat at his station like a cat ready to strike.

"Now all we need to do is wait for the light to get here," Frederick remarked.

Renee nodded. "Time?"

"Estimated five seconds if they left on time, ma'am," Hiroshi said. A moment later, he added, "New contact! New contact! It's the freighter!" A cheer went through the bridge. Even Carmen partook this time, but it was short lived. "I'm also reading a second contact in close escort with the freighter."

"Second contact? What the hell is it?" Terry asked.

Renee turned sharply to the Clairvoyants. "Did you know anything about an escort?" she asked.

"No," Inertia said.

Carmen also shook her head, but she didn't know what the issue was. They'd been able to handle that entire battle-group before. Why worry about one ship?

"It's...it's a fleet battleship," Hiroshi said mournfully, practically crumpling in his chair. "This is suicide," he added under his breath.

Renee sneered. "What was that, FCT? I don't understand that phraseology," she said firmly.

Hiroshi's body gave a startled shake, as if he'd been struck by lightning. "Nothing, ma'am," he said quickly. "I just said we'll find a way, ma'am."

"Better," Renee remarked. "Won't be easy, though," she agreed under her breath. She glanced at Inertia. "When I said anything, you really should have warned me it would be all of this."

He smirked. "Can you beat them?"

"I don't know," she whispered.

Carmen watched the exchange attentively. "What's a fleet battleship?" she asked.

"To put this simply, we're a cruiser, and we're meant to operate at long range by ourselves and only really fight ships our size or smaller," Renee said. "We can tackle larger prey with our missiles, but that's not really our role."

"And a fleet battleship, by contrast, is designed to take entire systems or fleets by itself. Size notwithstanding," Terry finished for her. Carmen nodded. Perhaps the sortens weren't so outgunned after all. "This really makes me wonder what the sortens have aboard that freighter to commit so much to protecting it."

"Me too," Renee agreed. "FCT, what's their track and speed?"

"The track needs a little refinement, but the Ghost Field was weak. Suggesting low speed," Hiroshi answered.

Renee nodded. "That's what I figured. They don't really have any place to go. They probably move about several sectors but don't leave that zone." She looked at Terry. "We can refine the track, no problem there. As soon as we do, place the ship a couple days ahead of them. That should give us enough time to game out a strategy."

"Aye, ma'am," Terry said.

"In the meantime," Renee continued, turning her attention to Carmen. The Clairvoyant looked back with surprise. She had never really spoken to her unless prompted. "I heard you'd like to schedule a surgery."

"You did?" Carmen muttered. She hadn't said anything. She looked at Inertia, who was back to impassively ignoring her, and then turned to Frederick. He gave her a thumbs-up and a big smile. She politely smiled back before she looked at the captain again. "It wouldn't be too much trouble?"

Renee playfully batted away her words. "Oh, please. We'd be on our way home right now if it wasn't for you."

Carmen smiled. Then she touched her burnt hand with her good hand and the burnt side of her face. There were other scars across her body as well.

"Yes, I would like that."

15

A SECOND OPINION

Everyone in the room watched the battle and hoped the inevitable could somehow be circumvented. Starships weren't easy beasts to kill, but the lucky shot or golden BB was still possible, though increasingly unlikely. The *Griffin* didn't have a chance any other way. Every simulation to this point had proven it.

She was just a step up from a hulk now. The ability for her to move under her own power was limited to only thrusters. The main engines had been blown away by a well-placed shot at long range. The bridge was also gone, destroyed by concentrated fire that had obliterated most of the top of the ship. Her back was also broken, her hull bent and twisted, swaying and gyrating in her pathetic attempts to maneuver. There was only one operational weapon left. The stern DED on the ventral side answered back with everything it had, but it was useless against the fleet battleship's shields.

"This is painful to watch," Frederick muttered.

No one said anything, but some jaws did clench tight in silent agreement. The sortens didn't even waste their time in taking away the *Griffin's* remaining claws. Instead, scores of shuttles descended upon the cruiser for a boarding action. Sortens weren't well known for being merciful to prisoners.

Renee had had enough. "Stop the simulation," she ordered.

The large three-dimensional display that dominated the CIC abruptly shut off. The entire engagement was recorded for later study, but there was little point in reviewing a one-sided slaughter. Tawny, who had played as the sortens in this battle, rose from her station and joined the group. There was no look of triumph on her face, even though she'd *won*. She'd joked grimly before the battle even began that she'd probably be able to win with her eyes closed. No one checked if her eyes were actually closed or not during the simulation, but no one doubted the claim was possible. Hiroshi, who'd played the *Griffin*, also joined the other officers and Inertia in the center of the room. Carmen was recovering from her surgery but was no great loss. She'd be the first to say she was no master of starship battle tactics.

Renee took a deep breath and let it out like a deflating balloon. "How many runs is that?" she asked.

"Seventy-three, ma'am," Terry answered. "Most were AI runs, though."

She glanced at her watch and cursed softly. Her hands transitioned to running through her shoulder-length hair. "Doesn't seem to make any difference, AI or directed," she remarked.

"Yes, Captain," he agreed, though he wished he didn't have to.

"Well, the only tactic that even lands a hit is disrupting their Ghost Field, timed with an alpha strike," Hiroshi said.

Tawny shook her head. "Didn't work this time or last time or the ten times before that."

"But it might eventually," he began. "We just have to get

the timing right, before they can raise their shields. That, combined with a lucky hit some place vital, is all we need."

"But if they get their shields up faster than we expect or we don't hit some place vital, we get plastered," Tawny countered.

Hiroshi's hands shook in tight fists before he spoke. The frustration was born from their increasing realization that there was no way to win. The simulated attacks everyone had witnessed for the past few hours drove the point home like nails in their coffins.

"We're past what could happen. We need to think about what we can do," he said. "There aren't any other options. Even if by some miracle we had enough firepower to take that ship one-on-one, the freighter would use the time to escape."

"I understand that, but when we actually fight, we can't just hit reset if we miss. It's one and done," Tawny said.

"It's a fighting chance. That's about all we've got left."

There was silence for a few seconds after Hiroshi spoke. Terry was the first to offer an alternative. "Destroy it," he said calmly. "We strike the freighter and destroy it...then run like hell."

Tawny considered the action but shook her head. "I don't think we'll be able to get enough separation from the battleship to charge our Ghost Drive. Her weapons outrange ours."

"Long range strike with Hammers then. We have a pretty solid track of the two ships, and the freighter will have lighter shielding and no armor. We won't need a picket," Terry said. "Major question is if we have enough Hammers to overwhelm their defensive fire."

"The strike would be on the freighter and not the battleship. It's possible," Tawny remarked.

Terry nodded, and Hiroshi hesitated to make his next

point. "We can use the Hustlers," he said. Everyone abruptly looked at him, but he'd expected as much. "Target the Hammers on the battleship to keep her busy and then have the Hustlers take out the freighter."

"That would be a suicide mission for them," Tawny said quietly.

At that moment, everyone wished Winter was still here. The Hustlers' XO was busy making sure their fighters would be ready for the coming strike if they were needed. The crews had been run ragged while serving as sensor pickets in the maelstrom that was Medusa. Even now they were tracking the progress of the freighter and the fleet battleship.

"It might be," Hiroshi said after a time. "However, if we engage that battleship, it certainly would be for us. They're small and there are many of them. They should be able to scatter and escape."

"We should sim it," Terry said after thinking the matter over. "Reset the sim for the following parameters," he said to one of the CIC crew.

"No," Renee said calmly, cutting him off before he could say anything else. She was still raking her fingers through her hair while her forehead rested in her palms. "No, we will not destroy the freighter," she continued, placing her hands down.

"Captain, it's the only way we can stop the sortens' plans," Hiroshi pointed out.

"And how many terran civilians will we sacrifice in the process?" she asked.

"There might not be any civilians on that ship."

"Yet there might be," she said with a firmer tone as she let the question hang. "Even as a last resort, I won't do it. Furthermore, whatever they are researching must be of some prime importance to protect it to this degree. If it's worth that much for the sortens to protect it, it's worth as much for us to capture it, whatever it may be."

"Captain, I agree—you know I do—but the situation is different from what we were briefed," Terry said, glancing at Inertia. The Clairvoyant glanced back but made no comment. "If there are civilians on that ship, I'm sorry to say they will probably be better off with the freighter destroyed than us dying to try to capture it."

"So, just kill them?" Inertia remarked. "If that's the course of action, at least give them the respect of not glossing over it." There was no anger in his voice, just a deep gravity behind every word that focused the room.

Terry looked directly at the Clairvoyant, and the Clairvoyant stared back. The Space Force officer did not waver. "Yes, kill them," he said pointedly. He then looked at Renee. "They are better off dead than as prisoners of the sortens. If they are subjected to even half their usual Clairvoyant research, no one could say otherwise. I regret it, but we can't save them all."

The commander looked at Inertia again and nodded. The Clairvoyant gave a respectful nod back but with downcast eyes. He could deal with the Space Force officers; they didn't mince words or pretend sentiment they didn't believe. They were probably right. There probably was no way to take the freighter, leaving its destruction the only option. He could agree to it; he could live with it; and he was also glad that Edge was not here. His partner always had trouble accepting the distastefulness of lamentable necessity.

"I understand that, but they will not be sacrificed," Renee said. "They might not be saved today, and they might not be saved by us, but they *could* be saved tomorrow or the day after. We don't know if they can't all be saved, and I won't presume they're lost just because *we* can't do it. The freighter will not be destroyed. End of discussion."

"We retreat then?" Hiroshi asked.

Renee glanced at him. "I didn't say that either."

"Do you have a plan?" Inertia asked, hope coloring his voice.

The captain leaned back in her chair, paused for a second, and then rolled her eyes. "No," she said after a groan. Everyone else in the room, other than Inertia, groaned as well, and she stopped the expression with a quick snap of her fingers. "Let's go back to basics and start from there. What is our mission?" she asked, the question instantly refocusing her team.

"To locate and then capture or destroy a sorten freighter concealing a research base, ma'am," Tawny answered.

"Yes, and what assets do we have?"

"One Peacekeeper-class cruiser with roughly a quarter complement of Mjonir missiles and nearly a full magazine of torpedoes. A squadron of Banshee starfighters, minus one ship. A battalion of Phalanx Troopers. Two squadrons of assault shuttles," Hiroshi said. "Plus two Clairvoyant mercenaries," he added, glancing at Inertia.

Renee nodded. "Our opposition?"

"One Blood-Dawn-class fleet battleship and a sorten heavy freighter, unknown complement or defensive capabilities for the freighter," Terry answered.

"OPFOR mission?"

"Presumably to conduct Clairvoyant research and—"

The captain silenced Tawny with a raised hand. "Only presume what you can reasonably be certain of."

The lieutenant nodded. "To conduct research of an unknown nature."

"Better," Renee said.

Tawny nodded again. "For the battleship, to protect the freighter against any hostiles," she continued.

"And hide the existence of the freighter," Renee added. "They are flying close enough together and the battleship is large enough to overshadow the freighter on sensors, unless you are close enough to discern two contacts and are specifically looking for two contacts. Most ships will just assume it's a battleship on maneuvers by herself." She paused before she spoke again. "Now that that's out of the way, assumptions?"

"The sortens would prefer to remain undetected, even by other sortens," Inertia said.

"Proof?" she asked.

"Both Solitary and this freighter are essentially alone in deep space. The nature of their research also requires anonymity. The abduction of terran civilians and attacks of planetside facilities are acts of war," Inertia said. "They cannot afford war with the UTE now, but they are working to gain a strategic advantage later."

"Seems reasonable," Renee said while she thought it over herself. "Conclusions?"

"If that's true, their teams on the freighter are probably small. They also probably have minimal defenses against any sort of boarding action," Hiroshi said. "They would proceed under the assumption that their escort can destroy any likely opposition before a boarding attempt could be made."

The captain nodded, and Terry took a turn to speak. "They probably can't call for reinforcements, at least not assets they directly control. Furthermore, they probably wouldn't appreciate any reinforcements that did arrive. They would have to explain the situation to a sorten military that might not be keyed in to everything that's going on."

"Like us with Space Force and this mission," Tawny remarked.

Renee ignored her comment. "I have to agree," she replied, "but there is one very important aspect of this that no one has mentioned. They won't be able to detect *us*."

"How do you figure that, Captain?" Terry asked.

"Their location makes it very unlikely that they'd ever encounter any hostiles," she began. "A battleship can output more sensor power than we can, but we're a smaller target. It evens out. We might even be slightly ahead. Anyway, and quite a decisive difference, is that we are looking for them and they are not looking for us. And also—"

"They don't want to be found," her brother finished for her. Renee nodded.

"Neither do we," Hiroshi pointed out.

"But they need more sensor power to detect a smaller target than a smaller target would need to detect them," Terry said. "That's why we use pickets. But they have no pickets. Even if they have embarked fighters or probes, a ship can't communicate while Ghosted. And—"

"They won't want to use active sensors anyway, as it would give away their position," Renee concluded for him.

"So…so what?" Hiroshi asked. "We still can't defeat that ship?"

"We can…we just need more ships," Frederick said, as if it were obvious. He looked at Renee, who nodded, her features growing increasingly grim.

"Where can we get more ships?" Hiroshi asked no one in particular. "We're on our own with this mission." He looked at Inertia. "Can you Rogue Wolves summon a fleet? You appear well connected."

The Clairvoyant shook his head and seemed both surprised and annoyed that the question was even asked. "We are just a band of mercenaries. If we had fleets of starships, we would have never come to you in the first place."

"We don't need any more ships," the captain interrupted. She took a deep breath and let it out sharply. "Unless someone has a better idea, we'll proceed with a fixed base attack," she said, though she sounded very much like she'd rather not go with that plan.

There was utter silence in the CIC after that. Everyone except Inertia and Frederick stared at her with eyes wide. There was no question that came to mind, no statement that made sense, against such a farcical line of reasoning.

"Can that work?" Inertia asked.

Renee nodded a few times as she stared off into the distance, her eyebrows working up and down. It seemed like she was trying to convince herself of her own course of action. "It can, though it won't be pretty."

"Captain, with all due respect, I think you should reconsider," Terry said.

She turned to him. "It can't be done any other way."

Tawny watched everything with mouth agape. She couldn't believe what she was hearing. "How can it be done at all?" she asked. "No one's ever even tried that before. No one's even considered it before. It's pointless against a target that can maneuver, ma'am."

"But they're not going to maneuver."

"You said earlier to only make presumptions you can be reasonably certain of. That's a hell of a presumption, Captain," Hiroshi said. "Why wouldn't they maneuver?"

"We pre-stage shots from multiple vectors—dozens, hundreds if we have to—from very long range. Light hours or better. All timed to arrive the exact moment we disrupt their Ghost Drive. They won't see it coming."

"Captain," Tawny began softly, "they can detect the

shots." Her tone was gentle and caressing, as if she were trying to sooth an utter imbecile. These were rudimentary starship tactics. How could she not understand that?

Renee shook her head while rolling her eyes. The impression she gave was one of wonder at how no one could understand her reasoning. But her officers merely thought she had finally cracked.

"They won't detect them because we won't use energy weapons. We'll use torpedoes."

"Torpedoes at a range of light hours? We'll be lucky to hit the broadside of a barn at that range," Terry remarked. "Not easy."

"As I said, hundreds of shots. And you don't know the half of it." She took a deep breath. "They could still detect the torpedoes if they use their active sensors. We have to make sure they don't."

"How do we do that, Captain?" Tawny asked.

Renee took another deep breath. Inertia began shaking his head before she even spoke; she saw it and grimaced. He usually connected the dots first. She didn't like the idea either. "We fight them close," she answered. "Very close. Close enough that they don't have to go active for a good track of us. The good news is that, at close range, only their secondary weapons will be effective. The bad news is that, at close range, *we* can't effectively maneuver to evade fire. The worse news is even with just secondaries, she can still stomp us like a bug. We only have to last a few seconds, though. Long enough for the torpedoes to hit."

Everyone in the room other than Frederick and Inertia stared at her again. Her communicator beeped just then, and they no longer drew her attention.

"Captain Brown here, go ahead," she answered after keying her collar.

"Captain, medical. You wanted to be informed when our patient was having her bandages removed. We're almost ready."

"Yes. I will be there shortly," she said. Then she shut off the communication system and turned her attention back to her officers. "While we're taking care of the battleship, the Hustlers will disable the freighter. Our assault shuttles will be pre-launched and will board as soon as she's dead in the water. I want to take her quickly to stop the sortens from destroying any research." Everyone continued looking at her as if she'd asked them to turn water into wine. She shook her head. "Of all the crazy things we've done, this is only a nine-point-five out of ten," she joked. No one laughed. Unfazed, she looked at Terry. "Sim it, both AI and directed. I'm going to go see Edge and then Colonel Lanser to go over the boarding plan. I'll help you refine the attack when I get back." The captain stood. "Any questions?"

No one said anything. The silence didn't appear to be caused by a lack of questions, though. Everyone seemed filled to the brim with questions, not about the plan, oh no, but about her sanity. They looked her in the eye in a state of horrified shock. No one moved. No one even blinked. They just stood there, frozen, comprehending and understanding but not believing. She looked at her XO again, and he immediately snapped out of it.

"No questions, ma'am. We'll get it done," Terry said.

Renee smiled and nodded. She had no doubt. She then looked at her brother. "Ready?"

It was brief, very brief, but she was sure she saw him hesitate. "It might be a better use of my time to assist Colonel Lanser with the boarding plan," he said.

"You don't want to go?" Renee asked, looking at him

sidelong with a raised eyebrow. "This should be quick. We can see the colonel after."

She gestured toward the exit. Inertia looked at her, and there was a moment of indecision. She didn't even know Clairvoyants were capable of indecision. Eventually he nodded, but it looked more like an admission of defeat than the acceptance of an invitation. Renee filed the episode away to reference later. Frederick followed them out, and before the hatch closed, she heard the rest of her officers start to get to work. She was certain she heard some curses.

She glanced at Frederick and said softly, "Some privacy please."

The political officer nodded then smartly moved ahead of them to get out of earshot. They were finally alone again, which was annoyingly rare, but as with every instance to this point, it was frustratingly awkward. It had been fourteen years at least since she'd last seen him. It was quite a bit of a time to pick up and carry on like nothing happened. She didn't know what to do or what to say, and neither did he.

She looked at her younger brother. She last saw him as a boy but he was now a man. She didn't know this person. How he walked, how he talked, and even the cadence of his breath was utterly alien from what she remembered him being. She didn't know if the sortens had any people captive on that freighter—she liked to think they didn't—but it was certainly possible. Edge had easily convinced her from the start that, if there were, they needed to be rescued. But here now, seeing her dearest family member missing in action, though he was walking right next to her, the mission became increasingly personal.

He wasn't all gone, however. Renee saw flashes of the boy she had known here and there—in his smile, and in a finely aimed barb she overheard him say to his partner from time to time. She remembered fondly, though not at that time, how expert he'd been at getting under her skin. She smiled as she thought of it and reflected, as she looked at him, that they hadn't been able to take his eyes. His gaze pierced through her and everything else. He'd always had a piercing gaze; she guessed it was a Clairvoyant thing, and perhaps she even did it herself now. There was even a deadly, if restrained, menace about it. It wasn't directed at anyone or anything in particular; it just wanted all to know that it was present.

Be that as it may, that wasn't all there was. No, it wasn't even a majority. Hidden beneath, perhaps visible to only her, was a boyish wonder and curiosity that couldn't be drowned out. She remembered it from the nonsense adventures and trouble they used to get into. She was surprised her backside didn't still sting from the whippings she'd gotten when their parent found out. She looked at him, and he glanced at her. The memory got her thinking.

"Mom and Dad would like to see you too," she remarked.

"They'd probably like to see you as well," he said back.

Renee winced. Yes, he always knew exactly how to get under her skin. She'd hated being home and left as soon as she could. Going to the academy had felt more like running away than a career choice.

"How closely have you kept tabs on me?" she asked.

"Just where you are and what you're doing, and only for the past few years," Inertia said after a shrug. "Didn't always have the means," he added.

"Before you joined the Rogue Wolves?"

He nodded, and she nodded in turn. She looked around before she asked her next question. Frederick was still well out of voice range, and she knew he would never violate her request for privacy. She didn't *feel* anyone around her, but that was too strange a sensation to really trust. She felt people all around all the time—she swore even in her sleep. Everyone was unique in their own rather beautiful way. But it was all so overwhelming, and she didn't know how Clairvoyants dealt with it. All she wanted to do was turn it off; it was just an annoyance. She looked at her younger brother and hesitated.

"If you didn't need me for this mission, would you have ever met me face to face?"

Inertia didn't say anything for a while. He looked like he didn't know the answer himself. Eventually, he groaned softly. "I don't know," he muttered. "I told myself I would see you when I was able, but with this war and you stationed on a starcruiser, it was a convenient excuse not to."

"I know what you mean," Renee said after a small nod. "If I knew where you were, I'm not sure I could bring myself to do it. I'd like to think I would—like to think I'd go leaping into it—but I don't know." She paused for a moment. "Used to have nightmares about meeting you," she admitted.

Inertia looked at her with a raised eyebrow. "Why would *you* have nightmares?"

"I was just a dumb kid. I don't know," she said with a shrug. She took a deep breath. "I didn't know what they do at those training facilities. In truth, I didn't want to know...still don't. But I always worried that maybe you wouldn't recognize me anymore or maybe I wouldn't recognize you. I worried that you'd die. I worried most that you wouldn't... you wouldn't, yet I'd still be an only child."

He looked at his sister. She slowly turned to look at him and then turned away sharply, bringing a finger to her eye and wiping something away quickly.

"Will, you don't know what it was like after they took you," she said. "From that moment, everything was different. I don't think I ever saw Mom and Dad smile again. They didn't even want me talking about you. They kept the door to your room closed; I wasn't allowed in there. Every picture, everything you ever made, every reference to you they threw away. The only thing left was a closed door of a room I could never go in," she said slowly. "You're right that I don't go home. I don't want to go home. I *can't* go home. I had to get out."

Inertia looked away in thought. Troubled worry grew on his features like rotten roots. Renee looked away as well. Her eyes turned upward as she closed them and groaned.

"Fuck," she muttered softly as her body shook.

He glanced at her then as she took a deep breath, held it, then let it go in a pant. "Well, at least you look sharp in a Space Force uniform," he remarked.

Renee laughed lightly and smiled as she turned to him. She wiped something away from her other eye. *Can get under my skin indeed,* she thought. "I'd hope so. I worked my ass off for this uniform."

"It suits you," he said. Renee smiled again. "Remember when we sat and watched the Battle of New York? How the sorten overseers ran around like chickens with their heads cut off, acting like it was the end of the world?" She laughed again, but it grew quiet as she thought about how long a time ago that had been. "It's surreal, thinking about it now," she said. "Hell, Winter flew in that battle. It was her first combat mission. Very surreal..." she repeated as she thought about it further.

"I remember but not that well. Only thing I can recall is sitting with you and watching the starfighters buzz over the city like fireflies," he said.

There was a long silence between them after that. They were getting closer to the med bay, and it got Renee thinking about something more immediate.

"So, what's with you and your partner?" she asked.

Inertia eyed her suspiciously. "What do you mean?"

Her eyebrows furrowed as her lips morphed into a disbelieving smirk. How could he not understand the question? "Will, I see how she looks at you. Even a blind person can see it."

He looked at her, rolled his eyes, and then looked forward. "Then be blind," he said pointedly with a small frown.

Renee barked a laugh that made even Frederick glance back. "You might be able to bowl over Edge with that strong silent crap, but not me. So…once again?"

Brother and sister looked at each other for a long moment as they walked, he with an annoyed grimace and she expectantly waiting. Inertia broke first by groaning loudly.

"She's my partner, but she is not a Rogue Wolf," he said as he looked away.

"She seems very much like a Rogue Wolf to me," Renee remarked.

"But she's not."

The starship captain thought about it and wondered what she had missed and how it was even relevant. "She's here, isn't she?"

Inertia groaned again. "And I wish she wasn't."

"Why? You two seem to work well together."

"That's the problem," he said.

"I don't understand," Renee said softly as she shook her head.

The Clairvoyant stopped in place. "Then understand this," he began. "This is a very mean, very dirty, very violent business—no honor in any of it. I do what I can to keep the worst from her. It's better she gets out of it before she gets completely sucked in and there's no way out. She could have a life away from all this, if she chose. Unfortunately, a major reason she's still here is because she feels she has to help me."

"Do you need her help?" his sister asked.

"Of course. She's been indispensable. I wouldn't…*we* wouldn't have gotten this far without her. But that's beside the point." His words became more and more frustrated as he spoke. "I've been trying to break any feelings she has for me; keep everything professional and then say goodbye once this is all over. I'm not sure it's working though. She just thinks I'm mad at her for some reason. I don't know what else I can do. She's better than this."

"I see," Renee said slowly. Inertia nodded, and the two started walking again.

The med bay was just down the corridor. Frederick had already stepped inside. The siblings approached in silence. Renee paused at the entrance.

"You know, Will, if it's as bad as you say it is…I'll just say it's good you two have each other." She looked away before she continued. "Not everyone is so lucky," she added, looking at him again.

The comment made the Clairvoyant pause as Renee entered the room. It seemed like a long time passed as he thought of her words, which he had never considered before, but it was really just a few seconds. He followed her into the med bay after a small sigh.

There weren't many casualties in the med bay. Thankfully the crew hadn't suffered any deaths in the preceding battles. Most injuries were from falls or falling objects caused by hard maneuvering. Items could be securely fastened, checked, double checked, and even triple checked, but something always fell. It was inevitable. The other patients were the pilots of the Hustlers, who were given drugs and checks to come down from the stimulants they sometimes used to stay sharp on long missions.

In her own section was his partner. Edge lay in bed wearing a medical gown with her head, an arm, and other parts of her body covered in bandages. She was obviously awake and sitting up, but with the bandages she couldn't see anything—for as much as that mattered for a monster of the Dark. Inertia took a place next to Renee and Frederick.

"Captain, perfect timing. We were just about to remove the bandages," one of the nurses said.

Renee nodded. "Proceed."

"Yes, ma'am."

Two nurses moved to Edge and began cutting away the bandages on her head and arm.

"Any problems?" Renee asked casually.

"Must admit, Captain," the nurse began as she continued to cut, "Clairvoyant patients aren't the easiest to work with. They can't control their bioelectric fields when they are sedated, and it is not easy to put them under sedation and keep them under."

Carmen's mouth was free enough to talk. "Sorry," she muttered sheepishly.

The nurse waved the apology away. "A couple shocks here and there are no worse than convincing a gung-ho trooper to rest and heal while their mates are still fighting. But, if you're asking if we were successful, look and judge for yourself," the nurse concluded as the last of the bandages were removed from Carmen's face.

Her blonde hair spilled out and over her, and she smoothed it back with both hands. Frederick whistled appreciatively after she did so. She smiled politely at him. The whistle was more a statement of fact than a leering invitation. Carmen then looked at her two hands. The skin of one looked as smooth and creamy as the other. She brought her unburnt hand to the unburnt side of her face and touched it tentatively. Then she stroked her face and enjoyed the curve of her cheek from her grin, which only made her grin more. A nurse handed her a mirror, and the Clairvoyant took a moment to study the handiwork of the medical staff.

"Will I always have only one eyebrow?" she asked.

"No," a nurse answered. "We were able to reconstruct new hair follicles and stimulate their growth for a time. The eyebrow and lost hair should grow to be even with your natural hair in about a week. After that, it will grow normally. Might itch during the stimulated growth, though. We can provide a cream if you wish."

"No thank you," Carmen muttered, as she turned her head to look at both sides of her face. She handed the mirror back and then took a peek under the bandages that covered the rest of her body. She'd remove them herself later, when she had more privacy.

"It's amazing," she said. "I can't tell the difference. Thank you."

The nurses nodded. "You're welcome. You may go when you wish."

She smiled and nodded at them. They nodded back at her and then at Renee, which she returned, and then they left.

Carmen looked at the assembled group before her. Frederick smiled broadly as he looked her up and down. She could read his thoughts. She didn't wish to as *they* approached a leering invitation, but she guessed he just couldn't help it. Renee smiled as well, pleased and proud of what her medical team could do. Then Carmen looked at Inertia. He looked back at her impassively but directly, staring her in the eye and nothing else. He didn't glance at her face, arm, or bandaged body as everyone else did. She couldn't help but stare back. It was like being caught in the gaze of a cobra.

One of the most powerful beings in the galaxy blushed then, and knowing it only made her cheeks flush more. She also bit her lip, which trembled nervously. She was still smiling, forcing herself to at this point. He was always ignoring her, always not even looking at her, always annoyed at her mere existence. But now that she quite obviously had his full attention, she didn't know what to do with it. Really, he was the only person to never comment on her burn scars. She was strangely transfixed, however, as she awaited his verdict now that they were gone.

After a soft sigh, he turned to a passing nurse. Carmen's breath caught in her throat. "She looks terrible. When does the surgery start?" he asked. Then he looked at her and smirked.

Carmen grinned with thin, tightly pursed lips as she slowly shook her head. If Charon didn't kill him, *she* would. If anything was certain in the universe, it was that.

16

BENEATH THE MASK

Widget boiled alone in a quiet corner of the rooftop. The troopers ate in their armor, they slept in their armor, they whined and complained about any and everything under the sun in their armor… And should couldn't blame them—their armor was equipped with air conditioning systems. She, in mere street clothes, wasn't as fortunately outfitted. *All the technology in the galaxy and the same problems remain,* she thought as she vigorously fanned herself with a hand. It was about as effective as cooling a glass of iced tea in a lake of molten lava.

She sighed as she typed notes to herself for next time. Knowing her luck, the next time she went out in the field would be on a frozen wasteland. She had the equipment for both environments when she needed it. She'd pre-scouted the climate and terrain of Planet Eris before they'd even left. But it was hard enough to get all her kit together and ship it on the short notice they had, and…well, anyone could commit a few oversights. She wiped the sweat from her brow and noted that included egregious oversights, regrettably.

Widget stood and retrieved a water bottle from her storage container. She ran the cold glass along her face for a few seconds before she drank it. Then she sat back down and continued her work on her computer. A few of the troopers glanced at her, but she ignored them. She hadn't acted like a stranger at the start of this; she'd talked to them in as open a way as she could manage. Talking to people in person was a bit different than on computer screens. She told them her name was Lucca, though it wasn't, and she'd even been able to join in their jokes, which were about as sophisticated as a rock through a window. But then they'd started getting annoyingly *familiar*, and that was enough of that. She wasn't one of those losers who played pretend with a virtual AI boyfriend or girlfriend. No, she had no time for it because she truly had no time for it—in reality and in cyberspace. In fact, she took pride in her plain, utterly forgettable looks. It took a lot of effort. With that in mind, she glanced through her notes to when one of the troopers had first started giving her eyes. It read: *Trooper looking at me, possible romantic/sexual intention, or the troopers are cannibals. Figure out way to get uglier or not tasty ASAP.* She had underlined the last sentence several times. She wore a small grin as she read the entry. *Maybe I really am crazy*, she thought. *Or the only sane one left.*

Since she didn't know how to get uglier or not as tasty, at least not anytime soon, she kept her custom M-12 assault rifle beside her just in case. Her sniper rifle still sat, dialed in, on the ledge.

"Well, Billy, another day," Quinn said through her computer speaker. "Never told you this, but there are a few bets going around on you and your cockamamie algorithm. Most don't think Charon and his army of clones are going to show."

Widget rested her head against the ledge of the building. "How many people did you share this op with?"

There was a laugh from the other end of the line. "Trade secret. Anyway, what say you? Did I bet the wrong way?"

"Which way did you bet? Or is that a trade secret as well?" she asked while she wrote a note to look into how many trade secrets her source had and what they were.

"I bet on it working, of course. I added a few contributions to it myself, remember. Besides, we've worked together for a while, Billy. Had to bet on you—it's professional courtesy."

"Yes, I remember," she muttered, though those contributions were the equivalent of placing a cherry on top of the baked cake.

"So did I bet the right way? What do you think?"

"How much did you bet?" Widget asked.

"Small bet for fun. A thousand credits. It's really just a way to test a money laundering program I made on the side."

"Can I check it out? The program, I mean?"

"Not a chance," Quinn answered almost instantly.

Widget gave a small frown. "What happened to professional courtesy?"

"Billy, I've worked against you just as long as with you. You know how this game is played."

Widget rolled her eyes. True friends were a rare commodity in this business. "Yes, I know," she said after a groan. "Then put me down for a thousand against."

"You don't think they'll show?"

"No, that's not what I meant with the bet."

"What did you mean?"

She used both hands now to wipe her brow. "It's peace of mind tax. I'll feel better knowing that, even if I cooked out here for nothing, I'll still walk away with some of your money. I half hope Charon doesn't show up now." She heard heavy laughing from her source and once again thought she heard more than one voice. Perhaps, he, she, they, or it, made little slips like that to annoy her? No matter. "Anyway, he'll show. You should double up."

"Oh? What makes you so certain?"

"I wrote an algorithm just for this search. I was up all night doing it. I don't lose sleep on a whim," she said very seriously.

There was more laughter from her source, and Widget pursed her lips. What she said was the honest truth. Her Clairvoyant boss could retire to his Clairvoyant dreams each night, but despite how much they talked about how powerful they were, she had yet to meet a Clairvoyant who could code. Most were complete technical nincompoops.

Just then, one of the troopers moved quickly past her field of view and began talking excitedly with another. He waved to a different trooper, and the group moved to the console they had set up at the other end of the roof for their orbiting drone.

"And if they don't show, it's your fault anyway. You blabbing to everyone with your stupid bets," she went on, turning her attention back to the computer. Her words cut with an extra annoyed edge.

More troopers joined the group. Widget watched them out the corner of her eye.

"Not everyone, only a select group. And the bet was incredibly nonspecific. 'Billy has a crazy idea. Will it work?'" Widget was paying less and less attention to the conversation as she now watched the troopers fully. "On to something a bit more important, I heard of two Peacekeeper-class cruisers dispatched to intercept one of our own deep in sorten space," Quinn said. "I believe they just left. Anything to do with you and your little group?"

"You asking out of curiosity, or is there a buyer for my answer?"

"Maybe one, maybe the other, maybe both. You know how the game is played," he added after a pause.

"Yes, as I said, I know. But as to what you're talking about, I have no idea," she replied, which was no lie. Out on this rooftop, she was cut off from most of her information networks. She had no idea how Inertia and Edge's search was progressing.

"Maybe you do and maybe you don't. I also know how the game is played," Quinn began. "Heard the ships are *Jaeger* and *Mercury*. They are set to join a sorten task force to hunt down this renegade ship. Don't know its name yet, but if it is one of yours, you should tell them to abort. They are set to be massacred. Free tidbit there, professional courtesy."

"Don't care," she said quickly as she moved to shut off her computer. "Gotta go."

"Wait, Billy!"

"Hey, do you want to collect that bet or not?"

She didn't even pause for the reply. The computer was off in seconds, and she was walking toward the troopers. The big, strapping soldiers saw her approach and subtly closed ranks so she could get no closer. She tipped her head as she wondered what the big deal was.

One of them glanced at her. "Hold there," the only female trooper in the platoon said. "We're getting telemetry now."

"I'd like to see the telemetry," Widget responded.

The trooper shook her head. "No can do. It's raw and unformatted. We can't let a civilian, even you, see exactly what one of our drones are capable of detecting."

Widget rolled her eyes. "Amateurs," she muttered dismissively. She then said a couple soft commands and, a moment later, all the data from the troopers' drone was transferred to her eyeglasses. She frowned. "Gungnir," she said, keying the communicator built into her helmet.

"Yes, Widget, go ahead," the Clairvoyant answered.

She started walking away from the troopers and toward her sniper rifle. "Do you have any handlers or assets out of the facility today?" she asked. Though unlikely based on what she was reading, it was good to be sure. They'd had a few false alarms already.

"That's a negative."

"Then get ready. I'm reading approximately forty Clairvoyants heading your way," she said.

Every trooper looked at her in that instant. "How does she know that?" one of them asked. "*We* don't even know that yet."

"Yes, we are just starting to sense them," Gungnir replied, oblivious of the stir his subordinate had just caused on the roof. "How much time do we have?"

"Best guess: a matter of minutes," she answered.

Gungnir made no other reply and neither did she. Direct and to the point was just how Clairvoyants were. The leader of the Rogue Wolves embodied those traits more than most. Widget looked through the scope of her rifle at the facility several miles down range. Every person there had long been tagged by her IFF systems. There was a green silhouette around each one, and she could see them scurry like ants through her scope in the defense plan Gungnir trained them on. She could even see him directing people.

The assets proceeded to their underground dorms in an orderly fashion. Some handlers also came out onto the grounds. Both didn't happen all at once—a prompt response before Charon actually committed to the attack could spook him away, and the hope was to capture him alive for interrogation. It was quite the risk. She might needle her boss and even be annoyed by his presence from time to time, but Widget didn't question his courage. There he stood, out in the open with no body armor or any other form of protection and with only about a dozen handler volunteers to face Charon and his horde of Clairvoyant clones. Body armor could have given away the trap as well. It was comforting to know that another group of handlers and the facility's suppression teams were standing by.

That comfort melted away, however, when her glasses reported a second group of clones following the first. She and Gungnir hadn't expected to face this large a force. It dwarfed the attack on the New Earth facility, which was a much larger complex in probably the most heavily defended region of terran space. Widget leaned away from the rifle and took a deep breath. There was no point in telling him; the Clairvoyant would be able to fully sense what he was up against by now.

She turned her attention to the Phalanx Troopers. "I have better processors and filters than the government crap they saddle you with," she said, answering the question of how she knew information before they did. "Lighter too." *Except way more expensive*, she didn't add.

"The only way that would matter is if you could download the feed directly from the drone. But that's supposed to be impossible," a trooper remarked.

Widget ignored the comment, choosing instead to bully her way past the troopers and into the center of the group. Time was getting too short to play nice. There was also no point speaking if they couldn't see what she was talking about. The troopers' console processed updates of the strategic situation painfully slowly, but at least it was large enough for everyone to see what was going on.

In the center of the display was Davison City's Clairvoyant training facility. Arrayed around it was the actual city itself. She surveyed the businesses and residences that were a virtual stone's throw from the facility. The line of fire for her and the troopers would even have their shots pass over a school. She bit her lip. Nothing they had tried could convince the mayor to evacuate the area of all but essential personnel. The mayor had wanted to know *all* the details of what was going on, but neither Gungnir nor the UTE was too keen on telling her for security reasons, and neither had the legal authority to force an evacuation. It was all too late now. Red dots that represented their Clairvoyant opposition were moving rapidly toward the facility. Widget couldn't see anyone in the air, so she assumed they were moving on foot.

She spoke a couple soft commands to change the display on her glasses. Once her suspicions were confirmed, she walked toward the console and almost politely pushed the trooper out of the way.

"Hey, you can't—"

Widget glanced at the trooper and then at Lieutenant Dewitt as she worked.

"It's all right, she obviously has something to show us," Dewitt said.

"I do," she said softly. She pressed a few more buttons and then it was done. "You see here?" she continued as she pointed.

She slightly altered the color of the approaching Clairvoyants. All the troopers leaned in to get a better look. She wished the console had a holographic display. Some bean counter somewhere had probably cut the feature. *The bean counter gets a raise and a larger office, and they get stuck on a rooftop, fighting for their lives, with substandard junk.* She always preferred custom hardware when she could get it.

"Yeah, and?" one of the troopers asked.

"The bioelectric signature of these clones is the same as the clones that attacked New Earth," she said. "This group is different, and this group is also different," she continued, pointing at each in turn. The groups were still marked in red, but she rekeyed each with a clear delineation in the shades. The troopers said nothing, and she nodded, figuring they understood. She then spoke a few commands under her breath to download the data to her glasses. It would only take a few seconds to update her IFF. "Concentrate on the first group, the clones that are similar to the New Earth clones."

"Why?" the lieutenant asked.

"It's pretty safe to say the sortens have made improvements since then. Those clones are probably the weakest. They might be here as fodder or a control group," she wondered out loud. Dewitt shifted uneasily and she saw several other troopers do the same. She didn't know why they looked uncomfortable and didn't really care if they were. "Definitely avoid these Clairvoyants," she continued, tapping the screen for emphasis. "I don't know why or how, but they aren't clones. Each individual's bioelectric field is completely unique. They might be mercs or some new type of Clairvoyant Construct or whatever, but don't engage them if you can. No way of knowing what they're capable of." *And Charon is probably among them,* she didn't add.

She looked at all the troopers, and they stared right back at her. They looked like they wanted to say something, but their lips held still. Yes, she much preferred talking on her computer than in person. On a computer, at least, she could play a quick video game to pass the time during an awkward pause. She gave them a few more seconds, but when it was obvious that they wouldn't release the comment struggling to escape their mouths, she decided to continue.

"I notice you don't have any TC2s," she said. "You'll have to work hard to mask your thinking. Focus on anything but the shot you're taking. Clairvoyants can passively sense you taking aim, which can give them enough reaction time to stop your bullet mid-air. Maybe try singing a song in your head to distract yourself." She paused for a moment to make sure they understood. As before, they looked like they wanted to make some remark, but nothing was said. "It's important to let go of your weapon if a Clairvoyant telekinetically grabs it," she continued. "They'll lift you right off your feet and possibly off the building. And—"

"Lucca," Dewitt interrupted.

"Yes?"

"We know how to fight Clairvoyants," he said plainly.

"Yes, you read tactics manuals. But that's different than actually facing the real threat."

"With all due respect, Lucca, you might be ace with the technical stuff, you have equipment I wish we had, and you can produce beer on a whim...but we are professional soldiers. You're in our domain now."

He spoke evenly. There wasn't a trace of anger or frustration; he sounded like he was trying to be patient more than anything. And it was obvious that patience had a limit. It reminded her of how Gungnir sometimes spoke to her.

Widget blinked a few times and then shrugged. "Okay," she muttered.

She walked back to her secluded section of the roof while he began giving orders. She listened only enough to discern that they made tactical sense. She didn't know how much experience he had—she hadn't checked. She could barely remember his name, now that she thought about it. But Gungnir would have insisted to Space Force a bare minimum of competence in whoever they assigned, despite the low rank. So at least they had that.

The troopers were quickly forgotten as she retrieved a new piece of equipment from the storage container.

"What in the world is she doing now?" a trooper said to one of his buddies.

It wasn't exotic and it wasn't flashy. In her hands was a set of what could best be described as leg braces. She placed a leg on the ledge and strapped the dull grey frame to one limb and then the other.

"Widget, we are in position. How much time?" Gungnir asked.

She took a few seconds to analyze the situation. "They've stopped. Maybe consolidating their position before the attack," she answered.

"Could they suspect something?"

"Doubt it," she said with a quick shrug. If they did, there was nothing she or Gungnir could really do to counter.

"One last thing… I need you to take care of the troopers with you." She didn't give any response, but there were some scoffs from the troopers who heard the transmission. "Widget?" Gungnir asked after a few seconds of her not saying anything.

"You know they might be plotting to eat me…or worse," she said quickly.

"No games. I'm holding you personally responsible for

them," her boss barked. "Not everyone is going home after this, but no one gets lost carelessly."

"Yeah, yeah. I'll tuck them in and kiss them goodnight."

The troopers aimed a few curses her way at that. Some of the comments even made her choke back a laugh. Why was everyone always so touchy?

"If it comes to it, you'd better," Gungnir warned. "Essential comms only. I sense them approaching again."

Widget saw the same through her glasses and rushed to the container to pull one last piece. It was a simple harness, which she strapped tightly on her chest. She then hopped vertically, and the troopers could only watch with eyebrows raised when she unnaturally floated back to the ground. They were managing their own equipment and watched her over their shoulder, but she always had at least some of their attention.

She went to the sniper rifle once she was done and flicked off the safety. A moment later, she tapped her helmet with annoyed closed fist. She'd forgotten to turn on her personal shield. Never mind the troopers; she wanted to go home too. She switched on the device and confirmed a good system test just as the battle began at the facility.

"There they go," one of the troopers announced to no one in particular as he began aiming with his rifle.

Widget brought the sight of her sniper rifle to her eye as well. She surveyed the scene like a gardener searching for weeds as she looked for a target. It took a few seconds for the sound of the fracas to reach her. Gungnir and his team of handlers refrained from using heat beams for fear of damage and injury to the surrounding civilian population, but that reticence didn't extend to the clones. Shafts of light pulsed from the facility and, from this distance, it looked like an exquisite pyrotechnic show. The screams of death and terror that were surely happening were too far away to be heard other than as a dull din.

Back and forth she scanned. She heard the troopers take shots all around her. There was no question of their aim—it was hard to miss even at this range with the systems at their disposal—but nothing resulted from their fire. The air on the rooftop eventually filled with as many frustrated curses as gunshots.

"Can't nail them even on full auto!" one spat.

"Watch your fire. Don't want to hit a friendly," said another.

"How do we do that? They're moving too fast and close together to pick a target."

Widget could no longer hear them as she concentrated. She was almost in a trancelike state as she slowly brought the crosshairs of her weapon onto her first target. She occasionally wondered if this state of focus was in the same realm Clairvoyants existed in. It was horrifying if that was true; she'd rather not be related to them in even that small way.

There was no trigger on any of her weapons. They fired via thought command. Clairvoyants had a tremendously annoying habit of making guns inoperable by using telekinesis to make the trigger unable to be depressed. The troopers took more shots which again counted for nothing. The reports of their rifles were drowned out by the loud bang of Widget's sniper rifle when she fired. She actually fired three times—twice in rapid succession, and the third was slightly off rhythm.

The bullets she fired were only slightly faster than an M-12, and both were hypersonic. Both had also been manufactured right before they were fired, and both bullets were accelerated electromagnetically. Her round, however, was much heavier and more accurate. The trooper squad also had a sniper, but Widget's rifle was in an entirely different class. It could drop a starfighter if, by some miracle, she could get one in her sights. Her target telekinetically stopped the first two bullets. The third was a grazing hit that nevertheless ripped his chest open in a shower of blood and gore. The bullet, as designed, disintegrated on impact to prevent hitting anything behind her target.

She lined up the next clone less than a second later. Gungnir was fighting this one and getting the better of him, but it would help to speed things along. She watched them trade blows, waiting for the right distraction. She saw it coming and timed her shot accordingly. The clone rolled with Gungnir's overhand right; the clone knew the punch was coming as well. He didn't, however, know of the bullet that tore off the top of his head right when Gungnir connected. Her boss paused when it happened. Clairvoyants could feel surprise but were annoyed by it. He reentered the fray a second later, and Widget looked for another target.

The troopers gawked at her and then a couple smiled.

"Professional, huh? Shit, get some, Lucca!" one of them yelled.

Widget never heard him. She was too busy dropping another clone. This one was yet another victim of the inability to read her thoughts due to her helmet, bullets too fast to react to, and her erratic shooting cadence that threw the Clairvoyant off rhythm if she was reacted to. The troopers were quick to adopt the technique. Automatic fire and single shots were replaced by alternating double, triple, and in some cases quadruple shots that were fired in no discernable pattern. Some were fired quickly, or there were wide, oddly timed pauses between each. They even began singing or humming. No choral master would hire any of them, but they were starting to take a toll on the clones.

The battle wouldn't and couldn't be won by Widget and the platoon of troopers alone, but that was never the intention. The rain of bullets was a distraction, nothing more and nothing less, but they were a crucial tactical advantage against the monsters of the Dark, who were defined by their unremitting focus. Punches the clones would have otherwise slipped or blocked found a home against a jaw or midsection. Fluid, coordinated attacks by the clones became wary, hesitant, and not fully committed. There was a distinct turn in the tide when the reserve handlers and the suppression team emerged as Gungnir rallied his team.

"Has Charon taken the field? I don't see him," he reported.

Widget scanned quickly with her sniper scope. "I don't know," she said before doing a quick survey with the glasses. "All Clairvoyants are at the facility now. Charon might be there, or he might not; we were never able to catalogue his bioelectric field."

Gungnir didn't respond right away. She watched him battle a clone, though she wasn't quite sure if that was a fitting descriptor. The clone, or more accurately, Construct, was tagged by her IFF as a member of the group that had a unique bioelectric field. He looked unique though broadly related to his clone brothers. That and the fact that the sortens would never be able to get this many natural Clairvoyants to fight on their side convinced Widget that she was looking at a Construct. It was a bit disconcerting how quickly the sortens had been able to advance their research. It was more disconcerting that Gungnir was having noticeable trouble dispatching him.

The leader of the Rogue Wolves wasn't exceptionally powerful. He was nowhere near the equal of Inertia, Edge, or other Clairvoyants in that class. His fighting style, however, was practically faultless. She'd personally seen him defeat opponents that should have been more than a match for him. She could tell by his demeanor and subtle shift to a more defensive stance that he realized he shouldn't endeavor to overpower the Construct. The sorten experiment increased the pressure at that, continually pushing Gungnir, who held his own. Unseen by all, even Widget, was the set up in the dance—the built-in flaw that Gungnir was baiting the Construct to exploit. The Construct attempted to seize that advantage with a powerful strike. Gungnir gracefully side-stepped the attack and ended the contest with one punch that cratered his opponent's skull.

"Find him, Widget," he said before pausing to catch his breath. "This is all for nothing if we can't capture Charon."

She made no reply back, but she did mutter to herself. "Find him. Find him, he says. I'm looking at the world through a straw!" She scanned the facility as best she could several times. "All right, where's the big scary Clairvoyant?" she continued to mutter.

She didn't see him. She didn't even know what he looked like, just the garb he chose to attire himself with for effect. But she did note that there was something different about the battle that she couldn't place her finger on. It looked like there were fewer Clairvoyants than there should be.

"It's about to hit the fan! Incoming!" one of the troopers yelled.

Widget didn't curse under her breath, though she very much wished she had the time to do so. She leaned away from her rifle and saw approaching in the sky several black dots that would probably doom everyone on the rooftop.

She dropped the sniper rifle and then spoke a soft command. A new, rather large weapon shot from the storage container and into her waiting hands. She grunted when she took its full weight. The troopers raised their M-12 and unleashed everything they had at the onrushing Clairvoyants. They screamed curses and challenges, but both were as ineffective as their wild shots. Widget took aim with her new cannon and fired. The noise was decidedly undramatic, just a loud pop. Her target was a group of three clones charging head-on. After the pop, there was a loud echoing detonation and puff of smoke from the exploding canister she had fired. Thousands of small flechettes expanded out at supersonic speed in every direction. One of the clones fell; the other two were able to escape unharmed.

More clones appeared, swarming and buzzing about the roof before they stung with searing hot heat beams. Several troopers were hit on their armored panel, which was able to shrug off the punishment. Others weren't as lucky. Glancing hits to the arm or leg burned the limb away. One trooper lost the top of his head. Widget dived out of the way of a heat blast. The beam still hit her foot, but her personal shield held firm. She turned and fired. Pop... Boom! Two clones fell, their bodies skipping along the adjacent building.

She knew they wouldn't be able to keep the offensive going for long, though. She felt her flechette launcher pull away from her and she let it go. The weapon shot off into the distance, propelled by telekinesis. She saw it eventually fall. When she spoke a soft command, it flew back to her waiting hands. Pop.

A trooper felt a Clairvoyant pulling on his rifle. From boot camp, one thing was drilled into him: his rifle was his life. He gripped it tightly and joined it as it shot into the sky before he fell to his death.

"Swigert!" a trooper yelled in despair as he watched his comrade fall.

Another trooper was pulled from his feet, but he let go

before he was half a body length off the ground. A different trooper dropped his weapon immediately when it was taken and smoothly pulled out his sidearm to continue fighting. Yet another trooper's weapon flew from his hands, but this time it bowled over two other troopers who got in the way. They shook their heads as they came back to their feet.

"What the fuck is with this taking our weapons stuff?" a dismayed trooper yelled. "Why don't they just throw *us* off the roof? Isn't that easier?" A second later, he fell to the ground, his neck broken.

Two more troopers dropped like a pile of bricks. A third dropped as if a felled tree. Several troopers screamed defiantly at the swarming Clairvoyants as they stood helpless against the force assaulting them. Widget didn't waste her time screaming, but she did let go a small yelp when it was her turn. Her head began to twist, yet it stayed on her shoulders—a feat only possible by the inertial systems and microthrusters of her helmet. Her glasses traced the force back to the offending clone, and she took aim to fire. It was the worst time for her to be distracted.

"Frag out!" a trooper yelled as he pulled a grenade.

Widget's eyes shot to him. "No! No grenades!" she screamed while she held her hands out, but it was too late.

The grenade left his hand and then floated in place. The trooper stared at the impossibility, unable to think of anything else to do. The grenade exploded in his face a second later. Widget looked away sharply, her shield flashing in bright splotches as it resisted the fragments of the explosive. A trooper closer to the blast was knocked off his feet, saved by his armor and no worse for wear. The trooper who threw the grenade wasn't as lucky. His arm was gone to just past the elbow, a bloody stump all that was left of it. The breastplate of his armor was ripped open and on fire, and his cracked faceplate was a mess of bloody shards. The trooper fell to the ground, screaming. His entire body shook in shock, unable to process what had just happened. A few troopers came to his aid. Widget wished she could—she had medical gear in the container. But they couldn't lose another gun, least of all hers.

Dewitt gritted his teeth. "Fire! Fire!" he cried, trying to rally his platoon. "Hold them!" He dropped his rifle a moment later. His hands went to his helmet, and he struggled to take it off. "What? No!"

He gave an inhuman, ear-piercing scream. Widget and the troopers watched in horror as his helmet collapsed in on his head, crushing his skull. Blood rained from it as he frantically tried to remove the helmet, but it was no use. The troopers stood by impotently with mouth agape when he hit the ground. His legs and arms still twitched, but he was gone.

Widget's eyes were wide. The clones didn't fight like normal Clairvoyants. Clairvoyants fought with rules—they restrained themselves. If they killed you, they just killed you. There wasn't unmitigated brutality. She wasn't sure they'd survive this, certainly not all of them. But there was a difference between defeat and a massacre. Just then, she felt something lifting her. Not her rifle but her entire body. She couldn't help a small whimper when it happened.

"Lucca!" one of the troopers screamed as he watched the Rogue Wolf being flung into the sky and then dropped off the side of the building. He and every other trooper froze after that. The half dozen clones that were their attackers landed on the opposite end of the roof. The fear lasted only an instant. "Firing line!" he ordered.

The valiant Phalanx Troopers responded immediately. The front rank kneeled while the rank behind stood, both with armored panels at the ready and M-12s aimed. Then they were joined by another. This Clairvoyant wasn't very tall, and he was actually quite skinny, though his clothes implied mass that wasn't there. On his face was a metal mask polished to a mirror finish, but it reflected the world imperfectly. The troopers looked at their twisted and warped reflection and swallowed hard.

"They took out the lieutenant. They took out Lucca. They took out most of the fucking platoon!" a trooper said, his voice wavering.

"We're getting annihilated," another remarked.

"You lot are more trouble than you're worth," Charon said coldly.

He folded his arms and motioned toward the facility with his head, and the clones flew off to rejoin the battle against Gungnir and the handlers. None of the troopers were heartened by their number of foes reducing to just one. Their grip on their weapons tightened.

"Shall we conclude the farce?" he asked.

"Open fire!"

The troopers unloaded everything they had. The Clairvoyant merc stood still, however. Their effort appeared no more than an expected annoyance. Their bullets dropped to the ground after stopping in place just before they hit their mark. Charon raised his hand slowly. Right as he was about to incinerate everyone on the roof, something long and fast shot from Widget's storage container. The troopers and the Clairvoyant watched it fly toward a woman who was flying— well, falling—toward the rooftop.

"Everyone down!" Widget screamed. Then she fired her rocket launcher.

Charon bolted to the sky, and the missile detonated where he had been. Widget landed on the roof and tracked him. She fired again and then glanced at the troopers, knowing she would miss.

"Everyone, get off the roof! Fall back! I'll hold him off."

"Alone?" a trooper asked.

"Yes, alone!" Widget yelled. She dropped the rocket launcher; it was out of ammo. After saying a soft command, her M-12 flew to her waiting hands. "Get off now!"

The Rogue Wolf laid a long stream of fire then ran toward the ledge and jumped. She didn't fly, nor did she fall to the ground. No, she leaped through the air and landed on the next building as if she were a frog leaping from lily pad to lily pad. Charon zoomed after her.

Widget breathed hard as she ran. Sweat burned her vision and her mind was a fog. Another ledge was approaching. She picked her destination and jumped.

"I know where Charon is," she panted to Gungnir while she sailed through the air.

"Where?" he answered quickly.

"He's after me!"

"Where are you?"

Widget looked around frantically. There were no land-marks she could use to guide the one person available to her who might be able to stand up to her opposition. Gungnir didn't have a datalinked map like her glasses.

"I don't know," she finally said.

"Hold him off. I'll try to find you."

Widget muttered curses almost as fast as her heart was beating. She slid to a stop and fired several times at Charon. The Clairvoyant pirouetted out of the way in so fluid a manner that the movement seemed almost preordained. She saw him raise his hand, and she jumped laterally before the heat beam hit. It followed her, cutting a large piece out of building, brick and metal exploding as it crumbled behind her.

She hadn't jumped in any particular direction; she'd just

jumped. She fell to street level and groaned when she saw the streets and sidewalks were full of people. They were already screaming and running, but not quickly enough. Some didn't even run; they just stood still and looked at the scene in dazed confusion.

"Run!" she screamed at them. "Get out of here!"

Her words snapped them back to the reality that they weren't just watching what was going on but actually living in it. They bolted, stupidly and haphazardly, but they ran. Widget ran as well, to as open a space as she could. Perhaps there, at least, no one would get hurt or killed. As she ran, she shot at Charon. She wasn't really aiming, just giving the Clairvoyant something to think about. It stopped when her rifle clicked, out of ammo. She dropped to one knee, slapped a new powerpack home, and then aimed properly. Charon was supersonic. She knew because he was encased in a vapor cloud. She couldn't hit him at that speed, nor could he hit her. Pointing with a palm or finger was decidedly less accurate than a rifle with a sighting system.

She jumped, twisting and spinning in the air to keep him in sight, shooting the entire time. It amounted to nothing, but her opponent did dart and dance to avoid her fire just in case. Widget tumbled end over end when she landed on the roof. She'd been unable to really control her flight in the air and had landed badly.

"Widget, I can't find you. I can't be certain which Clairvoyant to sense either. There are Clairvoyants all over the city now. They are retreating," Gungnir reported.

She needed some sort of signal, but she had no clue what. She didn't have time to think. The only thing she could do was try to last a little bit longer and hope Gungnir could find her.

She jumped, but a heat beam exploding behind her made

her stumble. She wouldn't clear the next building. Widget torqued her body to hit with her back instead of her face. Charon was in her field of view and she fired, as did he. Her shot came close. Charon also missed only slightly. The heat beam obliterated the side of the building next to her head right when her back rebounded against it. She tumbled to the ground, landing on her side with a grunt.

It didn't hurt, her antigravity systems made sure of that, but it wasn't pleasant either. Legs made far better shock absorbers than bone and organs. She scrambled to her feet and jumped vertically as hard as she could. When she looked around, there were still no landmarks her increasingly panicked mind could discern. This city was flat, nondescript sameness. There was nothing at all she could use to direct Gungnir to her position.

She hung motionless in the air for one brief instant at the apogee. Charon was waiting for her. The only thing she could think to do was drop her gun and raise her arms to cover her face; she didn't have enough time to shoot him. Widget screamed as the heat beam enveloped her. Her eyes were closed, but the radiation was so bright that she was blinded for a moment anyway. She fell out of the line of fire and back to earth without a mark. Her glasses reported that wouldn't be the case the next time—the shield had had it. Her rifle flew back to her hands after a soft command, and she landed on a roof with a distinct thud.

She brought the rifle to her shoulder, and right when she was about to fire, it was telekinetically crushed to a wad of alloy and composites. She dropped the weapon and pulled her pistol. Charon landed in front of her. The pistol was semiautomatic, for all the difference it made. She was frantic as she unloaded the weapon in less than a second, any thought of irregular cadence gone. Charon telekinetically stopped every bullet other than her first, which missed over his right shoulder. Widget reloaded the weapon faster than any other time in her life and fired again. She began regaining her wits halfway through the second magazine.

But before she could change her firing cadence, jump away, or do anything, her arm was painfully contorted and, right when she fired, the muzzle of the pistol was brought to her head. She gritted her teeth through the pain, tipping her head at the last moment to avoid shooting herself. Her dislocated arm fell limp beside her, but she didn't think about it. Instead, Widget shrieked from a new pain. She fell over as her right foot was slowly crushed telekinetically. It began with her toes. The octave of her cry grew higher and higher as her foot was flattened inch by inch. The world spun. Pain even colored her vision with bright, nonsensical explosions of light timed to her pulse. Charon finally stopped mangling her body just after her ankle.

Widget was a quivering mass and continued screaming. Eventually she was coherent enough to speak. "Fucking turtle!" she spat. Not one neuron was used when she said it; the words just flew out of her mouth.

"Indeed, how fast can a limp hare leap?" Charon mused. She looked at him, her eyes wide in terror, as she cradled her mashed foot. "The brains of the operation," he said to himself, pointing at finger at her. "Where shall it be then? The mouth? Gungnir might even thank me for this."

Her eyebrow rose at that. It had given her an idea. She ripped off her helmet and conjured the clearest, most Widget-like thought she possibly could. She knew it had worked when Charon suddenly shuffled away a moment later. Gungnir landed between them in a tight guard.

The two Clairvoyants didn't go at it as she had assumed they would. They simply looked at each other and hesitated.

She had no idea why. It lasted no more than a second, though. Charon blasted into the sky, and Gungnir streaked after him.

Widget watched them go, her broken body still trembling. It was only a few blinks until they could no longer be seen. She reached into her pocket. She'd prepared for situations like this; the essentials were always right at hand. She pulled out a fortune cookie, read its message, and then began hysterically laughing.

"Well, I think I will," she muttered, her voice shaking with pain even though she still laughed. With that, she laid her head down and passed out.

The fortune had read: *Be sure to rest after a hard day.*

* * *

The dueling Clairvoyants existed in the sky of Davison City as fleeting streaks. Charon was desperate to get away and Gungnir was desperate to catch him, though not for the reason he originally intended. The Clairvoyant liked to think he'd planned for every eventuality, but the current situation regrettably escaped his imagination.

The puzzle piece, however, fit perfectly. He realized now it was the only piece that could. It was the reason Charon couldn't be found—the reason his bioelectric field couldn't be discerned from the attack on the facility on New Earth. It was the reason he didn't exist until now and why no one could be found who knew him to name him...*her*. It all fit. The only thing Gungnir didn't know was why.

She sped, arced, and twisted through the sky. Perhaps she hoped to tire him out. He'd certainly fought longer than she had today. His face was bruised, and he probably had a cracked rib. In Charon's case, the troopers and Widget had fought bravely, but they were little more than a distraction for a sufficiently powerful Clairvoyant. Whatever the intention, Gungnir had enough reserve to keep pace. He even pressed a bit closer to drive that point home. At that, Charon dropped dramatically from the sky. He fell as well. Down and down they went, gracefully dodging aerocars while passing through clouds. Eventually Charon landed on one of the many flat rooftops of the city. Gungnir landed opposite her. He couldn't bring himself to raise his guard, though, despite how prudent it would be. Not against Kali.

"The Rogue Wolf hesitates," Kali said, her tone mocking and harsh. "Never thought I'd see the day."

Gungnir couldn't hear the voice of his old friend through the synthesizer that made Charon's voice menacingly deep. He couldn't see her either, with the mask that completely covered her face and twisted his reflection to that of a monstrous ogre. But he could sense her. No Clairvoyant could hide their bioelectric field. It was as identifiable and unique as a fingerprint.

"Ahh, speechless. I never thought I'd see that either."

He swallowed hard. "Kali, I don't know why you're doing this, but it's over."

"Don't know?" she questioned, slowly shaking her head. "With your mind of metal, of course you don't know. I'm stopping the sortens. No one else would."

Gungnir had no read on her. He'd never really been able to, but he'd never needed to before now. He had thought he knew her well. They were interned together. He'd even named her. But he did not know this individual standing before him. It seemed as warped as the reflection of her mask.

"I don't see how helping the sortens is stopping them," he pointed out.

"Of course, you don't," Kali replied. "But let me educate you."

Just then, there were muffled screams from the street level and even the building upon which they stood. Eventually hundreds of people levitated all around them, suspended by the invisible will of Kali. The intention was clear. Gungnir's eyes narrowed, and he finally assumed a guard.

"Exactly what I expected," she said as she observed him, her voice barely audible over the screams of the people.

"Don't do this."

"*I* am not doing anything," she said. "What were you and the brain intending? To capture me? To kill me? Well, to do that, you're going to have to make a choice. What's it going to be, Gungnir? I know you. I'm your mission," she said derisively. "That's all that matters, isn't it? Who cares about the collateral?" she said, gesturing to her hostages. "Prove me right, prove me wrong…either way, I win," she added coldly.

"Kali, don—"

He was unable to finish his sentence. If she had just dropped them in place, he could have telekinetically caught them without too much trouble. But she didn't. Instead, they were flung up and out in every direction. Kali blasted off the roof. There was a loud clap of thunder when she broke the sound barrier an instant later.

Gungnir swore under his breath. This would take focus. The Clairvoyant closed his eyes as he took in everything and nothing at the same time. The screaming, panicked terror of the civilians overwhelmed everything else. He concentrated on those closest to the ground first, slowing them gently to land without even a scratch back on the street level. On and on he went, methodically scooping up each person as if they were weary children and he a caring mother. The last were the people who were thrown vertically; a few were on the verge of cardiac arrest. But their mad decent slowed, and they were placed back on the ground without even having to bend their legs.

When it was done, Gungnir opened his eyes and looked in the direction in which Kali had flown. He couldn't see her and he couldn't sense her; his friend was gone.

17

THE LOST SIGNAL

Carmen paced slowly around her quarters. The pacing wasn't born from impatience, though the technicians repeatedly reassured her that they would be done soon; there was just nothing else for her to do. Her quarters were filled with not one personal item that could be used to pass the time, not that it really mattered, as she'd never had the means to develop any interests or hobbies. She wanted to get fully dressed. More accurately, she wanted to get out of her civilian clothes and into her body armor. But that would have to wait until they left. She didn't mind the delay too much, though. Perhaps a part of her was even thankful for it.

The mission, the entire endeavor, was coming to a head. It would be over, one way or another, in the next few hours. Strangely, though, she didn't think about any of it. She didn't want to. It wasn't from fear or anxious determination, both of which she'd experienced rather extensively since the moment she set foot on this ship. No, it was just easier to not think about it—easier to concentrate on swimming instead of wondering just how far away the shore was. She paced, though, lapping her quarters at least a dozen times. Renee often paced when she was deep in thought. Maybe the habit had rubbed off on her. It was possible, but even if it had, Carmen could never match that woman's unwavering focus. Her mind just wasn't built that way. If anything, the Clairvoyant looked forward to the distraction from the deep thoughts she wasn't thinking.

The technicians were installing a holo-communicator in the middle of her quarters. They had apologized multiple times at how many items they had to move out of the way to set up the pad, but she didn't care. None of it was hers, other than her clothes. In any case, the ship had been under strict EMCON almost from the moment it had arrived in sorten space. She'd never thought she'd be able to communicate with anybody until after the mission was over. Renee, however, was planning to send a status update to Fleet Command before the attack. There were no additional contacts other than the freighter and the battleship as the *Griffin* spent the last day or so preparing the trap, so the captain had deemed it worth the risk to send and receive transmissions, if only briefly. She'd then offered Carmen the opportunity to phone anyone she wished during that small window. The Clairvoyant had to keep herself from floating to the ceiling at that, but she also knew, though she couldn't read Renee, that the gesture was yet another "thank you." It truly was a small gesture, but Carmen appreciated it immensely—doubly so when she was told she'd be able to make the call from the privacy of her quarters.

The techs bantered back and forth as she paced and watched. Their words were pointed but friendly, and while she could read them, she had no idea what they were talking about. Technical gibberish always flew over her head. The pad was glowing now, so she assumed they were almost done. Indeed, one of them produced a test image on the pad with his PDD. The image disappeared a few seconds later, and the two techs turned to her.

"You're all set, ma'am," one of them said. "We'll retrieve it later, after you're done."

"Thank you," Carmen replied with a nod. The tech nodded as well and then began to leave. She looked at the pad and then at him and realized there was a rather critical problem that had yet to be solved. "Excuse me, but…how does it work?" she asked sheepishly. "I'm a complete nincompoop with this kind of stuff."

"Oh, it's quite simple," he said, walking toward the pad while gesturing her closer. "You control it from here." Carmen nodded as she examined the device. "Where are you looking to call?"

"What planet?" she asked, unsure of the question. The tech nodded. "New Earth," she answered.

She didn't know anyone anywhere else. She wanted to talk to Phaethon, if only to see how he was doing, but assets didn't get phone calls. The only other person she wanted to speak with, and desperately so, was Kali.

"Good. It's a posicomm—"

"A posi wha…" she interrupted but stopped herself short. She had no idea what that was, but didn't care to learn now. She could sense the tech was about to explain further and held up a hand to stop him. "Just tell me what it does."

"It will connect to Space Force directly and then, from there, use relays to your contact person. The transmission should be instantaneous at a great colony like New Earth." Carmen nodded. "It is hooked into the ship's emission control systems. You can start the call now and it will connect instantly when free to transmit. It will also give a warning before the transmission has to be shut off."

"How much time will I have?"

"Figured you would know better than me. Above my grade," the tech said with a shrug. "Probably no more than a couple minutes, maybe less. We try to keep data transmissions short."

She nodded again. "Thank you for the help."

The tech gave her a thumbs-up and smiled. He turned to the other tech, and the two of them left the room. *Only a couple minutes, if that,* Carmen thought with a sneer. She'd hoped for more, but she had to remind herself that some time, if however short, was better than no time at all.

She was on her knees, entering the information to contact Kali, a few seconds later. She didn't know specifically when the ship would be breaking EMCON, but it would be soon. Once done, Carmen went to prepare for the coming battle.

She took off her clothes and replaced them with the undergarments she wore beneath her body armor. Then the armor telekinetically flew to the Clairvoyant's waiting hands. As she held it weakly, she could only stare at it, her mind flooded again by the deep thoughts she was not thinking. The armor fit her perfectly; it always had. It was like it wasn't even there when she wore it. Phaethon probably would have killed her if she hadn't had it on back at Solitary. Everyone always knew she was a Clairvoyant, but she was perceived differently in her Rogue Wolf attire, even here on the ship. It wasn't a contemptible difference. It was like how people looked at firefighters in their gear while they stood next to a burning building versus any other person at the scene. She'd long since given up wondering how she'd gotten into this situation, because she knew that, if she lived it again, she'd end up right in this spot. What this path would lead to, however, was still up in the air...and very much the subject of several sleepless nights. She was glad Inertia was talking to her again.

"Edge? Edge, is that you?" Kali asked.

Carmen smiled before she turned around. When she did, her previous handler was presented perfectly by the device: skinny as a rail, shorter than her, and with soft features but challenging eyes. It seemed exactly like Kali was in the room, other than the inability to sense the Clairvoyant. Carmen hadn't seen or spoken to her previous handler since she left New Earth. With Kali's image right before her, there was only one thing she could think to do. That, however, was unfortunately impossible.

"I really wish I could hug you," she remarked. It took all of her being to suppress the urge to grab the incorporeal holographic image before her.

"I think I would like that," Kali said softly with a wistful smile. Her eyes dropped. "I didn't think I'd miss it this much."

Carmen's face was dominated by her wide, toothy grin. The speakers even captured her previous handler's melodic voice exactly right. But the hint of melancholy in the song would not do.

"Oh…why not?" she muttered. Then she leaned forward and tried to hug the image anyway. Her arms grasped nothing but air and then her own chest. A moment later, she began laughing at her silly stupidity. She leaned back to see Kali quite badly covering a grin with her hand.

The woman took a deep breath after a few seconds. "Don't ever change, Edge."

"Really, I distinctly remember you saying that I make life hard for myself," Carmen pointed out.

"You do," Kali said back instantly. "It's just…" Her voice trailed off.

"Just what?" Carmen asked, curious.

"Just…never mind. I'm sorry I brought it up."

Carmen nodded, curious what she was talking about. Her previous handler still appeared sad about something, despite her antics. "How's Phaethon?" she asked, deciding to change the subject. The holographic image captured Kali's hesitation perfectly as well. "Did something happen to him?" she asked as soon as she saw it.

Kali raised a hand. "He's fine, as far as I know. Don't worry about him."

Carmen's eyebrows scrunched together. "As far as you know? Why wouldn't you know?"

"Edge, did you talk to Gungnir before you spoke to me?" Kali asked, her tone so serious that the question sounded more like an interrogation.

Now Carmen scrunched her nose along with her eyebrows. "Gungnir? Why would I talk to Gungnir?"

"So, you haven't talked to him?"

"No, of course not."

Even Inertia hadn't talked to him, as far as she knew. There was no reason to, as Gungnir couldn't help with their mission. And if he wanted to contact them, the only way he might be able to would be through Fleet Command.

Kali nodded a few times when she heard the answer. The Clairvoyant, however, didn't appear to be pleased by it. She appeared contemplative if anything, and there was a long hesitation. The Rogue Wolf remained still as seeing it made her heart lurch. Kali eventually opened her mouth to speak, but Carmen spoke first.

"What does Gungnir have to do with Phaethon? Is something going on? Was he kidnapped again?"

"No, he wasn't kidnapped."

"So, why—"

"Edge, a lot has happened since you left," Kali interrupted. "I'm not even on New Earth. That's why I said he's fine, for as far as I know."

"How was I able to contact you then?"

"I made sure that, if you tried to contact me, your call would be forwarded to my current location."

Carmen nodded. "Is everything okay? Did Charon attack again? Where are you?"

"Where are you?" Kali asked back. "And why are you in nothing but your underwear?"

Her cheeks turned bright red. She'd been so excited to see her handler that she forgot she was in the middle of dressing. Cheeks still red, Carmen went to where she had dropped her body armor and began putting it on. The Rogue Wolf only dimly perceived that Kali had dodged all of her questions.

"It's probably best that you don't know where I am and what I'm about to do," Carmen began. "Don't want to endanger you. People will know you're my handler—bad people. They might even know I contacted you. I hope you have a secure connection on your end." She doubted it, though. Then she took a deep breath as she considered the matter further. "Perhaps I shouldn't have contacted you?"

"I'm happy you did." Kali paused for a moment. "I'm very happy you did."

"I'm happy I did too…but I don't want anything to happen to you," Carmen said after a shrug. "I don't think I could live with myself if I caused something to happen to you."

The woman shook her head. The holoprojector captured everything perfectly—the sway of her hair, the stress in her forehead as she shut her eyes, and a couple of small tears that flew out of view. Carmen didn't see those.

"You don't understand. I'm glad to see you, but it's more than that."

Carmen's eyebrows were starting to scrunch together again. "Kali, you've been very strange this entire time. It's starting to make me nervous. What's going on? You keep alluding to something, but you don't talk about it. Why aren't you on New Earth?"

There was a long period of silence between the women. Carmen froze again as she braced for the possible answer, and Kali stood there, visibly distressed at the prospect of giving it. Her previous handler's entire body seemed to shrink as her spirit diminished.

"Edge, if you're going to hear it from someone, it's best that it's from me."

"Go on," Carmen coaxed.

"It wasn't supposed to be this way. You were never supposed to find out."

"What wasn't I supposed to find out? Why are you telling me this now? Why is it so important?" she asked softly.

"I never wanted to tell you, and it has to be now. Circumstances have forced my hand." Kali looked away before she spoke again. "Damn brain. How did she figure out where I'd go next?" she muttered with curled lips.

This was fast becoming surreal. "Kali?"

"Edge—"

"Five seconds until transmission cut off," the holo-communicator beeped.

"I don't have a lot of time," Carmen said quickly.

Kali nodded, took a deep breath, and swallowed hard. "Edge, I'm sorry, but I'm—"

"Transmission has ended."

Carmen stared at where the image of her previous handler had been, unable to comprehend what had just happened and what it meant. It was too bewildering to even make a wild guess. The extra frustrating part was that Kali only needed an additional second or so to complete her sentence.

The Clairvoyant closed her eyes, took a deep breath, and tried not to think about it. Her partner was waiting for her outside the room. He knew she was going to make a personal call and wouldn't enter without her prompting. She didn't invite him in; there was no need. She was dressed and prepared—as well as she was able, anyway—and went to the door. He looked her in the eye when she opened it. She looked back.

"You okay?" he asked casually.

It was easy to hear the concern in the question, but it was asked with the intention that she would give him a quick assessment of her obviously bothered state more than as an offer of comfort. She appreciated it nonetheless.

"I'm fine," Carmen muttered, sure nothing else needed to be said.

Her partner knew her well by now. She wasn't going to shatter into a pile of glass before him. Inertia nodded, and she was aware that he knew she was lying. She was also aware that he knew she didn't want to talk about whatever was on her mind and wouldn't press the issue. She appreciated *that* quite a bit more.

He glanced at her again. "You're forgetting something."

Carmen tipped her head. *I am?* she wondered. She looked in her quarters and immediately spotted what he was talking about.

"Right," she said. Her sword flew to her a second later, and she strapped it on her back.

Inertia slowly shook his head. "I wasn't talking about your weapon. This is a bit more important."

More important? She had no clue what was a bit more important. There was nothing else she could bring. She hesitated to ask. Inertia didn't think she was an idiot, but it wasn't prudent to put that to the test. In the end, she figured it was better to be proven a nincompoop in all things than to continue standing there, looking lost.

"What do—" she began.

Inertia interrupted her by pretending to run his fingers through long, flowing hair. Carmen smiled. *Important indeed.* She tied her hair into a ponytail and was finally ready. Her partner smiled back modestly before he nodded, which only served to make her smile bigger. Then the Rogue Wolves started down the corridor.

They walked in silence as they'd done dozens of times before, both focused in their own way. Inertia stared straight ahead, striding forward confidently. Carmen was beside him, not his shadow but a companion, a confidant, and a second opinion. She trusted that he would take care of all the details —even the silly ones she missed, like tying her hair. He trusted that she would be there to respond and do what was necessary when the time came. The dynamic was comforting for both Clairvoyants to the point that they weren't consciously aware it even existed. Glances, nods, and tips of the head communicated vastly more than even telepathy. They didn't look at each other as they walked. They didn't say a word. They could sense each other, but the other's consciousness was beyond their Clairvoyant abilities to read. Nevertheless, information passed back and forth between them at light speed.

They entered then exited an elevator. Carmen didn't know where the launch bay was from her quarters. It had never crossed her mind to care to know. But Inertia knew, and they arrived not too long after. She knew intellectually what to expect. When she was confronted with the reality of what this mission would entail, however, she was taken aback.

There were hundreds of people in the launch bay. The ship's crew directed the tightly controlled chaos with crisp professional precision. She didn't know how to even begin to understand everything going on, but in broad view, all that was happening looked as choreographed as an orchestra. Once again, she wondered why her Clairvoyant abilities impressed so many compared to what some were capable of with humbler potential.

Phalanx Troopers arranged themselves by platoon and then squad before they filed into waiting assault shuttles. The pilots checked and double checked the craft before climbing into the cockpits and running further checklists. The sleek Banshee starfighters of the Hustlers were lining up behind the catapults for launch. Each fighter was fully armed with missiles under their wings and on their wingtips.

She watched one fighter in particular as it was guided into position. She faced the back end of the Banshee and had a good view of the exhaust nozzles for the twin engines. She didn't know much about starships, but she was well aware that, even at minimal power levels, the fighter could incinerate everyone and everything in the bay—even her with her bioelectric field. The aft thrusters could also do the same. Both were off for the moment. The thrusters only came to life with quick, miniscule burns when needed to taxi.

The crew hooked the nose gear of the fighter to the catapult and signaled to each other when it was done. After that, they signaled to the pilot to unfold the wings, which was done promptly. The Clairvoyant could feel a slight rise in the anxiety of all involved, but it was overpowered by training and experience. In a way, it reminded her of the state that had literally been beaten into her by her time at the facility. Once his final checks were complete, the pilot signaled that he was ready. The crew did their final check before there was a seemingly long pause, and then the fighter was shot into space. A loud thunk of the catapult shuttle reaching the end of the launch track completed the action. It was followed soon after by the thunk of a second Banshee being launched. Carmen could see both fighters float away; then there was the bright light of them activating their thrusters at high power as they jetted into the distance in formation.

The Clairvoyants turned at the same time to look at a woman walking their way. "Sir, ma'am, if you would come with me, your shuttle is waiting for you," she said when she was close enough.

It wasn't too loud in the bay, with only a dull roar every now and then from a shuttle or fighter taxiing with their thrusters. Carmen could sense what the ships were capable of—could feel the power of their systems. It was amazing that they could be operated with that level of precision. The measured control of such overwhelming power made her think of a giant picking up a single speck of dirt.

The woman began walking. Inertia gestured for his partner to follow with his head, and the trio made their way across the bay. Throughout, they garnered attention from anyone who was able to spare a glance. She drew more of it than Inertia. There were multiple reasons, some of which she worked hard at blocking out, but the heavily armed troopers couldn't help but stare at the sword strapped on her back. The museum piece didn't belong in a bay filled with high powered rifles, starfighters, and bleeding edge electronics, let alone as an instrument for one of the most powerful beings in the galaxy. There were murmurs she didn't hear but knew were going on about her and the sword. No one was scared of her or even of Inertia. There was only curious anticipation of what she could do, some of it quite ridiculous.

The woman led them to a shuttle that had most of the

troopers loaded. "This one's for you. Good luck, sir, ma'am," she said, nodding at both of them.

Inertia nodded back. Carmen did not. She was too busy watching everything in the bay. Tucked in the corner and out of the way, she finally realized, was *The Lady*. It was the biggest ship here by quite a margin and sat quietly alone.

The last of the fighters were away, and now the shuttles began to line up. Her conversation with Kali was long forgotten, and her worry of facing Charon was now but one of many anxieties. There had been a time not all that long ago when the biggest issue in her life was holding down a job. If she had to live it all over again, she was certain she'd do it again. She couldn't help thinking one thing, though. *How did I get here?* Carmen pondered while her eyes glazed over.

She felt a hand on her shoulder. It shifted slightly from the shock of her bioelectric field. "Edge, it's time," Inertia said.

Carmen couldn't stop a small shudder when she heard that. Her partner didn't notice. She didn't consciously notice either, other than that her body made some sort of reaction for some reason. It was forgotten in moments when the Clairvoyants walked up the boarding ramp and into the shuttle. They were the last to do so, and the door closed behind them. Every trooper stared at them all at once. Many were younger than she was, hard as that was to believe. They sat strapped into rows of chairs and, in their armor, looked more like robots than people. But she could sense fear, worry, and excitement behind their cool facades.

A man walked toward them. He was wearing a Fleet Command utility uniform, and there were chevrons on his shoulders. Carmen was bad at understanding ranks and had no idea what they meant. The only thing that ever seemed to matter was more chevrons, bars, or whatever meant more responsibility…and he had a lot of chevrons.

"Equipment storage is in the back of the bird," he said, looking at her and pointing with a thumb. His voice was gruff and meant to be heard. The Clairvoyant couldn't say she was intimidated by it, but she certainly paid attention. "There's a seat back there for you as well. Strap in as best you can and someone will attend to you. Got to make sure you're good and tight. We always dial it down for the troopers. They like the kick in the pants."

"*Dial it down?*" she asked Inertia telepathically. There was no reason to be ignorant out loud.

"*Inertial inhibitor, I think,*" he answered.

The chevroned man continued. "Sir, we have a place for you right up front here. Be quick about it; we're number four."

Carmen would rather sit next to Inertia, but it was a minor slight. She nodded to her partner and then started walking. The young troopers watched the Clairvoyant as she walked, both when coming and going, which made her raise her chin. If she was to be the center of everyone's attention, she may as well make a good show of herself. She secured her weapon and then sat in her assigned seat, which was the only one available in this section.

"Hey, if—" the trooper next to her began to say.

Carmen half turned her head and glared at him. She already knew what he was going to say; there was no reason to actually hear it. Oh, the Clairvoyant definitely produced fear then. The trooper's face even turned white. To her, it felt like a flare had gone off right next to her, and the feeling was almost as annoying as the words she cautioned him from saying. Almost. He sheepishly closed his mouth, and his comrades had a good laugh at his expense. Carmen ignored it to work on her belts. Someone came, just as the man had said, to assist her.

"Good," he said when it was done. "First time in one of these cans?" She nodded. "All right, let me give you a safety brief. First—"

"I think I got it all," she interrupted before he could really get going. It only took a quick read.

The man blinked a few times before he chuckled lightly. "If only all these rock-heads were Clairvoyants," he remarked. Carmen smirked modestly. "Anyway, enjoy the ride. We'll be going soon."

She nodded, leaned her head back, and closed her eyes. Then she took a deep breath and opened them again. "Maybe I should be on a beach, drinking a piña colada," she said softly to herself. "Whatever a piña colada is," she added. Her thoughts turned to Inertia, who she couldn't see but could easily sense, and the idea slipped through her fingers like sand and was forgotten. It was hard to imagine herself here right now, but it was harder to imagine him doing this all alone.

"This is the captain speaking," came a voice through the intercom. Carmen recognized Renee's crisp voice instantly. All the troopers became quiet and listened. "We were tasked with another impossible mission, and yet again the impossible has proved to be just another day in the office."

There was a loud whoop from the troopers and crew of the shuttle at that. Carmen looked at them and couldn't help a tiny smile as she rolled her eyes. They were all so eager while she second-guessed herself. She considered the contrast while she felt the shuttle begin to move. In the end, she figured Mel was right. She could kill—she had killed—but she was no soldier or warrior, and frankly she didn't want to be.

Renee continued. "We have triumphed against incredible

odds with your resourcefulness and courage. Both will be needed in the coming battle. We have truly come to it. One ship, a cruiser, undermanned and under-armed against a fleet battleship… Pity they never stood a chance." The troopers and crew laughed. Carmen did no such thing, but she could feel their tension lift like a blanket. They were eager, yes, but still afraid.

"By the odds, it's futile. Our beam weapons can never penetrate their shields or crack their armor. Our missiles will be destroyed by defensive fire long before scoring a hit. And we won't fight at range—no, we will dispel their Ghost Field and engage in close. Eight seconds. We're going to slug it out for eight seconds. If it gets to nine…well, I'll see you all in a better place." She paused for a long moment, and everyone was silent. "But it won't get to nine," she said softly but confidently. "The sorten captain only has eight seconds to fight, but we've been preparing the field for more than a day. Eight seconds should be long enough for those bastards to say their prayers."

There was more laughter in the shuttle. Carmen felt the craft shudder almost imperceptibly as it was hooked up to the catapult. "We will take the freighter after the battleship is down, and that will be our greatest test. We don't know her defenses or what horrors are concealed aboard. She might be able to launch against our boarding teams a legion of Clairvoyants, some of whom might even be civilians compelled to fight by means we couldn't conjure in our darkest nightmares."

Carmen swallowed hard. She hadn't thought of that. Fighting sortens was one thing, as was fighting Clairvoyant clones or even Charon. She wasn't sure if she could muster the will to even defend herself against innocent research subjects.

"Against such a force, you must rely on your prudence as much as your courage," Renee said seriously. "Our mission is salvation, not annihilation."

All was quiet in the shuttle as the catapult pulled tight. Carmen closed her eyes and bore down, steeling herself for what was to come. It was far too late to turn back—too late to change her mind. She was in this all the way, for her sake, for Inertia's, for Phaethon, even for Kali in a way, and for everyone else who'd been hurt, injured, or broken by those who preyed upon the monsters of the Dark. A second later, the shuttle was accelerating down the cat and into space.

18

EIGHT SECONDS

Renee took a deep breath after she was done and tried to relax in her chair. She wasn't one for speeches and could probably count the number she'd made on one hand. She wanted to make it very clear, however, that, as far as she was concerned, this was a rescue mission. It wouldn't do at all to have the troopers blow away everything they saw.

"All shuttles away, ma'am," Leena reported. "Fighters transiting to IPs."

The captain nodded. "Any change in our quarry?"

"No change in course, speed, or operation of Master One and Two, ma'am," Hiroshi said.

Renee glanced at her chair display. The two sorten ships were Ghosted and traveling at roughly twenty-four hundred times the speed of light. Wherever they were going, they weren't trying to get there in a hurry. Relatively speaking, she could get out of the *Griffin* and run faster than that. She paused a moment. The first casualty of battle was always the plan. It had been killed right before her eyes more times than she could count. But for now, her often murdered friend was alive and kicking.

"Navpoint One as briefed, execute when ready," she ordered.

"Navpoint One, aye, ma'am. Charging Ghost Drive," Tawny responded.

The captain continued thinking as her crew worked. The biggest question she had was if, or more worryingly *when*, the plan failed, could they escape? She was quite sure the sortens wouldn't call for reinforcements, and the *Griffin* could outrun a battleship if needed, but she would have to drop shields to charge the Ghost Drive. The ship would be obliterated in an instant without shields. Frankly, it would be obliterated in only half an instant more with them.

Just then, her display beeped from a text message. It was Frederick. "We're playing poker tonight, high stakes. I should win big with you blowing all your luck on this damn fool attack."

Renee worked to keep still when she finished reading. There was no reason to give the political officer the satisfaction of seeing her reaction. Frederick chuckled lightly behind her anyway, and no one else on the bridge knew why. She rolled her eyes—he couldn't see that—but she also noted he was more confident than she was that there would still be a ship left to play poker on.

He was more confident, yes, but one point needed to be made clear. "I don't rely on luck. Game on!" she texted back.

Frederick laughed outright. Terry shot him a quick sneer before he turned to Renee. "I've been running some projections on our torpedo tracks," he said.

"And?" she asked.

"And we've had good launches. All torpedoes should arrive within half a second of each other."

She nodded. However, she knew Terry wouldn't bother

her with minutia so trivial for no reason. "I sense a 'but' coming, Commander."

He nodded as well. "But we didn't nail accuracy as well as we hoped, ma'am. The bubble will be larger than expected. Should still have enough saturation for a good strike, though."

Renee considered the matter. The bubble was the rough approximation of where their hundreds of salvos of torpedoes would all pass through when they converged on target. For the attack to work, the sorten battleship had to be within that bubble when the torpedoes arrived. It was simple math that required tremendous coordination to pull off. The torpedoes traveled at a set speed and, in space, would never slow down. They were fired from different distances and from multiple angles. It was textbook tactics against a fixed installation, and it was why no one used fixed defenses against starships. A ship could fire and wait a month for the projectile or energy to actually arrive on target while the target would have no means to retaliate. With the added dimension of time, a starship could have multiple shots arrive at the exact same moment, overwhelming almost any defense. The tactic had never been used against another starship as far as she was aware. It was too bad that, if this worked, no one would ever know about it. The entire mission was classified.

"A bigger bubble might be a help," she said with a shrug. "Less margin of error."

Terry stared at her seriously. It was easy to guess that his report hadn't been given to deliver good news. "Yes, that's true. The problem is that *we* will now also be in that bubble. At the range we plan to engage, at least."

Renee rolled her eyes and dropped her forehead into a weary palm. She sighed softly before she sat up straight and looked at her XO. "What about the freighter? Will it be in the bubble?"

"No, Captain," he said, shaking his head. "Not if she runs like we expect."

I see, she thought. She was about to ask another question but figured it was more expedient to examine the data herself on her own display. The relevant page was called up in moments, and she took a second or so to study it. She turned back to Terry.

"We should be only on the outer edge of the bubble—moderately survivable," she said casually. "Consider it an occupational hazard," Renee added after another shrug. Terry nodded, and she continued. "Worst case, we both die and our boarding teams take the freighter and then take it back to terran space. Pyrrhic victory."

He looked at her seriously again. "Captain, you have an awe-inspiring ability to find the positive."

She smiled.

"Dispelling Ghost Field…now," Tawny announced.

The smile dropped from Renee's face instantly, replaced by focus. She glanced at the clock. By the numbers, they had only a couple of minutes for final preparations.

"Give me a fix," she said.

Tawny had already checked. "At planned coordinates within system margin of error, ma'am," she said with some pride.

Renee nodded. The pride was well warranted if she was that precise. "Master One and Two?"

"No change in course, speed, or operation, Captain," Hiroshi said. "One minute and twenty-eight seconds to intercept."

Good, she thought. So far, the plan wasn't only alive but

also high-fiving everyone in the room and boasting that it had everything under control. "Arm all weapons. Overcharge permitted on first shot only," she ordered.

Terry leaned closer to her while Hiroshi repeated the order. "Alpha strike?"

"Yeah, energy only. Can't hurt." He nodded, and Renee went back to business. "Time dilation?"

"System ready. It's set to active, ma'am," Leena reported.

The captain nodded and calculated her next order in her head. "Change time threshold to one thousand percent two seconds before intercept and set active." Leena made the necessary changes and announced when it was done. Renee continued. "Eight-second audible countdown after intercept set to standard time."

"Aye, aye, ma'am," Leena said.

Renee looked at Tawny before she spoke again. As always, the helm officer couldn't see when she had her captain's attention, but she was remarkably good at guessing when that was. The woman turned her head slightly to listen before Renee spoke.

"Ms. Crowe, everything depends upon us keeping the battleship in the bubble. Do not evade unless ordered. I will be sending you coordinates directly for any maneuvers," the Wiz Kid said. She took a deep breath as her mind turned to the torpedoes that were now coming for them as well as the sortens. "When I give the order to break-fast, you are cleared emergency G, whatever current heading is. Also cleared emergency engine limits. We won't have time to maneuver, we will have to evade with pure acceleration."

Tawny nodded and took a deep breath. Her hand gripped the control yoke in front of her. "Aye, aye, ma'am."

"Terry, fight the ship, energy weapons only. I'm going to

be concentrating pretty hard on the bubble," Renee said softly.

Her XO gave a determined nod. "Yes, ma'am."

At that, they both looked at the clock and swallowed hard. There were only seconds left. The next order was not inevitable but would more than likely seal their fate. Renee hesitated before giving it, her mouth opening several times until she groaned and rolled her eyes at herself.

"Set disruption field, state charge," she said sharply.

"Disruption field on, ma'am," Hiroshi said. "Sixteen percent. Twenty-three percent."

Renee heard him continually report the power levels of the field that would dispel the sorten Ghost Fields when the ships arrived, but she paid little attention to it. Her eyes were fixed on her chair display as she ran the engagement in her head over and over again. She noticed after a few seconds that one of her hands shook, and she could feel the same anxiety in her bridge crew. The sense sapped her focus, but there was nothing she knew to do to block it out. She'd never been particularly fond of her newfound Clairvoyant senses, but she absolutely loathed them in moments like these. She grabbed her shaking hand and rubbed it. At least she could stop that.

"One hundred percent, ma'am. Field established."

Twelve seconds left, she noted as her eyes narrowed. She half turned to Terry and glanced at him. "Mr. Fletcher."

Her XO nodded. "By my command, target Master One's expected emergence point, full salvo, energy only. Fire when ready." His words were crisp and professional.

Hiroshi repeated the order and then turned to look at Renee and Terry. "Sir, latest track shows the emergence point will *not* be in the bubble."

"Understood," he replied evenly, but his voice was a forced calm.

He looked at Renee and she glanced back, her mind racing but unable to conjure any solution. Tawny gripped her yoke hard again. It was silent on the bridge of the *Griffin* after that. Renee stared at the clock. She was the only person who didn't immediately have something to do. Hiroshi reported firing his first salvo, and just then the seconds were painfully elongated as the time dilation system kicked in. She couldn't help a small gasp when the contact report finally came.

"Master One and Two Ghost Fields dispelled at planned emergence point. Master One is raising shields and charging weapons," Hiroshi said.

The *Griffin's* alpha strike arrived before he was able to finish his sentence. The beam weapons erupted on bare armor with enough destructive force to level mountains. Molten metal surrounding the impact site was ejected into space. Armor directly struck was instantly vaporized. The hits were near the bow of the monster battleship, and there were dozens and dozens of them. Unfortunately, the effect was no more than insect bites on an elephant. A moment later, the energy splayed off the ship's powerful shield as if it were water hitting glass.

"One," the automated countdown began.

"Minimal damage to target, sir," Hiroshi reported.

Terry's eyes moved rapidly back and forth as he called upon the experience of countless battles while he considered his next move. "Target the bridge, energy only. All available power to weapons. Fire went ready," he said.

"Sir, DEDs are already approaching their temperature limits," Leena reported.

The XO gave a small nod. "Noted," he responded. He

wanted the sortens to think they were desperate. In a way they were, but it was controlled desperation.

Hiroshi fired as he was ordered to, sheets of blinding bluish-white light streaming from the cruiser to reflect off or be absorbed by its adversary's shield to no effect. The effort was almost pitiful against an enemy so capable. It was obvious that the sortens were surprised by the initial attack; there was a long moment, elongated to several seconds by the time dilation system, where the battleship and the freighter did nothing. But that soon changed. A powerful blast from the sortens' thrusters worked to turn the war machine broadside-to-broadside against the cruiser, which was only a fraction of its size and several orders of magnitude less powerful.

"All energy weapons overheated, sir," Leena announced.

"Two."

"Weapon power to shields," Terry ordered.

"Weapons to shield. Aye, sir."

"Sir, the freighter is running," Hiroshi reported.

"Have they started charging their Ghost Drive?" Terry asked.

"Negative, sir. They are just making distance," Hiroshi replied. "The battleship is firing."

"Sounding collision!" Leena yelled before the actual order to do so was given.

"Three."

Renee heard the klaxon and saw the flashing lights. She knew what was coming—her chair display presented the information quite completely, including the projected casualty figures. She ignored both. The battleship was being a frustratingly uncooperative dance partner. It wasn't in the bubble, and there was nothing she could do to force it to maneuver how they needed. A key part of the now dead plan was to disrupt the battleship's Ghost Field inside the bubble, not to make it fly into the bubble. She texted commands to Tawny that the helm officer only had to confirm. The ship flew to the given coordinates automatically after that, but they were minute maneuvers that continually failed to produce a meaningful result.

"Four."

"All hands, brace for impact!" Terry yelled over the ship's intercom, even though the klaxon was still wildly sounding.

The strike was devastating, despite being only the battleship's secondary batteries. The mounts weren't much heavier than the weapons the *Griffin* carried; however, there were vastly more of them. The shield resisted the onslaught as best it could, but it failed three-quarters through the first volley. Hits blew large holes out of the armored shroud that protected the vitals of the ship. It was that and because the sortens had fired with the expectation that the cruiser would maneuver that saved the ship. Renee texted an order to Tawny to invert relative to the battleship, presenting fresh shields and armor to the sortens. She then put the *Griffin* on an arcing vector that would hopefully allow them to escape the full fury of a second broadside. The battleship wasn't in the bubble anyway, and there was no way to place it there.

"Five."

Renee pulled her hair as ideas flashed through her head, but there were none that could avail her. The only positive thus far was that it was obvious the battleship wasn't going out of its way to destroy them. Its chief concern was sheltering the freighter. *That's it!* she thought. Her hands began flying over her display an instant later.

"The freighter is powering her Ghost Drive," Hiroshi reported.

"Looks like we might not even get that pyrrhic victory,

Captain," Terry said. "Signal all fighters to begin their attack."

"No, belay that!" Renee yelled. Her bridge officers look at her curiously.

"Captain, we have to disable the freighter before it can escape," Terry remarked.

"Not yet…only need a moment," she said more to herself than to him.

"Six."

She sent the coordinates to Tawny just as another volley from the battleship arrived. The effect was much the same as before. The lights flickered as primary systems failed and backups came online. Tremors were felt throughout the ship as hits slammed home. The mangled starcruiser, however, continued on her new course that brought her bearing down on the sorten freighter from a circuitous vector. The battleship hadn't maneuvered much during the battle. It never needed to, only turning and twisting as needed to bring the majority of its weapons to bear. It responded to this new threat instantly, though, jetting to place itself between the *Griffin* and the freighter.

Renee watched the progress on her chair display. Sweat beaded on her brow, and her heart was fluttering. *Now!* she thought. "All stop, anchor current position!" she screamed. She could speak faster than she could type.

"All stop! All stop!" Terry yelled as well.

Tawny jumped from both officers yelling at her and then shouted, "All stop, aye!"

"Send the fighters!" Renee said to Leena.

"All flights clear to engage. I say again, clear to engage. Fire to disable," Leena said at a rush.

"Seven."

The small Banshee starfighters streaked in from multiple

vectors. They were unseen by the battleship, who had been running with only passive sensors operating. The great ship could down fighters, but that was not its primary role. The fleet battleship was meant to take out vessels that measured in the millions of tons or lay siege to entire worlds. Its large size was its greatest defense against such a threat. But that was not the case for the freighter, and the battleship was too far away to lend much aid against so small an adversary. The Banshees' antiship missiles punched gaping wounds in the engines and Ghost Field emitter of the thin-skinned and lightly built freighter. The missiles could have destroyed the freighter outright, but the warheads were set to low yield. Nevertheless, rivers of fire poured into space before snuffing out an instant later when the oxygen was burned through. The freighter began to list and tumble as its main engines failed.

"Attack complete, ma'am," Leena reported. "The freighter is disabled."

Renee ignored her. The battleship was training all weapons upon them—secondaries *and* primaries. It felt like there was a bullseye on her forehead, though with the amount of energy about to be thrown their way, all that would be left of her would be atoms. She, her officers, and crew had done all they could do. It was all down to timing now and her guesstimation that the *Griffin* had better sensors than the sortens.

"Torpedoes inbound!" Hiroshi yelled.

"Tawny, break-fast," Renee ordered calmly.

The *Griffin's* three main engines blazed to life and the ship blasted forward on her current heading. The sorten battleship wasn't as fortunate. Renee's counterpart on the bridge of the battleship was caught completely off guard. He gave frantic orders to use defensive fire to down the torpedoes, but there were too many. Orders to maneuver to safety were confused and ineffectual, as there was nowhere to turn. Subordinates yelled various schemes to possibly escape, their voices becoming increasingly shrill the more they became aware of their hopeless predicament. Until finally, and the crew of the *Griffin* would never know this, the captain of *Lasting Glory* came to his hind legs and gave his foolhardy, brave adversary a respectful nod.

"Eight."

The shields of the sorten battleship did their best to resist the pressure of hundreds of torpedoes slamming into it at just under the speed of light. Each hit produced a flash of light, and it was only a moment before the several-mile-long starship could no longer be seen underneath that barrier of energy. It would not last, though. The shield failed, and the remaining torpedoes went on to drill deep into the ship before their antimatter warheads exploded. The warheads weren't very large, but they were buried in the target before they detonated. Parts of the hull bowed outward from secondary explosions that rocked the ship. A laser turret was blown apart in spectacular fashion, sending shards of metal into space that were larger than the *Griffin* herself. On and on the torpedoes came, hundreds and hundreds, and all in the span of half a second. The few that missed would continue on forever until they hit a planet, moon, star, or some passerby maybe eons later, making their day a very bad one.

"Heavy damage to target," Hiroshi reported. "Several weapon emplacements knocked out, fire control systems down, shields down but recharging, bridge intact, main power holding."

Renee cursed under her breath. "They can still fight. Finish them off, Mr. Fletcher."

"Aye, aye, ma'am," he said. "Mr. Fujita, I want that ship out of my sky. By all means, fire at will!"

The entire remaining magazine of Mjolnir missiles launched from the spine of the *Griffin* and streaked toward *Lasting Glory* without a thought of mercy or accepting surrender. The weapons that were still operational on the battleship made a last-ditch effort to stave off the inevitable, but the ship's fate was sealed. The heavy missiles didn't daintily punch holes through the armor; they plowed into it and blew off large pieces in nova-like explosions until all that remained of the awe-inspiring war machine was slag and subatomic particles.

The tension on the bridge of the *Griffin* erupted in a mass cheer just as great as the exploding battleship. Renee didn't even smile though. She was so exhausted and relieved that she almost melted into her seat. She couldn't even throw her head back and bask in the moment, however, as Frederick actually left his station and shook her by her shoulders.

"I knew it! I knew it! We can do anything!" her friend yelled.

Even Terry playfully cuffed her arm. "Sure made a fool out of me," he said. "I can't believe that worked!"

She brushed off Frederick's hands and smiled modestly. Then she smoothed her hair, which his shaking had messed, back into place. Her political officer slapped her hard on the back while he continued chuckling. Renee gave him a quick glare. Never mind that he had hit her hard enough to actually hurt, but he had messed up her hair again. She wasn't actually angry, though. It was simple exuberance, and it made her smile that a man old enough to be her father couldn't help himself. She also sighed, knowing she was going to be up all night to ensure he didn't drink himself to death while celebrating. But that was for later.

"Not over yet," she said to Terry.

"Right," her XO responded. "Send to all shuttles: Begin

boarding action immediately," he ordered. Leena nodded and began transmitting instructions. The senior officers didn't pay any attention to her after that. "What do you think they'll find on that ship?"

Renee thought about it for a few seconds and then tipped her head. "I don't know. Probably nothing good."

19

PAST VS. FUTURE

It was utter loneliness, even though she had always been surrounded by people. None of them knew her or understood her, and it had always been so. Every Clairvoyant would say the same—that she was certain of. There was never any fixing it. There was no way around it. And acceptance of that unavoidable truth was tragically bitter. Perhaps there were worse lots to suffer. Maybe. Maybe not. Those thoughts ran through her mind over and over again while she waited. It had been her life for longer than she could remember. It was all she knew.

* * *

Carmen smiled as the troopers whooped and hollered around her. Inertia was right, as he usually was, that the inertial inhibitor had been turned down. She'd be aware of every instant the shuttle accelerated even if the system had been at full power. Now each and every movement or burble the shuttle made was transmitted strongly through the transport pod and felt physically as well as through her Clairvoyant senses. The force generated wasn't anywhere close to causing a blackout. It was, however, quite a wild ride. She was already sore. The troopers loved it, though. She could see how it could be fun, but if given the choice, she'd rather fly by telekinesis than be in this tin can. Honestly, it was the control more than anything. Here, she could only react to what happened. She wasn't the one to decide where to go, when, and how.

She was more concerned with how the *Griffin's* battle went, though. No one on the shuttle knew. She hadn't asked; a quick read was all she needed to know. Every now and then, it was convenient to be a Clairvoyant. Besides reading everyone, she'd counted to eight, for all the good that did. After factoring in all this time dilation stuff, *her* eight seconds may not actually have been eight seconds. She sighed, wondering how the troopers could enjoy this moment so completely when, for all they knew, their fellows, all the officers and crew of the *Griffin*, could be dead right now. In times like these, she saw more upsides than down with the mentality. She could sense worry from Inertia, though he'd probably never admit it if she asked. But she was quick to note that this was one of the rare instances she sensed anything from him. He must have been feeling the emotion quite strongly. It was his sister on the ship, after all.

Just then, another emotion of completely opposite polarity spiked Carmen's subconscious. "The battleship is down! The battleship is down! They took it out!" one of the pilots announced excitedly over the intercom.

A loud cheer reverberated from the transport pod and seemed to shake the entire shuttle. Carmen made no noise, but she did grin from ear to ear. She tried to see her partner then, but it was completely impossible with how she was strapped in. She felt, however, his worry melt away into relief and then slowly into the casual focus and quiet intensity that was his trademark. That and the realization that the ship was safe were comforting.

"We're cleared to approach," the pilot continued. "No anticipated defenses, but be prepared for heavy maneuvering."

"Now it's our turn to get some," a trooper announced.

Carmen didn't pay much attention to their eager boasting for the coming battle. She instead took a deep breath and swallowed hard. It was their turn indeed. In all these fleet battles, strategy planning sessions, and critical decisions, both she and Inertia hadn't been much more than bystanders. Inertia knew vastly more than she did about most things, but even he could offer little help when the contest was between million-ton starships. That would soon no longer be the case. Soon, she and her partner would be the most important pieces on the board.

A small but controlled anxiety built. It wasn't fear—not in any way whatsoever. She knew fear and had swum its waters many times, but she was nowhere near those murky depths now. This was more preparation for the task than concern for the task itself. About then, she realized she'd probably been in more fights by the time she was eight than every trooper in this shuttle combined had ever been in. That truth wasn't evident by just looking at her. The scars weren't external.

The Clairvoyant closed her eyes then. Her mind drifted to nowhere as she thought of nothing. She didn't have the focused professionalism of her Rogue Wolf colleagues, nor the soldierly duty of Mel. She was still a monster of the Dark, however, and knew how to comport herself, even though she hardly ever wished to. Nevertheless, troopers stared at the woman with closed eyes as she took deep breaths. They pointed thumbs at her and openly wondered how she'd handle the next few minutes. She was aware of what the few troopers who didn't talk about her were thinking, and it was little different. None of them were aware, though, because of their armor, that their hair was standing on end. She opened her eyes, took another deep breath, and continued ignoring them.

"Prepare contact," one of the pilots announced. A few seconds later, the shuttle shuddered. "Contact."

There was a metallic hum as small high-powered lasers began cutting into the hull of the freighter. On and on they went for several minutes. With all the work that had to be done with getting past the freighter's escort and even getting on the ship itself, she'd been foolish to think she and Inertia would be able to do any of it with *The Lady*.

A multi-chevroned trooper unstrapped himself and stood. "All right, we're taking the main hangar," he said to everyone in the pod. "It has to be secured to make sure none of these bastards can escape. Other platoons are taking engineering and other vital spaces. After the hangar, we are to flow to the bridge." He took a quick breath. "You heard the captain— sortens can have anything waiting for us. We have no pre-scans of the ship, so we'll be advised as we go. For the breach, first squad will—"

"No," Inertia interrupted sharply. The Rogue Wolf unbuckled himself and stood next to the trooper. "No," he repeated, though softer than before. "Edge and I will handle the breach. That's why we're here."

"You're our best asset. Let us break out and have you reinforce us. No sense in you getting taken out at the door."

Inertia shook his head. "We'll be fine." Then he looked

down the transport pod for his partner. "Edge," he called, extending his hand as if offering an invitation for a dance.

Carmen was out of her seat in seconds. Everyone watched as her weapon flew to her waiting hand. The curious eyes continued following the Clairvoyant as she gracefully made her way to the front of the pod while strapping the sword to her back. There were soft murmurs in the background, to which she made absolutely no reaction. She stopped next to Inertia and glanced at him. That was all he needed from her to know she was ready.

"Here, take these," the trooper said. In his hand were two earpieces with a small attached microphone. "It will let us keep track of you and give directions."

Carmen hesitated. "*Do I really need that?*" she asked Inertia telepathically. "*I'll be with you.*"

"*It's a good idea. We might get separated,*" he spoke back.

She nodded and placed the communicator on her ear. The trooper turned around after that and continued to organize the platoon. The Clairvoyants ignored them.

"All right, let's save some lives today," Inertia said. She knew he was referring to the troopers, but she was hoping to save more lives than that. It was entirely possible that there were other abducted Clairvoyants here. She nodded, and her partner continued. "No holding back," he advised. Carmen nodded again.

The lasers finished their work a moment later. The platoon was up and standing at their back, rifles at the ready. There was no murmuring from the troopers now. Instead, tingly nervous hands gripped their weapons, silent prayers were made, and all tensely waited for the signal to go. They watched the Clairvoyants at the front who had volunteered for the most dangerous task of a boarding: the breach. The Rogue

Wolves stood casually, obviously ready but not spring-loaded for action. By contrast, the troopers were hunched behind their heavily armored and shielded panels that floated in front of them and looked ready to explode out of the shuttle on a moment's notice.

The freighter's hull had been melted away on the other side of the hatch. The techniques and procedures for boarding a starship had been refined over hundreds of battles during the first Terran-Sorten War, yet never had two one-percenters led the fight. The special hatch for the transport pod, specifically designed for boarding operations, appeared to open ever so slowly, though it only really took a second or so. A sorten squad was ready and waiting. They hesitated. The two Clairvoyants stared at them, not angrily and not with murderous intent; they just stared how one would at a patch of mold.

The hangar was easily larger than its overcrowded equivalent on the *Griffin*. The ceiling was quite high. Several shuttles were in the process of being loaded with equipment and personnel, but the crew and scientists froze in place when they spotted the Clairvoyants. After several terrified shouts, they rapidly fled. The noise of them dropping equipment and running into each other in their panic filled the space with a sharp contrast to the silence that was shared between the terrans and the sorten security team.

The male Clairvoyant took a step out of the shuttle first, followed by the female, which made the squad stiffen and retreat slightly. It didn't matter who led. Either was more than they were expecting. The sortens knew what they were just by looking at them, and they also knew the laser rifles strapped to their own backs were completely useless against such an enemy. There was a strong temptation to join their fellows fleeing the hangar, but the sorten squad leader glanced at them and then the Clairvoyants and knew that wasn't an option. The enemy had to be held here for as long as he could manage, otherwise his colleagues were surely dead.

"Reinforcements! Reinforcements!" he shouted into his helmet communicator. "Clairvoyants in the main—" Inertia ended the transmission by snapping the sorten's neck.

The squad fired their laser rifles; there was nothing else they could think to do. Inertia made no reaction. Carmen let go an annoyed sigh. The energy bent wildly around the Clairvoyants to vaporize bits of hull around them and the deck at their feet. They didn't even need to squint from the bright beams. The two took a few more steps forward. The squad retreated to keep the same distance. It counted for nothing as scores of sortens fell in place with broken necks. The remaining only increased the intensity of their hopeless defense before they too fell. In seconds, all that remained of the security squad was a pile of dead sortens on the floor.

"Move! Move!" the leader of the Phalanx Trooper platoon yelled from inside the shuttle.

Carmen stood still. She looked at the far bulkhead, which divided this section of the freighter from the next, and knew —by means that she could never explain—that the troopers had come out too soon.

"No, no wait," she said quickly while she held up a hand to try to stop them, but it was already too late.

A new sorten squad bounded into the hangar just as the last word came out of her mouth. They were already aiming their weapons at her and the troopers behind her. The Clairvoyant reacted instantly, flying away like a shot inches above the deck to draw their fire. Bullets followed her path as she twisted and turned between shuttles, equipment, and the sortens who had yet to escape. She sensed more than heard the troopers shoot back. It made the sortens' attention turn from her to engage the more pressing threat. That would not do. Carmen spiraled high in the hangar, acting more on instinct and intention than conscious force of will. Then she landed in the middle of the sorten team, completely disrupting their formation. The Phalanx Troopers stopped shooting for fear of hitting her and could only watch. Her partner occupied a second team of reinforcements in much the same way.

A surprised sorten lunged at her with a knife. The attack was so uncoordinated that she didn't even waste her time to dodge or redirect the blade, which sailed harmlessly over her shoulder. A strong telekinetic thrust sent the offending sorten thudding into the ceiling. His body crashed back to the deck with a thud just as loud as when he'd hit the ceiling, but he was already dead. She leaned back to avoid a hail of bullets that impaled the sorten behind her. Two fell at her feet with broken necks. A third's head was cratered with a punch—he had been too petrified to even react before the blow landed. Two more raised weapons on her, but she telekinetically smashed the sortens together and flung their bodies to the side. After that, some of the squad broke and ran. Carmen watched them go and hesitated. Their desperation stuck to the roof of her mouth with a taste that made her grimace. They looked over their shoulder at her, and the enemies locked eyes for a long moment. She said something under her breath that no one would ever know, but just then came a loud explosion. A rocket from the remaining squad members who didn't rout detonated on her head.

Smoke billowed and rolled where the Clairvoyant had once stood. The sortens readied another rocket, while the troopers took aim on the squad to avenge her. That was until their rifles started to shake to the point that they wouldn't have been able to hit a mountainside from point-blank range. She was still there and still alive. The pleasant young woman who had quietly sat with them on the shuttle, however, could not be seen. Or, more disturbingly, she was completely in view. The Rogue Wolf turned her head sharply to look at the sorten who'd shot her. There was a swish of her ponytail when she turned, but beneath the smoke and falling debris that shrouded most of her body glowed a pair of bluish-white eyes that made her seem more demon than girl.

The sortens frantically took aim, and she only raised her hand on them. Her heat beam exploded on their position, detonating their cache of rockets and sending a fireball back at her. Fire washed over her like a wave, yet she emerged from the flames as if stepping out of the surf. The troopers watched with mouths agape.

The two Clairvoyants looked at one another. It was hard for anyone watching to know what was transmitted between them in those moments as they communicated with only glances and nods. Inertia neither said anything nor gave his partner any expression for anyone else to go off of, other than to look at the entrance for the hangar. However, Carmen glanced at it and nodded, and it was clear the message had been understood. After that, her attention turned to the troopers, who were beginning to approach. Her eyes narrowed upon them, causing the platoon to stop in place. That message was understood as well, even though nothing had been said.

She turned around to face the entrance and, a second later, placed her hands on her hips. Inertia folded his arms, and both Clairvoyants waited. The troopers waited too, but for what they didn't know. In time, three new individuals walked into the hangar. They didn't move quickly, but their steps were so deliberate that they seemed to thunder when they landed. Their eyes were locked on the Rogue Wolves as they moved toward them. Carmen and Inertia stared in turn.

The men were quite large, easily bigger than Inertia and absolutely dwarfing Carmen. They wore body armor of similar style to the Rogue Wolves but of obviously less sophistication. It didn't move and conform to their bodies like air while still appearing firm enough to stop a hypersonic bullet. Their faces, machine chiseled with dark features, strong chins, and sunken eyes, were broadly similar between them, like they were brothers. The men even moved the same as each other, fluid, direct, and menacing, commanding a swagger that told everyone they were the apex of apex predators. Even still, their movement lacked the dynamic grace and precision of Carmen and Inertia. The Rogue Wolves made a few steps away from each other to set their respective battlefields, and the contrast between the groups was starkly apparent. There was something else too. It wasn't an element of the Construct's person but their attire. Adorning their right hand was a ring that contained what could best be described as a prism-shaped jewel. The jewel glowed brighter and dimmer rhythmically as they walked.

One of them approached Inertia. The remaining two towered over Carmen. Why two for her instead of him could not be ascertained. Perhaps she appeared to be the weaker target and, thus, could be quickly taken out. Perhaps she was the greater, and extra help was needed to take her down. Whatever the case, she made no reaction to it other than to assume a guard as she looked up at her opponents, glancing slowly back and forth between them. Inertia made no reaction either, for her stead or even for himself. He didn't even take a guard. Throats were dry and pulses raced as the troopers watched, knowing the outcome of the next minute or so would probably determine whether they survived the day.

The Clairvoyant Constructs struck first. Well, sort of. As soon as a muscle twitched in Inertia's Construct, he was staggering from a short, quick punch that short-circuited the attack. Carmen, unfortunately, wasn't able to counter before the blow was even given. A jab darted toward her face. She leaned and then stepped back before blocking a jab from the other Construct. Back and forth she weaved and retreated as the men used their superior reach to keep her at the end of their fists.

The troopers watched nervously, but there was no frustration or worry that her face could tell. She wasn't in a tracelike state. Behind her blue eyes, her mind was obviously thinking, but whatever stratagem she deduced had yet to prove effective. Farther and farther back she was driven by jab after jab, with the occasional straight or kick to vary the retreat. It was machinelike violence meant to grind up and break the talented virtuoso with mechanical certainty. Carmen may have been more powerful than them, but the anatomical reality of several inches of reach was apparently quite the advantage in its own right.

Inertia's opponent was never able to build that momentum. He wasn't able to mount any sort of coordinated offense. Every attempt was met by a masterfully timed counter. They weren't hard hits, but they were enough to make the Construct hesitate to continue an attack and then eventually hesitate to attack at all. The tide shifted then, and Inertia began an offense of his own. Once again, they were not disabling blows, but the collective damage was starting to take its toll. Blood stained the deck in short order.

The Rogue Wolves were dressed the same and had the same goal, but their respective battles were as dissimilar as their personalities. Inertia battered his opponent from the off, dominating and controlling the opposition in the same unmerciful manner of a cat toying with a crippled mouse. Carmen, by contrast, hovered just on the edge of danger. It was like she lived in that realm and either didn't know how or was unwilling to move from that zip code. She was pressed but not overwhelmed, under threat but not threatened. Worse, victory was in sight but just out of reach. In brief instants, though, the frightening totality of her power could be seen. When the Constructs became just a touch too aggressive, when a punch grazed a little too close, or when they were about to have her in their grasp, then and only then would she produce a quick burst of focused violence that quickly brought the enemies to heel. It wasn't enough to end the contest, though. One Construct had a split brow. The other had several broken ribs, and after those pauses, they kept coming.

Inertia finished his Construct with a combination of blows that reduced him to a bag of tenderized meat still twitching on the floor. The Rogue Wolf then folded his arms and watched his partner. The troopers glanced rapidly at him and at Carmen, sure he was going to go leaping to her aid at any moment. He had to—she was fighting two at the same time. But there he stood. His foot even started tapping.

Carmen leaned away from a kick. The second Construct was on her instantly. His fist came swinging down, and all she could do was lift her arms to block the blow. On and on he hammered her. Her legs buckled first, and then the force of the punches dropped her to one knee. For whatever reason, she looked at Inertia then. He stared right back. She couldn't say for sure what he was thinking, but she had a pretty good guess. She sighed and rolled with a punch that skipped harmlessly along her cheek before she flew away backwards.

There was a change in the air then that only one person in the room perceived. Inertia knew his partner well enough by now to tell when she subtly shifted gear. It was her final judgement, a tipping of the scale toward a concrete decision. He didn't know if that aspect of her was conscious or subconscious. However the process worked, it was maintaining that balance in seemingly all things that drove her half-crazy and caused her hesitation. It was also, however, what made her what she was, good and bad. Thankfully, that meant he'd only have to wait a few more seconds.

The Constructs bolted after her, but a spinning kick, beautiful and fluid in its execution, brought the heel of her boot to the Construct's jaw, snapping it like a twig and sending him tumbling out of the way. It happened just in time for her to duck under and inside the second Construct's punch, to which she countered with an uppercut that splayed him out on his back with legs in the air. The natural Clairvoyant then jumped and landed sharply on his throat. Every trooper winced. A telekinetic thrust vaulted her through a backflip, avoiding an onrushing heat beam. More jabs were sent her way. First one, then two, and she caught the third in the palm of her hand. Her bright white beam of pure radiation vaporized his arm to the shoulder an instant later. She angled her palm toward his torso and cut him in half. His armor counted for nothing. When it was done, she looked down at his broken body. The Clairvoyant pursed her lips, thought something she would never tell anyone, and then tucked a wayward lock of hair behind an ear.

Inertia took a deep breath and rolled his eyes. "You just can't help yourself, can you?" he muttered. Carmen looked at him and shrugged. "All it does is make the fight last longer," he pointed out.

"These Constructs are stronger than the ones on Solitary," she said, not as a defense but to change the subject.

He walked closer to her and nodded. That was true, but

they weren't really on his mind just yet. He looked at her, and with everything going on, he was certain of one thing. Despite what he'd said, the absolute last thing he wanted was for her to stop being *her*. She briefly looked him in the eye and saw as much, which prompted a quick smile. But then her face went neutral as her mind went back to business.

"Seems like they've made a lot of advancements quickly," he said as he finally considered the Constructs. Carmen nodded as well.

Both Clairvoyants looked at the troopers just before one of them spoke. "Outstanding. Fucking outstanding. Never seen anything like it."

The troopers approached hesitantly but then quickened their pace when it was obvious Carmen wouldn't glare at them again. They looked at both her and Inertia with quiet shock that they weren't even breathing hard. The realization made several smile. A squad tended to the sorten crew and scientists who weren't able to escape the hangar. The rest of the platoon examined the dead Constructs.

"What's with the rings?" one of them asked no one in particular.

"I was wondering the same thing." Carmen said, though her comment was aimed at Inertia.

None of the rings glowed now. A trooper went to one of the Constructs and tried to take it off. He pulled mightily, but it couldn't be removed.

"I don't know. Definitely something new. No mention of it at Solitary," Inertia said.

"We didn't get all their records, though," she pointed out. Her partner nodded seriously.

"I'll get this son of a bitch," the trooper trying to pocket the ring muttered under his breath. Then he pulled a knife, set to cut the finger off. Carmen frowned as she looked away.

"Knock it off," the multi-chevroned trooper spat. "Keep your head in the fight. This isn't over yet."

"Quite right," a different trooper agreed. She hadn't seen this one before. He had bars instead of chevrons, and she'd spent enough time around officers to know he was a lieutenant. He keyed his communicator. "This is Delta One. Hangar secure, several scientists and ship's crew in custody," he announced. "En route to take the bridge. Request vectors, over."

"Understood, Delta One. Stand by for vectors, over."

Carmen was able to hear both sides of the conversation with her communicator, as well as several others that she wasn't personally part of. It was nice to know what was going on without having to ask.

"This is Charlie Two. Meeting heavy resistance at main engineering. Requesting reinforcements," came another voice on the communicator.

The Clairvoyants looked at each other and then at the troopers. "Is it Clairvoyant resistance?" Inertia asked them instead of keying the mike himself.

"Or Charon?" Carmen added. She most certainly hadn't forgotten that she might have to face him in all this.

"Charlie Two, Delta One, what is OPFOR? Is it Clairvoyants?"

There was a long delay before a response finally came. "That's a negative on Clairvoyants. I say again, no Clairvoyants." In the background of the transmission, gunfire and laser blasts could be heard, as well as people screaming and shouts of casualties. "Their security teams are dug in and holding firm. We have too many wounded to fall back from our position. Charlie Two, over."

The lieutenant looked at the Rogue Wolves but said nothing. Carmen knew every thought that went through his mind, and they were conflicted.

After a few more seconds of silence, she asked both him and Inertia, "Do we go there?" It made no difference to her.

The officer shook his head. "Can't. We have to take the bridge. That's the priority." He sounded like he was trying to convince himself more than her. "They may have already set a self-destruct or triggered a SCS," he continued.

"What's a SCS?" she asked. She hated all their acronyms.

"Starship counter-boarding system," he replied. "Usually, it's a ship-specific viral agent that only the ship's crew are inoculated against. If they have something like that, *we'll* be fine—our armor is sealed. But it would kill the two of you, and the ship would have to be fully decontaminated before it's taken. Not an easy process." He groaned before he continued. "We have to take the bridge. Too much to risk otherwise."

Inertia listened and nodded. "Edge and I can take the bridge. You can reinforce the team in engineering, and we can link up later."

"Makes sense to me," Carmen said.

The lieutenant considered the plan for a moment. "Me too. Charlie Two, Delta One, hang on. We're on our way. Out." He turned to his troopers. "Staff sergeant, move 'em out!"

The chevroned trooper screamed several obscenities that made the Clairvoyant, who had just vaporized a man in half, curl her upper lip, but the colorful expletives did their job. The troopers filed out of the hangar in seconds, leaving only two from the platoon to watch over the prisoners.

Carmen looked at them and then at Inertia. There was only one question on her mind. "How do we get to the bridge?"

"I don't know," he said with a shrug. "Hopefully we don't have to figure that out on our own." He keyed the communicator on his ear. "Hello."

"This is Dungeon Master. Please identify yourself, over," came a quick reply. The male voice sounded quite young, but there was strong confidence behind it.

"*Dungeon Master?*" Carmen questioned with a bemused grimace. Inertia looked at her and rolled his eyes while he shook his head. She grinned.

"This is Inertia. My partner and I have separated from Delta One. We need to get to the bridge."

The reply didn't come right away like before.

"*I think you're supposed to say 'over' when you're finished talking,*" she spoke. "*They might think you have more to say.*"

"*I am* not *doing that,*" he spoke back after rolling his eyes again, which made Carmen grin once more. "*It should be obvious that I don't have more to say.*"

"Inertia, stand by. Okay, you are now designated as Wolf One, and Edge is Wolf Two. When together, you're designated as Wolf Pack. I have your position, and scans have found the bridge. I will be directing you the entire way. Wolf Pack, leave the hangar by the exit to your front, turn right and continue seventy-five meters, then stand by for further instruction. Over."

"Understood," Inertia replied.

Carmen nodded, though she wasn't part of the conversation, and just then a small wrinkle came to mind. "We probably shouldn't fly. Dungeon Master might not be able to keep up."

"Good point," he agreed.

She nodded one more time, and he turned and started off at a slow run with her beside him. She could feel the battles throughout the ship, the death on both sides, and worked to tuck the sensation into the back of her mind and forget about it. But just then was a flash of something small and fleeting that would have escaped her notice if only it wasn't so out of place. Her eyebrows furrowed, and she slid to a stop right just before she would have left the hangar. *Can't be*, she thought. What she had sensed was no more present than a ghost, but like those ethereal apparitions, she'd be hard pressed to say she hadn't sensed that which could not be.

Inertia stopped a few steps after her. He turned slowly. His partner's eyes were welded to the deck, and she looked like she'd just been told her mother had died. It was hard to tell if she was even breathing.

"What's wrong?"

Carmen looked at him with a start and then shook her head quickly. "Nothing. We're wasting time."

She ran past him and into the corridor but was so distracted that she turned left instead of right. She caught the error almost instantly and turned back the correct way. Inertia watched for a second before he began running again. She could feel him analyzing her, but she didn't care—not with what...*who* she sensed on the ship. *She can't be here. How could the sortens have captured her? I just talked to her!*

Inertia continued watching her while they ran.

"I said I'm fine!" Carmen snapped.

He no longer looked at her, but she knew she still had his attention. She sighed softly. *I'm not fine, I'm just crazy*, she thought. Clairvoyant intuition was annoyingly nonspecific. She must have just interpreted what she was feeling incorrectly. The only reason she was even aware of what she sensed was because it was so intimately familiar. Perhaps she was just wrong. She *had* to be wrong; there was no other explanation. Instead of driving herself more insane by wondering about it, she focused on the immediate instead: their pitter-pattering footfalls on the deck, her steady breath, and any opposition they may encounter on the way.

"Wolf Pack, turn left at the next hatch and continue."

Inertia acknowledged the command, and they did exactly as they were told. It was helpful that the freighter didn't have the meandering, circuitous corridors of Solitary. She still woke up in cold sweats from nightmares about being stuck there. The freighter was massive, but at least it was logical.

"Elevator on your right, twenty meters. Go up two decks then continue straight."

Dungeon Master appeared to be giving them a rather direct route. They made very few turns. Carmen didn't know how SCS or a self-destruct system worked. Would there be a count-down? If there was, would she even be able to hear it? Perhaps the ship would blow up at any moment. Perhaps she'd fall over dead after her next step from some unseen pathogen. All were uncertainties that made her swallow hard. They entered the elevator, she pressed the button for the appropriate deck, and they waited…and waited. It was only seconds, but each ticked by with the harrowing anticipation that it could be their last.

"Wolf Pack, be advised possible opposition just outside the elevator on your exit deck, over."

Neither she nor Inertia gave a reply. They could sense them—more Clairvoyant Constructs. The elevator stopped, but the doors didn't open right away. Instead, they glowed bright red. Her eyes went wide when she realized what it was, and an instant later, a pair of heat beams melted through the doors and blasted into the elevator. Inertia leaned out of the way of them. Carmen ducked as they scythed toward her. She telekinetically bent the door out of the way and then shot out of the elevator like a spear.

The Constructs were just down the narrow corridor. She curled into a ball, then twisted and gyrated in midair to turn perpendicular to the corridor walls. Then she extended her arms and legs and rolled along the deck. One Construct jumped over the Clairvoyant log-rolling toward him. The other was knocked off his feet. Inertia was already on the Construct who'd avoided her. She popped back to her feet just as the enemy that had been knocked off of his floated back to them. A few lunging steps was all it took to stand within inches. Carmen wasn't a small woman, she was average height, but against a Construct whose arm was only slightly slimmer than her waist, it was an advantage she pressed in this tight corridor. Punches she didn't duck under sailed harmlessly over her shoulders. The Construct didn't have the room to kick. He pushed her to gain space, and she used that force, combined with her greater leverage from her smaller frame, to throw him before she got right back in his chest. And there she struck with short punches, elbows, and knees when the opportunities presented themselves. The Construct had finally had enough and grabbed her in an attempt to crush her to death. He shocked her. She shocked him back. The one-percenter's current overwhelmed her adversary to the point that, when he finally let go, he fell over dead and was actually smoking. Carmen gave an annoyed sigh. She always hated doing that.

Inertia finished his Construct a moment later and looked at her when it was done. After glancing at the ring on her Construct's finger, she nodded sharply, and they continued down the corridor.

"Wolf Pack, corridor ends with a T intersection. Turn left. That corridor ends with an entrance for a large room. Enter it. Possible opposition inside, over."

"*Is it more Clairvoyants?*" Carmen asked. She didn't sense any, but it was good to be sure.

She'd asked Inertia in the intention that her question would be relayed to Dungeon Master, but he said nothing. He gave her a quick glance. "*You have your own communicator,*" he pointed out.

"*You can ask for me,*" she said back. It was easier to speak with telepathy while running than with actual words.

"*I can,*" he said, letting the statement hang.

Carmen waited a few seconds for him to oblige her and then groaned when it didn't happen. "Dungeon Master, this is Wolf Pack. Are the opposition Clairvoyants…um, over?" she asked.

Inertia slowly shook his head. "*You can be such a dork sometimes.*" She turned her head then and stuck out her tongue at him. He laughed lightly. She smirked

"Wolf Pack, Dungeon Master, unknown. We track you with your communicators. Ship's personnel are tracked by scanning local life support load. It's crude and can't be that exact. Over."

Carmen nodded, even though there was no way for anyone other than Inertia to know. His eyes strayed to her, and she knew he was going to comment on the pointless gesture. Her eyes strayed to him as a challenge to make it. They met in the middle. Nothing was said, though everything was. They slid to a stop just outside the room.

"I don't sense any Clairvoyants," she said.

"Neither do I."

"A lot of sortens, though, dozens…and they're nervous," she continued.

Inertia nodded. "Ready?"

"Yeah."

He telekinetically opened the door and stepped through.

She was right behind him. They were told it was a big room, and she had expected something like the hangar, but it was anything but. The room was large; however, the ceiling wasn't very high. Instead, the space stretched for quite a way in a long rectangle and was crowded with rows of computers. The Clairvoyants moved slowly. There wasn't the space to run. They weren't greeted by a security team as they'd expected. No one was immediately visible, in fact. Scientists and technicians hid behind desks and did their best to not make a sound. They, more than anyone, knew the effort was useless. Indeed, Carmen's eyes fell on each and every one of their hiding places. She didn't strike, though. Neither did Inertia.

"What is this place?" she wondered out loud while her eyes slowly scanned the room.

"Looks like a lab."

"Yeah, but for what? We never saw anything like this on Solitary."

"No, but here's a clue," he said, gesturing across the room.

Her eyes followed where Inertia was pointing until they came to rest on several large glass containers. Each contained a Construct in various stages of development, from embryo to full grown man. She walked hesitantly toward them, her partner just behind her. Yes, they needed to get to the bridge. And that weird, impossibly familiar feeling was still with her. Inertia had to sense it by now, but he didn't say anything. In any case, she was well aware of their situation—well aware that they could blow up at any second—but she had to take a moment to look.

"Are they alive?" she asked rhetorically.

They probably weren't; she didn't sense anything from them. They creepily seemed alive, though, as they floated naked in a bath of who knew what. Their eyes were closed and they weren't breathing, but it seemed like they could burst out of their capsules at any moment and grab her, or worse. It made her wonder how exactly it was done. What was the spark that made them living, conscious beings? Did they have a soul, or were they just mass-produced weapons? They felt pain and they could suffer. In all this, Carmen had never truly felt sorry for the Constructs. She'd never sought to rescue them, and in a way she still didn't. But now, looking at the unanimated monsters, she was resolved to end this for not just the sake of her natural brethren.

"Edge, we can't dawdle."

"I know," she responded before taking a deep breath. "What about the scientists?" she asked. They were still hiding. "We aren't going to kill them, are we?"

He shook his head. "No, we leave them. Come on." Carmen was pleased to hear it and nodded.

There was only one exit, which was at the other end of the room, and they moved toward it with speed and the fluid grace that colored their kin. When they finally stepped out, she took a deep breath and licked her lips. There was no denying what she sensed now. *Kali can't be here*, she thought —hoped. It was impossible. It *had* to be impossible, yet it wasn't. Carmen wanted to break away from Inertia and search for her previous handler. She even opened her mouth to ask to do so. Dungeon Master, however, spoke first.

"Wolf Pack, continue down the corridor to your right four hundred meters, over."

Carmen gasped. By great luck, that was exactly the direction Kali was in. Her partner said nothing, yet his eyes narrowed and there was a tense readiness about him. She had no idea why—he didn't know who Kali was—but it was safe to assume there may be abducted Clairvoyants here. There was a distinct but subtle perceptual difference in the bioelectric fields of natural and Construct Clairvoyants. Kali was obviously not a Construct and thus not their enemy. But Inertia looked ready for a fight for some reason. Perhaps he sensed something else with or near Kali and assumed Carmen had sensed the same thing. She never got a chance to ask, as he glanced at her and then went flying down the corridor. She flew after him, guessing four hundred meters was long enough for Dungeon Master to keep up. They flew not nearly as fast as they could, but the pace was easily better than what their legs could ever manage.

Carmen's skin tingled. She didn't know why or how Kali was here. First her charge and now her handler... Why did the sortens insist on targeting her so personally? It was a question as good as any, but the only answer she could conceive was that she was prepared to tear this entire rats nest apart to get Kali back, whatever the cost. At no other time in her life had she been this ready to fight. Rage made her skin hot to the point that she felt like it would split open at any moment and drip fire instead of blood.

"Wolf Pack, you're approaching a hatch to your left rapidly. Enter it. Medium sized room. Continue through the far door opposite your entrance, over."

"No opposition?" Inertia asked, just containing a snarl.

I'm going bonkers, Carmen thought. She was so out of it that the only person she could sense was Kali. There could be an army in the room for all she knew, with her thoughts and feelings bouncing back and forth as if demons were playing ping pong with her soul.

"That's affirmative, Wolf Pack. Room reads clear."

The Clairvoyants landed next to the door. "Well, someone is in there," he said.

She breathed rapidly. Yes, there was. Kali was in there,

and whatever force was holding her was going to pay. Carmen's heart thudded so hard that she was sure it was buckling her legs instead of just her shaking knees. She looked at her partner with clenched teeth. He looked back and seemed just as ready as she was. He opened the door, and the two bolted into the room.

In contrast to the lab from earlier, it had a high ceiling with padded walls and an observation booth high on one of them. But there was no army, no horde of sorten security and their Construct minions. Directly in front of them stood one solitary soul. The person was rather slimly built, but his tattered clothes hung off his body, giving size that wasn't there. A Taper was strapped to his waist, and on his face was a mirror-like mask made of metal that distorted their reflections until they couldn't even be discerned. Carmen's mouth fell open as her entire body froze. Inertia looked at his petrified partner and didn't know what to think. He knew she didn't like fighting. He could even respect it in a way. But he had never imagined ever seeing her actually intimidated by an opponent.

He stepped forward, every muscle ready for battle. "Charon," he said. "I hoped Gungnir would have taken care of you after Solitary, but I'll deal with you myself. Edge, once we start fighting, continue to the bridge."

"No!" she said.

He glared at her. Now was not the time to argue. "I'll be fine. Everything depends on you taking the bridge."

"No," she said again. "It's…it's Kali."

"Kali?"

"My old handler." She swallowed hard. "So this was what you were trying to tell me," she said softly.

Kali leaned forward, ripped off her mask, and threw it to the side. Her eyes were wild with an emotion that couldn't be placed. There was anger, furious anger, but not at Carmen or Inertia. It churned and fed upon itself like a hurricane and seemed to exist for no more reason than that force of nature. It was destruction set in motion.

"Now you know," her previous handler said. Her voice was the same as it always was, melodic and smooth. The difference between what Carmen saw and heard, though, made her want to throw up.

Inertia looked back and forth between the two women. "Edge?" he questioned out of the side of his mouth.

"Oh, Inertia, don't let me keep you. That way to the bridge," Kali said, motioning with her head.

He was now even more confused. He looked at his partner. She took a deep breath and nodded for him to go. He nodded hesitantly himself and then began walking, looking at Kali when he went by. She appeared more ready to thank him than fight him.

"Make sure you don't spare any of them when you get there," she remarked.

He gave Carmen and Kali one last backward glance and then left the room. Carmen heard Dungeon Master give him more directions, but she turned off her communicator and threw it away. This mission, capturing the ship, everything— it no longer mattered now.

She took another deep breath. "What…is…this?"

"Edge…my dear Edge, I'm proud of you."

Carmen's breath caught in her throat. "Proud of me?"

"Of course. I knew I could count on you—"

"Count on me for what?"

Kali shook her head, and it was obvious that she wondered how her former charge could be so lost. "To stop the sortens. What else? I told you before that we deserve blood for blood for their crimes. There were sacrifices, but this war was a godsend. They may never recover now that their home worlds are annihilated.”

Carmen trembled in confusion. Her previous handler’s voice had gradually lost it melodic sweetness. She’d heard the tone before and had always hated it. Now the harsh venom echoed off the walls.

“The war is over. What does any of this have to do with me?”

“Nothing, not directly,” Kali said. “The sortens surrendered, yes, but I was able to learn about their research—what the rats were doing here and at Solitary.” She paused for a moment. When she spoke again, her voice was quiet. “I knew I wasn’t strong enough to stop them. I needed you. I saw how you acted at Crystal Palace. You didn’t want to fight Artemis, but you went. You didn’t kill her, *but you went*. I didn’t think you would at the time. I’ll never forget that day. That’s why I knew that, with the proper motivation, I could get you to commit to stopping the sortens. And here you are. Let’s end them once and for all.”

Carmen knew what the word *motivation* actually entailed. Her blood chilled to ice. “Why me? Why not go to Gungnir?”

Kali sneered, seemingly repulsed by even hearing the name. “Gungnir,” she uttered. “You don’t know him like I do, Edge. The robot has a mind of metal. It wouldn’t matter what I said; he would never bother unless there were credits in the deal.”

“He’s helping now,” she pointed out.

“And he’s getting paid for it. The UTE basically gave him a blank cheque.”

“You could have gone to the UTE.”

Kali groaned loudly. “And what would the bureaucrats have done? Start the war all over again on the word of a random Clairvoyant and her sources? If they really cared, they would have sent a fleet here instead of one ship commanded by a disgraced captain."

Carmen shook her head slowly. "I don't believe Gungnir is like that. He would have helped if you had asked."

"And you don't know what you're talking about," the woman shot back. "This is about justice, not profit margins. You've seen Solitary. They're nothing but violent, destructive monsters. It's what they are. It's what they do."

Carmen swallowed hard but still tasted bile. "People say the same thing about Clairvoyants."

"Yes, but perception isn't always reality," Kali said strongly. "We don't abduct and butcher the helpless for sadistic experiments, for one."

There was a pause. "You did."

Kali gave a start, as if she'd been slapped. "I had no choice," she said quickly. "I needed them to trust me so I could penetrate their organization. It was the only way..." But her voice trailed off as her former charge stared at her with wide, pleading eyes while she slowly shook her head. Kali sneered again. "Don't you judge me, Edge!" she spat. "Don't you dare judge me. Nothing, nothing you ever went through compares to what the sortens did to me."

There was so much Carmen wanted to say—so many words that wanted to gush out her mouth. It took almost all of her discipline to dam the river to a trickle. "How does becoming them bring justice against them?"

"I've done nothing of the kind," the woman said, batting her words away. "If I've done anything, I brought them to the brink. We're at the final push."

Former charge looked at former handler. Carmen's lips trembled and her tongue seemed paralyzed by the words she was hearing. It was too much to believe, but the horror was reality. And in the chaos, one thing swirled in her mind greater than all else. It needed to be said, though she didn't wish to bring herself to say it. She shook her head as she couldn't hold herself back anymore.

"You took my charge," she said softly. "They tortured him." Her voice was barely above a whisper. "They tortured him!" she shouted as anger bled into her voice. "And how many others?"

"And that's exactly why they need to be stopped!"

Carmen looked away as she shook her head again. A few seconds passed, and then there was a change in the air. She looked at Kali. "Not just them," she said as she drew her sword and assumed a guard.

Her former handler took an unknowing step back and gasped. "You've never picked a fight ever in your life and your first is with me? Don't you see what they're doing to us?"

"Not you but what you've become," Carmen replied evenly.

Kali's eyes narrowed. "I haven't *become* anything. And if I did, it was because they made me this way. What else can any of us do? We don't know anything else! That's the evil of the sorten beasts—they take everything about you, everything about your past, and destroy it to control your future."

Carmen exhaled sharply as her eyes fell. "And you agree with them," she said. "If they made you what you are, that doesn't mean you have to stay what you are."

The woman's lip curled. "Noble Edge," she mocked. "Let me tell you one thing. There are horrors of all kinds in this world. Yes, I helped them, but my actions were justified. What does it matter anyway? No one, not even you, can save everyone. You're stupidly foolish if you think you can."

"I've heard that before," Carmen said, "and no, I can't save everyone. But it certainly matters to the ones I do save."

No more words were said after that. Kali saw the seriousness in her eyes and sighed. Her hand went to her Taper and retrieved it, telekinetically spinning the weapon to its full length as the sound of loud cracks filled the fight room. Her former handler assumed a guard, and both women stood tense and unsure but ready. The Rogue Wolf gave an anguished yet determined cry and went on the attack.

20

BREAKING THROUGH

Inertia could sense the battle between Edge and Kali. He'd hoped they didn't have to fight, for his partner's sake more than anything. Now he tried not to think about it. He occupied his mind with his own predicament, and frankly the massive size of the freighter was fast becoming its own annoyance. The bridge was buried deep, near the center of the ship, which was why it couldn't be breached directly. It was just that, by his reckoning, he should have already been there.

"Wolf Pack, Dungeon Master. I only read one of you on planned route. Wolf Two, has your communicator's locator failed? Over."

"It hasn't failed; we were forced to separate. Ignore her for now."

"Wolf One, copy. Be advised, possible significant opposition along planned route, over."

"Is there a way around?" he asked.

"That's a negative, Wolf One. It appears the bridge is protected by defense in depth. You'll have to break through each layer directly."

Inertia found out exactly what that meant before he even

had time to ask. A heavy bulkhead shut before him. Even exerting every telekinetic joule he could muster didn't keep the corridor from sealing shut. Another bulkhead closed behind him, trapping him in place. A second later, there was the sound of moving air. *They're trying to suffocate me*, he realized. Already his lungs were beginning to burn as they gasped for air that was less and less there.

The most expedient option seemed best. He raised a palm to the bulkhead and fired. The blinding, hot shaft of radiation glowed bright purple. Such was its intensity that it was actually invisible for a least a foot from his palm. The strain of the effort showed on his face with pointed eyebrows and gritted teeth. Then, a few seconds later, he stopped, unable to sustain the effort. Inertia breathed hard. The room felt like it was spinning, and he was unsure if he was about to pass out from lack of oxygen or from the stress of the heat beam he'd just unleashed. Either way, he groaned when it was obvious that his plan didn't work. The bulkhead glowed an angry red, but it refused to buckle.

"Wolf One, reading life support failing in your corridor!" Dungeon Master reported.

Inertia was more aware of that than they were as his increasingly numb mind raced. He doubted that, even if Edge was with him, the two of them combined could break through. He hadn't thought about his death much. It had never been something worth worrying about. But it was quite ignoble to meet it by being suffocated in a corridor on a freighter. Just then, he considered another possibility. The bulkhead was rapidly cooling, but his beam had been hot enough to make the entire corridor glow, even though there had been no direct contact. And the rest of the corridor didn't seem as sturdy.

"Dungeon Master, what's beneath me?" he asked.

"It appears to be a commissary, over."

He needed hear no more. He pointed both palms at the deck before him and got to work. It was helpful that a Clairvoyant's heat beams were pure energy instead of fire, sparing the little oxygen that remained for him. He could already tell that he was having an effect. The deck first glowed brighter and then began giving way as it started to melt. Air rushed into the corridor from the room he'd just accessed, and he took big mouthfuls of it. Finally, when the hole was large enough, he jumped through and into the commissary room, just as Dungeon Master described.

Inertia leaned forward and rested a weary arm on a nearby table as he felt the odd tickle of reabsorbing the energy he'd just spent. It was an extremely inefficient process and not one he could consciously control, but it was enough to give him a second wind. He swallowed hard and stood up straight.

"Wolf One, stand by. Rerouting… Okay, to your right there is a door. Go through it and continue straight, over."

Inertia couldn't see the door. The room was well stocked with rows and rows of food and supplies. Nevertheless, he navigated as directly as a shark sensing blood and found the door in seconds. There was no one in the next corridor that he could see or sense, and he continued as he was instructed, running at an easy pace. He was still not fully recovered from the effort earlier and probably wouldn't be for some time. The fatigue an overtaxed Clairvoyant felt wasn't the pain and burning of exhausted muscles. It always started subtly and then came all at once, feeling more like a growing need to sleep than a physical or mental breakdown. His normally sharp, lucid perceptions took on an ethereal haze, and that told him rather clearly that he needed to be careful.

"Wolf One, we need to get you on the correct deck.

Multiple security barriers are in place, and the only way we can do that is to have you double back, over."

"I don't think we have the time," he said.

"Agreed. Are you able to force your way to the deck above, like what you did to get to this deck? Over."

Inertia stopped running and thought about it. He was breathing hard now, despite his pace, where before his breath came calm and steady. His fingers also tingled. "I don't know," he finally answered.

"Wolf One, wait one. We're going to see if we can hack the doors, over."

Inertia nodded and then groaned. Edge's ridiculousness was rubbing off on him. If he didn't watch himself, he'd start saying "So, what now?" all the time.

"Wolf One, we're having trouble interfacing with their system. Continue to stand by."

A few seconds later, there was a new voice on the communicator. He hadn't heard it before. "Attention all callsigns, tracking ability degraded due to interference from localized energy buildup in the freighter."

They set a self-destruct, Inertia thought with widening eyes. "Dungeon Master, we don't have the time to wait to hack the doors. I'll attempt to blow through. Can you still direct me?"

"Affirmative, Wolf One. Signal weak but stable. Unlikely to able to give you any more opposition reports, over."

"I don't need those anyway," the Clairvoyant said evenly. "Where do I go?"

"Continue down the corridor. Right turn at intersection then stop. I need to direct you precisely for deck breach, over."

Inertia began running hard, but not before another nod.

He was too focused this time, however, to chastise himself for it. "Time for self-destruct?" he asked.

"Wolf One, unknown. We've never seen an energy signature like this before, over."

The information, namely the lack of it, pushed him harder. The Rogue Wolf was just short of sprinting when he came to the intersection. He stopped, as he was told to do, but weary hands came to rest on tired knees as he panted. His throat felt like it had been dipped in acid.

After pausing a few seconds to catch his breath, he asked, "Where?"

"Wolf One, continue seven paces forward and one to the left, then stop, over."

Inertia did precisely as he was instructed. There was nothing visibly different about the section he stood under now versus any other corridor in the ship, but Dungeon Master had probably identified some weakness that he was unable to detect or some oversight in their security barriers.

"Wolf One, target directly above you. You may fire when ready, over."

He had assumed as much and was already preparing with several deep breaths to help muster the effort. Then he pointed both palms at the ceiling and unleashed. Small bits of melted slag dropped on his head and shoulders, but he barely noticed—a Clairvoyant couldn't be affected by their own energy. It was done in a few merciful seconds, and Inertia gasped when he was able to stop. Everything went black for a second, and then the world was blurry. He slapped the side of his head, shook it, and a moment later, his vision turned back to normal. He was quite sure, however, that he wouldn't be able to do that again.

He looked up, flew through the hole he'd made, and

entered a large bathroom. It was not a facility he'd ever be able to use due to the differences between terran and sorten anatomy, but as was fitting of sorten efficiency and procedural alacrity, the place was spotless. Renee would probably break down in tears of joy if the *Griffin's* bathrooms were ever as clean. There were no sortens here, but Inertia could sense several in the corridor outside.

He approached the door cautiously, unsure of whether the security team were able to track him, or if they even were a security team. It was a bit surprising how eager the sortens were to go down with the ship. He'd assumed the corridors would be filled with panicked hordes making for the escape pods. Perhaps they figured they had no other choice. They would only be captured by the *Griffin* for interrogation if they did escape. That didn't matter for this group in the here and now, though. He intended to take them quickly. There was no time for anything else. The increasing focus on the coming fight made the feelings of fatigue fall away, though he was wise enough to know it was still there. The Clairvoyant took a deep breath and then exploded out of the bathroom.

The sorten squad jumped before screaming in terror as he set upon them. They had been facing the wrong way, aiming to take him down if he broke through a security bulkhead. Dungeon Master, either knowingly or otherwise, had placed him at their rear.

A kick broke a sorten's leg and two quick punches brought him to the ground. It was a common misnomer for many that Clairvoyants always used their abilities in a fight. In reality, other than those senses and skills which operated subconsciously, they often didn't use their abilities, other than in quick spurts. Inertia made sure he didn't now; he wanted the reserve just in case. Sortens weren't a hardy people. He knifed through the squad and dropped them with blows powered by sheer muscle alone. The almost preordained dodges and subtle changes in positioning to keep the advantage happened as they always did, with no conscious thought.

The sortens' response, by contrast, was completely feckless. They fired where he'd used to be, they fired where he'd never be, and some of their fire even hit each other. This wasn't the drilled soldierly excellence of the sortens of Solitary. It seemed obvious after a time that they weren't well equipped at all to face someone like him. They had probably never thought it would happen. Eventually he killed the last sorten by telekinetically snapping his neck. He had been clawing at the bulkhead in a panicked attempt to get away.

Inertia turned coldly from the bloody business without thought as he keyed his communicator. He didn't notice that he was frowning when he did so. "Dungeon Master, Wolf One. Continue."

Dungeon Master responded with a series of directions, which caused him to run again. It was only a matter of time until he happened upon another squad. This one was more prepared than the previous had been, more than likely because he came upon them from a direction they expected. It didn't make much difference in their ultimate fate. They managed to actually land a shot on his shoulder, though. The bullet didn't penetrate, and he silently thanked Widget for always spec'ing great gear, but it told him he couldn't be too lax.

That was true in more than one way. The sortens couldn't beat Inertia, but they did slow him down. He could even sense from them that slowing him down was their ultimate objective. They bravely threw away their lives with eyes wide in terror right before the end, but behind the fear was a dogged determination bordering on desperation to keep him from reaching the bridge for even one extra second. The feeling served to drive him forward with renewed vigor. But then came a wave of Clairvoyant Constructs.

They leapt upon him in a furious attack that even managed to push the one-percenter back several paces. It helped that, in the narrow corridor, they weren't able to surround him, but they kept coming in a continual relay that gave no respite. Inertia gritted his teeth. He could see the sortens begin to rally and another wave of Constructs rushing to the battle behind them. He wished Edge was here to help him. It would have been prudent for the two of them to take out Charon...*Kali*, together and then move on. But his partner's conflict was personal, and he didn't want to get in the way of that, even if the ship blew up right now with everyone on it.

A Construct's punch grazed his chin, and Inertia knew now was the time to call upon the reserve he'd been saving. He dodged out of the way of the next, stepping forward as he did to trip his opponent and send him crashing to the deck. The Construct behind him wasn't prepared for Inertia's combination, which made him stagger. Another sidestep brought him to the next Construct in line. His adversaries behind him weren't dead—far from it—but they floundered while the momentum of those in front was disrupted. The natural Clairvoyant drove forward, landing quick, precise hits with each step. At last, those behind him bolted forward to join the fight, but he was ready. He used their force against them, throwing or redirecting them to run straight into the Constructs at his front. Their offensive was now completely broken, and he took the opportunity to kill as many as he could. The sorten security teams watched in horror as limbs were broken, necks were twisted, and blows crushed skulls and cratered midsections. It was all fluid, purposeful violence. Not one movement was wasted as Inertia flowed from attack to attack, deftness and poise making the scene look almost scripted, until at last only one Construct remained crawling on the deck. Inertia pointed his finger at him and blew the back of his head open with a heat beam.

The sortens opened fire in a panic. Horribly aimed bullets ricocheted down the corridor. Puffs of blood were kicked up by shots landed on the dead Constructs, yet the Clairvoyant stood firm, if barely. It was a relatively basic skill to telekinetically stop a bullet you knew was coming. It was also relatively basic to stop a magazines worth from an entire platoon; however, it was not effortless. His vision turned grey as the sortens rushed a reload. It was now or never. Inertia telekinetically sent the bullets he had stopped back at the sortens. The lean aliens with fur that implied mass that wasn't there were ripped apart. Several screamed, still alive despite their gruesome dismemberment. He hadn't aimed and had just sent the bullets as a cloud down the corridor. He mercifully finished the living sortens by telekinetically snapping their necks. Then he took a deep breath as all became quiet.

"Wolf One, Dungeon Master. Bridge to your first left. Energy readings still building, appear to be approaching critical. May not be able to continue communications. Good luck, over."

Inertia heard the transmission and flew, even though he was barely able to. He ripped through the door and was rewarded for his haste by immediately landing flat on his back. He'd been shot. It was hard to know if the bullet had penetrated; the right side of his body was numb. What he did know, however, was that he wasn't dead. He snapped back to his feet just in time for a foam cannon to trap his right arm and leg.

"Hold him! We only need a few more seconds!" a sorten shouted.

He guessed the bullet hadn't penetrated, as the sorten who'd shot him looked to defeat his body armor by aiming at his head. Inertia showed him his palm and burned him down in place. His beam then cut the sorten with the foam cannon in half. A particularly valiant sorten, who was unarmed, began beating the trapped Clairvoyant. He didn't wear the armor or uniform of the security teams, and Inertia guessed he was a member of the crew or a scientist. Either way, he landed the best hits Inertia had felt since he boarded the freighter. He shielded himself as best he could with his free hand. He could have melted the sorten where he stood— could have snapped his neck. But natural Clairvoyants preferred to fight on their opponent's level. The sorten had been fighting on his hind legs and was pummeling with both his graspers and forelimbs. Inertia grabbed a grasper, twisted it till it broke, which made the sorten give a pained yelp, and then pistoned the sorten hard in the abdomen with a punch. It wasn't as forceful as Inertia could manage, as his trapped arm and leg didn't allow him to generate the proper torque behind the blow, but the sorten staggered away anyway while clutching himself.

The others weren't as brave to try their luck, but there was another soul who wasn't a sorten—though the use of the term *soul* was a bit of a misnomer. Boom…boom…boom. The Eternal pounded toward him, its weight shaking the equipment on the bridge.

"Surrender, terran, and you will be spared!" it said. As was usual for the machines, its voice changed stress and tone as it spoke. Inertia worked to free himself from the foam as the Eternal approached. The colossal contraption could crush him with one blow. "We wish to keep you for study. Surrender!"

The Eternal was almost on him, but the unofficial rules Clairvoyants used to limit themselves only applied against *living* creatures. In an instant, the machine shook violently. Everyone in the room was sure that only scrap would be left when it was over, but the Eternal rose to its full height without even an oil leak.

"This unit has been hardened against that form of telekinetic attack. Now—"

Inertia tipped his head in acknowledgement as the machine spoke, and before it finished speaking, it was thrust into a wall…repeatedly. Over and over again, the Eternal was rammed against a wall, the ceiling, and the deck, as if a child's play toy. All the while, the Clairvoyant calmly freed himself. At last, the Eternal fell to the ground as a pile of parts.

The Clairvoyant ran toward the main console just as the sorten leader pulled a pistol. "Stay back!" he yelled as he fired.

Inertia was too focused on stopping the countdown to even bother killing him. The weapon was telekinetically crushed, as was the sorten's grasper that held it, which produced a piercing scream.

How do I stop it? Inertia thought as he scanned the console. There were actually two countdowns, and he had no idea what that meant, but one of them was about to expire. His eyes scanned back and forth and found nothing. He hit dials and switches that looked promising, but none availed him. The sorten leader, who was sitting next to him, started laughing.

"Stupid terran!" he spat.

Inertia looked at him with narrowing eyes, and his hands found the relevant screen he needed. The sorten had been so worried about him stopping the countdowns that it only took a cursory read to figure out how, exactly, to do just that. The sorten's eyes grew wide when he realized what had happened. There was only a moment to spare, and Inertia cursed softly when he hit a delay.

"Security code required to abort displacement," the computer told him.

He had no idea what that meant, but the sorten was more concerned about that than anything, so it had to be stopped. Inertia looked at him again, plucking the code from his mind as if a rose, and began inputting it. Sweat beaded on his forehead. Fractions of a second were all that were left. He typed in the code, but right when he pressed enter, the time expired. The sorten began laughing again.

Inertia froze when the time went to zero. There wasn't the flash and fire of the ship blowing up. He looked slowly around the room, and nothing had changed. He'd assumed that countdown was tied into some sort of self-destruct or defensive system, but he was still here. He didn't think about it as he got to work on the second countdown. This one had a bit more time remaining.

"Attention all callsigns, energy buildup from the freighter has dissipated. Interference abated. Full comms and scanning capability restored," he heard Dungeon Master say just before he stopped the second countdown.

The sorten leader glared at him but seemed otherwise pleased. "Know this, terran," he said. "You may take the freighter, but you will never find it. Archangel will continue, and there is nothing you can do to stop it!"

Inertia was tempted to kill him right then and there out of spite, but he knew he needed to keep him and as many sorten scientists alive as possible for interrogation. For one, the Clairvoyant had no idea what he was talking about, but whatever it was seemed quite important. What was more important to Inertia now, though, was his partner. Unfortunately, he had to stay on the bridge and babysit the sortens until the troopers could arrive and relieve him.

21

THE FINAL MERCY

If a passerby casually walked into combat lab 2337, their hair would stand on end. Well, it would be standing on end far down the corridor, but once inside, they might look like a hedgehog. It was likely they'd even vomit uncontrollably. All of that would probably happen, but what was certain was that they would be transfixed by what they saw. It was the most common side effect of a duel between two Clairvoyants. This contest, more than most, was marked by its distinct contrasts.

One stood almost completely still, resolute, firm, and unyielding. She hadn't taken a step since the start. So rooted was she in place that it would be a wonder if she could even be moved. Her defensive was impregnable, letting her give attack after ferocious attack by a weapon that could hardly be seen. The Taper whirred and spun around the Clairvoyant, cracking and slicing the air in mad chaos that stood quite apart from the person who wielded it. Her expression was oddly detached. She looked more observer than participant with a serene air that made her appear above it all, or at least trying to remain above it all. Indeed, there were clear instances in which she seemed to look down on her former charge, yet they were so slight that they graced Kali's soft features without even catching her notice.

Carmen had yet to stop moving. Her weapon didn't work effectively in the same hands-off telekinetic nature of a Taper. As always, she held the weapon almost weakly, her hands and arms operating more as a subtle guide to the telekinetic impulses that flowed through her subconsciously. Her sword was nearly as difficult to follow visually as the Taper, but unlike Kali, she flowed from step to step, stance to stance, retreating and advancing in a deadly dance that looked as beautiful in its grace and precision as exhausting in its execution. The young Clairvoyant's face was about as calm as a roaring ocean. Frustration was beginning to show through despite her best attempts to keep it at bay. Her eyes had the laser focus of a hawk about to dive on its prey; above them, however, her eyebrows folded in on themselves more and more, like a tightly wound spring. The same tension mounted on her jaw and lips, where a grimace became increasingly defined on her otherwise pleasant features with each thwarted attempt to reach her former handler.

Carmen parried a thrust from the Taper that would have impaled her throat if it connected. She began twisting her body out of the way of the counterstrike without even a conscious thought. She knew, however, even with her reflexes boosted by telekinesis, that the traditional defense of just not being there was too slow against a Taper. That reality was confirmed when the weapon bounced off the broad of her sword with a block as she failed to completely get of the way. She moved forward slightly, as it was the best she could manage, and parried the next strike with a flick of her wrists. She didn't have the time for anything else. An opening presented itself. She saw it. She might have even known it was coming, which may have been why she moved forward, but it passed too quickly to do anything with. Carmen's grimace got just that little bit bigger.

She glided back swiftly and used the reach of her weapon to threaten with the point. Kali's Taper batted away her feeble thrusts like they were insults. The woman even tipped her head slightly while rolling her eyes. Carmen could agree that the attacks weren't worth much; she'd never intended for that, but she did need the breather.

She'd never used a Taper before and had never had the inkling to try. She'd never fought against someone who used one either. It was quite apparent now why they were the preferred weapon of a telekinetic. The limitations and strengths of the weapon seemed tailor made for Clairvoyants. Carmen's sword, while made specifically for her, was ultimately an instrument meant for someone bigger and physically stronger than herself and was to be used in war instead of a one-on-one duel. It could be used for the purposes she intended, but that was not its inherent purpose. Kali's Taper fit comfortably on her belt but was longer than she was tall when fully extended. Its perfect symmetrical balance made it easy to wield telekinetically, and its reach wasn't limited by the length of Kali's arms, as she never touched it. Carmen didn't need to hold her sword either, but it would have been awkward if she didn't, as the precise movements she used to cut or thrust relied on the feedback from the weapon as well as pure technique.

She retreated a bit farther to the degree that no attack by either party would be viable. Carmen looked her former handler in the eye then, and Kali glared back at her former charge. The young Clairvoyant had spent her every day with the woman for six years, and they'd remained close after that. Not every pairing was so fortunate. Artemis had outright killed her handler, as had Phaethon to two of his. For her part, she still had nightmares about Janus to this day, but perhaps she'd been too quick to judge. Yes, he had practically tortured her. Yes, he had broken her. Yes, he'd tricked her into killing her dog, Mikayla. But in the end, he'd resigned instead of continuing the work. Kali, on the other hand, had been there right to the end. Carmen had been thankful for it at the time. But in retrospect, the person she thought had done less had in reality done quite a bit more, though in a more subtle and skillful manner.

As she looked in her previous handler's eyes, she felt a small amount of hope that the person she saw now was not the same person she was working to still remember fondly. That the genuine affection she'd felt over the years was not for someone who would so casually manipulate her to satisfy a vendetta. That somehow, someway, Kali had been transformed into the demonic monster bent on killing her. But behind the wrath, and sadly, even contained within the wrath itself, was the calm and serene but fiercely challenging gaze Carmen knew from all the way from when they'd first met.

Kali's eyes narrowed. She looked annoyed that her charge had backed off, but it was hard to tell the reason. Carmen could read her—she'd always been able to—but she rarely had and certainly didn't want to now. Just seeing Kali look at her like a fly she wanted to crush was heart stopping. It made Carmen's eyes grow wide while she worked to catch her breath. However, her former charge's shock only served to add a sneer to Kali's countenance. The Clairvoyant took a few quick steps forward, the first time she'd moved during the battle, and then she renewed the attack. Carmen wasn't ready for it.

The Taper came at her in a fast swipe she could only perceive, not see. She ducked it and the other end that came right after. She had to get so low that she fell flat on her butt, but both attacks missed. Then she rolled out of the way of a hit that cratered where she had been sitting. Kali darted after her, no longer remaining still. Her hands now guided the weapon as it spun and thrust. She still didn't touch it, but the effort added extra speed and violence behind every action.

Carmen parried a half dozen strikes along the length of her blade. She'd long been unable to actively think about anything she was doing, but now she felt just a step behind with everything she did. It was all a matter of inches as she deftly moved the point of her sword to keep herself safe. The sound of clanging and sliding metal filled the room. Hits from the Taper visibly bent her sword to the degree that it was a wonder it didn't outright snap. And her former handler kept coming. Carmen took a few risks to counterattack when she could; all were batted or swept away with ease. She closed the range in an attempt to grapple with their weapons instead of keeping the contest to strictly striking, but the effort came to nothing.

Kali telekinetically held the Taper in front of herself crossways. Carmen pushed against it, but an instant later, both it and she were flying toward the opposite wall. The impact knocked the wind out of her, and she guessed the technique wasn't breaking any of the unspoken rules that governed how Clairvoyants fought. Kali hadn't telekinetically pushed her former charge—she had pushed the Taper, which then pushed her former charge. Either way, Carmen was now pinned against the wall with the edge of her sword just off her throat. She grunted and strained against the force. Then, out of the corner of her eye, she saw Kali raise her palm. Carmen screamed as she pushed the Taper just far enough away from her to fall to the ground. Kali's heat beam exploded against the wall a second later, but the young Clairvoyant was already running toward her.

Kali pointed her palm again. Her former charge did the same. They fired at the same time, and the one-percenter's beam held firm as the other beam was redirected to melt the deck. Carmen missed anyway as Kali dodged out of the way of the attack. Carmen dodged as well with a forward roll a moment later when the Taper speared toward her from behind to return to its owner's grasp. Carmen gracefully came to her feet and immediately went into an attack. The Taper blocked the blow, and Carmen immediately continued with the opposite edge. That attack was batted away and, in an instant, the next edge was coming in a feint before attacking with the other edge. The effort was as balanced as a throwing knife, executed like a poem, and was unarguable, but it came to no effect. Kali went on the attack. She wouldn't be driven from her position. She couldn't be driven from her position. The Rogue Wolf held her place as well. The women's gazes were locked on each other while their weapons debated and danced around the issue. Then it happened. Carmen's sword came to her defense just a touch too late. She tried to turn with the attack to limit the damage. Nevertheless, she yelped as the tip of the Taper grazed her cheek and then sliced her ear in half.

She staggered away as her hand went to her face. When she pulled it away, it was covered in blood. The cut to her cheek and ear soon began to pour onto her shoulder and stain the ground. Kali didn't continue, but it wasn't out of concern for Carmen's wellbeing. She looked at her former charge with a fuming rage that Carmen had never seen before. She was no longer surprised, though. Perhaps she hadn't been surprised once during this whole ordeal, though she worked mightily to pretend she was. There was no hiding the truth. The anger, the wrath—Carmen had known it was there, as it had always been, just covered by a calm veneer that had always smoked ominously. It was undeniable, and now the molten lava was erupting in full flow.

"You're pathetic, Edge, you know that?" Kali screamed. "You're fucking pathetic! You want to fight me? You've never been able to commit to anything ever in your life. What would you be without me?" she continued, letting the question hang. "Still stuck on New Earth, your life a dead end, pining for that stupid, stupid boy you never even actually loved! You're nothing! You've always been nothing! All that potential wasted! Now, for once, finish what you started. Help me finish off the sortens, and then you can go back to your mediocre, meaningless existence!"

Carmen said nothing. Her bloody hand went back to her sword's hilt, and her eyes became even more dead-set as she took a deep breath. Kali sighed softly when she saw them but missed the ever so slight tell that signaled a change in their intention. There was probably only one person in Carmen's life who would have noticed.

"Fine, I'll just kill you. If that's what it takes for you to finally learn some sense, that's what it takes. Just know I gave you a choice."

"As did I," Carmen replied softly.

Kali sneered when she heard her and then spun the Taper above her head as she took a stance. Both women paused for a long second before they went into action. Kali struck first with an impossibly fast swing that her former charge easily parried out of the way. The second was coming when the woman felt her leg explode. Carmen had parried the attack and countered all in one motion, angling her blade to split Kali's femur. A second cut almost severed her arm at the shoulder, and a third movement impaled the Taper into the far wall, taking it out of the fight, as Kali dropped to the ground.

Carmen pointed the tip of her sword at her fallen

handler's chest. Kali looked at it and then at her charge as she breathed hard. She looked around the room for a second, as if lost, and then back at her Carmen. The face of her former charge reflected no expression other than that of indifferent judgement. She had never seen it before. She'd never seen her charge fight before. The look chilled the heat in her blood to ice. Carmen's conclusion was final, complete, and absolute. Kali had been wrong about her. Edge wasn't unable to commit to anything—it was exactly the opposite. Janus had named her perfectly.

She took a deep breath. There was only one thing she could think to say, and in all this it needed to be known. "I love you," Kali said.

Carmen licked her lips and bit something back. "I loved you too."

She then touched a finger to the edge of the blade, which was sympathetic to her bioelectric field. Kali gave a quick scream when Carmen blew a hole in her chest, and then there was nothing. Her work done, the Rogue Wolf silently walked out of the room, her sword telekinetically returning to its sheath as she went.

22

THE CAUSE OF DEATH

"Wolf Two, please respond. Wolf Two, please respond, over."

Inertia listened to the transmission and waited anxiously for Edge to say something, but the only answer was static. This wasn't the first such call, and unfortunately there was nothing he could do about it, other than to wait and work to keep his rising anxiety at bay. Thankfully, he could sense his relief approaching.

"Wolf One, Dungeon Master. Sorry we're unable to reach Wolf Two. She hasn't moved since the two of you separated, over."

Inertia took a deep breath and let it go through barred teeth as he considered the possibilities. Either she took off her communicator and forgot to put it back on, she was hurt and couldn't respond, or she was dead. He didn't think Kali could defeat her in a straight fight, but he remembered how his partner wouldn't even raise a hand to defend herself when she'd had to fight Phaethon. Anything was possible.

"Thank you, Dungeon Master," he said with a calm that didn't reflect his actual state of mind.

"Wolf One, be advised, organized resistance is breaking

throughout the ship. We should be able to send a squad to her last known position in about five mikes, over."

The door to the bridge opened just as Dungeon Master finished speaking and a group of troopers entered. They walked in with a crisp phalanx formation and rifles at the ready, but they broke ranks and lowered their weapons when they saw the Clairvoyant and the cowed bridge crew beside him.

"Dungeon Master, that won't be necessary. I'll find her myself."

"Wolf One, understood. Will you need vectors? Over."

Inertia considered it. "No, I think I'll be able to find my way back on my own."

"Wolf One acknowledged. Medical teams are available if necessary, out."

He hoped they wouldn't be. The troopers on the bridge were busy subduing and restraining the sorten crew. Their conduct was gentler than Inertia was expecting. The sortens would be quite sore after, but their terran hosts made no show of the act; there was just professional efficiency. A different team was already beginning to work on the computers. He didn't know how much data was left, maybe all or maybe none, but he didn't much care. His mind was already out of the room, but he needed to give a report before his body could join it. He walked toward the trooper in charge, who was a major, though he didn't know his name. The major saw Inertia coming and turned from his team.

"Will you be able to hold the bridge without me?"

The trooper nodded sharply. "No problem. There is still some sporadic fighting, but the ship is essentially ours."

Inertia nodded as well. "There were two countdowns when I entered the bridge. One completed, but I stopped the other. I do not know what the completed countdown was for. I didn't wish to read the crew to find out. But, by their reaction, it seemed the more important of the two. I fiddled with the computers a bit, couldn't find anything."

The major's lips became thin lines while his mind worked. "Sergeant Cortez," he called.

"Sir!" Cortez responded when he appeared at the major's side. The sergeant looked about Edge's age and had a wide-eyed boyish quality about him.

"The Rogue Wolf said there was some type of countdown that completed. It obviously wasn't a self-destruct or SCS, but the crew were pretty happy about it. Get on it."

"Yes, sir," Cortez said before he immediately began delegating the task to the rest of the squad.

The major glanced at him for a second and then back at Inertia. "He's the best trooper in the battalion with tech. We'll also interrogate the crew after they're processed. Whatever that countdown was, we'll figure it out." Inertia nodded respectfully and began walking out. "Good luck," the major called.

The Clairvoyant heard him but made no reaction as he maneuvered around the consoles and troopers in the bridge. He was in the corridor after only a few seconds. He keyed his communicator. "Edge...Edge, I'm on my way," he said. He didn't wait for a response. He didn't expect one. But just because he couldn't hear her didn't mean she couldn't hear him.

He moved at a fast walk, still fatigued from his fight to get to the bridge. More troopers were arriving. He would have made way for them, but he knew—as always by means that couldn't consciously be discerned—that they would make way for him. Indeed, the squad came, ran by on either side of him, and went. It didn't take him long to see that the security bulkheads had been deactivated. That was helpful in a way but also not. He was largely retracing his steps, and the landscape was quite different now that the corridors were completely open. More troopers were busy cataloguing and sorting the bodies of the security teams and Clairvoyant Constructs he'd killed. They talked quietly amongst themselves as they worked, barely noticing him as they paused and frowned at some of the more gruesome injuries he had inflicted. Blood was splattered throughout the corridor, which he had not noticed at the time.

Another team was trying to remove the ring on each Construct's finger. It didn't appear to be for trophies but for study, and their spat of cursing was an obvious tell that they weren't having an easy go of it. Inertia could hear on his communicator that other teams elsewhere on the ship were reporting the same trouble.

He entered the bathroom soon after. Everyone in the corridor raised an eyebrow at that, but it was the only route he knew. It was quite easy to find the hole he'd made, and he dropped to the lower deck without a second thought.

"Edge? Edge, do you hear me?" he asked, in the blind.

Perhaps there was some sort of interference that blocked the transmission? Perhaps, now that he was closer, she'd be able to respond? But there was nothing. Inertia sighed softly. It was a dumb idea anyway. Soon, though, he was occupied with remembering the many twists and turns he'd made to get to the bridge now that he had to follow the path backwards. He found the next hole without too much trouble and flew up to the next deck. The security bulkhead was still in place here. It seemed like his beam had deformed it enough that it could no longer be retracted, though it had not buckled. He was tempted to walk up to it and give it a swift kick for all the trouble it had caused, but that was also a dumb idea.

He wasn't too far now. The corridor was rather empty at

this point, which made sense, as there was nothing really here for anyone to bother with. That lab he and Edge had gone through earlier certainly had to be a hot spot. But completing the mission held no great importance for him now. He took a deep breath before he entered the fight room.

There was no one inside, save one departed soul. He approached Kali's body, looking down upon it. Her chest was blown apart from a heat beam, and there was a pool of blood from a cut leg and shoulder. All three injuries led Inertia to believe she'd been executed more than defeated. There was more blood a few steps away and a trail of it leading out of the room. It wasn't smeared in any way, suggesting that his partner had been able to walk away. Inertia's eyes grew serious as he studied it. The amount of blood made him guess it wasn't a superficial injury, but he could see her communicator lying on the ground. It just sat there, away from everything, and looked undamaged. She would have called for assistance, either from him or someone else, if she were truly hurt.

Where are you? he wondered. He could follow the blood as if she were a wounded animal, but he'd rather not. He didn't want to think about what may have happened to her. The Clairvoyant closed his eyes instead. He should be able to sense her if she was still alive and close enough. His mind shifted through the ether. The process was never as clear cut as a compass and a map. It was a feeling—one that drowned out the many others to produce a niggling urge. Inertia opened his eyes and started walking.

"Where are you?" he said out loud this time.

She wouldn't leave her communicator if she intended to join him on the bridge as planned. The device didn't look broken, but if it was, she would have stayed either in or near the room and waited for him to come back for her. There was one conclusion, however, that he hadn't considered yet. Maybe Edge didn't want to be found. Any other time, in any other situation, he'd respect that. But not now and not here. They were still aboard a freighter with unknown traps and defenses behind enemy lines.

He could sense her clearly now that he was closer, which was heartening. She had to know that he was coming, too. But there was no change in her demeanor that Inertia could tell. He could never read her anyway. This section was a bit more active. The crew from the *Griffin* were even helping the troopers now. Any other time, he would have been right with them, cataloguing everything on this ship—figuring out what merited immediate study, what could be disassembled for review later, and what was a complete dead end. But his thoughts stayed with his partner. The technicians and engineers worked without concern for either of them. It was known by all with a communicator that she was lost, and they would have reported seeing her if they had, which meant she had to be completely out of view, possibly even hiding somewhere.

Inertia entered the next corridor, and it almost felt like she was next to him. He scanned the surroundings until at last his eyes came to rest on a door. He entered without pause, and there was nothing—at least nothing that he could see. A soft, subdued whimpering couldn't help itself from being heard. He walked deeper into the room, which was a large personal office, and could now say it sounded like someone was crying. It wasn't hysterical weeping or mad tears, just sadness. He opened his mouth to call to her but then immediately thought against it. Inertia walked slowly forward, yet his head was half turned to look over his shoulder at the door as he considered walking back out. The idea left him instantly when moved around a console and saw her. Carmen looked up at him at the same time.

She sat on the ground with her arms wrapped around her knees. Her cheek was bloody and her left ear was a complete mess. Tears were streaming down her face, which she hastily moved to wipe away. The effort was for nothing, as her face was soon wet again from a fresh trickle. If anything, she seemed annoyed that she couldn't stop herself, especially with him looking at her. And look he did at his partner, his fellow Rogue Wolf, Edge. He knew that, if he exited the room, she'd join him in a minute or so, pretending that this had never happened. That might have even been for the best. Inertia made a decision then, one he knew couldn't be taken back.

He walked toward Edge, paused for a moment, and then sat next to her on her right side. She looked at him, but he stared straight ahead calmly, expectantly. She took the silent cue and rested her head on his shoulder while wrapping her hands around his arm, which was placed loosely on his knee. They sat like that for who knew how long. Carmen wiped the last tears from her eyes then took a deep breath and let it out slowly.

"Thank you," she said softly.

Inertia took a deep breath as well. "I don't know if I'm the best person to find comfort with. I'm fucked up," he said evenly, almost matter-of-factly, but somewhat mournfully.

"I don't think I'm much of a prize there, either," she said after a sigh.

"I'm sorry about your handler. I know the two of you were close."

"We were, but that wasn't why I was crying. Not completely," Carmen said. "I don't regret killing her," she continued. "I wish I didn't have to, but I don't regret it. It's just…there was nothing else I could do."

"I understand."

Carmen closed her eyes and took a deep breath. "You don't," she said. Her voice was calm, but her tone was heavy. "*There was nothing else I could do*," she repeated, her words increasingly desperate and hopeless. He glanced at her, and she knew she would have to find some way of explaining the hundreds of thoughts running through her mind that even she didn't fully grasp. "I used to think the facility had taken my life. Scared me more to think that it didn't. Now I don't even know. Everything I've ever done, before or since, has been because of Janus and Kali…even when I didn't realize it." She paused for a long moment. "The sortens made them, and they made me. I don't want to be like her, but I don't think I know how to *not* be like her."

"But you're not like her," Inertia replied.

"I'm not so sure. We aren't alike now, but how did she start? She thought she was doing the right thing. I think I'm doing the right thing. Part of me even agrees with her, if not her with methods. That can change, though. When I had to face Phaethon back at Solitary, I was completely comfortable with him killing me. When I had to face Kali, I knew I had to kill her to stop her, and I don't even regret it." Carmen closed her eyes and gritted her teeth through a shudder. She then took several deep breaths. "You know I don't like fighting, but did I ever tell you why?"

"No," her partner said.

She swallowed hard. "I don't like it because it *doesn't* bother me. What's driving me crazy right now is that I don't feel any guilt. I don't feel anything. After the shock of it wears off, it's just gone. Nothing. That's terrifying."

"You were crying when I entered the room," he pointed out.

"Yes, and do you know why? I was crying because I couldn't help imagining how horrible it would be to live as she did. Her…quest," she said, searching for the right word, "was all she had. What's worse is that it's all *I* have. I really *don't* have anything else. What is my life right now, other than this?" She wiped a fresh tear from her eye. "It's pathetic. It really is pathetic." She paused and said softly, "I'm pathetic."

Inertia was quiet for several seconds while he felt his partner tremble on his shoulder. He sighed softly before he spoke. "Edge, I don't even know your real name, but I've never thought you were pathetic."

She smiled weakly. She'd tried to make the movement small, but her cut cheek still made it hurt. "It's Carmen," she said.

"Carmen. Well, my name's Will. It's nice to finally meet you." She smiled again, as did he, but then there was another long silence. "I'll say you shouldn't stay in this line of work, though," he added.

"Not if I can help it."

"That's good." He took a deep breath as his eyes went to the ceiling. "As for the rest, I don't really know. I'm not the best person to talk to about it. I don't really have anything else either, and I kill without even wondering why I don't give it a second thought." He stopped speaking after that. She glanced at him, and for the first time since he'd sat down, it seemed like he wasn't thinking about her. Inertia blinked slowly, his eyes fell, and the moment passed. "But perhaps it's a good thing to know what you don't have," he continued.

"How's that?" she asked.

"Because then you can seek what you need."

"Didn't help Kali," Carmen said with a shrug. She groaned loudly. "It's so easy to do what she did, though, blaming the sortens for everything. It's even truer for me than her. There's hardly anything I've ever done that wasn't influenced by my handlers and my time in that awful place. I'm past it, I really am…or at least I'm trying to be. But I never will be, not completely. It will always linger."

Inertia nodded. "I can't disagree with you. However, they were what they were made to be. You might be as well, but it doesn't mean you have to stay that way."

"That's what I told Kali, for all the good it did." Edge sneered while she shook her head. "The galaxy is a very mean, cruel place. I'm tired of being lost in it."

He nodded one more time and then glanced at her. "Major difference, then, between you and her. You're not alone."

She looked at her partner while he glanced at her. "No, no I'm not," she said, squeezing his arm tight. She sighed softly. "If anything is regrettable, it's that. She was completely alone, always alone. She didn't need to be. I was there… Gungnir was there. There had to be others, but she couldn't see it." She sat quietly for a few seconds. "I hope that's enough."

"I think it's a large piece of it."

"Feels like it. Always has. Thank you again, Will."

"And I thank you, Carmen."

They looked away from each other and sat, her mind clear for the first time since they'd set foot on the freighter. The calm silence was eventually broken by a wayward transmission.

"Wolf One and Wolf Two, please respond. Your presence is requested at the main research lab, over."

Inertia moved to key his communicator, and Carmen

groaned when the movement disrupted her head on his shoulder.

"Dungeon Master, I've found Wolf Two, stand by," he said.

Then he groaned too as he stood up. He turned and extended his hand to Carmen, who was still sitting. "All right, let's go see what these Space Force geeks want," he muttered while he pulled her to her feet. Carmen gave a dutiful nod, though she'd very much rather continue sitting.

"I screwed up my face again."

"I noticed," he remarked after taking a moment to study the damage more thoroughly. "They should be able to fix that, no problem. But don't worry. Even if they can't, that political officer of theirs will still look at your ass."

He began exiting the room, expecting Carmen to follow him, but she didn't. "And where will you look?" she blurted out.

Inertia stopped abruptly. *Got him*, she thought. Every time, over and over again, he knew just the right words to send her for a loop. It was annoying in an oddly comforting way. But just once, she'd like to get the upper hand. He turned to face her slowly, and it looked like now would finally be the time. He looked quite surprised at what Carmen had said—even shocked, hidden behind a serious façade—as he walked toward her. The expression made her smirk like the cat that finally swallowed the canary, despite how painful it was with her stinging cheek. She was still smiling triumphantly as she looked up at him when he stopped within a breath of her.

He slowly and powerfully but gently grasped her chin and aimed her face at his. "In the eye, Carmen," he said, staring at her directly while he spoke. The smile faded from her face as her body went still. She wasn't stiff. No, an odd numbness that felt like a pleasant tickle spread from where he touched her. She didn't notice that she was blushing. "Always in the eye," he continued. Then he let her go and began walking again. "Come on, this might be important," he said. Carmen could only nod as she joined him.

Inertia asked for directions just as they reached the corridor. The activity level was easily higher than before he had entered the room. The freighter now swarmed with officers and crew from the *Griffin*. Troopers led scores of bound sortens. Caches of sorten weapons were organized in multiple piles. But by this point, everyone had given up on removing the strange rings from the Clairvoyant Constructs.

Dungeon Master led them deep into the ship, nearer the engineering spaces. Carmen couldn't hear the various reports of new discoveries in the multiple labs throughout the ship, but she was also spared the callouts of a trooper or crewman falling from a well-placed ambush by the remaining security teams. Those, however, were occurring less and less frequently, and no one they could see appeared concerned about any enemy action. The state of the corridors changed the farther they went, though. The heavier fighting that had taken place here was quite obvious. Bullet holes and laser blasts stained the walls. Their feet crunched on grenade shrapnel. Medical teams tended wound troopers and even wounded sortens. Last, and most painful to see, some troopers openly grieved fallen comrades.

Carmen tried to ignore it all, instead hyper-focusing on keeping to her partner's side. Eventually, Dungeon Master directed them to enter a room. Carmen paused after she did. It was large and circular with computer consoles filling the space, but what had her complete attention were two large, vertical plates that stood in the center of the room on an elevated platform. There was a soft hum from them, and she swore they made her skin tingle. Whatever the case, she and Inertia weren't in the room alone. Troopers worked at the computers, as did *Griffin* crew. Tawny directed the effort while Renee and Frederick observed.

"Medic!" a trooper called when he spotted Carmen.

A different trooper went to the Clairvoyant and immediately began working on her cheek and ear. She was thankful for it, but there were other things on her mind. "What is that?" she asked.

"The source of the interference blocking our signals and the countdown we didn't stop," Renee said.

Carmen looked at Inertia, having no idea what she was referring to. "I'll tell you later," he said quietly.

She nodded but felt the classic Clairvoyant annoyance of having to repeat herself. "So, what is it?" she asked again.

The captain took a deep breath and let it go sharply. "It's a time machine."

23

PROJECT ARCHANGEL

It was sometimes strange to be a Clairvoyant. In many instances, you knew more about a person than they even knew about themselves—fears, desires, all the unspoken urges that lay just beneath the surface. Sometimes those urges weren't so hidden, just unsaid, and sometimes they bubbled so violently into the foreground that it was more than a wonder how no one else noticed. That was certainly the case in the main conference room aboard the freighter. Everyone, save for maybe her partner since Carmen could never read him, was contemplating, in explicit detail, how exactly they were going to murder Commander Frederick Reeves.

"No, you can't go back to kill your ex-wife," Renee said, rolling her eyes.

Carmen smiled. She couldn't read the captain either, but what was on her mind for the moment wasn't a mystery. The woman's tone of voice changed often to subtly and sometimes not so subtly underline or reinforce whatever she was saying. Carmen swore she could make a simple "hello" crack like a whip if needed. There was a warning and threat behind her words now. Even Carmen would hesitate to challenge it.

Every syllable practically screamed "knock it off!" But Frederick either didn't get the hint or didn't care. It was more fun to avoid reading him and not know for sure.

"But Captain, she wouldn't be missed—real harpy, that one. Maybe go back for her mother and get both at once," he proposed.

"We've been over and over this. It doesn't work that way. You can't go back in time and do anything you haven't done before. If you killed your ex-mother-in-law, you already did it. Your ex-wife exists, so you never killed her mother. You *can't* change history," Renee said.

"That's only because you won't let me. Come on, it'll make the world a better place…at least my younger days."

She gave a loud, dejected sigh and the conversation circled to the beginning again. They'd been at it for at least the past half hour. Renee spoke in technical and philosophical terms that Carmen had never heard before. Several at the table nodded in agreement as she spoke. The Clairvoyant herself didn't think the issue was that complicated. A child could understand.

Gathered at the table with them were Tawny, Mel, and Terry. The conference room was a space enclosed by glass, and beyond it the time machine and the techs working on it could be seen. She didn't pay much attention to them, enjoying her ice cream instead. She didn't know the flavor. It was…red, but it was quite good. She'd never had the money to afford ice cream, since she had saved everything to help Michael.

"There's no such thing as a time paradox," Tawny agreed.

Carmen looked at her with a bemused wrinkle on her nose. The lieutenant had quite the imagination for stuffing Frederick into airlocks. The idea of the small woman forcing the rotund man into one was amusing.

"Can I have more ice cream please?" she asked a passing attendant.

The man shook his head. "Sorry, ma'am. There is no more," he said.

"Oh? No one really had that much."

"Yes, but some had more than others," he replied, glancing at Frederick.

Carmen looked at Frederick sitting next to her. Inertia was on her other side. What the attendant said was true; the political officer had eaten more than one bowl. She hadn't thought about it at the time, though she no longer wondered why Terry had shaken his head when Frederick was served twice then thrice. In any case, Frederick did still have some ice cream left. He was busy saying something about keeping the universe in balance and various pieces of assorted nonsense. Her colleagues looked angry enough to melt into puddles in their chairs. As far as Carmen was concerned, however, he could keep right on talking, because she spooned herself a quick scoop from his bowl and ate it. Frederick stopped mid-speech.

"You want to lose your hand, girl?" he spat pointedly.

She smiled and made a show of slowly taking another scoop from his bowl. She ate it while staring at him hard. The overweight, middle-aged political officer stared back at the Rogue Wolf. Her eyes began to narrow.

"That gives me an idea," Renee began. She looked at her brother. "Inertia, how much do you charge for a hit? I might have a contract for you."

Frederick looked at the captain with a start and then at Tawny, who grinned wide evilly. Last, his gaze fell on Inertia.

"Considering past services rendered, I'll consider doing it for free," he said.

Frederick swallowed hard. He pushed the bowl of ice

cream toward Carmen. "Hey, let's make a deal. I'll let you keep all of that if you fight for me."

She said nothing, but she did push the bowl back toward him while she leaned to be closer to her partner. Then she rested her chin on an open palm. Frederick looked at her and swallowed again when it was obvious that Carmen was inexplicably more loyal to her partner than to the promise of sugary, frozen desserts. He sat up straight and cleared his throat.

"Captain, in light of recent events, I've decided to table the discussion of Operation Kill Ex-wife."

"Good," Renee said.

"Would have worked though," he added under his breath.

Carmen heard him and chuckled lightly. He smiled at her and pushed the bowl back toward her. "Thank you," she said softly as she began eating again.

Terry groaned, Tawny laughed to herself as she thought about what Inertia or Edge could do to Frederick, and the non-Rogue Wolf Clairvoyant sat impassively.

"If you can't change history, why would the sortens build a time machine?" Frederick asked.

"From what we can tell, they weren't trying to change history," Mel said. "Their research was almost completely on these." He produced a ring much like what the Clairvoyant Constructs wore and placed it on the table. "We found this example in a research lab. We've also learned that they can't be forcibly removed once placed on the hand. Even when we cut off the finger with a ring on it, it regenerates in place in only a few seconds. Amazing technology."

Carmen telekinetically retrieved the ring and examined it closely. It didn't seem very special, just a gold colored band with a large, diamond-shaped jewel. She remembered the jewel glowing. This one did not.

"What's it do?" she asked as she handed it to Frederick just before he said he wanted to see it.

"It appears to enhance a Clairvoyant's bioelectric field," Mel answered. "It probably won't do anything for one at your level, but it would greatly strengthen their Clairvoyant Constructs."

"We noticed," Inertia remarked.

Mel nodded. "It more than likely also has enough power to instantly make an…average person a Clairvoyant," he added, searching for the right word.

Carmen looked at Frederick, whose curiosity was about to have him try the ring on. "Do you really want to be a Clairvoyant?" she warned. He stopped instantly, then placed the ring down and pushed it away.

"That still doesn't answer the commander's question. Why would they build a time machine? What do the rings have to do with that?" Terry asked.

"They don't. From what we can tell so far, the sortens were sending teams back in time to study humans in an age before any genetic massaging ever occurred," Tawny said.

"Back at Solitary, Caelus said he wanted to study terrans who haven't been genetically modified as a baseline. He spoke like it wasn't possible," Carmen remarked.

Tawny nodded. "For him, it probably wasn't. The sortens' research was very compartmentalized. The scientists at Solitary might have been aware of what was going on here and might have been given some research notes, but they wouldn't be able to study anything directly."

"Are there any abductees here?" Inertia asked.

"No," Mel answered. "We've swept the entire ship from bow to stern and found none, nor any facilities to hold captives. We only just started interrogations, but so far the research teams have indicated that the subject is taken, studied, and returned all in their own time and are largely unharmed. No one is ever brought here."

"All of that is possible?" Carmen asked. "That they have a team doing this back in time and no one ever knew about it?"

"Well, the time travel part is relatively easy. We technically do it every time we Ghost," Renee said. "The technology is broadly similar. The hardest part of it is the tracking."

"Tracking?" Terry asked.

The Wiz Kid took a deep breath before she answered. "It's not just time; it's time and space. It's not possible to send someone very far forward in time from the perspective of the time machine. But backward is relatively easy. The problem is *where* do you send them and at what point in time? Everything is in a constant state of motion. If, for instance, I were to send any of you back in time by ten minutes—"

"You'd need precise coordinates on where the ship was ten minutes ago, or we'd appear in space," Terry finished for her. She nodded. "And that would get harder and harder the farther back you go."

"Exactly," Renee said. "Now imagine sending someone to a planet a week ago, a month ago, a hundred years ago or more. You need amazingly precise tracking ability of the target stellar object, a problem the sortens were able to solve. Going into the future is impossible, though, as the location of any given object would be a matter of probability, not history."

"That's not the only issue," Tawny began. "Think of time like a river. Think of the current in the river as some sort of temporal inertia. Objects and people will resist being sent back and will, in fact, revert back to their initial state unless they are actively kept in place."

"Like tying a log to the bank so it doesn't get swept away?" Frederick asked.

"Essentially yes," Tawny answered, though she was unable to help a bit of surprise at a coherent question from him. "That's a relatively simple prospect for an object. Living things are more difficult."

"All right, then who or what did the sortens send back with the countdown I didn't stop?" Inertia asked.

"We confirmed the second countdown was a self-destruct," Mel said. "The first was to send two rings back."

"Why would they care about them?" Carmen asked. "Couldn't they make them somewhere else?"

"Not these two," Tawny said.

Carmen looked at her and silently begged her to elaborate. The lieutenant deferred to the colonel, who took a deep breath. "One of the rings wasn't created by the sortens. It appears to have been made by the arkins."

There was silence at the table after that. Renee leaned back in her chair as everyone looked back and forth, unsure of how to proceed. At last, Carmen broke the silence with an innocent question.

"So, what do we know about them?"

"Very little," Renee remarked. "We don't even know what they look like. We've fought them with the *Griffin*, though, and barely survived." Frederick glanced at her and smirked, which made the captain smirk as well. "More so than usual. Anyway, as for who or whatever they are, all we can really say is that they are far more advanced than…anyone. The only reason we haven't lost the war is because they haven't attacked in force yet."

"Why not?" Carmen asked.

"No idea," Renee answered with a shrug. "Either they can't or won't, or they're getting ready to. But there's no doubt that they aren't shy about helping the sortens technologically or possibly materially to fight us."

"The arkins gave the sortens one ring: Phoenix," Mel said, smoothly continuing after Renee. "The sortens have been working to copy the technology for mass production. The closest they've gotten thus far is Archangel Prime. Both were sent back in time to safeguard them."

"Meaning the sortens have a time machine somewhere else," Inertia remarked.

"Or a team already operating in that time period," Terry mused.

"Any data?" Carmen asked.

Tawny shook her head. "If there was anything in their computers about operations other than here, it was wiped. But as I said, very compartmentalized."

"Do we know, at least, when and where they were sent?" Carmen asked.

"That we do know," Tawny began. "More than a thousand years ago, early twenty-first century Earth."

"What do we know about then?" The Rogue Wolf asked after a shrug. She knew next to nothing about ancient Earth history.

"Very little," Tawny said. "Much of our history was lost during the sorten occupation. What we do know is that it was an extremely debauched period in history at almost every level, filled with unspeakable vices and corruption," she continued, her tone grave.

Frederick cleared his throat. "Captain, in light of the dangers involved, I must volunteer for this mission. I doubt other crewmembers are up for the challenge."

Carmen smiled, but several at the table were less than

amused. Renee rolled her eyes, though with a slight smile she tried to hide. Carmen noticed; Frederick noticed, which produced a pleased twinkle in his eye; and Inertia would have noticed if he cared. But no one else did. It was amazing how the buffoon flew rings around everyone while they thought *he* was the one who couldn't keep up.

"I couldn't send you even if I wanted to," Renee began, shaking her head to hide her growing smile. "As Lieutenant Crowe said, it's no simple task to send people back. For now, the only individuals we can send are Clairvoyants."

"Why?" Inertia asked with a start.

"It's something to do with your bioelectric field. Elements of it are used kind of like a Ghost Field for the time-space displacement," Renee said. "Anything more than that we don't know. The sortens, by their research notes, were able to send themselves back, but we don't know how."

"So only me, Inertia, the colonel, and...well you," Carmen said.

Renee opened her mouth, and it looked like she was going to correct her, but then she immediately thought better of it. Carmen didn't really know how what she had said could be considered wrong, other than that the captain didn't think of herself as a Clairvoyant, but that was an utterly trivial detail. The woman must have come to the same conclusion, as she nodded before saying, "Yes, exactly."

"Edge and I can handle this...if you're up for one more?" Inertia said, turning to his partner.

Carmen glanced back. He really did look her in the eye most of the time. She hadn't thought about it before, but now that she was aware, she couldn't stop thinking about it. She looked away before she started blushing again.

The feeling left her quickly as she hesitated to answer. It had all been theory up till now. But, when faced with the cold hard reality of what this trip would entail, she didn't want to go. It felt like it would be a mistake to go. This entire endeavor had taken pieces of her with only a few rewards, and in fact the only reward she could think of was rescuing Phaethon. Her partner watched her, as did everyone in the room while they awaited her response. She could refuse. Inertia would probably push her to if she paused a few seconds longer. But she looked at him then and knew she had to agree. A part of her, small and mostly ignored, was screaming at the top of its lungs for her to stay. However, she didn't know if she could live with herself if something happened to him just because she got cold feet when he needed her.

"Sure," she said with a shrug. "How many more bases can the sortens have?"

Inertia eyed her carefully. *I waited too long*, she realized. She glanced at him and gave a confident nod. She knew she wasn't much of a liar, but after he watched her closely, he gave a small nod in return and looked away.

"That's all well and good, but is it the best idea to send anyone?" Terry questioned.

"How do you mean?" Renee asked.

"Current scans from the *Griffin* and long-range probes don't detect any sorten patrols, but we don't know how long that will last. Fleet battleships don't go up without someone noticing," he advised. "*Jaeger*, *Mercury*, and the fleet are still hunting for us."

"Can the time machine be disassembled?" Frederick asked before anyone could say anything else.

"Presumably, but we shouldn't need to go that far. It's all relative," Tawny said. "Whoever we send back can spend months—years—in that time period, but when they return, it will be instantaneous for us."

"I don't want to spend years in debauchery land," Carmen said quickly. Her eyes turned to Frederick before he spoke, and she grinned. It felt good to do so after the past few moments. She appreciated his company for much the same reasons Renee did.

"Speak for yourself," he muttered, though easily loud enough for everyone to hear.

"There is more risk in not going," Mel began. "The lieutenant is right that it *is* all relative, meaning there's no increased chance of us getting detected by waiting. But if we don't go and the sortens are able to retrieve these rings, them combined with their Clairvoyant Construct technology will mean they'd have the ability to manufacture the most powerful army the galaxy has ever seen." He paused before he continued. "Yes, the sortens have surrendered, but there have been reports of the Eternals trying to develop a Clairvoyant countermeasure. Perhaps this is it."

Renee nodded several times. "I think the matter is pretty well decided. Does anyone have anything else?" Frederick meekly raised his hand, making the captain roll her eyes and groan loudly. "Anything that's relevant to this discussion and which would not cause me to shoot you," she clarified. The commander put his hand down.

Carmen watched the back and forth and would have grinned again if there wasn't something else on her mind that she'd only just now considered. "What if someone from that time picks up one of the rings and puts it on? They couldn't become a Clairvoyant, could they?"

There was silence at the table as everyone looked at each other. It seemed like no one else had considered the possibility either.

"We don't know," Tawny said. "No one knows if it was an ability unlocked by genetic massaging or if it has always been part of us. That's the entire point of the sortens' study," she added with a shrug.

Carmen nodded solemnly and then swallowed hard. "No one in that time even knows what a Clairvoyant is. I can't imagine what it would be like to have that suddenly thrust upon you."

"It wouldn't be pleasant," Renee said softly. Carmen looked at her and wished she could have worded what she'd said differently. The captain, however, didn't appear unduly bothered. She took a deep breath and sat up straight in her chair. "Ms. Crowe, make the preparations to send the Rogue Wolves back. As soon as you're ready, they'll go."

"Aye, ma'am."

Carmen nodded and looked at Inertia, who did the same.

"Mr. Lanser, I want anything of value that can be salvaged from this ship, including the time machine, if possible."

"Captain, what about the prisoners?" he asked. "We don't have any legal right to hold them. Are we to eliminate them?"

"No," Rence said quickly. She looked away for a second as she thought. "When we leave, they'll be placed in the freighter's escape pods. The freighter itself will be scuttled. We'll transmit their location when we're back in terran space." She took a deep breath to allow time for her mind to change gears. "Mr. Fletcher, go back to the *Griffin*, coordinate our retrieval efforts there, and immediately report any contact of any type. We don't have much in the way of weapons left; we need sufficient early warning to run."

Terry nodded dutifully. "Aye, ma'am."

"I'll remain here, assisting with any analysis and making final decisions on what's worth keeping," she concluded.

Then the captain stood, as did everyone else, and the officers left the room in seconds as they went to carry out their assignments. Carmen and Inertia lingered, though. There was nothing immediately they had to do. She silently looked at the time machine. It was such an outwardly simple device for such a complicated piece of technology. No one here really understood it, but she guessed you didn't need to know how an aerocar actually worked to drive one. Carmen touched the bandage on her face and ear. Thankfully there'd been enough time before the meeting for her to wash the blood out of her hair. The bandages could be taken off in less than an hour, and there wouldn't even be a scar or mark left. She had countless such invisible wounds. She considered the new additions to her collection and sighed softly while she looked at her next challenge. *Last leg*, she thought—hoped.

Inertia appeared next to her. "We're just getting two rings. Shouldn't be hard."

"I hope you're right.

24

OUT OF THE FIRE

As the crew and officers of the *Griffin* buzzed around Carmen, she paid attention to none of them. They spoke to her in their usual acronyms, jargon, and shorthand. Perhaps they figured she would read their minds and know what it all meant. The Clairvoyant didn't bother, though. There wasn't really that much to know. What it basically boiled down to was that everything she was about to do she had already done. What already happened could not be changed. Space Force had a knack for complicating the simple with plans, contingencies, and simulations. The professional thoroughness had its place, and there were times that she appreciated it, but Carmen's thoughts were too scrambled to focus on them with the required precision.

In less than two weeks, she had rescued her charge and killed her former handler, and now she was about to go back in time by more than a thousand years to retrieve a pair of all-powerful trinkets. When she'd told Gungnir, seemingly a lifetime ago, that she was in this all the way, she had absolutely no clue what that meant at the time.

"Edge. Edge… Ed—"

"What? What is it?" she asked quickly.

The technician briefing her looked at her with a raised eyebrow, as did everyone else in the room. Carmen sighed. It was possible for Clairvoyants to get distracted. People were surprised when she knew everything and were just as shocked when she was just as much of a dullard as they were. There was no way to win.

"Sorry, I'm just distracted," she said.

"I understand, but pay attention to this. This part is vital," the woman said. Carmen nodded, and the tech held up a new device she had never seen before. It was small and boxy with several lights, and it had a couple buttons to input something she was sure she was about to be told. "This binds you to the time period we send you to. It's call a—"

"Let's just call it a binder," Carmen remarked. She'd read enough to know the proper name was a long series of numbers, dashes, and letters that would boil her brain to try to remember.

The woman briefing her nodded. "It's keyed to your bioelectric field. If it gets damaged, loses power, or otherwise shut off, you will be instantly sent back here." She strapped it tightly to Carmen's arm over the body armor. "It's effective within half a meter of you, in case you need to change clothes or anything like that. It will give a proximity alert if you're about to get too far away. If you do—"

"I'll instantly be sent back. Got it," Carmen replied.

"Right. According to the sorten research notes, it may be painful when you emerge in your target time. It will pass in a few seconds. There will be a bright flash and the sound of thunder from the air you displace. Consequently, we aimed your emergence point to be at altitude, approximately three thousand meters at night. Should be enough to avoid any attention, aircraft, or buildings." Carmen nodded. "The sortens were able to erase the *exact* time and location where they sent Phoenix and Archangel Prime. We're doing the best we can to narrow it down. Lastly, you don't have to worry about getting any inoculations. Our immune systems are genetically massaged to be better than a human's. Worst you should get from any ancient plague or disease is a runny nose. Can't say how you'll take their food though."

"I'm sure I've cooked worse," the Clairvoyant muttered.

The woman didn't even crack a smile. Carmen wasn't one to *try* to be funny, but she was missing Frederick's levity about now. The technician seemed to have the regs and her tech manuals tattooed on the inside of her eyelids.

"Now's the time if you have any questions." Carmen shook her head. "Okay, you'll step between the plates when you're ready. The other Rogue Wolf will be with you once he's finished his brief. We had to have you two far enough apart to key your…binders. Once again, you two won't need to do anything other than stand between the plates. One last thing, though it doesn't matter much to you. You're set to return five seconds in the future from when you depart, just so it's not instantaneous for us." *That would be a little weird,* Carmen thought. It would look like they'd never left. "Good luck."

The Clairvoyant took a deep breath. She wasn't sure if they needed the luck. Every little bit helped, though. She stood and then exited the room. The small ready room she had been in led directly to the embarkation room where the time machine was housed. Everyone turned to look at her. Renee was here, as was Frederick, Mel, Tawny, and a gaggle of techs. Frederick gave her a reassuring nod with a broad smile, which Carmen ignored. She looked for her partner and walked quickly to him when he finally emerged from his ready room. The eyes followed her as she went, but

Carmen paid no attention to them or the thoughts behind them.

There was a rising anxiety then, one which she hadn't felt for a long time. It made her think of those times she'd sat on the bluff back at the facility and stared far into the horizon. Her fingers began to tingle. Despite all that, however—despite everything telling her that this was a step too far and that they would be better off forgetting this entire scheme—she looked at him, took a deep breath, and nodded. Inertia nodded back.

"Did they tell you how we actually find the rings? They didn't say anything to me…for as much as I paid attention."

Her partner looked at her and playfully rolled his eyes, which made her guiltily purse her lips. *"We find the sortens. They are looking for the rings. We find them, we find the rings."* Carmen nodded. It made sense.

He looked at Renee. "We're ready," he said.

"Ms. Crowe," Renee said softly.

"Aye, Captain. Inertia, Edge, please step between the plates." Inertia motioned with his head, and they started walking, stopping between the two large, vertical plates of the time machine. They faced each other as they waited. "All systems on!" Tawny ordered when they were in place.

"Beginning energy transfer," a tech announced a moment later.

Carmen felt more tingling, but this time she was sure it wasn't her nerves. First her hand and then the rest of her body felt like it was submerged in a vat of spiders. The lights on the binders glowed brightly.

"Power to full," Tawny ordered.

The feeling instantly grew worse. She couldn't help but rub her arms and hands, though she worked very hard to not make it obvious that's what she was doing. Her lips curled as she tried to keep herself from groaning out loud. Then she looked at Inertia. He stood perfectly still. He had to feel what she did, but there was no reaction on his part. It made her think of something Kali had told her long ago. "You're one of the most powerful beings in the galaxy. You should act like it." Carmen stopped rubbing herself, as it wasn't helping much anyway, and stood up straight. Inertia winked at her. She smiled. She didn't know if it was right to go back in time, but she was certain she was doing it for the right reasons.

"Power at sixty percent...seventy percent," a tech announced.

Just then, she and Inertia were surrounded by a warm, ethereal glow.

"What is that?" Renee asked.

"Excitation from the time machine has pushed their bioelectric fields into the visible range, ma'am," a tech answered. "It was expected."

Everyone involuntarily stopped what they were doing and what they were thinking and could only watch. The fields flowed from each Clairvoyant as if water, ever changing and always moving, surrounding them in an expanding bulb that filled the room and seemed to penetrate the walls and even the people. In time, the fields of not just them but of everyone in the room, even the non-Clairvoyants, were visible. The fields of each individual pulled, teased, and flowed through and around one another. Each person was unique, and in more than just magnitude. Carmen and Inertia overpowered everyone, save for Renee.

Carmen's field seemed to swirl around her in rhythmic dance, producing eddies and currents which merged along a defined axis that became flowing symmetry. Inertia's field began in calm, wafting back and forth as if smoke. There was no telling where it ended really. Instead of diffusing to nothing, his field seemed to break apart into angry tendrils that came back together into a stronger whole. Renee's field, by contrast, was a tight ball, subdued to almost no bigger than her person. Fields flowed around it, never through it and never pushing it aside. But from time to time, it exploded outward with enough force that it looked like it would flatten everyone in the room. On and on for each person, their unique signature was displayed for all to see.

"Is this what you always sense?" Frederick asked.

Renee licked her lips. "Yes."

"It's beautiful," Tawny said breathlessly.

"Lieutenant, we have a warning light with the displacement initiator," a tech reported.

"We can't stop now," Tawny said, turning her attention back to her station. "More—give me more power."

"Roger!"

There was a loud hum as the entire room vibrated. The plates glowed, forcing all but the Clairvoyants to look away. Carmen and Inertia couldn't even be seen in the brightness. Then the room filled with the sound of a loud explosion like a thunderclap, and the light and the Rogue Wolves were gone.

"We did it!" a tech said.

Tawny swallowed hard. "Reemergence in…four…three… two…one…no—"

Another loud thunderclap drowned out her final call. After a bright flash, Inertia appeared between the two plates on his hands and knees. His shoulder and back were on fire as he groaned loudly.

"Put him out, put him out!" Renee yelled in surprise as she rushed toward her brother.

The Clairvoyant telekinetically damped the flames on his own before anyone was able to respond. She knelt next him. His body armor was heavily damaged, and there were bruises on his face as well as a few cuts. He continued resting on his hands and knees while his entire body trembled. She didn't know if that was a side effect from the time displacement or from injuries she couldn't see.

"What happened?" she asked.

"We failed," he said after a few more groans. "The situation has gotten worse."

Renee nodded with wide eyes. "Where's Edge?"

Inertia looked slowly around the room and seemed surprised that he was alone. His entire body wilted. "I…don't know. I fear she's dead."

ABOUT THE AUTHOR

Yup, I'm the evil guy keeping you up all night to read, "Just one more page." A storyteller from birth, it was inevitable that I'd find my way to writing books. All of my works have a very strong focus on character and believable worlds.

Other than books, I'm a licensed pilot and certified jet nerd. I'm also interested in motorsports and a lover of the "sweet science."

Check my latest updates and join my newsletter at ktbeltbooks.com

Lastly, honest reviews are vital to helping others make informed reading decisions. Please consider leaving a review of this book on your favorite booking buying websites.

CREDITS

Fire Shape made by FreePik from
www.flaticon.com

www.ingramcontent.com/pod-product-compliance
Lightning Source LLC
Chambersburg PA
CBHW030628190726
48286CB00008B/2446